'When you ma**r**[...] it was me you[...] really matter wh**o my father was?** she asked forcefully.

'In this case, yes, it does. Before this, to me you were one person—now you are someone else. I cannot reconcile myself to that just now.'

'I realise how difficult it must be for you and I do not ask your forgiveness at this present time. But no matter who or what my father was it does not make *me* less worthy. My feelings for you remain unchanged. Can you not feel the same? Can you not accept me with all my faults—all my disgraces? Must you despise me?'

The pleading sadness in her voice and her obvious distress made Stuart pale and he moved slightly, as if to go to her, but he checked himself quickly. 'Last night I was not aware of your disgraces when you so excited my desire. But since learning who you are I cannot help feeling that I have betrayed my brother's spirit...'

Helen Dickson was born and still lives in south Yorkshire, with her husband, on a busy arable farm where she combines writing with keeping a chaotic farmhouse. An incurable romantic, she writes for pleasure, owing much of her inspiration to the beauty of the surrounding countryside. She enjoys reading and music. History has always captivated her, and she likes travel and visiting ancient buildings.

Recent titles by the same author:

LORD FOX'S PLEASURE
JEWEL OF THE NIGHT
HIGHWAYMAN HUSBAND

THE PIRATE'S DAUGHTER

Helen Dickson

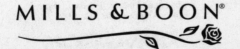

MILLS & BOON®

All the characters in this book have no existence outside the imagination of the author, and have no relation whatsoever to anyone bearing the same name or names. They are not even distantly inspired by any individual known or unknown to the author, and all the incidents are pure invention.

First published in Great Britain 2003
Harlequin Mills & Boon Limited,
Eton House, 18-24 Paradise Road, Richmond, Surrey TW9 1SR

© Helen Dickson 2003

ISBN 0 263 83522 7

Set in Times Roman 10½ on 11½ pt.
04-0903-94196

Printed and bound in Spain
by Litografía Rosés S.A., Barcelona

THE PIRATE'S DAUGHTER

Chapter One

November 1671

The time for the hanging of Captain Nathaniel Wylde, the notorious pirate, was set for twelve noon at Execution Dock on a bend on the north bank of the River Thames at Wapping. It was here that the gallows stood on the muddy shoreline near the low tide mark, the usual place for the execution of pirates who infested the seas. Once captured, they came under the jurisdiction of the Lord High Admiral, who was responsible for all crimes committed at sea up to the low-tide mark. Above that, all felons were dealt with by the civil courts.

The gallows was a simple structure of two wooden posts, made to look monstrous and sinister by a hangman's noose suspended from the wooden cross beam. After the hanging the body would slowly become submerged by three consecutive tides washing over it, before being taken down and fitted into iron hoops and chains and suspended from a gibbet on the lower reaches of the Thames—as a dire warning to seamen who have a mind to fall foul of the law.

Colourful and exciting tales of the exploits of Nathaniel Wylde, the handsome, charismatic pirate, were talked of

from the Caribbean to the South China Seas. A huge crowd
had gathered on the shore, and some had taken to boats on
the river, to witness his hanging, to see for themselves the
man who was a living legend, captured by pirates while
crossing the Atlantic to the Caribbean to start a new life
following the defeat of the Royalists at the Battle of
Worcester twenty years ago.

He had survived two brutal years as a galley slave with
the Barbary Corsairs in the warm, sparkling waters of the
Mediterranean, before escaping and capturing his own ship.
With the lure of adventure strong in his veins and mastering
the skills of navigation and seamanship surprisingly
quickly, he proceeded to sail the oceans unchecked, preying
on heavily laden merchant ships, and answerable to no law
or code of conduct but the pirates' own.

Unlike most pirate captains who were notorious for their
ruthlessness and unspeakable cruelty, Nathaniel Wylde—
unprincipled swashbuckler and undoubtedly a rogue—had
acquired the reputation of a 'Gentleman Pirate' owing to
the charm and courtesy he showed towards his victims,
which tended to cloud the serious nature of the crimes perpetrated against them. His crew, although illiterate men,
were unusual in the fact that they were not the typical miscreants as on other pirate ships, renowned for their foul
language and drunken debauches.

Standing on the edge of the crowd stood Cassandra Everson, the hood of her cloak pulled well over her head—
partly to protect her from the steady freezing rain falling
out of a leaden sky, but more to shield her from recognition
by the man, her father, who would soon become the focal
point of the crowd's attention when he mounted the ladder
and prepared to breathe his last.

'I wished to spare you this,' murmured the tall, thin man
by her side, his hand on the hilt of the dagger he carried
at his waist, concealed beneath the folds of his cloak. 'We

should not have come here. I promised Nat to keep you away—not to let you see him die.'

'I had to come. You, more than anyone, should know that. We will not have to wait much longer. It is almost time.' She fixed her steady gaze on Drum O'Leary. His features were concealed by his cloak, for with a price on his own head it was imperative that he wasn't recognised. Drum had taken a great risk in coming to the execution, but when he had arrived at Everson House in Chelsea to break the news of Nat's capture and impending execution, against his wishes she had insisted on accompanying him.

Drum O'Leary was a fearsome-looking individual, an Irishman, an arch-villain, and to cross him was to court a dagger between the ribs. An old cutlass wound on his cheek pulled his mouth upwards slightly, causing it to be permanently fixed in a lopsided grin, giving him a sinister appearance. Outwardly Drum acted and spoke politely, but beneath that calm façade was a man who would show no mercy when crossed.

He had acquired the name 'Drum' while serving in the King's army as a drummer during the Civil War. He was Nathaniel Wylde's most faithful and trusted friend, and he had been by his side for twenty years. Forced to leave England after King Charles's defeat at Worcester, they had both been captured and served as galley slaves together, but Drum had not been on board the *Dolphin*, Nat's ship, when she had been captured, owing to the fact that he had been on the Cape Verde Islands off the coast of West Africa visiting his Portuguese wife.

A line of suffering appeared around Cassandra's mouth and Drum was touched by the grief he saw in her eyes, which were so like Nat's. Execution Dock was not a place he had brought her to without qualms.

'Don't worry, Drum. He will not know I'm here.'

Cassandra was insensible to the bitterly cold November

day and the stink of foul odours coming from the river as she strained her ears and eyes, searching the road for the cart that would bring the condemned man to this awful place of execution, until, at last, she heard the hollow rumble of wheels and it came into view.

It had crossed London Bridge from Marshalsea Prison on the south bank where, after Nat had been intercepted off the coast of West Africa by an English privateer, a heavily armed vessel licensed by the Admiralty to attack and seize the *Dolphin*, he had been confined for the past three months. Having been tried and convicted of piracy at the Old Bailey Sessions Court, and unprepared to confess to his crimes, Nat had been sentenced to hang.

The cart was in a procession led by the Admiralty Marshal on horseback. Cassandra had not laid eyes on her father for nigh on fifteen months, but she recognised him immediately. His familiar mane of silvery blond hair was like blazing sunlight on this dismally cold November day. A heavy growth of beard covered his usually clean-shaven face, and his skin, turned golden brown by many years at sea and hardened to the texture of leather, had paled after his long weeks of incarceration.

Cassandra pulled the hood of her cape further over her face and gripped it together across her mouth and nose so he would not recognise her when the cart came close, for he would not want her to witness his final degradation and humiliation. When she looked on his beloved face, scalding tears burned the backs of her eyes and she almost choked on a lump in her throat which she swallowed down, angered by her own weakness, for it was not in her nature to cry.

When the cart reached the river side he climbed out, followed by the prison chaplain who had accompanied him, hoping the prisoner would see the error of his ways and repent of his sins before the end. He was given the chance to address the crowd but refused. Fixing his eyes on the gallows he strode forward, giving everyone watching the distinct impression that he was as eager to depart this world as he had been to enter it.

There was a swagger to his gait and a carefree dignity, for as he had lived his life so he would meet his death, tall and unbowed, his pale golden hair flowing free like the dancing pennant of his ship, the *Dolphin*, and as imposing as a tall poplar clothed in shimmering leaves of summer glory. Villain and blackguard he might be, but at his moment of death he exuded an air of panache which could bring a macabre smile to the lips of even the most hardened, sanctimonious spectator.

A cold fury washed over Cassandra as she watched the ghastly scene being played out before her eyes. She was angry and frustrated by her inability to speak to him, to say goodbye. Digging her fingers into the palms of her hands, she heard the words of the chaplain reciting the prayers as he followed her father across the mud. She was insensible to the stirrings of the crowd, which moved like a storm-tossed ocean, as she watched her father climb the ladder and the executioner place the noose around his neck. At that moment she felt as if she were dying herself. Drum stood beside her, as immobile as a figure of stone.

'Give him courage to show no fear,' Cassandra whispered, her life and soul concentrated in her eyes as they remained fixed on the condemned man. 'Let this soon be over.'

Nathaniel Wylde seemed not to hear the chaplain asking him to repent of his sins as his eyes did a broad sweep of the crowd, suddenly becoming fixed and intent on someone standing apart. His expression froze, but then his eyes narrowed and a slow smile curved his lips as he raised his hand in a courtly flourish of a salute.

Curiously Cassandra turned and followed the line of his gaze, wondering what it could be that had caught his attention and caused him to smile at the moment of death. She saw a man who stood alone, away from the crowd, shrouded in a black cloak and wearing a tall crowned hat. She could not make out his features, but she could see he was as dark as her father was fair. She felt a strange, slithering unease. The man had an air of command she had never encountered before, not even in her father. Everything about his manner warned her that he was an adventurer.

As if the man sensed she was staring at him, he twisted his head towards her. The meeting of their eyes was fleeting, and before Cassandra could take stock of his features he turned quickly and walked away with long ground-devouring strides. The man's self-assurance was infuriating. Feeling the tensing of Drum's figure beside her, she tore her eyes away from the man's departing figure and faced the gallows—just in time to see her father swing to his death.

A violent pain shot through her and she turned away. 'It is done,' she said through her breath to her companion, whose pain was as great as her own. 'This is the darkest day of my life. Come. Let us be gone from here. I have seen enough.'

Together they walked away from the river, away from the crowd, and, although her body still functioned automatically Cassandra walked with blind steps, for her father's death hung all about her.

Drum broke the silence. 'I must return you to Chelsea.'

'No.' The strangling tension in Cassandra's chest began to dissolve, and she drew a long, full breath.

Drum halted his stride and looked at her sharply, warily, waiting for her to continue, sensing she had something other than the execution on her mind.

'I don't want Nat to remain hanging on that rope for the tide to wash over him,' Cassandra said, her voice quivering with deep, angry emotion, 'for the crabs to eat at his flesh, and then to be hung in a metal cage at some point in the estuary for the crows to pick at. When the water covers him I would jump into the Thames and cut him loose myself if I could.'

Drum paused and looked at the lovely, spirited, unhappy girl. There was such a fierceness about her that he didn't doubt her words. 'There's nothing you or anyone can do for Nat now.'

'Yes, there is, Drum,' she said, turning to look at him, her features swept clean of sorrow and a decisive hard gleam in her eyes. 'There is one last thing. There is still his ship—the *Dolphin*.'

'The *Dolphin* has been impounded and is moored further up river awaiting her fate.'

'Then you must be the decider of what her fate will be, Drum. Get her back—and then she is yours. Does that not appeal to you?' she said forcefully, trying to infuse some of her enthusiasm into the lofty pirate. 'Imagine it! That is what Nat would have wanted.'

Drum stared at her incredulously. 'Forget it. It's not possible.'

'Not possible?' Cassandra argued heatedly. 'Why, Drum, I'm disappointed in you. Since when has anything been impossible for you? Come, now. Do not tell me your spirit of adventure has deserted you,' she mocked, with a smile to take the sting from her words.

'Me and my spirit of adventure departed company when I heard Nat had been taken,' Drum grumbled. 'Besides, where will we find the men to sail her? Half the crew who were captured along with Nat have already been hanged.'

'That may be, but there must be scores of out-of-work seamen and dockers living among Wapping and Rotherhithe's rat-infested streets and alleyways who would be willing to join you—for a price.'

'Aye, and a high one at that if you want them to assist in stealing Nat's ship from under the nose of the authorities.'

'And Nat's body. Find someone to recover it at high tide when it's submerged by water. Let the sea be his final resting place—not some gruesome gibbet at Tilbury Point, for all to see and gloat at. Were I a man I would do it myself,' she said, her eyes blazing with the fighting spirit of a rampaging firebrand, 'and see to it that all those responsible for bringing Nat to this suffer the same fate.'

Drum regarded her with disdain. 'You are loyal, but misguided, and very much like Nat.' Deep in thought, he began to pace to and fro, for it would be no easy task to carry out beneath the eyes of the night watch. Once his mind was made up to do as she suggested, his attitude changed radically. After weeks of lassitude he had something to focus on, a goal, and he would pour all his energy into achieving it. 'There are some I know hereabouts who remain loyal to Nat.'

There was something in his voice that made Cassandra's heart beat afresh. 'So you will do it?'

'Aye—I'll do it—but it will be a desperate, dangerous undertaking. Let's hope that providence favours us and the heavy cloud remains, making it a moonless night.'

'You'll succeed. I know you will. Oh, how I envy you. There are times when my life spent at Chelsea stifles me. How I long for the kind of freedom my father enjoyed. It was kind of you to think I should know of his plight, and kinder still to risk coming to tell me.'

At this time Cassandra didn't know how she would cope with a world without her father in it. She had few friends, and cousin Meredith had been in Kent visiting her paternal grandmother for weeks now. When she was at home, fond though Meredith was of Cassandra, the house and garden and entertaining her brother John's friends were her passion—and the extent of her interest. A terrifying vista of emptiness lay before Cassandra. On the plus side John was on an island in the Caribbean. She fixed Drum with a steady gaze as a wave of recklessness came upon her, and she said bluntly, 'Take me with you.'

Drum ceased pacing and looked at her as though she'd taken leave of her senses. Her words set his mouth in a thin line. 'Out of the question! What you ask is absurd.' His voice began to rise and he checked it. 'Women don't belong on pirate ships,' he told her firmly, unable to hide his opinions where women and ships were concerned.

Cassandra's eyes widened with pleading, and she smiled in a way that had never failed to melt Nat's heart.

'And don't look at me like that,' Drum growled, hardening his heart against the coercion of her smile. Such sentiments spelt his ruin. 'I'm not like Nat, who you could wind round your finger like a strand of cotton.'

'Please, Drum. There's nothing for me here. Time and again I've sworn to leave when the opportunity presents itself—and this is it. Following Nat's last visit—a visit that was witnessed by our neighbours—some people have come to know who I am, and they're not kind. They call me names, the favourites being that I am a bastard—a pirate's spawn—and there are worse.' There was an edge to her voice that hardened her tone. 'Oh, my Lord! How I hate those people. Until then I hadn't realised the extent of John and Meredith's protection.'

Drum checked the words of sympathy that rose to his lips. She had no need of them. There was nothing self-pitying in her, in the anger that flamed on her cheeks and set her eyes on fire. Beneath the serene grace was a soul craving excitement and adventure, a spirit struggling to be set free. Drum shook his head, his brows drawn together, for it boded ill, he was certain.

'Nat wouldn't thank me if I put you in danger. Do you

think he would have allowed you to leave your Cousin John's protection?'

'Domination,' Cassandra countered coldly. 'I love John and Meredith dearly, but the kind of life they plan for me—married to some man I would never set my cap at—fills me with dread.' Secretly she dreamed of marrying a man who was dashing and handsome, bold and with a sense of adventure—a man like Nathaniel Wylde.

Drum squinted at her sideways. 'And what makes you think life on the high seas is a playground? Although I suppose the tales Nat filled your head with would have you think so.'

Drum was right. Cassandra had fallen beneath the spell her father wove. The stories he had regaled her with had been more potent than the strongest wine. But she was neither deceived nor disillusioned by them and had long since decided that the dashing heroes of Nat's tales were outlaws, careful to keep well ahead of the law.

'Nat's life was fashioned by his own hands,' Drum continued. 'We were alike. Our souls fed on the same spirit of adventure and a desire to succeed in all we set out to do. Nat was a man of fire, who thought nothing of life if it held no challenge—and such consideration he felt for his daughter was a twist of character you would not expect in such a hardened rogue. But I knew him too well to interpret it as weakness.

'Regardless of the risks, he was drawn back to you time and again like a lodestone, and there were times when it almost cost him his life. I loved Nat like a brother, but that doesn't change the fact that he was a notorious pirate with a well-deserved reputation for villainy.'

The colour slowly drained from Cassandra's face. Drum saw it and forged ahead, refusing to spare her, determined to get it out in the open and make her see Nat for what he was. Too much sentimentality was unthinkable.

'You've convinced yourself Nat was practically a saint, who could do no wrong. The truth is he was much closer to a devil than a saint, and everyone knows it. You were naïve enough to believe his boast that he would never harm anyone.'

'He was still my father and I loved him,' Cassandra remarked defensively.

'You loved an illusion, an illusion you created out of the tales he spun because you were innocent and idealistic.'

'I know that,' she said, fighting to control the wrenching anguish that was strangling her breath in her chest, 'and blind, gullible and stupid. But I refuse to believe that the man my mother fell in love with was all bad. He was my life, my king, and the sea was his own special realm into which I have always dreamed of being initiated.'

'Love blinds you. There's much you don't know about Nat.'

'I know, which is why I want to feel what it is like to experience a little of what he did.'

'And risk capture—even death?'

'Yes. Please, Drum, take me with you.' Her eyes implored him to comply. 'I don't fear the consequence of my actions. I don't care if I die tonight or tomorrow or in the weeks to come.'

Drum looked at her, and then away again. 'That is why I want you to stay here, for the same reason.'

'Cousin John is in the Caribbean at this time on Company business. Meredith is in Kent visiting her grandmother and isn't due back for ages yet. I'll leave her a note explaining where I have gone. She'll be angry, I know, but I'll be halfway across the Atlantic by the time she returns to Chelsea.' She dismissed her cousin without a second thought as she concentrated on the reckless, foolhardy plan forming in her mind, which was beginning to take on a positive shape.

'You have it all mapped out, don't you?'

When the good side of Drum's lips turned down in censure, Cassandra's resolution to stay calm faltered and she fixed him with a fierce stare. 'I'm not so chicken-livered that I will faint on finding myself the only woman aboard with a shipload of men,' she said, voicing her impatience. 'Besides, if they respect Nat as much as you say they did, as his daughter I'll be safe enough.'

'I expect you would.' Drum raised a brow in mock reproof. 'I was considering your sensibilities.'

'Then don't.' Drawing a deep breath, she controlled the urge to shake him. 'I shall go to Barbados—to John, which is where he will be for the next twelve months at least. Oh, Drum—' she sighed when she saw doubt cloud his eyes '—I want to feel the deck of the *Dolphin* beneath my feet— to feel the pull of the wind in my hair and smell the sea. I want to know how it was when you sailed with Nat. You of all people should be able to understand that.'

'Aye, you'll know how it was when you feel the deck heaving beneath your feet. Not many people can stand the motion of a ship's deck. You'll be sick right enough.' Despite his exasperation over her stubbornness, Drum was filled with admiration for her courage, but the rigid, unyielding expression on his scarred face as he looked at her revealed none of this.

Cassandra met his stare, equally resolute. 'If I am, I'll get over it. When we reach Barbados the *Dolphin* is yours to do with as you please.'

Despite his misgivings, Drum gave a twisted grin and a wicked, twinkling gleam shone in his eyes. 'I would give a thousand pieces of eight to see your cousin's reaction when you arrive on Barbados unheralded.'

Cassandra sensed he was weakening and seized the advantage. 'Then you agree to take me?'

He laughed quietly and rubbed his chin, his expression

resigned. 'You have a persuasive tongue—but I don't like it. I still say a woman has no place at sea. If I do succeed in securing the *Dolphin*, your presence on board will be a complication. You are an innocent and as such will need vigilant protection. I don't relish the role of knight-errant being forced on me. God willing we'll encounter fair weather that will enable me to deliver you to your cousin before too long.'

As they walked on Drum's eyes were bright with anticipation as he became infused with Cassandra's enthusiasm. She was Nat's daughter all right—tall, graceful and lithe, as slender as a wand and as agile as a faun. There was an arresting quality about her face and an inner vivacious light shone from her eyes, showing a passion for life—fire and ice. Her mind was strong, her manner bold and determined—a legacy of Nat's.

'There's one thing we must speak of. Your father amassed great wealth over the years. The authorities have been unable to lay their hands on it. Only myself and the remaining members of the crew know where it is to be located. What is to be done with it?'

'As to that, I want none of it. It can sink to the bottom of the sea or be given to the authorities. Do what you will with it, Drum. It was obtained illegally and by force. I did not condone Nat's way of life—and I have to confess that oft was the time I wished it had been different.'

'His way of life was set from the day he seized the *Dolphin*.'

'That I know. Undoubtedly he was a villain—bold and decisive, and he cut a dashing figure—although his daring deeds made him a charming one, and the scale and brilliance of his villainy elevated him to the rank of one of the most notorious pirates that has ever lived.'

'Aye,' Drum agreed with a touch of sadness. 'It did that.'

Tears clouded Cassandra's eyes, dampening her lashes.

'He always made me feel ten feet tall, Drum, and I loved him dearly—pirate or not—to my grief and shame. But he never hurt me so I cannot speak ill of him. When I was thirteen years old and my aunt died and he came to see me, the times I spent with him were the happiest of my life.

'Until then, my life under Aunt Miriam's dominance had been a complete misery, and she never let me forget the stigma of my birth. There was never a day went by when she didn't remind me I was her dead sister's bastard child. Everything I did I did out of a sense of obligation, but, on getting to know Nat, everything I did was to please him, out of love. Now, come,' she said, walking on with a new spring to her step, the crowd behind them at Execution Dock beginning to disperse. 'What about these recruits? I must return to Chelsea to get some things and instruct the servants, and in the mean time you have much to do.'

Drum was of a mind to object, to insist on her remaining at Chelsea, and he would undertake the task of finding men who would be willing to take the risk of releasing the *Dolphin* from her moorings, men who would know how to keep their mouths shut for a price, but he remained silent, knowing the futility of uttering any protestations.

There was only one man who could tell Cassandra Everson what to do—only one man she had wanted to please, who she would ever listen to. But he was hanging from the end of a rope at Execution Dock. It would take an exceptional man—the like of Nathaniel Wylde—to master her, to tame Nat's illegitimate, wilful daughter. It would have to be a man who loved her, a man who could not be swayed by the false promise of a coercive, dimpled smile.

Captain Sir Stuart Marston strode away from Execution Dock with a profound feeling of relief that it was done. At last he had seen his foremost enemy suffer the punishment he deserved.

On the restoration of Charles II to the throne of England, Nathaniel Wylde had ignored a Royal pardon to surrender himself and continued taking and plundering ships bound for the West Indies. Initially, having no love of Cromwell's protectorate in England, he had preyed only on Parliamentary ships, but over the years, as his enthusiasm for piracy flourished and his gains became richer, in his greed and lust for more it had come to matter little what flag a ship sailed under if her cargo was worth the taking.

It was almost a year ago that Stuart's elder brother had been on one of the ships bound for Jamaica to visit his uncle who owned a plantation there, when his vessel had come under attack from pirates. In a heavy mist the heavily laden merchant vessel, having sailed wide of the convoy in which it was travelling, had stood little chance of outrunning or outgunning the two pirate ships—fast single-masted sloops with forty guns between them.

Only a handful of those on board had survived to tell the tale, and Stuart had learned that the captain of the vessel that had led the attack was Nathaniel Wylde, and that after removing the cargo he and his cohorts had left the stricken ship and nearly all those on board to sink to the bottom of the sea. News of this sinking had shocked the Admiralty and public alike in England. Driven by a need to avenge his brother, Stuart had approached the Admiralty and been granted his wish.

He was issued with a privateering mission allowing him to seek out Captain Nathaniel Wylde with his ship, the *Sea Hawk*, to arrest and bring him back to London to stand trial for his crimes—an unusual concession, for such licence was usually issued to a Royal Naval vessel, but the ships of the Royal Navy were needed in the long-running fight with the Dutch.

After drawing Captain Wylde out of his lair in the Gulf of Mexico, Stuart had hounded him across the Atlantic to the coast of West Africa, which had fewer hiding places than the islands of the Caribbean.

Wylde had put up a fierce fight, but eventually Stuart and the seamen under his command had managed to capture the *Dolphin*, her captain and half her crew. Along with his ship, Nathaniel Wylde had been brought to England in chains and hanged.

In possession of a feeling of deep satisfaction that he had avenged himself on Captain Wylde for the death of his brother, Stuart proceeded towards the Pool of London where the *Sea Hawk*, chartered to a private English mercantile company, was moored.

He had only one more mission to the West Indies to carry out for the Company before he was to retire from the sea and settle down to a life of ease at Charnwood in Kent, home to his family for generations, where he would satisfy his mother's desire that he find himself a wife and provide her with grandchildren and an heir.

Absently his thoughts turned to the tall, slender young woman he had observed from a distance watching the execution of Nathaniel Wylde. There had been an intense look of concentration in her eyes, which had turned to open curiosity when they had met his. Each had briefly assessed the other with an unwavering stare, and the woman's steady gaze had taken on an iron nerve. It was the measure of a woman confident of her own worth.

Her eyes had been the only feature exposed, but he recalled the long strand of pale gold hair escaping the confines of her hood. It had drawn his gaze like a moth to a flame, for it was the only bright feature to lighten the dreariness of the day until Nathaniel Wylde had appeared, and his own mane of hair had shone to equal that of the woman's.

It was then the truth burst on him—that the young woman he had seen could in all probability have been

Wylde's daughter. At first his brain refused to accept it and he smiled at his foolish, fanciful thoughts, for not by any stretch of the imagination could he visualise a man's daughter coming to watch her father hang. However, recollecting tales told by mariners that Nathaniel Wylde had a daughter of spirit and great beauty, and that she lived with relatives somewhere in London, perhaps he was not mistaken in his suspicion after all—and with Wylde's blood in her, she would feel neither distress nor out of place at a hanging.

The more he thought about it—having observed her as Wylde had mounted the gallows, he had seen her knuckles showing white from the force with which she had gripped the hood of her cloak across her face, and recollected how both she and her companion had gone to great lengths to keep their features concealed as they remained hovering on the edge of the crowd—the more possible, the more probable it became that the woman he had seen was indeed the pirate's daughter.

He could have turned back and denounced her companion, who was undoubtedly one of Wylde's associates, but for some reason unknown to him he hired a hackney to take him to his ship, eager to put the unpleasant episode behind him and slake his thirst and eat his dinner in the warm comfort of his cabin, reluctant to condemn another man to the same gruesome fate as Nathaniel Wylde.

But the following morning he had grave misgivings and was compelled to examine his failure to turn back and denounce the man when the bosun informed him that, unobserved, the *Dolphin* had slipped quietly from her moorings in the dark of the night and was last seen heading down river towards the sea—a woman, with pale blonde hair flowing down the length of her back and dressed in breeches, her feet planted firmly apart, standing in the prow of the ship.

When the tide had receded it was also revealed that Nathaniel Wylde's body had been cut free of the hangman's noose at Execution Dock.

Chapter Two

After encountering severe storms off the mainland of South America, which severely damaged the *Dolphin*'s hull and forced her to put in at the first landfall, which happened to be the island of Trinidad, it was with sadness and reluctance that Cassandra, eager to reach Barbados and her cousin Sir John Everson, parted company with the *Dolphin*.

The burial they had given her father at sea had been a particularly poignant moment for her. She had watched through a mist of tears as the corpse of the man who had been tied to her by blood had slipped beneath the grey waters. 'Goodbye, Father,' she had whispered, and in the soulful wind blowing over the sea came the tempting strains of an answering farewell, strains that filled her heart, a sound heard by her alone.

And now Cassandra was glad to be moving on, to put the tragic memories of those terrible last days in London behind her. She acquired a passage on a large English merchant vessel, the *Spirit of Enterprise*, bound for Barbados and Antigua. During the same storms that had battered the *Dolphin*, the merchantman, which had been travelling in an organised convoy, since lone vessels were in danger of being attacked and plundered by pirates, had been blown se-

verely off course, and the ship's commander, Captain Tillotson, had put in at Trinidad to take on fresh water.

Uneasy at Cassandra being the only woman on board the
Dolphin, Drum had insisted that his daughter, eighteen-
year-old Rosa, accompany her. She was a quiet, comely
girl, with dark features like her Portuguese mother. Drum
had taken her on board when they had made a lengthy stop
at Praia, his home in the Cape Verde Islands.

In desperate need of provisions, and to carry out urgent
repairs to the badly leaking *Dolphin*, Drum was to go on
to one of the neighbouring islands—an island that was a
favourite haunt for pirates. Contrary to his misgivings when
he had taken Cassandra on board, the sailors had taken to
her like seals to the ocean, and the entire crew would mourn
her departure.

Drum bore a deep and abiding love for his daughter;
when the moment came to say farewell, he stood still for
a moment while Rosa rested her head against him, then he
patted her and said gruffly, 'Be a good girl, Rosa, and do
as Cassandra tells you.' Promising dutifully that she would,
lifting her arms she put them round her father's neck and
kissed his scarred cheek. He held her tightly for a moment
and then stepped back and turned to Cassandra.

'Try not to worry about Rosa, Drum,' Cassandra said,
aware of his concern and touched at how much feeling this
hard-bitten pirate possessed for his daughter. 'Captain Tillotson is to give us his protection until we reach my cousin.
I promise to take good care of her, and ensure her safe
passage back to Cape Verde. Where will you go, when the
Dolphin is repaired?'

'Who knows?' he said with a roguish, Irish grin. 'The
ship will sail, winged by her oars, and go wherever the
wind will take us.'

If Captain Tillotson thought it strange for an English
woman to be travelling with just one female companion so

far from home, he was too much of a gentleman to show it. However, the occupants of the *Dolphin* stirred his curiosity and he suspected they were sea rovers, but the captain, though fearsome to look at with his scarred face, seemed a reasonable enough individual and was clearly concerned that the young lady and her companion be delivered safely to her cousin on Barbados.

It was with the dawn on a morning in April, almost five months after leaving England, that Cassandra glimpsed the coral island of Barbados, its encircling reefs giving her a degree of security and immunity. It was a large island, hanging like a teardrop one hundred miles east of the Caribbean chain. Well situated in terms of the north-easterly trade winds and ocean currents that enabled the island to receive shipping from Europe, it rose on the horizon wreathed in a golden mist, like a mirage, bewitching, peaceful and powerfully hypnotic, and, the closer they sailed, the air blowing from inland was heavy with a thousand scents.

The ship anchored in the commodious bay at Bridgetown. The glittering waters were dotted with all manner of craft, from fishing ketches and lighters to huge merchantmen that docked at Barbados frequently. Barbados was successful in its manufacture of sugar, and Bridgetown, bustling to an ageless quick tempo, was the island's trading centre.

The noise and colour assailed Cassandra's senses, and the hot Caribbean sun gilded the town and warehouses that lined the waterfront in a silver glow. Everywhere disorder reigned. A never-ceasing army of bare-chested black slaves worked laboriously, driving wagons and manning the oars of the lighters—sturdy vessels utilised to transport cargo to and from the ships anchored in the bay. They were built to carry twenty to thirty tons—and in many cases passengers and cargo would be lucky to escape a drenching.

The figures on the beach were a blur in the trembling heat haze as Cassandra was rowed in a precariously laden lighter from the ship. With no room in the boat for another person or piece of baggage, Rosa had been left with no alternative but to take the boat behind. When they were halfway to the shore, the boat carrying Cassandra began to list precariously to one side as it was tossed about on the choppy water, causing the baggage to shift. Everyone in the boat realised it was about to capsize.

Overseeing the unloading of his ship, the *Sea Hawk*, Stuart Marston stood on the shore, momentarily distracted from watching his cargo of much-wanted metals and broadcloth being taken to the warehouses, when his attention was caught by a female occupant in one of the boats advancing towards the shore. A wide-brimmed hat with a sweeping white plume sat on top of her silvery blonde hair, and she was lavishly attired in garments that would have graced the Court of King Charles in England, yet which looked incongruously out of place on this tropical island.

Her beauty was apparent and he could not tear his eyes away from her. She seemed to exist in a shimmering pool of silver light radiating all about her. His dark gaze swept over her features appreciatively, for like all hot-blooded men he was easily moved by the beauty of a woman. Observing that the boat she was in was about to cast her into the sea, immediately he strode into the surf and began wading through the shallow water towards it.

Taken completely by surprise as two tanned hands reached out and hauled her from the boat just as it keeled over, spilling occupants and baggage into the water and causing a general turmoil, Cassandra gasped and began struggling against the person who had taken such liberty, but it was like trying to prise herself out of a steel trap.

'Be still,' commanded the masculine voice of her captor, his hard arms tightening about her waist and beneath her knees, 'or you'll have us both in the water.'

Startled by the harsh, deep resonance of his tone, Cassandra did as he ordered, torn between amusement and a certain amount of consternation, but, on seeing her captor's handsome features and encountering an amused dark stare, she relaxed and, reaching up, placed her arms about his neck.

Smiling up at him, she let her eyes dwell on the tiny beads of perspiration, which glistened like delicate pearl drops on his brown flesh. Nothing had prepared her for the thrill of excitement that travelled deliciously throughout her body at finding herself pressed against the broad chest of such a powerfully attractive man.

'I realise that you must have feared for my safety when you saw the boat list, and I am grateful to you for coming so swiftly to my rescue, sir,' she murmured, feeling the hardness of his body and the tightening of his sinewy arms supporting her, and conscious of the faint scent of sandalwood, which he favoured. 'It was extremely gallant of you. However, I can swim and the sea in this part is not nearly deep enough for a person to drown.'

'Then I am glad I was ignorant of that fact since it would have denied me the pleasure of carrying you to the beach. Unless, of course, you would like me to put you down into the water—which I do not recommend,' he said, the quirk in his lips deepening into an amused, one-sided grin, and his eyes sparkling with devilment, 'for it is not unknown for sharks to swim in the shallows in the hope of obtaining a tasty meal.'

'Then it would appear I have no option but to remain where I am. I have no mind to be eaten by the sharks, so I am perfectly happy for you to carry me all the way to the shore,' Cassandra replied softly, falling under the influence of the stranger's slow and easy smile.

She was content to let her eyes linger on the deep cleft in his chin, which emphasised the strength of his jaw. His mouth was wide, his lips firm, and she conceived that it denoted humour as well as hardness. The only imperfection was a small scar, which curved down one cheek, yet even that could not mar his handsome face. His eyes were impressive, fierce and black, their smouldering depths seductive and enticing, and totally alive.

Cassandra judged him to be in his late twenties or early thirties. There was a certain arrogance and aggressive quality to his features, and he was self-assured and attractive enough to turn any woman's head. His hair was thick and unruly and shining black, and a heavy wave fell with careless unrestraint over his brow. His skin shone with a bronzed, smooth, healthy glow and he looked magnificently virile and masculine.

Feeling himself undergoing her close scrutiny Stuart looked down at her. Their eyes met, his bolder and more penetrating than any man's who had looked at her before. They openly and unabashedly displayed his approval as his gaze ranged over her face. The slow grin that followed and the gleam in his dark eyes brought a stinging heat creeping over Cassandra's skin and her heart turned over beneath the warmth, the power of it. Realising she was staring at him with a brazenness that was immodest, she lowered her eyes. Her sudden discomfiture broadened his smile, displaying two even rows of white teeth.

'Do I unsettle you?' he enquired quietly.

'No. Not in the least.' That was not quite true, for he did unsettle her. Having no experience of men like this, she was not at all sure how to handle the incident.

'If so, I beg your pardon. You are an extremely beautiful young woman—indeed, it would be ungracious of me to say otherwise—and I fear I have been on board ship too long. My manners appear to have deserted me,' Stuart confessed, looking down into her eyes raised to his, bright and vivid blue—periwinkle blue, the bluest eyes he had ever seen, the pupils as black as jet. From that moment he was intrigued.

Held in his arms, she was as light as swan's-down and he could feel every slender curve of her body, hinting at hidden delights. The fresh delicate scent of jasmine rose from her skin that was burned golden brown, which intrigued him more, since all the young ladies of his acquaintance deemed it shocking to expose one's flesh to the sun.

But Stuart suspected this was no ordinary young woman. He sensed in her an adventuresome spirit, which had no room for convention or etiquette. There was nothing demure about her, as was the case with the young ladies who flitted in and out of his mother's circle back in England, whose eyes would be ingeniously cast down, even among those they knew, which was proper. This young lady showed none of the restraint instilled into young girls of good family. She stared directly into his eyes. Her own glowed with an inner light and hinted of the woman hidden beneath the soft innocence of her face.

Around the slender column of her throat she wore a diamond-studded velvet band that matched her oyster silk gown. Despite the searing heat of the day and the heavy clothes she wore, she looked cool and completely at ease, not in the least embarrassed or discomfited at being carried in the arms of a half-dressed sea captain in full view of sailors and townspeople, or concerned by the capsizing of the boat, which its occupants were trying frantically to correct.

'So—you are English,' he said at length, his curiosity matching his growing ardour.

'Does that surprise you?'

'Considering we are on the other side of the Atlantic in the West Indies, then I have to say it does, Mistress…?'

'Everson.'

'I am most pleased to meet you, Mistress Everson.'

'I am here to visit my cousin, Sir John Everson.'

'Is he a planter on the island?'

'No. He is a director and shareholder of a mercantile company based in London—the Wyndham Company. Perhaps you know of it.'

'There are few in the trade who don't. Its commercial success has attracted understandable envy and admiration from its rivals. The Company has expressed an interest in expanding eastwards—to the Spice Islands and India, I believe.'

'Maybe so. I couldn't say. John doesn't often discuss Company business with me. For myself, I had a mind to pay him a visit—to see something of the West Indies and widen my horizons. Should I find Barbados as pleasant as it's been portrayed, then I shall be in no hurry to leave,' Cassandra told him lightly, as if she were speaking of nothing more interesting than visiting the county next to the one in which she lived in England, instead of an island on the other side of the Atlantic Ocean.

'And you live in London?'

'More or less. I live in the village of Chelsea.'

'Then being from Chelsea, you'll find this climate and its people very different.'

Bathed in a tropical heat, Cassandra gazed along the shimmering line of sand. It was a vibrant and colourful scene, an unfamiliar one, with people who were strangers, not only white but black, too. These black people were slaves, of a different culture, who spoke an unintelligible language, brought over from Africa to work the labour-intensive sugar plantations.

Slavery might have economic advantages but it involved

cruelty. It was a system that restricted the human rights of individuals owned by the white planters. John had explained that without slaves the plantations could not exist, which was the sad reality of the island's success. It was a system Cassandra found abhorrent, and she was glad the Wyndham Company's operations did not extend to the triangular route.

The triangular route began in Europe with ships loaded with trade goods bound for Africa. These goods were bartered or sold for slaves. The second leg of the journey— known as the Middle Passage—was across the Atlantic to the Caribbean, where the slaves were offloaded and sold at auctions or privately. Laden with tropical produce, the ships then returned to Europe on the third leg of their journey.

Cassandra knew that in the weeks ahead she would see slavery in all its ugliness, but today, beneath a blue sky and the white-capped sea pulsating with the forces of wind and gravity all around her, the island seemed to hold a special allure. Already she could feel herself falling under its spell. She breathed in the air of the future in the making, the strange, unfamiliar scents borne on the breeze that blew from inland, which in her ignorance of a place she had only a rudimentary awareness of she could not put a name to, but which, altogether, became the essence of the Caribbean. It was exciting and made her feel vibrantly alive and set her blood racing.

'Oh, I think I shall come to like it very well,' she finally replied quietly. She eased against the stranger as he continued to wade through the shallows, intensely aware of the immediate effect of her movement as she heard him catch his breath and felt his arm tighten about her waist. How was it possible that the warmth of that corded arm burned through her dress and into her flesh? She looked at his face, just inches from her own, and the bold gleam in his eyes almost halted her breath. 'And you, sir? What is your business on Barbados?'

'My ship, the *Sea Hawk*, is chartered by a mercantile company back in London—the Wheatley and Roe Company—not as successful as the Wyndham Company, I grant you, but it does well enough. I am Captain Stuart Marston, and glad to be of service.'

They had reached the shore but he continued to hold her, seeming reluctant to put her down—and it shocked Cassandra to find she was thoroughly enjoying the experience and the sensation of having him hold her so close.

She smiled up at him through her long, thick lashes. 'We have reached the shore, Captain Marston. I think it's quite safe to put me down now. Do you know my cousin?' she asked as he set her down on the sand, experiencing a feeling of regret when he relinquished his hold on her.

'No, I can't say that I do. I did not arrive myself until yesterday.'

'But you are no stranger to the West Indies?' she asked, smoothing her skirts and quite unconcerned that they had been doused in seawater, for they would be dry in no time in this heat.

'I have made frequent trips over the years—both to the Indies and America.'

'And accumulated exciting tales to tell, I don't doubt,' Cassandra teased. 'What a pity I don't have the time to stay and listen to them. I do so enjoy tales of adventure and valour and daring-do.'

A lazy grin swept across Stuart's tanned face, and he smiled deep into her eyes. 'Would you make of me a braggart, Mistress Everson?'

She inclined her head in response to his disarming smile. 'I would not be so bold, Captain Marston. Tell me, as someone who is familiar with the island, what do you think of Barbados? Can you recommend it? My cousin says you have to experience it for yourself, to take in the powerful flavours of the island, and form your own opinion. Would you agree with him?'

'Your cousin is right. It is true that the Caribbean Islands are quite splendid—unique, in fact—and you must be prepared for a strange new experience. Their mystique has attracted travellers from all over the world.' He glanced at the *Spirit of Enterprise* out in the bay, squinting his eyes in the sun's glare. 'I see you sailed on the *Spirit of Enterprise*, commanded by my good friend Samuel Tillotson. I'm glad he made it after being blown off course, when he might have fallen into the hands of buccaneers that infest these waters. Unfortunately these lawless, uncontrollable desperadoes are capable of attacking and stripping some of the greatest ships when they're without the protection of the convoy, and think nothing of slaughtering everyone on board.'

His words were spoken with some deep-felt emotion, and there was an underlying bitterness that was not lost on Cassandra. Her conscience smote her and she averted her eyes, her thoughts locked upon her own involvement with such men. 'Yes. We must be thankful he made it.'

'And are you travelling alone?'

'No,' she replied, moving a little away from him, finding that being in such close proximity was curiously disturbing. He was uncommonly tall, a little over six foot, she thought. He wore a loose-fitting coarse linen shirt, which flapped open to expose a broad expanse of bronzed chest covered with a dusting of black hair. A thick leather belt with a silver buckle circled his waist, and beneath his black breeches, rolled up above his knees, his calves bulged and the sand stuck to his wet feet. She had seen men on board the *Dolphin* similarly dressed, but none had affected her in quite the same way that he did. 'I—I have a companion with me.'

'A lady?' he asked, cocking a quizzical dark eyebrow.

'But of course,' she laughed. 'I could not possibly travel halfway across the world on a ship with no companion other than seamen, now could I? It would be unbecoming for me to travel unattended.' Suppressing a smile, she wondered what his reaction would be if she were to tell him she was no stranger to life on board a ship with only hard-bitten pirates for company. No doubt he would be horrified and want nothing more to do with her.

'And your cousin—he is expecting you?'

Cassandra's eye's clouded and her expression became serious, for she was apprehensive of what John's reaction would be on seeing her. 'On the contrary. In search of adventure and to carve myself a mark in the world, when I left England I cast aside the security of home and family, knowing I faced the censure of my cousin John, who is also my guardian. I dare say he will be horrified to see me and his anger will be ferocious indeed, especially since I have no defence for my actions.'

'And you don't expect to escape retribution.' Stuart's eyes scanned her face, the twitch of his mouth revealing his amusement, while at the same time the thought did cross his mind that the young lady might be in love with her cousin.

'Unfortunately no. I fear the consequence of my actions. John will be unable to refrain from showing his displeasure—and no doubt I will be thoroughly admonished for my unsuitable, impetuous behaviour. But once he is over the worst of his anger and has calmed down, I know he will be pleased to see me.'

A breeze rippled through the plume in the brim of Cassandra's hat and she turned her face better to feel its coolness on her cheeks, offering some relief from the heat and humidity, finding as she did so that her eyes were drawn to Captain Marston's irresistibly. His steadfast gaze held hers so she could not look away. She saw his face was not lacking in interest for he was beginning to realise he had met a real phenomenon.

'So, your stay on Barbados is indefinite, Mistress Everson?'

The smile returned to her lips. 'It is my wish to remain for as long as possible—but then, regrettable though it will be when the time comes, I must return to England with my cousin. How long that will be I can't say until I've seen him. And you, Captain Marston? How long are you to remain on Barbados?'

'When my ship has been relieved of its cargo I have to go on to Jamaica. I have relatives there I wish to see, and I have to collect a fresh cargo—mainly sugar. I expect to be gone several weeks, but I shall return to Barbados in time to join the convoy back to England.'

They turned to watch the boat that had capsized being hauled on to the beach, and the one carrying Rosa and the young midshipman Captain Tillotson had ordered to escort her followed close behind.

Stuart looked at Cassandra. His black eyes narrowed as he studied her with unnerving intensity. 'I am reluctant to see you go, Mistress Everson. Perhaps you will allow me to escort you to your cousin?'

Cassandra averted her eyes. Being flesh and blood, she could not remain unmoved by the attentions of such a devastatingly handsome man. The feelings he roused in her were unsettling and outside her experience. 'Thank you— you are most kind, but—Captain Tillotson has instructed one of his midshipmen to take me directly to him,' she explained hesitantly, watching the young man of whom she spoke assisting Rosa from the boat.

'And you know where he is to be located?'

He moved closer to her, a towering masculine presence who filled her sights. Close to, his ruggedness seemed more pronounced, and the broad expanse of his chest and arms reminded her rather forcefully of how his powerful body had felt pressed against her. Unexpectedly Cassandra found herself the victim of an absurd attack of shyness, and she suddenly felt extremely uncomfortable with the dark way he was regarding her, his gaze narrowed and assessing.

'Y-yes,' she stammered. 'He—he is staying at the Courtly plantation, which is the home of Sir Charles Courtly in the parish of St George. Sir Charles is John's long-time friend, who also has large investments in the Wyndham Company.'

Stuart nodded. Her confusion showed on her face. She was very young, her face that of a guileless child, and his own became warm and gentle, and yet at the same time ardent. He drank in her presence, quelling the insane impulse to bend his head and slowly, endlessly, kiss the smile from her soft inviting lips, to carry her along the shore away from prying eyes and make love to her.

She had no conception of her own beauty or the impact it had on men. No woman had ever affected him so deeply on first meeting. He must see her again, and the knowledge that he would exhilarated him. She fired his blood. He wanted her completely and irrevocably—with a need that defied all reason.

'Then at least allow me to arrange some transport to take you out there.'

Cassandra accepted gracefully. There was a vigorous purposefulness in his long quick strides as he headed for the waterfront, and an air of carefully restrained power, of forcefulness, emanating from him. She stood rooted to the sand, while all of Meredith's dark warnings about being acquainted with men such as Captain Marston rushed through her mind.

He spoke with a silver tongue, and his words, like his bold stare, set her blood aflame. He had told her he would be reluctant to see her go, and she was surprised how reluctant she would be to leave him. She told herself she was being foolish, that she was overreacting to what was nothing more than empty flattery, that it could not matter to her. Despite what he thought and said, she could not link her future with that of a reckless sea captain. In no time at all he returned.

'It's all arranged. A carriage is waiting to take you out to the Courtly plantation. It's hardly a vehicle fit for a lady, but it will get you there.'

'Thank you. You have been most helpful.'

'I hope we will meet again before I have to return to England. Perhaps when I return from Jamaica. Everything about you intrigues me in a way that makes me want to get to know you better.'

Suspicious of his flattery, Cassandra laughed nervously, though a traitorous part of her responded to the low caress of his voice. She had to get away from him—to escape the intoxicating madness he was plunging her into. She needed all her willpower to dispel the assault on her defences. This man was too assured, too handsome, too irresistibly exciting by far.

'And I think you are an outrageous flatterer, and capable of luring helpless females into a game at which you are obviously a master, Captain Marston. Yes, I can well believe that you are capable of charming a snake out of its basket. How many female hearts have you stolen with such honeyed sentiments?'

His look was swift and predatory, and a roguish gleam brightened his eyes. 'Some—although I see nothing helpless about you. However, most women would think such thoughts but never utter them.'

Cassandra saw laughter lurking in the depths of his dark eyes. He was mocking her. Annoyance stirred and her eyes flashed. 'I am not most women, Captain Marston.'

He raised an eyebrow with an amused admiration. He hadn't missed the flare of temper in her eyes. 'I couldn't agree more. You are unaware of the potency of your charms that makes you different, Mistress Everson, and I meant no insult.'

Cassandra smothered a smile at the man's outrageous audacity. 'None taken.'

'And you will allow me to call on you when I return?'

'Yes, of course. I shall look forward to it,' she murmured.

'Thank you. Duty may take me away from you now, but not for long. I will not lose you. If you are not here when I return, then I will find you in London.' His voice was low, urgent and persuasive, and he was studying her from beneath his strongly marked eyebrows, watching her face as he bowed his dark head politely, his expression appraising as she turned and began to move away and followed the young midshipman and her companion off the beach.

Stuart's eyes continued to watch her. Her step was one of confidence, as if she sensed hidden dangers ahead but determined nevertheless to enjoy them. She moved gracefully, with an added fluency that drew the eye to the elegance of her straight back and the proud tilt of her head. In those first dazzling moments when he had scooped her out of the capsizing boat, neither had been prepared for the impact of their meeting, for the attraction had been mutual and instantaneous. The unexpectedness of it astounded Stuart, and Cassandra would have been surprised if she had known the depth of his feelings as she walked away from him. Suddenly, this, his final trip on the *Sea Hawk*, had begun to take on a certain appeal.

Young, original and fresh, Mistress Everson possessed an indescribable magnetism in abundance, with that unique quality of innocence and sexuality rarely come by. She was a woman, hardly more than a child, with a combination of youthful beauty and an untouched air of shy modesty, and yet she had about her a primitive earthiness that sat strangely at odds with her well-bred gentility. When she smiled a small dimple appeared in her cheek, and her rosy parted lips revealed perfect, small white teeth. Stuart was enchanted. He thought he had never seen anything quite so appealing or irresistibly captivating as Mistress Everson. Women like her were as scarce and as hard to come by as a rare jewel and must be treated as such, and he was determined that she would not escape him.

He knew practically nothing about her, but the violence and depth of his attraction, and his instinct, told him he had met the woman with whom he wished to spend the rest of his life. He had always avoided any sentimental attachment, yet here, against his will—for he had not thought to look for a wife until he returned to England—he found his head filled with thoughts of Mistress Everson, and he became determined that as soon as he returned from Jamaica he would embark on the most exhilarating and exciting chase of his life.

As he was about to turn away he stopped in his tracks and looked at her again, checked, suddenly, by a memory when he saw a thick strand of her silvery gold hair, having come loose from the pins securing it beneath her hat, become caught by the breeze. It toyed with it and raised it high, and it rippled and danced behind her as she walked like a ship's pennon borne on the wind. His brow became creased in a puzzled frown when the memory stirred once more. He tried to think what it was and to remember of whom it was Mistress Everson reminded him. He got no further, for at that moment he was distracted when one of his crew drew his attention, and he was forced to turn his mind to other things.

Cassandra knew Captain Marston was watching her as she walked away through the vibrant, colourful profusion of people thronging the beach. She was tempted to turn her head and look back, but for some strange reason that was beyond her she kept her eyes focused ahead.

How could it be that after a few minutes away from him she was already craving his company once more? When he had looked into her eyes she had felt the intensity of his regard, and had known that he was passionately aware of her. Their meeting had left her tingling with pleasure, for she had never met a man so fascinating, stimulating and exciting. That he was a man of power and accustomed to obedience from others was clear.

She very much hoped they would meet again—or did she? She sighed, totally confused. What was wrong with her? Had she lost control of her reason? Was the island getting to her already? Was it the heat or some temporary madness? No one had ever made her feel this way. Could it possibly be that she was falling in love with a man she had met just once?

Chapter Three

The Courtly plantation lay some four miles inland in the parish of St George, a broad lowland area separating the higher central uplands from the southern region. Since the settlement of Barbados by English colonists in 1627, the island had developed with astonishing rapidity, as forest clearance had proceeded apace, and the production of sugar, and its by-products, rum and molasses, had become the island's principal economy. Barbados was politically stable, with the institution of slavery dominating every aspect of life on the island.

Protected from the sun's hot rays by a parasol she had acquired in Trinidad, seated beside Rosa in the swaying carriage, Cassandra had a good view of the sun-drenched island. At the back of her was the jewel-bright sea, and before her stretched an undulating landscape of small settlements, modest hills and a patchwork of flat, tidy sugar fields, with the sight of expansive sugar plantations and poorly maintained settlers' cabins dotting the verdant landscape.

Winding footpaths cut through brush and forest, thick with tropical foliage. The size and shapes of the trees, many of them towering fringed cabbage palms, were awesome.

Leaving the road, they travelled down a wide track. Ahead of them were the outbuildings and the main house of a sprawling plantation. The three-storey stone and timber house, sturdy and handsome, which had been built on a rise above the cane fields to catch the cooling breezes and to look over the estate, was a stately English manor house in a tropical setting.

The plantation consisted of boiling houses and distilleries and other factory houses necessary for the manufacture of sugar, along with the squalid rows of palm-thatched slave huts, which were at the rear of the big house. They were partly hidden from sight by a barrier of trees and far enough away so any unpleasant odours did not offend the refined noses of the gentry who inhabited or visited Courtly Hall.

John had told her a little of Sir Charles Courtly, whose father, backed by merchant capital in England, had arrived on Barbados in the 1640s. Growing sugar had been his carriage to wealth and he had amassed a fortune, which, on his demise, had passed to his son. The family had become one of several that had come to dominate the island's economy and politics. When he wasn't in England—where he displayed an ostentatious lifestyle—Sir Charles Courtly hosted some of the most elaborate social gatherings on the island.

The carriage travelled up a long, narrow avenue lined with fringed palms. As they neared the house Cassandra's reaction to the heat, the smell, the noise and the people she saw going about their work was almost physical. She breathed deeply with pleasure, for nothing had prepared her for this, but when the carriage stopped at the door of the house her heart throbbed. Knowing the painful interview with her cousin was close, a tension began to build inside her.

The door was opened by a servant, a man resplendent in pale blue silk, and when he saw Cassandra and Rosa, a wide, incredulous smile of welcome split his black face. The man, whose name was Henry, was so polite and his smile so infectious, that the two women were put at ease immediately.

When Cassandra introduced herself and Rosa and told him who it was she wished to see, he bade them enter. Cassandra paused to enquire of the young midshipman about paying the driver of the carriage, only to be told that the fee had been settled by the gentleman who had hired it. Cassandra's heart warmed with gratitude for Captain Marston. If she should meet the handsome sea captain again—which she sincerely hoped would be the case—she would thank him for his kindness.

After unloading the carriage and placing the baggage in the drive, the midshipman climbed back on to the seat beside the driver and headed back to Bridgetown. At the same time as the visitors entered the house, a petite, elegant lady with a vivacious air, in middle age, breezed into the hall. The faint scent of roses surrounded her, floating from her lilac silk gown. It was the fragrance that always reminded Cassandra of Meredith, the scent of home, comfort and love. A host of memories stirred in her heart, and her conscience pricked her, sharp in its sting, for she sincerely hoped Meredith had forgiven her for disappearing like she had.

'I am Julia Courtly,' the lady murmured, introducing herself immediately and greeting Cassandra with unfeigned pleasure, a delighted smile dawning on her face, much of her youthful beauty still very much in evidence.

Cassandra felt a pair of brown eyes scrutinising her curiously. 'I am Cassandra Everson, Lady Courtly, and this is Rosa, my companion. I must offer my deep apologies that we should impose ourselves on you uninvited, but I am here to see my cousin, Sir John Everson. I believe he is staying here at Courtly Hall.'

Lady Courtly looked most surprised. 'He certainly is, my dear, but John never said you were coming.'

Cassandra had the grace to look contrite. 'He—he doesn't know. I thought I would surprise him.'

'And he will be. I can't tell you how pleased I am to welcome you to Courtly Hall,' Lady Courtly said effusively. 'We will not trouble ourselves as to why you have come to Barbados or how, but will see that your visit is an enjoyable one.'

'John—is here?' Cassandra enquired tentatively.

'Yes, I do believe so, but not here in the house. He prefers to stay in a bungalow in the grounds.' Her eyes went past Cassandra to Rosa, who looked as if she were about to wilt. 'Mercy! You must think me atrociously lacking in manners. Please forgive me. You will be tired and in dire need of refreshment after your journey. Come into the drawing room.' She ushered them inside, turning to Henry and instructing him to have refreshments sent in.

The interior of the room was cool and elegant, with exquisite silk hangings, pictures and gilt mirrors, carpets and furniture shipped over from England and France years before, a tribute to the family's good taste.

'You must be made comfortable at once,' Lady Courtly said. 'I shall see that rooms are prepared while you take some refreshment.'

Cassandra smiled her gratitude. She hadn't expected to be greeted so warmly. 'I thank you for your kind thought,' she said in a low voice, 'but Rosa and I really don't wish to be any trouble. It was an exceedingly irresponsible action on my part to come here without a proper invitation. We will be perfectly content to stay with John.'

'What! In that poky bungalow where there isn't room for a body to turn round? Absolutely not. I'll not hear of it. You are John's cousin and there is no better place for you to stay than under this roof. Besides, with my son and his wife away in England at present, the house is much too quiet.' Impulsively Lady Courtly put out her hand and laid it on Cassandra's, her smile warm and entrancing. 'I shall so enjoy having you stay and introducing you to our friends, and you can tell me all about what is happening in England.'

'Thank you, Lady Courtly. I will speak to John.'

'Of course you will, and I know he will agree that it is best you stay here. Oh, and my name is Julia, by the way. Lady Courtly sounds pompous and so formal, I always think. The three of you will dine here later—and then you can meet my husband.'

After partaking of much-needed refreshment, Cassandra and Rosa were directed to John's bungalow some distance from the house by a shy young houseboy. The small building was almost hidden by the surrounding trees and sweet-scented flowering shrubs, and all manner of hanging and climbing creepers, with blossoms as dark as crimson or white as snow. The air was heavy with their perfume and the droning of bees.

Thanking the boy, who scuttled away, Cassandra stepped on to the verandah, welcoming the cool tranquillity of the shade it offered. Two bamboo rocking chairs stood side by side, and a hammock hung from a nearby tree. Gingerly she stepped through the open door, unprepared for the exotic strangeness of the bungalow, of its smell of lemons and musk. The polished wooden floor was strewn with gaily-coloured woven mats, and curtains fluttered in the gentlest of breezes at the open windows. Brocade upholstered divans scattered with corded and tasselled cushions stood against the walls.

Emerging from an adjoining room, hastily fastening his breeches, John's appearance was dishevelled, his eyes languid. Cassandra laughed with delight on seeing her cousin, of whom she was extremely fond. Her delight was short-lived. The effect her arrival had on the man who was twelve years her senior was one of incredulity and absolute horror. Despite the heat and John's natural high colour, his rapidly whitening wide-eyed face was enough to unsettle Cassandra's composure.

Smiling apprehensively, she moved towards him, hoping for an embrace, but John did not laugh, and nor did the coffee-skinned, scantily clad young woman who had come to stand behind him, who was staring at Cassandra in wondrous awe.

John's righteous display of anger fairly shook his body, for the mere fact that Cassandra had arrived unheralded on Barbados at all was bad enough, but that she should come upon him while he was savouring the welcoming and undemanding delights of his native mistress in the middle of the day was embarrassing to say the least.

'Cassandra! Confound it!' he exploded. 'What in damnation are you doing here?'

'Please, John, don't be angry with me. Let me explain—'

'Explain? Explain what?' he shouted as the young woman behind him slipped back into the bedroom, her bare feet a whisper on the floorboards. 'Nothing you have to say can justify your appearance. How dare you come all this way without my knowledge or approval? It simply will not do. Your astounding conduct is reckless and foolhardy to say the least. You always were too stubborn and headstrong for your own good, but I thought you'd more sense than to do something like this. What if I had returned to England— or been carried off by one of the infernal diseases that are forever rampant in the tropics?'

'Then I would have no choice but to return to England myself. Oh, come now, John,' she pleaded. 'Tell me you are pleased to see me.'

John was unappeased by her apparent calm; in fact, it only increased his anger. He moved closer, glaring at her.

'Have you taken leave of your senses? Have you gone mad? How can you expect me to be pleased to see you when you arrive unheralded and unattended? What in God's name possessed you?'

Ignoring his anger, Cassandra risked a little smile, hoping that with a little gentle coercing she would succeed in placating him. After all, it had always worked in the past.

'I am not unattended, John. As you see,' she said sweetly, indicating her young companion who was hovering fearfully in the doorway, afraid to enter further inside the room lest he vent his anger on her also, 'I have Rosa as my companion.'

John's eyes merely flicked to Rosa's stiff figure before it returned to savage his cousin. He continued to glare at her, the taut set of his face warning her of the control he was holding over his temper. He kept his voice steady when he next spoke, but its tone, like his expression, was like steel. 'Then tell me, what has brought you to Barbados?' Suddenly his eyes filled with alarm as a thought occurred to him, and he took a step closer. 'Is it Meredith?' he asked, thinking something terrible might have befallen his beloved sister. 'Has something happened to my sister?'

Cassandra was quick to reassure him. 'No—no, of course not. Do not worry yourself. When I left London Meredith was away visiting your grandmother. The last I saw of her she was quite well. My—reason for coming here was because—well—I had a desire to see something of the Caribbean for myself. That is all.'

'Do you mean to tell me you have travelled all this way on a whim?' John demanded, astounded.

'No, not a whim. Oh, I know my arrival must come as something of a surprise to you—'

'Surprise is putting it mildly,' he ground out.

'I know—but I promise not to make a nuisance of myself. In fact, I promise you will hardly be aware of my presence.'

'That I very much doubt.' Placing a fist to his temple, John turned away, slowly becoming resigned to the fact that he had no alternative but to let her remain for the present. Turning his back on her, he strode to the window. Of medium height and reasonably attractive—although his features were too thin to be described as handsome, his dark brown hair lightly sprinkled with grey—he stood for a moment in silent contemplation before turning to face her once more.

Her deep blue eyes bright with expectancy and warmth, she presented a perfect, delightful vision of womanhood in the centre of the room, but beneath the slim, rounded beauty she was as spirited as a young colt. She possessed a certain wilfulness—a disquietingly headstrong quality, which called for firm handling. John was a strong-minded, experienced man of the world, but he hadn't known how to hold his young cousin in check, and with cynicism he wondered if there was a man who could. No man would better her or bridle her free spirit.

'You are not the kind of woman it is easy to ignore. I long ago ceased to be amazed by anything you do, Cassandra—and you always did have the ability to adapt to your surroundings. However, it appears that the fact that you have incurred my deep displeasure weighs little with you. Is it your wish to embarrass me by coming here?'

Cassandra composed her features gravely and shook her head dutifully. 'No, John. That was not my intention. I was miserable and lonely. Meredith wasn't there and wouldn't be back for weeks. I—I came because I wanted to get away from England for a while. I—I had to, you see,' she murmured hesitantly, quietly.

Cassandra did not know that her expression had changed, that reverie had brought a sadness to her face which John quickly interpreted. His eyes turned cold. 'Could your leaving, by any chance, possibly have anything to do with Nathaniel Wylde?' He was unable to hide his scorn. His dislike of the man, the outlaw who had sired Cassandra, ran deep.

Cassandra looked at him steadily, engulfed by a deep despondency, for thoughts of her father and the cruel manner of his death awoke turbulent emotions inside her. 'Nat is dead, John.'

Totally unprepared for this pronouncement, John stared at her in astonishment. 'Dead?'

'Yes. He was captured and hanged at Execution Dock on the day I left London.'

Quickly and without emotion she related the events of her father's last weeks, of which John was totally unaware. He listened to her in silence, a mixture of feelings passing over his face. Only when she had fallen silent did he speak.

'Then I cannot say that I am surprised. He got what he deserved.' When he saw the pain his words caused Cassandra, he placed his arm tenderly about her shoulders and drew her down beside him on to one of the divans.

'I apologise if that offends you, Cassandra, but I never made any secret of what my feelings were regarding Nathaniel Wylde. When my own father died, followed so quickly by my mother, and he reappeared in your life, I was unable to refuse to allow him to see you. But I did so most unwillingly. I know that after living under the strict rule of my mother's household, being with your father was like breaking out of prison.

'But you let your love for him cloud your mind to the true nature of his character. After being denied access to you while you were an infant—and to appease his selfish desire to have you with him—he filled your head with things no properly raised young girl should listen to. He was a villain whose world was inhabited exclusively by pirates—ruthless criminals, Cassandra, who deserved to hang for the crimes they perpetrated on others.'

His voice was quiet and sombre. Cassandra's eyes narrowed and her lips compressed. She was hurt but not offended by John's attack on Nat because, after all, he was only repeating what he had said many times in the past.

'Yes, I know it is over, John, and for what it's worth I have accepted it. But I was deeply affected and revolted by the manner of his death.' Not wishing to incur his wrath further, she omitted to tell him that she had been present when Drum had sliced through the ropes securing the *Dolphin* to her moorings and had Nat's body cut down from the gallows, but she was unable to keep from him the manner of her journey to Barbados. His anger reignited and his face suffused with angry colour.

'By God, you came to the islands on a pirate ship? Archvillain he might be, but I gave O'Leary more sense than to take you with him. He will pay for this. If I ever get my hands on him… And Captain Tillotson? Was he aware who O'Leary was—that he was a murdering scoundrel who should have hanged with his master?'

'No, I don't think so,' Cassandra answered, her eyes going to Rosa perched stiffly on a chair across the room. The young woman's cheeks flamed and her eyes had narrowed and gleamed with anger on hearing John's scathing attack on her father. Thank goodness she didn't say anything. She must have a word with Rosa when they were alone. Perhaps it would be best if John didn't know she was Drum's daughter. 'Please, John, let the matter rest. Does it matter?'

'Of course it matters. While men such as O'Leary are at liberty to roam the seas at will, no ship, cargo or man are safe. All colonists who rely on the merchantmen to carry their produce live in fear that they will be attacked. It's hardly surprising that they regard such men as common murderers and robbers and hold them in the deepest contempt. It is imperative that while you remain on the island no one must discover your identity and your involvement with O'Leary. How else can you stay here without becoming the subject of a scandal? I won't have it, Cassandra. Do you hear?'

'I'm sorry, John. I don't want you to suffer on my account.' Usually Cassandra knew better than to argue with him when he used that tone, but now she looked at him mutinously. 'I'm not going home, John. I want to stay here with you. You will let me?'

'You leave me with no choice. You and your companion can stay for the present—here in this house,' he conceded, rising quickly. 'I am often away for days at a time, in Bridgetown or meeting with plantation owners—on Company business, you understand.'

He looked towards the young mulatto woman who had emerged from the bedroom. Swathed in a heavy lime-green silk dress with a contrasting border worked in gold, she stood quietly watching them at the far side of the room, and Cassandra noticed how her cousin's gaze softened when they rested on her.

'Elmina will remain to take care of you. She—she is my servant—prepares my food—my clothes, you know, that sort of thing,' he explained, coughing nervously and averting his gaze, becoming awkward and embarrassed suddenly, and seeming unable to look at Cassandra, who had risen from the divan and was watching him closely. 'As you see the bungalow is small—though comfortable. You will find Elmina helpful. She will minister to all your needs and her English is very good, so that will not be a problem.'

'There is no need for you to put yourself about on our account. Lady Courtly has kindly offered to let Rosa and me stay at the house. She is having rooms made ready as we speak.'

John's relief was evident. 'I see. That's very gracious of Julia—and, yes, I suppose that would be for the best.'

Cassandra allowed her gaze to dwell on the mulatto woman. She had fine dark eyes and an abundance of lustrous short black hair. Her coffee-coloured skin was without a blemish, and her full ripe lips and slightly flattened nose showed her Negroid ancestry. She had a slumberous, languid grace, and possessed the requisite warm softness and the firm-fleshed litheness of youth, which was capable of awaking all too easily the carnality of the opposite sex. Having already guessed at the relationship that existed between her cousin and Elmina, Cassandra was surprised but unaffected by it. She smiled inwardly, for she could well see why John was so taken with her, and why he favoured the privacy of the bungalow to the house.

She knew interracial liaisons were not uncommon on the islands, giving rise to a mulatto population and creating a new class of coloureds. However, it would be indelicate for her to discuss the situation with her cousin for, after all, if he chose to keep a native woman in his house as his mistress then it was entirely his own affair. She felt no resentment towards the woman, but it raised a complication she had not bargained for.

'But make no mistake, Cassandra,' John went on, 'you cannot remain on the island indefinitely. You will return to England as soon as I can secure you a place on the first available ship.'

Swamped with disappointment, for she had hoped to remain on Barbados for as long as her cousin, Cassandra stared at him, her face crestfallen. 'But why can I not remain here until it's time for you to return?'

'No,' he answered firmly. 'I want you away from Barbados before the rainy season. Often the devastation wrought by the high winds and rain defies exaggeration. For the island's planters they can spell disaster.'

'But that is too soon,' she objected, her thoughts turning to the handsome Captain Marston, for she had hoped to still be on Barbados when he returned from Jamaica. 'Do—please let me stay longer, John,' she begged sweetly. 'I shall be no trouble to you—I promise.'

John sighed, shaking his head in defeat. 'As to that, Cassandra, I doubt it very much. We'll see how things turn out—but I will stress that your behaviour will determine the length of your stay. Is that understood?'

'Oh—yes, very well,' she replied, appeased by his concession.

'Good. As for myself,' he said, his gaze dwelling softly on Elmina's appealingly beautiful face, 'I do not intend returning to England until much later.'

There were parties and stylish gatherings of local gentry given by Sir Charles and Lady Julia Courtly while Cassandra was a guest in their house. John lost no time in pointing out that it was necessary for her to replace her pitiful, pathetic belongings before he could introduce her to his friends. He would not have her appearing like a drab and was determined that she would look her best. It made him proud to know she was admired—and maybe attract the eye of one of the island's rich planters.

Julia whisked her off to Bridgetown, where they purchased materials of every shade and light fabrics to be made into gowns by Julia's sempstress and her chattering helpers. Cassandra stood for hours on end as they fitted and pinned and snipped and stitched, until each gown moulded her slender form to perfection.

Barbados was a strange and exciting place to be—glamorous too, in its own way, and Cassandra enjoyed it with the reckless pleasure of a pardoned convict. The island was inhabited by merchants and many wealthy planters, who had made good and clearly tried to live like kings, setting their eyes on building palaces in the tropics, filling them with fine furniture and silver and lavish banquets served to their guests.

The people the Courtlys and John introduced her to on the whole belonged to the island's aristocracy. They all had money and the women wore fashionable gowns and showed no signs of the hard work done by others in their fine houses. The men she met were eager to be introduced to her, paying her the most extravagant compliments as though they hadn't seen a pretty woman before.

These men all had the same hard, alert look Sir Charles Courtly wore, like men who have much on their minds. Charles Courtly was a man of average height, with sandy-coloured hair and a rakish moustache, and his figure was as slender as a man's half his age. He was a member of the parish vestry—one of sixteen of the elected property owners of St George empowered to collect parish taxes and rents.

He had an intimidating air of command, derived from years of managing his plantation and administering to island affairs. The charm he exerted was effortless, but Cassandra began to realise, as the days passed and she got to know him better, that he ruled his plantation as much from general fear of the retribution he could wield upon his slaves as from respect.

As the days drifted by in an untroubled haze, Cassandra dare not let her thoughts dwell too deeply on her father since they awoke turbulent emotions within her, and yet she felt that fate was not unjust, for she would be content to remain on Barbados for now, to bask in its warmth, its enchantment—and to gather fresh enthusiasm and strength to face what it had in store for her when she returned to England.

As the weeks went by and September came to Barbados, when the parching drought of summer was frequently followed by the heavy rains and wind, John often allowed her to accompany him to Bridgetown, and on his evenings at home he brought guests to dine at the bungalow—men attached to the Wyndham and other mercantile companies attending to business in the Caribbean islands.

Tonight he informed her there was to be only one guest. She watched the visitor enter and remove his wide-brimmed hat with its dancing white plume and hand it to Elmina. Those languid movements were all at once familiar. When he raised his head, she encountered an amused dark stare. Her initial surprise was quickly followed by a wild beating of her heart. A soft flush sprang to her cheeks as her eyes softened with recognition. Then they blazed with a fierce light.

John's guest moved closer, his tall, broad-shouldered figure seeming to fill the room. As on the beach all those weeks before, his nearness was disturbing, and on meeting the dark irresistible gaze of Captain Marston, Cassandra felt that maybe she would not have to wait until she returned to England to find out what fate had in store for her after all.

Rarely had the lovely Mistress Everson been out of Stuart's mind since he had plucked her from the capsizing boat. Throughout the weeks he had spent on Jamaica she had never left his thoughts, and he had been sorely tempted to cut his visit short and return to Barbados. Thinking of her forced him to recognise and reflect on all the things he had missed in his life and the things that would be lacking in it for all time if he didn't give up the sea, which strengthened his decision to do just that.

On returning to Barbados and meeting her cousin Sir John Everson in Bridgetown, he had lost no time in enquiring after his charming cousin and was absolutely delighted to find she was still on the island—and he had truly thought his luck was in when Sir John asked if he would accommodate that same young lady and her companion on his vessel when it returned to England.

Sir John's invitation to dine with them at his house and return to his ship the following morning was too tempting an offer for him to resist. Had it been anyone else he would have declined the invitation, for after a busy day overseeing the loading of more of the cargo, he could think of nothing better than going straight to bed. But his fierce desire to meet the delightful Mistress Everson again—curious to see if she really was as lovely as he remembered—was too attractive an invitation to turn down.

She stood against the light, unconscious of the spectacle she offered, magnificent and ravishing in her shimmering saffron gown, her hair, a mixture of silver and gold, hanging loose down the length of her spine and gleaming like polished silk. Her face was serene and radiant—the face of an angel. She was even lovelier than he remembered, an enchanting temptress, her beauty full blown. And he wanted her.

He sensed that it would require time and courtship to lure her into his arms. However, time was something he did not have, and having given up trying to understand the reasons for the step he was about to take, he had made up his mind not to leave Barbados without making her his wife.

Facing weeks ahead on board ship, of seeing her day after day and not being able to touch her, would be a living, frustrating torment. So fragile would be the hold on his self-control that it would be impossible to restrain the urge to drag her into his arms and make love to her. His intentions were nobler than that. With a woman like her by his side, in his bed, he would experience something better, more profound, more lasting, than the mindless pleasures he had experienced in all his affairs with others.

And so, as he deliberately set himself out to charm this adorable creature, not for one moment did he think Sir John would refuse his offer, nor did he have the slightest doubt of his ability to lure Mistress Everson. He wanted her and he wanted her immediately, and he would be damned if he'd wait until they were in England to court her. Besides, he had never actively had to pay court to a woman in his life—they were usually all too eager for his attentions.

Chapter Four

Cassandra met the pair of black eyes levelled on her, unprepared for the effect on her senses. Captain Marston did not move, and there was a repressed sexuality almost tangible in his stillness. Already the impact of his charm was burrowing through her reserve.

His immaculate outfit in black velvet and white silk shirt emphasised the shining blackness of his thick hair and tanned skin, and in his eyes, which held her gaze, the smouldering dark depths were seductive and enticing. There were tiny lines around his eyes from squinting at the hot, tropical sun, which gave strength to his handsome face. She smiled at him with pure, unbridled happiness, but when she remembered the flirtatious mischief and his bold manner that had hung over their first encounter, a stinging heat crept over her flesh.

'You are already acquainted with my cousin, Captain Marston,' John said in a jovial voice. 'I have not thanked you for saving her from a drenching on her arrival to Barbados.'

'I did little enough. I was glad to be of service.' Taking Cassandra's hand, Stuart bowed casually, raising it and brushing her fingers lightly with his lips, his eyes never leaving hers for a moment, and he found the calm boldness with which she was gazing at him encouraging and far from displeasing. His lips curved, assured in the knowledge that his smile had melted many a woman's heart. 'Please say you are happy to see me again?' he asked softly.

'I think you already know my answer to that, Captain Marston.' Cassandra had not meant to sound so forward, but the words seemed to slip from her lips. It took a conscious effort for her to draw her hand away. He was exactly as she remembered, vital and exciting, with a deep, vibrant note to his voice, his eyes as bold and black as any pirate's. 'You met my cousin in Bridgetown, I understand. I'm delighted you accepted his invitation to dine with us this evening.'

'It's not in my nature to turn down an opportunity to dine with such charming company. I had hoped to have the pleasure of meeting you again, Mistress Everson, before I leave for England—so I was more than happy to accept Sir John's invitation to dine with you both. I must compliment you,' he said, his gaze travelling slowly over her body from head to toe with bold appraisal, his eyes lingering overlong on the gentle swell of her breasts. 'You look exquisite. The Caribbean obviously agrees with you.'

'Thank you.' She smiled. 'I would be content to remain here indefinitely. I like it very much indeed—at least, what I've seen of it. The beauty of Barbados, which at first renewed my spirits after the long voyage out here, is growing stronger. I often go into Bridgetown and ride short distances with John, but I long to be able to see more of the island. Occasionally I visit the homes of other planters who live close by with Sir Charles and Lady Julia—but John does not allow me to venture far.'

'And I should think not,' John commented sharply, handing them both a goblet of wine. 'It would not do for you to go wandering about by yourself. With a hundred and one fevers forever rampant in the slave quarters, you'd be sure to go down with something or other.'

'There you are, you see, Captain Marston,' Cassandra said laughingly. 'That is what I am up against.'

'Nevertheless, there is something in what your cousin says. To my cost I have already lost several members of my crew to one or another of the fevers that prevail in the tropics.'

When his host went to speak to the serving woman Stuart drew closer to Cassandra. His expression changed. It was sombre, his eyes compelling, his voice low and serious. 'How lovely you look. Never have four months seemed such an eternity. When I left Jamaica, for days the winds were against us. I feared I would never get here. I also feared the heat and the sun were beginning to affect me— that I had been staring at the stars too long, and was half afraid I had imagined our encounter on the beach that day.'

Cassandra favoured him with a dimpled, teasing smile. 'At least you didn't suffer a lapse of memory and forget me altogether—although it does not mean I can forgive your forwardness on that occasion.'

The Marston brow quirked in sardonic amusement. 'I would not expect otherwise. You must allow me to redeem myself in your eyes.' He looked neither chagrined nor apologetic. Instead he regarded her with an infuriating grin. 'Are you surprised to see me?'

'Of course. I'm extremely flattered that you came all the way from Bridgetown to see me.'

'I said I would.'

'I thought you'd forget, Captain Marston.'

'Forget someone like you? Never. You made a deep impression on me.'

Cassandra fully understood what he was saying. Her cheeks grew warm.

'It is not so strange that two people should feel an instant attraction. When I want something, I'm a very persistent man.' Stuart's voice sounded like a caress, his eyes, after leisurely lingering on her parted lips, meeting hers. They glowed, telling him that she was warmed from within by his words, and he found himself wanting to draw her to him and kiss the ripeness of her full, soft mouth, to sweep her away and imprint himself on her with a fierceness which was hard to quell.

Fully aware of the effect he was having over her and totally without contrition, Stuart smiled, a smile that softened his features and creased his eyes—and almost reduced Cassandra to near panic. No man had ever affected her like this, and he was right, she was attracted to him, unbelievably so.

'I would be more than happy to dispense with the formality of you calling me Captain Marston. My name is Stuart. Your cousin tells me you are called Cassandra. I may call you Cassandra?'

It was a command rather than a request. 'But—we hardly know each other.'

'That is a matter soon remedied,' he told her, with absolute confidence that he could.

Cassandra felt a perverse desire to shatter a little of his arrogant self-assurance. 'I'm afraid that's impossible. You have to leave for England with the convoy, and I will not leave Barbados until John does.'

His lips quirked in a smile. 'You may find your cousin has other ideas.' Before she had time to take him up on this, he asked, 'Am I the only guest to dine with you this evening?'

'There will be just the three of us. Sir Charles and Lady Julia are not at home this evening, and Rosa, my companion, is indisposed.'

What Cassandra said was true. Rosa had retired to bed with a headache during the afternoon—in fact, she had looked most unwell. Cassandra was concerned about her, and she was relieved that Julia had promised to send for the physician to take a look at her if she got no better. She looked towards the table where John was pouring more wine into his goblet. 'Please take a seat,' she said to their guest. 'The food is ready.'

Over a meal served by Elmina and consisting of aromatic and delicious dishes of fish and vegetables, they talked of inconsequential things. The candles shone with a sharp brilliance, the flames fluttering and dancing in the gentle draught. The lattice shutters had been pulled open to admit the perfumed smell of the garden, the warmth of the night air, and the occasional breath of a chill wind blowing overland from the sea. Now and then the call of a night bird pierced the air, and the rustle of palm fronds could be heard brushing against the walls of the bungalow.

As the meal progressed and the evening wore on, Cassandra saw all the signs in John's flushed features, and his voice raised louder than usual, that he had imbibed too much wine, which he was in the habit of doing, whereas Captain Marston looked cool and composed, unaffected by the liquor. Throughout the meal he appeared to drink, but in fact he imbibed far less than John. Unfortunately, the mellow influence of the wine released John's inhibitions and loosened his tongue.

'Fond as I am of my dear cousin, Captain Marston,' he laughed when Cassandra gently and tactfully suggested that he might have drunk enough wine when he was about to replenish his empty goblet, 'she is a determined and wilful creature and used to having her own way in most things. The sooner she returns to England and acquires herself a husband the better it will be for my peace of mind, I don't mind telling you—although marriage to her should be approached with a good deal of caution.'

Cassandra gave him an annoying glance while managing

to force a laugh. 'Faith, John, I have precious little to recommend me to any man. Who would have me? You are forever telling me I am lacking in social graces, and I am as poor as a church mouse.'

'What you lack in wealth, my dear,' he said, leaning over and patting her hand affectionately, 'you more than make up for in other ways. You do have other attributes to your credit—apart from the obvious, of course,' he said, smiling, referring to her beauty.

'My dear cousin is quite unlike any woman you are ever likely to meet, Captain Marston,' John continued unabashed, 'whose whims and fancies must be humoured at all costs. I tell you, all her life she has thwarted my every wish with her stubborn ways—which always bordered upon disobedience and disrespect for my authority—but without exceeding it, I must point out.' His words did not serve as a rebuke and he finished on a softer note with a little twinkle dancing is his eyes, for he was exceedingly fond of his pretty young cousin.

His host's fondness for Cassandra was plain to Stuart, and he found himself wondering if what he felt for her was something other than cousinly affection—and if the attraction was mutual. Experiencing a sharp twinge of jealousy that this might be so both surprised and annoyed him.

Glancing towards Captain Marston's sober countenance, Cassandra detected a hard gleam in his coal-black eyes. 'I beg you to take no notice of John, Captain Marston. He speaks in jest—and I think has drunk a little too much wine. I do not believe we should be discussing this subject in front of our guest, John. I would not wish to cause him any embarrassment.'

Seated across from Cassandra, Stuart lounged back in his chair, his arm stretched across the back, his hand idly turning the silver wine goblet in his fingers. His expression was thoughtful as he listened with interest to their light-hearted banter. When Cassandra laughed her face lit up and her eyes were like two sparkling sapphires, and her rosy lips stretched over her small white teeth. He was enchanted, and he wondered if she had any idea how beautiful she was. He smiled, a slight, crooked smile.

'I assure you that I am not in the least embarrassed—and I would like to know more about the young lady he speaks of.' Her eyes regarded him calmly and steadily. She had such beautiful eyes, he thought as she gave him a mocking smile.

'And what exactly would you like to know about me, Captain Marston?'

'Something of a more personal nature, I think,' John commented, laughing jovially. 'You see, Captain Marston, Cassandra was considered to be an extremely difficult child by my mother before she died, and later I came to share that opinion—and most sympathised with me as an unfortunate man who had taken over the guardianship of a rebellious, unbiddable girl of an unpredictable disposition—'

'Nevertheless, I do have some things in my favour,' Cassandra interrupted crossly, irritated by what she considered to be a harsh and unfair analysis of her character. 'I am reasonably well read and well educated, and, contrary to John's opinion that I lack social graces, my manners are perfectly acceptable to society. Come, admit it, John?'

John chuckled. 'Aye,' he conceded, 'I'd say your account is entirely accurate.' Leaning back in his chair, he stretched his legs out in front of him, replete and satisfied after his meal. 'So, Captain Marston, your ship is loaded and ready to leave with the convoy.'

Cassandra already knew Captain Marston would have to leave Barbados soon, but nevertheless she was unprepared for the sharp stab of disappointment that pierced her heart. The pleasure of the evening withered. 'How long will it be before the convoy sails?'

'Very soon—days—no longer than two weeks at the most,' Stuart replied, having noticed her dismayed reaction and feeling well pleased by it. 'We await Captain Tillotson's and several other vessels' arrival from Antigua, and then we sail for England.'

Trying to overcome the awful feeling of regret because he was to leave before they'd had the chance to become better acquainted, Cassandra smiled softly. 'And what exciting and exotic cargo will you be taking back with you to England?'

'Nothing as exotic as what you might have in mind—just the principle articles of trade such as cotton and sugar and other commodities. Things which are always in great demand by the British market.'

'There is little wonder the pirates lay in wait to intercept the ships in order to steal their cargoes.'

'Regrettably that is true. It is a fact that piracy takes place on a massive scale—which is why mercantile ships have become warlike and the reason why they almost always sail in convoy.'

'And how long will it be before you return to the West Indies, Captain Marston?'

'This is to be my final voyage. My seafaring days are at an end.'

His reply surprised Cassandra. 'Oh! Why is that?'

'I have duties in England that dictate I spend more time at my home in Kent. Because my time has been taken up with the sea for many years, I'm afraid my estate has fallen into a sorry state and is in dire need of attention.'

'Forgive me if I seem surprised, Captain—it is just that you give me the impression of being a sailor born and bred. Having spent a number of years on board your ship, I suspect you will find it difficult to retire from it.'

Stuart cocked an eyebrow, assessing her. 'I admit it will not be easy.'

'Do you not employ a bailiff—or have brothers who can take care of your estate back in England?'

Stuart stiffened. 'I have a bailiff—but no brothers,' he replied, his voice sounding strained and his expression becoming closed suddenly, as if she had intruded on to something private. 'There is only my mother, and she prefers to spend most of her time in London.'

'I see.' Cassandra was curious as to what it could be that had brought about this apparent change in him, but she let it rest, not wishing to pry further. 'And what will you do with your ship? Will you sell it?'

'The Company is to buy the *Sea Hawk*. But what of you, Mistress Everson?' Stuart leaned back in his chair, regarding her with a frown, tactfully directing the conversation away from himself before she felt inclined to ask questions about his family that he preferred not to discuss with anyone. 'Your cousin tells me you are to leave Barbados, also.'

Cassandra glanced sharply across the table at John, the meaning behind the remark Captain Marston had made earlier becoming clear. 'He did?'

'Yes,' John said quickly, looking flustered all of a sudden, wishing he'd taken the time to tell Cassandra of his intention before Captain Marston's arrival. 'I've asked Captain Marston if he will be so kind as to accommodate you and Rosa on board his ship for the journey back to England.'

'You have?' she gasped, her startled gaze flying from her cousin to Captain Marston, who was calmly watching her reaction to this with an infuriating wicked gleam dancing in his black eyes.

'Yes. I told you when you arrived that you cannot possibly remain here indefinitely. I would prefer it if you were back at home with Meredith, which is where you belong.'

'I see,' Cassandra said stiffly, looking directly at Captain

Marston. 'I trust you have room to accommodate me and my companion?'

'Yes. Ample. I shall be delighted to have you on board.' The haste with which Sir John was sending Cassandra back to England was beginning to cast doubt on Stuart's suspicion that his feelings for his cousin were anything other than that. He smiled inwardly, beginning to feel easier.

'Thank you. Then it would seem there is little more to be said.' Cassandra looked away from the dark gaze that was studying her intently, and she had to admit that if she had to return to England then she could think of no other ship she would rather sail on than his.

The conversation was interrupted when Elmina entered to speak to John. Cassandra chose that moment to excuse herself, moving out on to the verandah and welcoming the cool night air after the heat of the room. Oil lamps hanging from a low beam against a curtain of scarlet blossom gave off a flickering light, which drew dancing moths, mesmerised by the flame. She was only aware that Captain Marston had followed her when she heard his light step behind her.

He moved a little away from her to lean casually against the wooden balustrade and looked to where she stood, her profile etched against the star-strewn sky, her face gleaming like alabaster in the white glow of the moon that bathed the garden in an incandescent light. Neither seemed in a hurry to speak, the silence stretching between them broken only by the creatures of the night.

In the dim light Stuart savoured the soft ivory tones of Cassandra's flesh exposed on her arms and neck. The long gracious lines of her lithe young body were evident beneath her gown. His experiences had taught him to be no admirer of the standards or social graces of English society ladies—although his mother, with her gracious, single-minded devotion and dedication to her family, he did not class as one of them. He despised their indolence, their perpetual preoccupation with matters of fashion, and their endless, meaningless gossip.

But Cassandra Everson was so unlike them. In fact, she was unlike anyone he had ever known—for he could think of no other woman of his acquaintance who would have the courage to sail across an ocean to visit her cousin on a fancy. She was perhaps the most beautiful woman he had ever seen, and he gazed at her as though his eyes could not get their fill of her, as though he were looking on beauty for the first time in his life.

He wanted more than anything to take her hand and raise it to his lips, to kiss it reverently, to treat her like a delicate, precious work of art, to tenderly cherish her, but at the same time he felt the urge, the need, to place his hands on her arms and draw her towards him, to press her to his body where the increasing heat of his manhood stirred.

'What are you thinking?' he asked at length.

'Oh…' she sighed '…of how beautiful the night is—and how soon I shall have to leave. I shall regret that.'

'Does it upset you having to return to England? Or perhaps you have an aversion to travelling with me on my ship?'

Cassandra turned and looked at him. 'An aversion? No. Why on earth should I? It's no fault of yours if my cousin has no desire for me to remain here with him.'

'I understand that you were brought up by your cousin.'

'I was brought up by my aunt and uncle—John's parents. They both died when I was a child. Since that time John has been my lawful guardian.'

'And were you close to your aunt and uncle?'

A look of desolation entered Cassandra's eyes as she reluctantly retreated back into her past. 'No. Quite the opposite, in fact. My uncle was a hard man and paid me scant attention—but my aunt…I hated her,' she said quietly, her voice quivering with deep emotion. 'Her dislike of me was intense and she made my life intolerable. During the years of the Civil War our families were divided in their loyalties to King and country, which did not help my case.

'However, without my parents, there was no one else to take care of me. My cousins John and Meredith were the two people who sustained me. My determination to survive my aunt's oppression during the early years of my life taught me to be my own person—which has always been my greatest strength. And, as you see, Captain Marston,' she said with a cynical smile, 'my spirit remains un-crushed.'

Her simple, toneless voice, giving him without emphasis a brief insight into her past, of how she must have suffered pain and humiliation at the hands of her aunt and uncle, wrung Stuart's heart with pity, and the look in her eyes told him much more than any words she could have uttered.

'Your cousin tells me your father was killed at Worcester fighting for the King—and that your mother died when you were born. It cannot have been easy growing up without knowing either of your parents.'

Cassandra's eyes narrowed warily as she gave him a level stare. So, she thought, that was what John had told him, what he wanted him to think, for, apart from a few gossiping, speculative neighbours in Chelsea, himself and Meredith, Rosa and the crew of the *Dolphin*, no one knew she was the daughter of the infamous pirate Captain Na-thaniel Wylde.

John was deeply ashamed that he bore any connection to such a man and was constantly reminding her that, for her own sake, on no account must she reveal the identity of her father. Her heart twisted with pain, for much as she would like to speak of him, she knew it was in her best interests that the part of her life she had shared so briefly with him must remain locked in her heart for ever.

'No—no, it wasn't,' she replied in answer to Stuart's

question. She smiled suddenly when a soft breeze blew the
folds of her skirt. 'My aunt and uncle were Puritans and
fanatically dedicated to God. Their religion dominated
every waking moment of our lives. If they knew what I
had done—coming to Barbados without telling anyone, to
live on a Caribbean island and surrounded by slaves—without doubt my sin would be great indeed and I would be
severely chastised.' She grinned wryly. 'I think she might
have a few choice words to say to John, too, concerning
his relationship with Elmina.'

Stuart frowned curiously. 'Elmina?'

'The mulatto woman who served us at dinner. She is my
cousin's housekeeper—and I strongly suspect she is also
his mistress and the reason why he is so reluctant to return
to England. The looks that have passed between them all
evening cannot have escaped you. You must have noticed.'
She smiled.

'I have to confess I did not,' he murmured softly, his
voice suddenly grown deep and husky and his eyes focusing on her lips. Her revelation dispelled his suspicion that
she might be in love with her cousin, and he with her. 'My
eyes were more favourably employed.'

Cassandra felt the impact of his gaze and caught her
breath, flushing softly, understanding the meaning of his
words and flattered by them. 'John has not admitted their
relationship as such. I'm sure he would consider it too delicate a matter to discuss with me.'

'Nevertheless, you do not appear to be unduly disturbed
by the closeness that exists between your cousin and his
servant, which I consider strange. Most young ladies of my
acquaintance would be scandalised by such a relationship.'

Cassandra's eyes narrowed and she glanced at him
sharply, her cheeks flaming suddenly, for she was stung by
the irony and what she considered to be an underlying note
of reproof in his voice. For the first time a constraint had

come between them. 'Then the young ladies you speak of must be exceedingly dull company, Captain Marston, who no doubt spend their time talking of tedious matters like the state of their health and the clothes they wear. I am not like that.'

'It wasn't a reproach, but I am beginning to realise you are quite uninhibited.'

'That is a natural characteristic of mine. Perhaps I should not have silenced my cousin when he was giving such a vivid account of my character, for then I think you would know me a little better.'

'So there is some truth in his description of you,' Stuart remarked, stifling a grin at the complete absence of contrition on her lovely, upturned face and jutting chin. 'You are a stubborn and disobedient woman, whose whims must be humoured at all cost.'

Her unabashed gaze locked on his. 'Yes—all of it. And if I had allowed him to continue you would have learnt that some of my pastimes are considered by our neighbours in Chelsea to be quite shocking.'

'I would?'

'Yes. John is forever rescuing me from one escapade or another. I hunt, I fish, I wear breeches like a man and ride about the countryside at home like a gypsy—which drives my cousin Meredith to distraction. I also speak my mind, for since my aunt and uncle died I no longer feel I have to curb my tongue. I do not feel the need to apologise and nor am I ashamed of what I am or what I do, so if this does not meet with your approval, then it is just too bad.'

Stuart cocked a sleek black brow, a merry twinkle of amusement dancing in his eyes. 'I do believe you are trying to shock me, Cassandra,' he said calmly. 'But there is nothing about your character that I do not already know.'

'You can read my mind?'

'You might say that. I am beginning to feel heartily sorry

for your cousin. You appear to be quite a handful.' He chuckled. 'There's little wonder if he is eager to have you off his hands, for you to wed.'

Cassandra glanced across at him. His face was in shadow, but she could see that he was smiling. His eyes glowed and he looked at her appreciatively as he continued to lounge with careless ease against the balustrade, his arms folded across his chest. He was all lean hard muscle and for a moment she forgot her outburst and wondered what it would be like to love and to be loved by such a man.

He was strong, his manner one of complete assurance— and a cynical humour twinkled in his black eyes. There was also a dangerous, cool recklessness about him and a distinct air of adventure—a trait that so reminded her of her father. They might have been cast in the same mould except that Stuart Marston would despise her father's chosen, unlawful way of life.

'Aren't you shocked by my unseemly behaviour, Captain Marston?' She met his eyes and saw they were teasing and suddenly he laughed outright, a deep, rich sound, and she relaxed.

'Not in the least—and I asked you to call me Stuart. It is part of your make-up that attracts me to you, and you know it. And I do not believe I am mistaken when I say the attraction is mutual.'

Cassandra turned her face away from his close scrutiny. There was an unfamiliar look in his eyes that turned her into a woman she no longer recognised. She was weakened by it and did not understand what was happening to her— the result being total confusion.

'I—I really don't know what you mean.'

'Oh, I think you do, so do not be coy with me. Tell me, what is your opinion of me?'

'This is our second meeting—which is hardly time for me have formed an opinion of you,' she answered primly.

'But each has been no ordinary encounter. I think you have formed a very strong opinion of me, and for my part I find you an immense challenge. You intrigue me. So, tell me, how would you feel about agreeing to become my wife?'

Cassandra stared at him in a kind of disorientated, bewildered state. Their gazes held, the silence punctuated by the persistent call of a night bird.

Stuart's eyes smiled, but his voice was quiet, seductive. 'I can see I have rendered you speechless.'

She spoke, but her voice was a strangled whisper. 'Sir— you—you jest.'

'I would not jest on so serious a matter to me.'

He was smiling, a mocking smile, calmly watching her from beneath his lowered lids, but Cassandra sensed he was alert and that an unfettered power struggled beneath his calm. His tone was perfectly natural, as if he were merely asking her to take a stroll around the garden with him, but its very ordinariness caused a feeling of panic and the mystery of the unknown to flow through her.

Without logic or reason she was drawn to Stuart Marston as to no other and she experienced a moment of terror when she was with him, for the sheer magnitude of her feelings threatened to overwhelm her. She felt weak, vulnerable, suddenly—at his mercy and standing on the threshold of something new. He was essentially worldly, emanating raw power that was an irresistible attraction to any woman. She was stimulated by him, he excited her, and he exuded an element of danger that added to the excitement.

But this was not just another adventure and if she entered into any kind of commitment with him then there would be no escape. He had asked her to be his wife, and in this she wanted to follow her heart, no matter how impossible that might be. But she could not.

'If you are seriously interested in acquiring a wife, will

any woman do?' she asked, knowing the words sounded flippant, but thinking it wise to keep their interchange as light hearted as possible.

'No. Only the woman I have a yearning for.' His eyes captured hers and held them prisoner. He went on speaking with slow deliberation. 'My experience cannot truthfully be termed lacking, yet you far exceed any woman I can call to mind. In the past I have sailed the seas and seen many ports—often confined to the ship for long periods while under sail. Of late other matters have commanded my attention, and until now I have failed to meet a woman worthy to be considered.'

'There are things about me you don't know. If you did, you wouldn't want to marry me.'

He laughed, thinking she was referring to nothing more serious than past childish escapades. 'I'm willing to take that chance.'

'Maybe, but I am not. It's impossible.'

'Impossible? Why do you say that?'

'I—I cannot tell you. Please don't ask.'

In her eyes Stuart thought he glimpsed a pain, a memory, she was fighting to suppress. 'Whatever it is, it makes no difference.'

'Yes, it does. Did you really expect me to say yes to your wild proposal?'

'Not wild. I've thought about it, and I had hopes of your acceptance.'

'But—you do not know me. We are mere strangers who met by chance. Forgive me if I seem somewhat astonished—but naturally I am confused by your offer made on so short an acquaintance.'

His voice was seductive, persuasive, and in the moonlight his eyes gleamed darkly. 'I don't believe our lives are ruled by chance. When I plucked you from the boat in Bridgetown Bay, I figured I must have done so for a reason.

Maybe I'll discover the nature of that reason given time. When I see something I want I act on it immediately—and I want you, Cassandra Everson. My opinion of you was decided from the start—and I always believe in first impressions.' He was calm, his manner easy as he continued to watch her closely with a steady gaze.

His dark, compelling eyes held hers attentively, an inner passion glowing in their sombre depths. 'You are beautiful, exciting and mysterious, and you possess a natural independence of spirit and single-mindedness that I admire. Your eyes are as blue as the Caribbean Sea, and as compelling. No woman has affected me so profoundly.'

Cassandra laughed aside his flattering remarks, and the glint in his eye was proof that he had more than praise on his mind. A traitorous part of her responded to the intensity of his gaze and the warm caress of his voice. 'That is nonsense, sir—but a pretty speech none the less.'

'I'm not one for pretty speeches, Cassandra. Think of the pleasure we will have getting to know one another—endless weeks on board the *Sea Hawk*. It could be quite enjoyable. I do not think either of us will be disappointed.'

'You are very bold, Stuart Marston.'

'I'm no saint, that I freely admit. I told you, when I want something I'm persistent, and I do not intend letting you escape me.'

'Escape? Are you saying that I am your prisoner?'

'No.' His lips quirked. 'But I believe I am fast becoming yours.'

She laughed, shaking her head in disbelief.

His white teeth gleamed behind a devilishly wicked grin. 'You are a cruel woman, Cassandra Everson.'

'I don't mean to be, but I have to wonder at your motives for wanting to marry me. You know I have no dowry. I am penniless.'

'That matters little to me. I have more than enough

money for both of us. Before I left England my mother made me realise that it is time I married—if only to satisfy her demands for a grandson and heir. I know she would be delighted with my choice—if you accept my proposal of marriage, that is.'

He was standing very close. Cassandra could smell his skin and feel his presence. Like a magnet it was drawing her to him, and she took a step back before the will to resist failed her. She saw the anticipation in his dark eyes as he watched her, waiting for her answer to his question that would affect both their lives. She sensed there were two contradictory sides to his character, that there was so much that remained hidden behind his dark gaze.

But whatever mysteries might lie beneath the surface of this strange man, she could not marry him. In fact, with cold clarity she was beginning to realise that she would have to think very dispassionately before she entered into marriage with any man. There was the complication of her identity and the personal notoriety that went with it. John had told Stuart that her father had been killed at Worcester, but what if by some quirk of fate he discovered that was a lie, and that her father had belonged to that breed of men he so despised?

Apart from his own kind, there wasn't a man or woman alive who would knowingly claim friendship with Nathaniel Wylde's daughter. How would a man like Stuart Marston feel when he discovered that same woman was his wife? He would be appalled and outraged and harden his heart against her, and rightly so. He would hate her for being who she was, for lying to him, for deceiving him, and she could not bear that.

'You are obviously a man who has been accustomed to having his own way in most things, I can see that, and adept in getting it—but I meant what I said. I won't marry you. I'm sorry.'

Stuart's eyes searched hers, but their dark depths were deliberately shuttered. For a long moment his gaze lingered on the elegant perfection of her face, and then he murmured, 'So am I, but it does not end here. I have a yen for you, Cassandra Everson. I will not give you up, and I am confident of a flawless success. I shall begin my persuasion tomorrow.'

'Tomorrow?'

'I am to spend the night here in the bungalow, and your cousin has invited me to ride with you in the morning. I accepted.'

The thread of confidence in his tone and his calm dismissal of her refusal to marry him stirred Cassandra's resentment. 'I see. Is it your intention to make me one of your conquests?'

Her chilled contempt met Stuart face on. He moved closer and towered above her. 'Conquest? You mistake me, Cassandra. I do not ask that you yield to me—nor do I desire to conquer you. The moments that are cherished and treasured are the moments that are shared, not taken. I want you to be my wife—my partner in all things.'

It took all Cassandra's will power not to give in to the persuasion of his words. 'It changes nothing between us. I cannot marry you—ever.'

Stuart considered her for a moment. 'Then be wary, Cassandra, for I shall win you, by fair means—'

'Or foul.'

A slow smile spread over his features. 'Whatever. Indeed, I can be steadfastly persistent in what I want, and never waver from my purpose. I won't be satisfied until it's done.'

Chapter Five

Lingering on the verandah staring into the dark, Stuart's jaw was hardened with resolve. Just why he wanted Cassandra so passionately was something that confounded him. He told himself that he couldn't bear to think of her belonging to anyone else. But it was more than that. She was in his blood.

Dear God, what was the matter with him? He was thirty years old and had known and made love to more women than he could possibly remember, and yet here he was, mooning over a child woman like a callow youth. There was only one remedy to win her in so short a time, and normally it was one he would not hesitate in taking—he would relish it, in fact—but he could not in all decency seduce the delectable Cassandra Everson, even though he was very good at seduction and an accomplished lover.

Or could he? His eyes narrowed and after a moment's careful thought he decided that, yes, he could.

Looking forward to her ride, Cassandra rose at sun up. She was apprehensive at meeting Stuart again, and was relieved when Julia said she would accompany them. Thankfully Rosa was feeling better, but not well enough to join them on their ride. John and Stuart were waiting for them in front of the house with the horses, and, on meeting Stuart's open appraisal, she was glad she had groomed herself carefully and wore her best attire of scarlet silk.

'How becoming you look this morning, Cassandra,' he remarked smoothly as she settled herself into the side-saddle. 'I can see I am in for an extremely pleasurable ride.'

Cassandra did not miss the meaningful sparkle in his eyes. She had intended to treat him with cool formality, but his grin was so boyishly disarming that she smiled. 'I'm sure it will be. I believe the countryside north of St George is worth seeing.'

John introduced Stuart to Julia, who looked as cool and elegant as ever, no matter how hot the temperature. Her eyes swept over the handsome sea captain appreciatively. Riding beside Cassandra, she smiled surreptitiously across at her and winked. 'He's wondrously handsome, my dear, in a dark, frightening sort of way. There's also something dangerous about him, too,' she added, 'that puts me in mind of a buccaneer. Don't you think so?'

Cassandra smiled, tending to agree with her. With his dark looks and wicked smile, Stuart Marston only needed a ring in his ear and a cutlass in his hand to be a swash-buckling pirate—like Nat.

John glanced up at the sky, where fitful drifts of dark clouds were being blown restlessly along on an easterly breeze. 'A pleasant morning for a ride,' he commented, 'though I suspect there might be rain later. Best not go too far.'

Cassandra's gaze was constantly drawn to Stuart, who rode a little way ahead with John. Mounted on a huge bay, and clad in black from his boots to his wide-brimmed hat that shaded his powerful shoulders, he was the most over-powering figure she had ever beheld—a stranger bent on making her his wife. She could think of little else. Her resolve to stand firm was set, but in some naïve, gentle part of her heart, she had an uneasy feeling that she was becoming his victim, as he had all the time intended that she should.

The track they followed through the fields of swaying sugar cane was cool in the early morning hour. Entering the parish of St Thomas, winding paths led them through dense green shade of palms and ferns, past brightly coloured flowering and herbal treasures. Exotic butterflies fluttered by, and overhead, singing their hearts out, was an orchestra of brightly coloured warblers and mocking birds.

They encountered several people out riding. Julia was acquainted with most of them, and they stopped to speak to one group. After introducing Stuart and Cassandra, Julia and John stayed on chatting, while Stuart and Cassandra rode on side by side at a leisurely pace.

They entered a gully that was awash with shadows and a tangled overgrowth of trees. The sudden quiet and seclusion sent a trickle of apprehension down Cassandra's spine. Glancing across at her companion, she wondered why he hadn't stopped to wait for John and Julia to catch up with them before entering the gully. There were any number of tracks they could have taken, which would certainly confuse John.

They had ridden some considerable distance when she turned, hoping to see John and Julia close behind, but something inside her told her they wouldn't be. She was right: the track behind them was deserted. All her instincts bade her turn her horse around and gallop back the way they had come, but Stuart was close enough to stop her.

'Don't you think we've ridden far enough?' she dared to venture. 'John and Julia will never find us if we don't go back. Does that not concern you?'

Stuart said quietly, 'Not particularly. But there is no cause for alarm. You are quite safe.'

She tore her eyes away from his sombre smile, unable and adamantly unwilling to be charmed into believing such an implausible lie when she recalled their conversation of the previous evening. He had told her in no uncertain terms that he would make her his wife—that he would win her by fair means or foul. The memory brought a stirring rush of excitement searing through her, and her own need was there to answer him, but the sudden intrusion of Nat into her mind quelled the onslaught. She looked ahead, her cheeks ablaze with the ferocity of her own ardour. He was set on a course in which she was to play a part, she could see that—and he seemed completely assured of finishing it.

'You have brought me here deliberately, haven't you, Stuart?'

He challenged her with a mocking grin. 'I can see you have read my mind.'

'You tricked me. You must think me a stupid, gullible fool.'

'Nay, Cassandra, never that. I sought you out to get to know you better, and in the course of that venture your fairness seized my heart. You entrapped me as surely as any sea siren. When you turned down my offer of marriage your refusal chilled my hopes, and yet I glimpsed in you a chance that you might in time yield to me. When your cousin and Lady Julia hung back, I realised an opportunity had been presented that could aid me in my desire, and allow me to court you at my leisure.'

Cassandra's voice was ragged with emotion as she struggled desperately to ignore the sensual pull he was exerting on her. 'You have a nerve taking such liberties. You will certainly incur John's wrath if you continue to indulge in such foolery.' Her rebuke only seemed to amuse him, for his grin deepened, making her doubt that she would be effective in discouraging his arduous tendencies.

'When you know me better, Cassandra, you will realise

that when I set my mind on having something, I am not easily dissuaded from that end.'

There was a sudden change in the light as the dark clouds became an indistinct mass, blocking out the sun. The air had grown increasingly chilly and an occasional heavy droplet of rain struck at Cassandra's face. Reining her horse to a halt, she glanced across at Stuart, who looked remarkably unperturbed by the forces of nature gathering overhead.

'We must go back. There's going to be a downpour any minute and, besides, John and Julia will be frantic with worry.'

Stuart merely glanced at the frenzied sky and cocked a handsome brow. 'There's no time. We'll be soaked before then.' As if in collusion, the rain chose that moment to fall in big, fat drops. 'We must find shelter until the rain's passed over.' He smiled leisurely as he gave her a lengthy inspection, and even through the material of her dress his eyes burned her and her cheeks grew hot.

'I can't. I can't stay here alone with you. It—it wouldn't be right.'

The black eyes sparkled and danced with unbridled humour. 'This is no time to argue. I happen to have a well-developed instinct for self-preservation, and even you must see the logic of seeking shelter. Come, I know the perfect place.'

Cassandra was too alarmed by the prospect of being alone with him to stop to wonder how and when Stuart Marston had become so familiar with the highways and byways and the secluded haunts of Barbados. 'No, I can't,' she said in a shaky, breathless voice, knowing she was being completely irrational, but even she was not naïve enough to ignore what might happen if she were to be alone with him.

Cassandra's panic stirred and rapidly grew as Stuart

calmly ignored her pleas to turn back and led her towards what looked like a curtain of vines on the rocky wall ahead of her. He told her the long green vines, wrapped and interwoven one into another, covered the mouth of a series of caverns, which would offer them protection from the storm. By the time they reached them lightning was streaking across the sky and thunder rumbled over the low hills. The rain had become a steady downpour and they were quickly becoming soaked. Dismounting with the agility of an athlete, Stuart dragged a still reluctant Cassandra from the saddle. Pulling back the vines of the nearest cave, he gave her a gentle push inside.

'Wait there while I tether the horses beneath that rocky overhang.'

Half blinded by the rain and her own hair, Cassandra stumbled through the yawning mouth of the cave. Adjusting her eyes to the dim interior, she had enough light to see the size of the limestone cavern. It was large, large enough to hold four to five hundred people, she thought, and there was more than one cavern, carved by the slow but steady work of underground streams over the centuries. She stared at the fascinating rock formations and at the huge stalactites hanging from the roof. The caverns tapered away into a dark, brooding stillness, and somewhere from the interior could be heard the sound of rushing water.

Removing her hat, she shook the water from the brim before setting it down on a rock. A footfall behind her swung her round to face Stuart. Legs slightly apart, tall and wide, he filled the narrow entrance, and with the light behind him, his presence seemed to invade the whole cave.

'We'll be safe enough until the storm has passed over.'

His voice was soft and rich with resonant strength, reminiscent of sultry nights beneath open skies. To allow more light inside the cave he pulled back some of the vines and secured them with a rock. Removing his doublet, he threw it down along with his hat. With her breath locked in her throat, Cassandra watched him. Beneath his loose shirt his muscles flexed as he moved. Her gaze took in the sheer male beauty of his wide shoulders and narrow waist. Something in the sombre way he was looking at her as he walked towards her made her tremble.

'H—how did you know about these caves?'

'I've been to Barbados several times. They were pointed out to me by an acquaintance, who was showing me the island when I had some time on my hands four years ago.'

'I see. What is it?' she asked, meeting his inquiring frown. She watched him warily, dwarfed by his towering height. The very air bristled with the energy sparking between them.

'Take off your dress. It's soaked through.'

In a sudden panic she grasped the neck of her gown, shaking her head and stepping back. 'Certainly not. I prefer to keep it on,' she said quickly, aware that she must look a sight, with her hair hanging down her back and clinging in wet strands to her face.

'Remove it,' he insisted quietly. 'You'll catch your death if you don't.'

To Cassandra's horror, without preamble he turned her round and began to unfasten the tiny buttons up the back. She struggled to keep the bodice in place, protesting most objectionably, but her gown slipped down over her hips to her feet. With only her shift as protection from his burning eyes, she tried to cover the gentle swell of her creamy breasts with her hands. Stuart picked up her dress and draped it over some rocks close to the entrance of the cave.

Coming back to where she stood, his hand reached out and touched her cheek tentatively, and before she could put up any resistance his lips claimed hers, warm, passionate and demanding. In the dim light Cassandra caught a flash of steel in his eyes. She pulled back.

'No, Stuart. Stop. Would you dishonour me?'

He captured her face between his hands, his eyes dark with desire, his voice when he spoke smooth and persuasive. 'Nay, Cassandra. I would not do anything that is against your will. I will take nothing you do not freely offer when you are in my arms. But you cannot know the torment I suffer of wanting you. How could it be otherwise?' Caressing her cheek with his thumb, the movement sent shock waves through Cassandra's body. 'What we have is too special to deny, but wanting you is torture, my love.'

Lowering his lips, he brushed the flesh where his thumb had been before. Raising his head slightly, he met her gaze, his look stealing her breath and robbing her limbs of power, his lazy, amorous smile almost destroying her resolve.

'I—I would not wish you to suffer because of me, but this is madness,' she gasped, desperately hanging on to the fragile thread of her sanity.

'I agree, but 'tis the kind of madness that appeals to me.' His lips made contact with her face once more, moving to her ear, his breath warm. 'A kiss, Cassandra,' he breathed huskily. 'Just one more kiss. Would you deny me that?'

Cassandra closed her eyes. Her thoughts were scattered and her heart pounded. One kiss, he said. Just one more kiss. If that was all he wanted, where was the harm in that? Some small, insidious voice inside her head urged her not to do it and she hesitated, torn between right and wrong, between honour and dishonour—but where was dishonour in just one kiss?

Stuart felt her hesitation. Even then he knew that he could conquer his mounting desire and step back, but he also knew that the triumph he would feel at conquering her rejection would be equalled by the pleasure she would give him. 'Sweet Cassandra,' he breathed, ardently placing kisses on her burning cheeks, 'I want you. You want me.'

She swallowed nervously. 'No—no…'

'And there speaks the lie.'

It was his tone, not his words, that conquered her. She was being drawn by a stronger will than her own—drawn by the heat of his lips and the magnetism of his eyes. Surrendering to the call of her blood, resting her hands on Stuart's chest, she offered him her lips. The touch of his mouth on hers brought a soft sigh to her throat—the scent of sandalwood hovering like a seductive whisper between them.

His lips moved over hers with an expert thoroughness, kindling a fire she had not guessed existed. With his hand gently caressing the nape of her neck, his kiss was a masterpiece of passion and persuasion, his lips seeking, finding, provocatively caressing as he proceeded to use every nuance to bring the woman in his arms to submission. His mouth was firm upon hers, infinitely coercive, demanding her surrender.

Beneath such mastery Cassandra's innocence was being drawn like a moth to a flame. Inexperienced as she was in the ways of love, she was being lured into a situation she could not control, and so potent was the spell that Stuart wove, she had not noticed how skilfully he had pulled her down with him on the floor of the cave—which was to become a bed softer and more sumptuous than any she had ever lain on.

Caught in a web of his own desire, impeded by their garments, Stuart quickly stripped them away. As he looked down at Cassandra's naked form his breath caught in his throat. Her hair was a pale shadow against her flesh, her stomach as flat as a boy's, and her small proud breasts were tipped with pale pink. The gentleness and yielding in the melting dark blue depths of her eyes nearly unmanned him. She was beautiful, utterly so, and he knew instinctively that no man had ever seen her like this, naked and in the full bloom of womanhood—and he swore that no man other than himself ever would.

Cassandra gazed up at the iron-hard, bronzed figure looming over her, and in the watery light what she saw made her heart beat harder. Stuart's face was all angles and shadows, hard and dark with passion, and the dark eyes looking down at her were blazing with it—and yet there was as much tenderness in them as desire. The combination made her body ache with sudden yearning, and when he stretched out beside her and caught her warm, inviting body in his arms, his touch was fire. They clung together, neither of them speaking, losing all sense of time, content to let their bodies touch, but the sudden trembling of her limbs awakened Stuart and he kissed her.

It was hard and violent, relentless in its demand, and Cassandra felt a burgeoning pleasure and astonished joy that was almost past bearing. She did not draw back as their uncontrollable hunger for each other took command, for she was lifted beyond herself by a desire stronger than fear or modesty. Unashamedly she pressed herself into him and clung to him as he moulded her pliant body to his rigid contours, feeding his hunger, feeling the agonised need in him. The moment was a feverish crescendo of desire and desperation. The pain of ecstasy was increasing, and Cassandra could feel something wild and primitive building deep inside her, racing through her veins. The brief frenzy ended and her lips became soft and pliable and warm as her whole being turned to liquid.

With extraordinary skill and prowess Stuart's hands moved over her gently and with deliberate slowness, exploring the secrets of her body with the sureness of a knowledgeable lover, savouring what he found and feeling her skin ripple and come alive under his slightest touch. He reminded himself that this was her first time, that he must be gentle with her, not to succumb to the tempest of the moment. Raising his head, he gazed down at her, seeing her eyes large and dark with need, and when she reached up and dragged his head down to hers once more, the touch of her fired him and he groaned, driven to unparalleled agonies of desire. His breathing quickened against her cheek as he surrendered to a primitive, powerful need to possess her.

Her lips were soft, her body too yielding, and he responded to their spell with a wild passion, his lips becoming hard, almost cruel in the savagery of his need. He was amazed and delighted by her sensuality as he covered her body with his own, ignoring the moment when she felt pain, which momentarily jerked her out of her passionate haze, her natural instinct compelling her to cry out and try and pull back. But instinctively she relaxed and wrapped her arms around him, lost in coherent yearnings to have this moment continue for evermore.

Cassandra learned in that single, joyous and irrecoverable moment what it was to become one with another human being, what it was to be a woman. Stuart was implacable, loving her with an ardour that, with his guidance, she became caught up in. Enveloped in the heat of his body, life began to surge anew in Cassandra; never in her life had she believed the act of love could be like this—all consuming, so that she became convinced she was possessed by a madness, by a delirium beyond anything imaginable so that there was nothing else.

With waves of pure physical pleasure washing over her, and lost in the sheer beauty of what Stuart was doing to her—something she believed was unique to themselves— her world began to tilt, and she knew it would never be the same as it was before she had met Stuart Marston.

In the afterglow of love, their passion spent, they lay together, limbs entwined. It was an enchanted time, a time set in a vacuum of peace, with no end and no beginning, and yet they both knew it could not last, that they could not remain as they were forever. Stuart was in awe of what had transpired as he marvelled in the tranquillity of contentment. He realised it had stopped raining, and that it must have done so some time ago, but he couldn't remember when. Dappled sunlight streamed through the opening, warming their naked bodies.

Holding Cassandra close, he clung to the euphoria of the moment as he tried to keep the reality of what he had done at bay, for with his passion spent, there was no hindrance between his brain and his conscience. The sickening truth was that he had deliberately set out to seduce this beautiful, defenceless, virginal young woman, and succeed admirably.

With self-disgust he decided that *seduce* was perhaps too polite a word to describe what he had done, for he hadn't even had the decency to seduce her in the soft comfort of a bed, but had stripped her naked and taken her on the hard floor of a cave like the meanest beast. The fact that she hadn't fought him and pleaded with him to stop, and that she had given herself to him willingly, did nothing to assuage his guilt.

The responsibility of what had happened was entirely his, and it didn't take a genius to work out that John Everson would be well within his rights to run him through for what he had done, which, he now realised, was what he deserved.

With aching gentleness he kissed the top of Cassandra's shining head. She shifted slightly and he felt a dampness on his chest. That was when he became aware that she was crying. Placing his hand beneath her chin, he tipped her face to his.

'Please don't cry. I'm sorry. For what it's worth, what I have done was inexcusable. If I could undo the wrong I would, but it's too late.' Brushing wayward strands of hair from her wet cheeks, he swallowed down a knot of re-

morse. 'Why do you weep? Did I hurt you?' Shaking her
head, she smiled through her tears. It was the sweetest smile
Stuart had ever seen, and the relief that flowed through him
acted like a balm on his guilty heart.

'That isn't why I'm crying. I often cry when I'm happy.
I came to Barbados because my life seemed so empty—so
meaningless and hopeless. You have made me happy because, for the first time in my life, when you made love to
me I knew what it was like to feel wanted—to feel needed.
It was a special feeling and I shall never forget it. Thank
you. Whatever happens after this, I want you to know that
I have no regrets.'

A reprieve was certainly not what Stuart had expected.
Humbled by the raw emotion in her voice, he gazed into
her glowing eyes with disbelief. The shattering tenderness
of her words caused his heart to contract with an emotion
so intense it was painful to bear it. 'Under the circumstances you are being extremely generous. I don't deserve
it. If you had resisted—struggled and begged me to stop—
I would not have forced myself on you.'

Cassandra lowered her eyes, unable to resist the memory
of what she had done, and how glorious it had been—a
sensuous, wondrous experience. The wantonness she had
displayed shocked her. How abandoned she had been, how
eager to share the pleasures of the flesh—already she ached
for it to happen again. The magic of his body filling hers
was still there, and she could still feel the heat of his seed
inside her.

'You were very sure that I would want you—and I did.
I wanted you so much, without thinking what I did. My
self-control was well and truly toppled beneath your deliberate attack on my senses. I yielded to you willingly and
without thought. Your forceful persuasiveness was my
downfall.' She saw him wince at her brutal honesty, and
she smiled. 'I'm being frank, I know, but if two people

can't be frank with one another at a time like this, I don't know when they can be.

'I was unable to withstand your ardour. You brought me to sweet fulfilment, knowing full well what you were doing to me, and that it would leave me hungering for more of the same.'

He turned his face into the rumpled mass of hair spread over her throat. 'And do you still hunger for me, Cassandra?' His voice was deep and husky as he inhaled the sweet scent of her.

'Yes, but I doubt I am strong enough to withstand another full-fledged attack of your ardour at present,' she remarked on a suffocated laugh. Reluctantly she left his arms and scrambled to her feet. 'We must be getting back. John is bound to ask questions, so we must have our answers prepared.'

'And we will be as circumspect as we can be. It will be our secret delight when we look at one another in the days ahead, and remember the pleasure we have shared. No matter how unconventional our beginning, we will always have this. The short time we have spent in this cave will be a time encapsulated in our memories for all time.'

Having pulled on her silk stockings and donned her shift and dress, which had dried remarkably quickly in the hot sun at the cave's entrance, Cassandra paused and looked at Stuart. He had stood up and was fastening his breeches. She caught her breath at the marvellous perfection of the powerful man displayed before her eyes. Her body was still tender from its contact with that magnificent, virile flesh, and she marvelled at the way they had fitted together. It had been perfect, as if God had intended that it should be so.

Suddenly a plain and simple fear gripped her heart. 'You do you realise what this means, don't you, Stuart?'

'Fully, my love,' he murmured. Pulling her into his arms,

he shoved her hair aside and trailed his lips down her neck, his breath feather-light on her flesh. 'Now you will have to marry me—but the way I see it, you and I are as married now in the eyes of God as if any priest had already joined us. The ceremony will be a mere formality.'

Cassandra's eyes pricked with tears at the simple statement. This was no pretender, who would abandon her after taking her body. 'Thank you,' she whispered simply.

'You're welcome. A love like ours was destined to be. We belong together now. Nothing and no one can take this away from us. You are the woman I want to spend my life with, and I want all of you—heart, mind and body.'

She smiled tremulously. 'I find it hard to believe that anybody could want me that much.'

'Do you need convincing still?' he murmured, claiming her lips once more.

She drew back in his arms and stared up at him, thinking how handsome he was, with his dark eyes and an errant wave falling rakishly over his brow. 'I don't know.' This was a man she hardly knew, a stranger still, despite what they had done, and yet she wanted to know this man to whom she had just given her maidenhead better.

Stuart grinned at her frowning face. 'You will. However, until you are my wife, my love, celibacy will be the order of the day. My intentions where you are concerned will be entirely honourable from now on and will have to wait until after the wedding. I shall try to restrain myself, difficult though that will be, but I shall start to conserve my strength, since it is obvious I'm going to need it in our marriage.'

'Why, does it wain so quickly?' Cassandra asked lightly, a gurgle of laughter bubbling to her lips. She could see a mischievous gleam lighting up his eyes, and her heart beat quickened when he placed his lips in the warm, pulsating hollow of her throat.

'It renews itself with astounding fortitude, thank the

Lord, as I shall delight in proving to you when we are wed. Before I return to Bridgetown I will speak to your cousin,' he said, thrusting his arms into the sleeves of his shirt. 'The sooner the better.'

'What if he refuses?'

Stuart's brow quirked in sardonic amusement. 'He won't. He'll agree for your sake. I shall damn anyone who stands in my way.' Seeing the apprehension on her face, it hit him then that her reason for refusing his proposal last night had not been removed. He was curious as to what it could be, but decided not to pressure her into disclosing it. Maybe it would become clear in time. Gently cupping her chin in his hand, he gazed deep into her eyes, understanding the direction of her thoughts. 'No matter what it is that troubles you, Cassandra, do not fear me. Do you want to be my wife?'

When Cassandra looked at him, it came with a slow dawning that she wanted this more than anything she had ever wanted in her life before. She would marry him, but may God help her if he should discover her secret. 'Yes, I do. I shall be content to be your wife, Stuart, in every way.'

John and Julia had taken refuge from the storm at the plantation home of one of Julia's friends. John felt some concern because Cassandra was alone with Captain Marston, but he was confident they would find shelter until the storm had passed over, and that Captain Marston would take care of her. After all, he was an honourable man—a gentleman who acted like one—and John was assured that no man of breeding would take a young unmarried girl of good family to a private place and treat her wantonly.

When they met up with them on the road he accepted their explanation that they had sought shelter in a cave and waited for the rain to subside, and he was satisfied that Cassandra showed no aftereffects of the storm. Although when he looked at her more closely as they rode side by side back to Courtly Hall, he realised that wasn't quite correct.

She was unusually quiet. A small, secretive smile played on her lips, and her eyes were brilliant and warm with emotion, looking away into some world where he was forbidden. In fact, she was positively glowing. Only once did her eyes meet those of Captain Marston, and the look that passed between them was the gleaming look of successful conspirators. The resulting suspicion was farfetched, yet the moment it entered John's mind it nagged him and filled him with unease.

Cassandra was young, inexperienced in the ways of the world, and not even Captain Marston would have the temerity, the sheer effrontery, to interfere with the cousin of a man who had invited him into his home. Not in his worst fears did he imagine that Cassandra might have given more than a kiss, but whatever it was that had occurred between the two of them, as the days passed there seemed to be a new maturity borne of the time she had been alone with Captain Marston.

John was surprised—and more than a little relieved—when Stuart Marston asked for his permission to wed Cassandra. Elated by this unexpected turn of events, he had no hesitation in giving it, and was delighted that the marriage was to take place before the convoy sailed for England.

On the day of the wedding Rosa bathed and covered the bride's body with lightly scented jasmine before dressing her in a shimmering gown of creamy white silk gauze, embroidered all over with tiny pearls. A gold and pearl necklace of the utmost delicacy adorned her throat. Her head was modestly covered in a cloud of diaphanous material for the ceremony, which was then folded back to reveal her shining wealth of hair hanging down the curve of her spine.

The wedding proved to be an exciting diversion for John's and the Courtlys' many friends and acquaintances, with Sir Charles and Lady Julia providing an excellent wedding feast.

Stuart's attire was unostentatious. He wore black knee breeches and a handsome knee-length black coat with broad scarlet-and-gold embroidered cuffs. With pride mingled with joy, he only had eyes for his bride, and he was impatient to return with her to his ship where they could be alone at last. She looked positively radiant and his arms ached to hold her.

It was not until they were climbing into the boat that was to take them out to the *Sea Hawk*, when the sun was a crimson blaze of glory on the horizon, that Cassandra experienced a feeling of doubt, of alarm, as she considered the enormity of the step she had taken, when she realised it was too late to turn back, and that she was to spend a lifetime with this man she knew so little about.

She looked towards where he sat across from Rosa, his profile turned away from her towards the sea, his finely etched features inscrutable in the fading light. Unconsciously she fingered the ring he had placed on her finger, a ring composed of a circle of diamonds of an extraordinary size, its centrepiece an enormous sapphire exhibiting a deep, exotic lustre.

She recollected how Stuart's dark gaze had held hers when he had placed it there, and she also recollected how soft his lips had been when he had placed them on hers, sealing their union with a kiss. With these thoughts filling her mind, any doubts she might have were expelled.

On the point of leaving the shore, she turned to John, who had accompanied them to the boat. He was to remain in the Caribbean on Company business, and to continue to enjoy the uninterrupted favours of Elmina until the time came for him to return to England. He must have sensed Cassandra's slight hesitation and the doubts passing through her mind, for he leaned forward and hugged her, kissing her cheek with deep tenderness.

'Go, Cassandra, my dear, dear cousin. Go with your husband and be happy. He is a good man. He will take care of you. See that my letter is given to Meredith, and give her my love. I will contact you as soon as I return to London.'

John watched the boat leave the shore. The convoy of something like forty heavily laden merchantmen was assembled out in the bay, among them the *Sea Hawk*, which he hoped would take Cassandra to a new and happier life from the one she had known. He prayed most fervently that she would come to love her husband, and in so doing put the memory of Nathaniel Wylde behind her. Let him sink into oblivion. Wasn't that where most legends went?

Chapter Six

Cassandra climbed the rope ladder flung over the ship's side with ease, stepping on to the scrubbed deck and breathing deeply the familiar, comforting smells of hemp and pitch. They welcomed her like old friends. The crew lounged about on piles of rope or drums of tar as they sang sea shanties to the tuneful quivering strings of a lute, making the most of their last hours of ease before the ship set sail.

After having a quiet word with the first mate, James Randell, who was waiting to welcome them on board, Stuart escorted Cassandra down the companion ladder to his cabin. It adjoined the great cabin, which served as a communal dining saloon for the officers, at the stern of the ship.

The huge vessel, manned by eighty mariners and additional surgeon, sailmakers, smiths, caulkers and joiners, to name but a few—as was the case with most great merchantmen sailing across the oceans of the world—moved gently beneath their feet on the swelling sea. The tall masts swayed with the motion, the timbers creaked, and the holds were packed with all manner of goods, from food and drink, tar and oil, powder and ammunition for the forty guns, and a hundred other things, not counting the precious cargo.

Silver moonlight shone through the wide window of Stuart's cabin. A huge globe stood in one corner and a table was littered with log books, tables of latitude and tides, charts, a compass and a quadrant for measuring angles and lengths in observing the sky—all objects Cassandra had become familiar with when she had sailed on the *Dolphin*.

She felt strangely elated after the day's events. The heat and her heightened sensibilities had brought a pink flush to her cheeks. Stuart poured each of them a goblet of wine. Handing one to her, his fingers brushed hers briefly, long enough for her to feel their warmth, their strength. His body was sensuous and taut with vigour, but he behaved towards her with an instinct that showed restraint.

'A toast to you, Cassandra—my dear wife,' he said, raising his goblet. 'May we always be as happy as we are tonight.'

His voice was soft and deep. When he looked at her, his dark eyes glowed with highly charged emotion that contained a deep satisfaction, for it was difficult to believe his good fortune that this beautiful creature was his wife, that the conquest had been easier and more pleasurable than he had at first envisaged. He was seized by a passionate longing to protect, to take care of her, and to treat her with the reverence she deserved, for, despite her determined, forthright manner and strong personality, she had the soft vulnerability of a young fawn.

'You're not nervous, are you, Cassandra?' he asked, seeing a shadow of apprehension in her eyes.

She said the first words that entered her head. 'A little. I've never been married before. I'm not sure how I should behave.'

'I've never been married before either, so we will have much pleasure learning together.'

Cassandra lowered her gaze. 'Nevertheless…it's different for a man. They know the ways of the world—they know women. I—don't want to disappoint you.'

Stuart laughed softly, tipping her chin so that she met his understanding gaze. 'Do you honestly think I want a wife who is experienced in the art of loving? If I did, I would have looked on the streets. It is your naïvety I love, Cassandra, your innocence—and I know from experience that it belies the fires of a passionate and sensual woman. I regret we have to sail early in the morning—but it gives us a little time to be together.'

'I thought you were awaiting the arrival of Captain Tillotson with the rest of the convoy from Antigua.'

'The ships were sighted nearing the island earlier. It's fairly certain they will put in an appearance before dawn. But, my dear, beautiful wife,' he murmured softly, taking the goblet from her hand and placing it aside before drawing her into his arms, 'we do have the night to ourselves— and it was made to enjoy. A night made for love.'

Cassandra sighed with a smile when his long fingers touched her cheek, slowly turning her face to his. When his eyes darkened with desire she felt no fear, only a sweet anticipation, and that all those wondrous sensations she had experienced with him once before were about to be rekindled. 'All too soon it will be light.'

'Not for hours yet. But we have many nights to enjoy, to get to know one another on our journey to England.' His teeth flashed pearl bright as he smiled. It was the smile of a rogue. 'No doubt in time you will become familiar with my selfish manner and all my past indiscretions and chastise me as is now your right.'

'I would not presume, for they are no concern of mine.' She laughed, a delightful, sensuous sound, which never ceased to enchant Stuart.

'Our relationship has strange beginnings, does it not?

There has been no courtship for us to get to know one another as other couples do, no preliminaries of gentle woo-ing.'

'And yet you married me without your family in England around you. What will your mother say when you arrive on her doorstep with a wife in tow?'

'She will be highly delighted, and so relieved to see me wed at last that she won't mind that she missed the cere-mony. I look forward to introducing you to her. Had we been in England, no doubt I would have sought your cousin's permission and there would have been an accep-tance followed by a long betrothal and finally marriage. But there was no time for that.'

'Does your mother live at Charnwood?'

'We have a house in London which she prefers to Charn-wood. Unlike myself, she has an aversion to the country. She likes to be close to the court, and most of her friends live in town. But don't be alarmed,' Stuart said when he saw her look of consternation. 'You will like her. It's im-possible not to. And I know she will be happy with my choice of bride.'

'Then I shall look forward to meeting her very much.' Cassandra felt his arms tighten around her and she raised her lips to receive his kiss, which was a masterpiece of passion and subtle restraint. Start moved with expert thor-oughness, kindling a fire that had laid dormant for too long. He did not release her until she was breathless. 'Your lips are so gentle, so tender,' she murmured, unable to hide the yearning in her eyes, the vulnerability and the passion.

'I cannot promise they will always be so.' Stuart's voice was deep with desire. His eyes darkened and, plunging his fingers into her silken hair, he kissed her again. When his mouth left hers he smiled, holding her away from him.

'I always knew the kind of woman I wanted as my wife,

but I thought she could never exist, except in my mind— and suddenly I find that she does.'

'You make me sound a paragon among women,' Cassandra whispered, her eyes dark and dilated.

He took her face in his hands, his dark eyes tender, but commanding her to submit to him. 'And that is what you are, Cassandra—to me. Now come, my love. I have no desire to delay any longer what is fast becoming inevitable. Inhibitions are meant to be lost on your wedding night.'

'And here was I thinking I had already lost them in a cave on Barbados.'

Her teasing reply brought a low chuckle to Stuart's throat as his hands methodically, and with as much care as if he were unwrapping a precious object, divested her of her clothing. Lifting her, he carried her into an adjacent cabin and laid her on the bed, leaving the door ajar to allow the moonlight to invade their privacy.

It was a time of exploration and unhurried discovery for both of them, of delights and pleasures to be savoured. Stuart's kisses were slow and deliberate as he sought to awaken her to desire, delaying and lingering over the performance. But desire and passion were already vibrating like a harp inside Cassandra, setting both their bodies aflame. No one else had seen her like this or touched the secret places of her body, which Stuart brushed and squeezed lightly with his fingers, causing her to utter a groan of pleasure as a rush of flame tore through her.

She shivered, carried away by his maleness and his caress, by the strange attractions of this man, her husband, of his lips travelling over and burning her eager flesh. Of its own volition her body offered itself eagerly to his. Every touch was one of infinite tenderness, heightening their senses, each responding to the other's sensuality, their bodies communicating with growing fervour, which became a frenzy of passion, until they surrendered at last to the primeval force that possessed them. Their senses ripened and swelled until they were scattered in a storm of passion of such magnitude that they both thought they could bear it no longer.

The sky was beginning to grow light when Cassandra— cocooned in lethargy and contentment, satiated and replete—at last fell into a deep and blissfully untroubled sleep, with dreams of a wonderful voyage back to England, unable to see anything but smooth sailing ahead.

But long before they reached its familiar shores she would have given everything she possessed to exchange the perils that would beset her on the ill-fated *Sea Hawk*. She was unaware when Stuart rose and left her to visit his friend Captain Tillotson on the *Spirit of Enterprise*; he had hoped to meet up with him when he had arrived at Barbados with Cassandra all those weeks ago, but had failed to do so.

When Stuart returned to his ship, his whole world had been unbelievably shattered and his heart was filled with a terrible, impotent black rage as he considered the hideous truth Samuel Tillotson had divulged as to Cassandra's true identity.

His face had been grim as he'd listened in frozen silence, feeling as if an iron band around his chest was being tightened with every condemning word his friend uttered. At first he had felt there must be some mistake, but the one irrefutable fact he could not ignore, or disprove, was that it had been Cassandra he had seen at Execution Dock when Nathaniel Wylde was hanged. That was why he had sensed there was something strangely familiar about her when he'd met her for the first time. Her features and silver and gold hair resembled the pirate's. Why hadn't he had the sense to see it?

After all his experience, he thought as his wrath continued to grow, he'd fallen like an ass for the oldest trick in the world, and he cursed himself for trusting her. What a brilliant, scheming little opportunist she was, a consummate actress, and, like the fool he was, he'd been taken in by her, been transfixed by her beauty when he'd first set eyes on her, acting like a knight errant when she'd been about to be tipped into the sea. He'd been duped—not only by Cassandra, but also by John Everson. The man must have been laughing himself into a seizure when he'd offered to marry his cousin. No man in his right mind would want her, knowing she was the spawn of Nathaniel Wylde.

Everson had deliberately lied when he'd told him Cassandra's father had been killed while fighting for the King at Worcester, and Cassandra had looked him in the eye and endorsed this. Damn her! Damn her cheating, deceitful heart.

Despite her strong protests when he'd asked her to marry him—which, to be fair to her, might have had something to do with Nathaniel Wylde being her father, and her conscience—that fair-haired sorceress had agreed to marry him in the time it had taken him to make love to her. She hadn't resisted, hadn't protested or tried to fight him off—in fact, she had been wanton, as wanton as sin. He hadn't stolen her virtue, she had *given* it to him, driving him to a violent compulsion to possess her, making sure he would want to go on possessing her—and he had, he thought, admitting the truth to himself. He had wanted her more than he had ever wanted anything in his life. Parading before his eyes were visions of an enchantress, of a bewitching young woman—Cassandra lying in his arms, Cassandra looking at him with her melting eyes…laughing up at him…

Samuel had asked him to have another drink before returning to his ship, but Stuart had refused. There was no way to avoid the truth. No amount of liquor could douse the pain and the anger that were burning like an inferno inside him.

And now, as he looked down at Cassandra's sleeping form amid the tangle of sheets, at the smoothness of her belly and the upward thrust of her breasts, he remembered vividly how soft, how slender, her arms had been when they had twined themselves about him, captivating him, making him her pliant, willing slave.

His throat ached as his eyes drank in her alluring beauty, but then a white-hot fury unlike anything he'd ever experienced consumed him, turning his mind into a furnace of boiling rage. Unable to bear looking down at her and not drag her from the bed and send her packing back to John Everson, he turned away and left her. It was a long time before the pain inside him began to dull as a cold, black rage swept over him.

It was much later when Cassandra awoke and stretched, luxuriating in a delicious feeling of warmth and well being. Rolling over, she found the bed next to her was empty. Sleepily she opened her eyes, letting her gaze wander through to the main cabin. Stuart was standing by the window, already dressed.

Climbing out of bed, she draped a sheet about her nakedness and went to him. He stood with his back to her, giving no indication that he was aware of her presence as he stared out to sea, one hand raised and resting on the window. Sliding her arms tightly about his waist, she rested her head against his back, uttering a deep, contented sigh.

'Why didn't you wake me?' she murmured.

She felt his body stiffen within the circle of her arms, felt the tension rock solid inside him, and when he firmly took hold of her hands and disengaged them from his waist, instinctively she felt that for some reason all was not well. It was warm inside the cabin, but a creeping chill stole over her. When he turned and faced her, she saw the tender gaze of a lover had fallen away, and in his eyes there gleamed a cold, unrelenting light. For the first time she saw behind the masquerade of a dashing sea captain. She saw the real Stuart Marston, a man devoid of emotion—merciless and dangerous.

Looming before her in a midnight blue jacket and breeches, he emanated a wrath so forceful that she gasped and instinctively stepped back, her heart beating like a battering ram in her chest. Never in her life had she witnessed such controlled, menacing fury.

'Why—Stuart! What is it?' she asked, trying to combat her mounting alarm. 'Is something wrong?'

'You could say that.'

His voice was calm, much too calm and carefully modulated, and that alarmed her. She was suddenly afraid and there was a tremulous feeling inside her, but she knew she could not give in to it, not when he was looking at her like that. She took a deep breath, and when she spoke her voice was as calm as his own had been.

'Has something happened? Why do you look at me like that?'

'My compliments,' he emphasised contemptuously, 'on your duplicity, your deceit, and your disloyalty.' When she paled, he nodded. 'It would seem our marriage began on a lie. Yes, Cassandra, I accuse you of having deceived me, of pretending to be what you are not. Why did you not tell me you boarded Captain Tillotson's ship at Trinidad?'

Completely taken off guard, Cassandra stared at him, speechless. The light went out of her eyes as she was brutally roused from her happy state. Her heart contracted painfully, for there was no sign of the love they had shared. None of that was evident in the cold, marble severity of her husband's face. His bronzed features were a dangerous colour, his dark eyes snapping furiously as he glared at her.

She wanted to turn and flee from him, but she stood, facing him with perfect composure.

'Why did you lie to me?'

'I—I did not lie. You did not ask and I did not think it was important.'

'No?' His voice was chilling, with all the deadly calm of approaching peril. He moved closer, his eyes hard and compelling, holding hers so that she was unable to look away. Cassandra was fearful of what he was going to say next, suspecting the worst. 'Then answer me this. Are you the daughter of Nathaniel Wylde—the bloody barbarian who was hanged at Execution Dock in London in November of last year?'

Cassandra's face went white, her throat going so dry that she was unable to answer. He knew! The question hung in the air between them like a threat, his tone telling her he would allow her no respite until she'd given him some answers. Her silence maddened him. Losing control of his precariously held temper, he lunged out and seized her shoulders in a bruising grip, his iron fingers digging deep into her soft flesh, but so great was the panic inside her as she looked up at him towering over her that she was unaware of the pain this caused her.

'Answer me, damn you,' he lashed out furiously. Close to tipping over the edge into a pit of madness, he shook her hard. 'And if you lie to me I'll throttle you, so help me God! You are a conniving, deceitful little bitch, but just once in your misbegotten life, I demand that you tell me the truth.'

Shuddering violently, denial sprung to Cassandra's lips, but still she uttered no sound—what was the use? He wouldn't believe her and it would only add insult to injury. A wave of terror passed over her and she was afraid, terribly afraid, for she had never felt like this in her life before. All the fury Stuart was capable of feeling was concentrated in his face, making her realise that in failing to tell him about her father she had unleashed in him a fury so profound and terrible that a man of his inflexible nature would find hard to forgive.

'I am asking you again. It is true, isn't it?' he persisted ruthlessly. 'Nathaniel Wylde was your father?'

She nodded slowly. 'Yes.'

'So—you do not deny it?'

She shook her head, her hair falling about her face, and said with quiet resignation, 'No, I don't. I have no reason to.'

Stuart stared at her hard for a moment before letting his hands fall to his sides and stepping back, as if he couldn't stand to be close to her, as if he couldn't stand the sight of her. No one had ever looked at her with such scathing contempt, such loathing. Cassandra saw the savage, scorching fury that was emanating from every pore of him. His jaw was taut with rage, his mouth drawn into a ruthless, forbidding line, and his expression was as murderous as his feelings.

'Why was I not told? Why did you keep a matter of such importance, of such magnitude, from me?' he demanded.

'I am sorry. I—did not think it important, but I should have told you, I realise that now. How did you find out?'

His eyes were merciless. 'You did not think it important to tell your husband that your father was a vicious pirate? Really, my dear—you astound me,' he said with scathing sarcasm. 'When I awoke early I decided to pay a call on Captain Tillotson, who arrived to take his place in the convoy during the night. He congratulated me on my marriage, as one does—but can you imagine my shock and amazement when he expressed his surprise that I had married the daughter of a pirate—and not just any pirate, but the infamous Captain Nathaniel Wylde?'

Cassandra stared at him in disbelief. 'Captain Tillotson knew?'

'The man you were with at Trinidad aroused his suspicions—along with the fact that you and your companion were travelling to Barbados alone. After making enquiries and giving a description of his character to some of his seafaring friends—for a man who bears such a marked facial disfigurement is not easy to forget—he knew beyond doubt that the man you were with was none other than Drum O'Leary—Nathaniel Wylde's closest confidant— with a price on his head to equal his own. I also believe your companion travelling with you on board this ship to be his daughter. Is that correct?'

Clutching the sheet about her nakedness, Cassandra's anger was swift. The bewildered terror that had seized her initially evaporated. In a blinding flash she understood that he wanted to degrade her because she had kept the truth from him, that his monstrous pride would wreak some unspeakable revenge on her for her father's crimes. She searched that hard, sardonic face for some sign that he felt something for her, anything, but there was nothing but contempt. Bile rose in her throat as she realised she did not know him after all. Tossing her head, she stared at him, her eyes scornful, her pride forbidding her to bow to his harsh interrogation.

'Yes. Rosa is Drum's daughter,' she admitted coldly. 'What of it?'

'I am your husband,' he ground out, 'much as I have come to regret that unfortunate state of affairs since my encounter with Samuel Tillotson. It comes as a hard lump for me to swallow that my wife has been *queening* it among an ill-disciplined, murderous rabble—that she was so well acquainted with them as to collude in the stealing of a ship from her moorings, and cutting down a dead man from the gallows who had been justly hanged.

'No doubt there are those among the criminal fraternity who would compliment and applaud such feats of daring and success—but I cannot. I shudder to think what kind of education you received while you were living with a bunch of cut-throats, whose way of life depended on the use of force and extreme violence, torture and death. I understand perfectly now why your guardian spoke so disparagingly of you—no matter how light-hearted he sounded at the time—and why he was so eager to get you off his hands.'

'That's a lie,' Cassandra snapped, glaring at him.

'Is it? I don't think so,' Stuart remarked with cool mockery. 'You, my dear, are a virtuoso of deceit—which, because of your past, is a fair assumption. Little wonder your cousin wants everyone to believe your father was killed honourably in battle whilst fighting the King's cause, to conceal the fact that he was a pirate, an arch-villain—a butcher whose hands were stained with the blood of a thousand innocents. There isn't a man alive who would knowingly take Satan's spawn for a wife.'

His bitter insult finally snapped Cassandra's fragile self-control, sending her into a fury that was almost uncontainable. Her eyes flashed a dangerous, steely blue as she took a step towards him and slapped his face so hard that his head jerked sideways and she feared she had broken her wrist. The sound of her hand striking his cheek echoed in the cabin.

Stuart stepped back, absolutely appalled, his face turning white with rage. 'You little hellcat.' He caught her wrist when she would have slapped him again, and in the next instant she was crushed unmercifully against his chest. 'Be warned, Cassandra, if you were a man I'd kill you for that,' he rasped hoarsely, before thrusting her away from him.

Cassandra held her ground, her chest heaving with anger, her eyes locked on his. 'If I were a man I'd kill you myself. You bastard!' she burst out mindlessly, too infuriated to care what she was saying, or that a muscle had begun to tick in the side of Stuart's jaw and that he looked murderous. 'I did not deserve that. Don't you *ever* call me that again, ever—do you hear? You are heartless and cruel, and I cannot believe I let you sweet talk and seduce me into marrying you, and I will never be able to forgive my stupidity in trusting you—in loving you,' she confessed, without knowing what she said in her impassioned moment. 'And I did not steal *any* ship. The one you speak of was the *Dolphin*—my father's ship—which became mine on his death.'

Stuart stood perfectly still, giving no sign that her confession of love moved him. He stared at the tempestuous beauty with blazing eyes and a face alive with fury, unable to believe the alluring, impulsive girl he had married had become this furious, self-possessed young woman. 'The *Dolphin* was impounded, so the crime was theft. And your father? Do you deny that you colluded in having his body removed from the gallows?'

'No. I have no reason to deny it. He may have been a notorious pirate, but he was still my father, and I was determined he would not be stuffed into an iron cage and hung on the marshes for the crows to pick at. His body was buried at sea, which was his wish.'

'No matter how staunchly you try to defend what you did, you should know that since your hasty departure from England, the Lords of the Admiralty had no doubts as to the identity of those who stole the *Dolphin* from her moorings. Drum O'Leary was seen on board as she slipped down the Thames—and also a young woman, who those who saw her said bore such a strong resemblance to Wylde she could have been his daughter.'

'They have no proof of that. It is mere supposition. As far as I am aware, apart from a small number of our neighbours in Chelsea, there are few that know Nathaniel Wylde had a daughter, let alone what she looked like.'

'I did,' he countered bluntly. 'The Admiralty knew he had a daughter living with relatives somewhere in London.'

'That may be so but, never having been seen, I could not be recognised. What people saw was a woman with fair hair. She might have been anyone—a sailor's moll, perhaps.'

'The Admiralty might take some convincing of that. A proclamation has been issued giving details of the ship— and that Drum O'Leary and Nathaniel Wylde's daughter are pirates and enemies to the crown. Substantial rewards have been offered for your capture.'

Cassandra stared at him in shock, the remainder of what colour she had left draining from her face. 'And knowing what you do, no doubt you would be happy to put the noose around my neck yourself in order to be rid of me,' she scorned, her voice as cutting as steel as she met the accusing eyes of her husband without flinching.

'Don't tempt me,' he growled.

Proud and determined, she did not resemble any supplicant. Anger and pride strengthened every fibre in her body and sent a sudden surge of blood pumping through her veins—Nathaniel Wylde's blood, which would never bow in the face of intimidation.

The force of her personality that burned in her eyes gave Stuart an insight of the woman who had sailed on the *Dolphin* to Trinidad, who must have looked as she did now, with her solid will and defiance in every line of her body. She looked magnificent and a flood of admiration he was unable to prevent washed over him. Quickly he recollected himself and drew himself up sharply, his features convulsed in a spasm of anger and exasperation.

His cruel remark pierced Cassandra to her very soul. With a mixture of pain and anger she looked on her husband's handsome face, at the thin line of his lips—lips that just a short while ago had courted hers and sent her into such raptures of delight. She searched his eyes, for there must be something there left over of their night of love. But there was nothing. They looked on her coldly and without emotion or love.

'I deeply regret that I concealed the fact that Nathaniel Wylde was my father, but I saw no reason to divulge it. He is dead and can have no relevance to the future.'

Her ability to mock his fate and ignore her father's crime was too much. Stuart's gaze snapped to her face, and Cassandra recoiled in shock from the scorching fury in his coal-black eyes. 'You dare say that to me, when any children we might have will have his blood flowing through their veins? Can't you bring yourself to admit that his choice of profession was indefensible—or were you so completely under his domination, and possibly as much a victim as any of the honest, unoffending mortals who had the misfortune to cross his path?'

'It affected me deeply when I discovered the truth about him. I do not condone any of his actions—but nor do I have words with which to condemn him. However, I realise you must despise me for what I've done, for being who I am.'

'You're right.' His voice cracked like a whiplash. 'So savage were Wylde's crimes that there are those he wronged who still seek to avenge themselves. There are also those in the Admiralty who would not believe you played no part in them. Knowing of your presence on board his ship—that alone would be enough to condemn you.'

They looked at each other but did not speak, for his words reeked horror deep within Cassandra's troubled heart. Pain and silence stretched between them so complete that it was almost audible. What stood between them was bitter and ugly, and she could not see how it could ever be any different.

'Yes,' she said quietly, so quietly that Stuart almost failed to hear her. 'You have made me aware of that. Initially I did not know of my father's reputation—I was too young. I only became aware of the fact that he loved and cared for me and had only stayed away until after my aunt and uncle died, when I was thirteen, because they had forbidden him to come near me.'

'The reason being?'

'Their divided loyalties at the time of the Civil War.'

Stuart's lips curled scornfully. 'Their loyalties to each other cannot have been so divided, for how else did your father get your mother with child?' He spoke sarcastically, with a cold contempt.

His aggressive manner brought an angry gleam to Cassandra's eyes. 'Against my uncle's wishes they met secretly, for they loved each other deeply. It only added to my own misfortune that my mother died in childbirth, denying them any chance they might have had of marrying.'

'Your misfortunes! Your misfortunes bring tears to my eyes,' Stuart scoffed, turning from her and striding across the cabin to look out of the window, at the ships beginning to manoeuvre about in the water as they prepared to get under way, reminding him that his presence would be required on deck. He turned and looked at his wife coldly, and with deliberate cruelty he carefully enunciated each vicious word. ''Tis you who are the bastard, Cassandra, not I, as you accused me of being. You should have told me that your father was the infamous Captain Wylde and relieved me of the embarrassment of making you my wife.'

His harsh words cut deep into Cassandra's heart. 'Since you find marriage to me so distasteful, do whatever you think must be done. Since there can be no annulment, if it is to be divorce—then so be it.'

'I will not sully my family's name with a divorce,' Stuar remarked coldly. 'It is quite out of the question. Events must take their own course and we must learn to make the best use of them. It is a situation we must learn to live with. There are going to have to be compromises on both sides.'

Puzzled, Cassandra stared at him. 'Compromises?'

'We will both have to learn to compromise. I should have guessed who you were when I saw you on your arrival on Barbados. There was something about you that stirred my memory—but I could not think why at the time. You were careful to keep your face concealed, but now I know that it was you I saw at Nathaniel Wylde's execution that day.

Cassandra stared at him in disbelief. 'You! You were there?' Like a flash she remembered the man her father had made his final salute to. 'Yes—I remember you, also. I was you who captured my father's attention when he was on the scaffold. You he looked at and raised his hand to with an air of a salute. I turned and saw you leave—but did not see your face. You knew him, didn't you?'

'To my everlasting regret,' Stuart replied, striding towards the door, 'and, on returning to my ship afterwards when I became certain I had seen his daughter in the crowd with one of his associates, I almost turned back and denounced him. Had I the sense to have done so, it would have saved me this embarrassment. Should it become public knowledge that I have made Nathaniel Wylde's daughter my wife, then a mighty scandal will ensue and cause immense pain and embarrassment to my mother. That is something I intend to avoid at all costs.'

'Before you go, please answer me this.' Cassandra moved quickly to stand in front of him as he was about to go out. 'What did my father do to you that was so terrible that it makes you hate him so much?'

Stuart's cold eyes became locked on hers. 'Did no one

ever tell you who it was who tracked your father to his haunt in the Caribbean? Who it was that hounded him to the coast of West Africa before capturing him and bringing him back to London to hang?'

Cassandra shook her head, but then realisation of what he was saying flooded her whole being. 'It was you,' she whispered, her face as white as the sheet she clutched around her. 'It was you, wasn't it?'

'Yes.'

Her laugh was choked and bitter, her voice when she spoke quivering with anger and pain. 'Then you should be proud of yourself.'

'I am not proud,' Stuart replied without emotion. 'Were you proud to be a part of it all? I sought justice, that was all. Your father was as much my enemy as Cromwell was the King's—and he remained ruthless, remorseless and relentless right to the end. I had my reasons for making sure Nathaniel Wylde was captured and hanged for his crime.'

'Tell me?'

'He killed my brother. It forged a hatred between us. Having strayed from the convoy which was sailing to the Caribbean, my brother's ship was attacked and plundered by pirates. According to evidence given by a handful of those on board who managed to survive in the water until they were picked up by the convoy—unfortunately too late to be of assistance to the stricken ship—the attack was led by Nathaniel Wylde. He callously left every man, woman and child on board to drown when it sank to the bottom of the ocean.'

This smote Cassandra's heart and she lowered her eyes, unable to meet his direct gaze, to look upon the hatred he possessed for her father mirrored in their depths. 'I am so sorry,' she murmured. 'I didn't know.' At last she understood completely the reason for his anger, his hatred. She was beginning to see her father in the same light as others and her love was soured. She felt betrayed, suddenly, abandoned; the image she had carried in her heart was shattered for ever—as, it would seem, was her marriage, which wasn't even twenty-four hours old.

John was right—she had been influenced by her father, allowing her love for him to cloud her mind to the true nature of his character, to the violence and wickedness of his chosen profession. But she had been young, naïve, a willing victim ready to fall prey to his charismatic charm and the doting, lavish attention he showered on her after years of neglect. And yet deep inside her heart she had always known the truth but had refused to acknowledge it, knowing that, on doing so, the pain would be intolerable. Stuart was completely justified to feel as he did.

'He raised his hand to me in a final salute in grudging respect for the way I had succeeded in capturing him and his ship after playing a cunning game of hide and seek with me across the Atlantic Ocean,' Stuart went on. 'And though it pains me to tell you, considering he had no seafaring background until he became a galley slave, his navigational skills were quite exceptional. Now do you understand what I meant when I said we will both have to make compromises? It will be no simple matter for either of us having to live together, knowing what we do.'

He continued to look at her coldly. 'The implications of your background and involvement with the pirates—not forgetting the seriousness of the conviction hanging over you—I cannot begin to contemplate at this moment, or what my feelings are towards you and the kind of future we will have together with this lying between us.

'It will be a long time, if ever, before I shall be able to forget that you are the daughter of the man who killed my brother—as it will for you, whenever you remember that I am the one responsible for the death of your father. And now you must excuse me. I have some important matters to attend to.'

The implication that she was not an important matter was unmistakable, and Cassandra tensed at the deliberate, un-provoked insult. 'Don't let me detain you,' she said tersely.

'I won't. My crew will be waiting for me to give orders to sail. If you are wise,' he said in a blood-chilling voice as he towered over her, 'you will avoid me very carefully while you are on my ship.' His eyes swept over her con-temptuously. 'Dress yourself. I will inform one of the crew to bring you some breakfast.' Clamping his hands on her shoulders, he moved her out of the way.

In stunned silence Cassandra watched him go. She stared at the closed door. The cabin was suddenly larger, emptier, somehow more lonely. Shock had formed a merciful co-coon around her, which, as it melted away, would give place to real suffering in all its terrible anguish. She could not think what she was going to do, what would happen now. At that moment nothing mattered except the pain within her.

Chapter Seven

Weighing anchor and hoisting her sails, the *Sea Hawk* took her place in the convoy that left Barbados and began to glide beneath an azure sky towards the open sea. The chances of a propitious passage for the slow-moving merchantmen were largely dependent on favourable winds.

Cassandra, deeply distressed by the memory of what had transpired between herself and Stuart, remained in the cabin, blindly watching the activity taking place through the window as she tried to put some semblance of order back into her crippled emotions.

For the first time in her life she was truly afraid, afraid because until now she had given little thought to the seriousness of the situation she had placed herself in. If she should return to London and her identity was exposed, she would be arrested and hanged. If she had dissociated herself from any criminal action after her father's execution and gone home to Chelsea, she would not be in this predicament.

Washed and dressed and with no appetite for food, she stood alone with her wretched thoughts. With hindsight she realised she should have told Stuart who she was, and now she was tormented by the thought that she might have lost him forever—just when she realised how deeply she loved him. Her gaze drifted through the open door to the bed where they had made love. In that bed all her hopes and desires had blossomed and then shrivelled away like summer flowers when winter frost sets in. Was it to be over so soon? Were there to be no more nights spent in his arms?

Rosa, who was feeling homesick and happy to be leaving Barbados, came to help Cassandra with the unpacking of her trunks. She smiled, pleasantly surprised to see how large and light the cabin was. Her own was next door and much smaller.

'I can see you are going to be comfortable,' she said, her eyes sweeping the well-furnished cabin, its brasswork gleaming like polished gold. However, her smile was quickly dispelled, for one look at Cassandra's pale and wretched face told her something was wrong, as well as the red eyes which meant that she might have been crying.

Despite the sadness that had descended on her, Cassandra managed to bring a smile to her lips on seeing her young friend. Rosa possessed a quiet sense and wisdom—and an understanding of the unprincipled life to which she had been reared on the Cape Verde Islands—way beyond her years.

They had become close friends during the months they had spent together, and Cassandra was glad that Rosa had agreed to accompany her to London before returning to her home. However, Rosa had not been blessed with a robust constitution and her general health gave Cassandra cause for concern. From the moment she had left her home, the young woman had been susceptible to many minor ailments, each one taking her longer to recover from than the one before. Her face was pale and she was thinner than she had been when Cassandra had first met her.

'I know how relieved you are to be going home at last, Rosa—to be leaving Barbados.'

'Yes. The distance between the Caribbean and the Cape Verde Islands is too great by far for me,' she replied, her voice rich and deep with an attractive trace of Portuguese. 'On reaching London I'm sure I will soon obtain passage on a ship bound for the East Indies. They often call at the islands to obtain water. But why aren't you on deck to see the convoy get under way?'

'I can see everything pretty well from here.'

The sadness that weighed heavy on Cassandra's heart could be seen in her eyes and affected her voice, which brought a shadow of concern to Rosa's dark, almond-shaped eyes. She moved to where Cassandra stood and turned her round to face her. 'What is it? Has something happened to upset you? When I went on deck earlier for some air, I saw Captain Marston and he appeared to be in an extremely bad temper—hardly the kind of behaviour one would expect from a bridegroom the morning after his wedding. What is it, Cassandra?' she asked gently. 'Something awful must have happened to distress you so.'

Cassandra sighed, knowing she could not hide the truth from Rosa's sharp, inquisitive eyes. Besides, what had transpired affected her too. 'Stuart has discovered who I am, Rosa. He—he paid a visit to Captain Tillotson earlier, whom, it would seem, having somehow found out who we are, lost no time in telling him.'

In a few words Cassandra quickly told Rosa what had taken place between them on his return to the *Sea Hawk*, and the part he had played in capturing her father and the reason for his hatred. As the story unfolded Rosa listened in horrified silence.

'Then there is little wonder your husband is angry,' she whispered when Cassandra at last fell silent. 'I can understand completely the hatred he must have felt towards your father that drove him to avenge his brother. You must try to understand how he is feeling. This cannot be easy for him.'

'I do understand, and it makes me feel quite wretched. He was none too pleased either when I confirmed what he already suspected—that you are Drum's daughter. I fear we are both in for an unpleasant voyage home.'

'As his wife, your situation is far worse than my own. What will he do, do you think? What are his intentions?'

'I don't know. At the moment I should imagine he is trying to come to terms with the mistake he has made in marrying me. He is so furious that I believe him to be capable of anything. I did not know the man his anger unleashed, Rosa, and for a time I was afraid of him. He was a stranger to me—which makes me realise just how little I know him.

'What I do know is that by keeping the truth of my identity from him I have placed him in an impossible situation. I should not have done it. It wasn't right. Because I was party to the taking of the *Dolphin* from her moorings—and having my father's body cut down from the gallows, in England—there is a price on my head. If I am handed over to the authorities, I will hang for sure.'

Rosa was appalled to think that something so terrible might befall her friend. 'Don't say that. Don't even think it. Captain Marston would not let that happen. Wait and see, Cassandra. I'm sure that by the time the ship reaches England he will have put all this behind him.'

'I wish I could be sure of that, but I can't,' Cassandra said bitterly. 'I've tried to put myself in his place. At first I was shocked and angry because he did not even trouble to discriminate between Nat and me, the guilty and the innocent, but when he left me and I pursued my reflections, my attitude to him gradually became more sympathetic. Perhaps, in his place, I would feel the same. After all, why should he trust me? I am the daughter of a man on whom he had sworn vengeance and whom he had seen hang.'

'Come now, Cassandra. You are being too hard on yourself.'

'Am I?' She sighed deeply and shook her head. 'I don't think so. The first time Stuart met me he made no attempt to disguise the fact that he was attracted to me. He didn't stop to think, and simply because he wanted me he made me his wife. without bothering to find out more about me. But from the moment in which spontaneous attraction drew us together, fate stepped in and took a malicious pleasure in separating us. He will never be able to look at me without being aware of who I am—without seeing my father.'

'One day he will.'

'If he doesn't, and we are to remain man and wife, then there is little hope of happiness for either of us.'

'Has he mentioned divorce?'

Cassandra shook her head slowly. 'To avoid any scandal that will bring discredit to the name I now bear, he has made it quite plain that divorce—which cannot be brought about without an Act of Parliament anyway—is out of the question. Maybe when we reach England he will send me away somewhere and we will live apart.'

'I cannot believe he would do that. To do such a thing would be bound to cause comment among his friends, and be sure to cause him embarrassment.' Taking her hand, Rosa drew her down beside her on the cushioned seat in the window recess, letting her eyes linger on her unhappy face. 'He must love you, Cassandra. What other reason could there be for him wanting to marry you with such haste? And you love him, don't you? It's fairly obvious to anyone seeing you together.'

Cassandra nodded slowly. 'Yes. I confess I do love him. I love him so much that if he sends me away—if he banishes me from his life totally—it will tear me apart.'

'Then be patient. For the time it is going to take to reach England he will see you wherever he goes. He can't put you entirely out of his mind. When he has come to terms with who you are, his love will overcome all this, you'll see. Love moves mountains—at least, that is what my mother is always telling me, and my mother is never wrong,' Rosa said with a smile, her eyes looking tenderly into Cassandra's own, and Cassandra read in them a softness and a sympathy that comforted her.

She did her best to smile. 'Your mother sounds very wise. Both our fathers have much to answer for, have they not, Rosa?'

Later, when her unpacking was done and Rosa had retired to her own cabin to rest, Cassandra went up on deck to breathe in the fresh sea air. She attracted stares and smiles from members of the crew, to which she responded pleasantly. But none of them seeing her could possibly be aware of how miserably unhappy she was as she moved to the rail. The sea was silky smooth and dotted with fishing boats. Idly she let her gaze wander along the deck towards the poop, her eyes lighting on Stuart standing next to the wheel, where he was immersed in discussion with James Randell.

She longed to go to him, but pride and the uncertainty of what sort of reception she would receive held her back. He had discarded his coat, and above his breeches he wore a sparkling white loose linen shirt with the sleeves rolled up over his forearms. It flopped open to the waist to reveal the deep tan of his broad chest. His shining black hair was tied back at the nape, the breeze playfully teasing a heavy wave that dipped over his brow. Cassandra could have stood there for hours gazing at him, remembering what it had been like to have him hold her, to run her hands over his muscled chest. He seemed to sense her presence and, raising his head, looked to where she was standing.

Immediately he excused himself to Mr Randell and walked briskly towards her, his expression grim. Cassandra met his gaze squarely. She tried to smile, but she could tell by the way he looked down at her, studying her with an implacable coldness and barely contained anger that sent a chill through her heart, that nothing had changed, and she knew with a feeling bordering on despair that he despised her. Tilting her chin, she looked at him with ironic concern.

'The atmosphere is quite stifling down in the cabin so I thought I would come on deck. I am allowed on deck, I hope?'

'Of course you are. What possible pleasure could it give me in denying you the freedom of the ship? However, now we are under way, there are matters we have to discuss. Come,' he said, taking her arm none too gently in a firm grip. 'Let's go below. What I have to say I prefer to say in private.'

Without protest Cassandra allowed him to escort her along the scrubbed deck and down to the cabin—which she had vacated just a short while before because the atmosphere inside hung as heavy as an opiate in the mid-day heat. As though Stuart could not bear to be close to her, when the door was closed he strode towards a small table and poured himself a goblet of wine. Drinking deep and placing the goblet down, he moved towards the window and stood with his back to her.

Cassandra could see he was as taut as a bowstring and that he was clearly battling with his feelings. She had an impulse to go to him and place her arms around his neck, but she was in no doubt that he would be repulsed by such an intimate display of tenderness. The heavy silence that stretched between them preyed on her nerves as she waited for him to speak, and when he at last turned and looked at her his face might have been carved out of stone.

'Because of who your father was…who you are…I will not touch you again. What happened between us last night will not be repeated until I have considered how best to proceed.'

Anger and confusion were warring inside Cassandra's head. 'You are saying that you will not share my bed.'

'Exactly. When we reach England I will have decided on the course our future will take. I will tell you then what we will do,' he said dispassionately, immune to the wrathful expression on her lovely face.

'I see.' Cassandra was more disturbed by this than anything else. Tears pricked the backs of her eyes, and in an effort to hide her hurt and disappointment she forced them back and held her ground. 'I am not some mindless article to be used and disposed of at will. If this is how you see things, then our marriage is a sham and better ended.'

'I've told you there will be no divorce. For the time being this matter is between you and me—no one else. Is that understood? Should it become known that I have taken the daughters of two of the most infamous pirates of the age on board the *Sea Hawk*, then it would lead to certain mutiny.'

'I understand that. But what if Captain Tillotson makes it known who you have on board?'

'He won't. I have his word on that. I would also prefer that my officers and crew do not suspect there is anything amiss between us.'

Cassandra's smile was one heavy with irony. 'That will be rather difficult, don't you think, if you are to sleep elsewhere. That alone will tell everyone all is not as it should be between us when you occupy a separate cabin to your wife.'

'There is another bunk in the adjacent cabin, which I

shall use to allay any suspicion. When in the company of other members of the crew—which will be often, since there will be a large complement at dinner each evening—for the sake of appearances you will act as a wife should and with due respect for the name you now bear.'

Immediately Cassandra tensed, her eyes jewel bright as she met his gaze. 'Whatever my faults, Stuart, I hold loyalty and honour in high regard,' she remarked sharply, buffeted by a myriad conflicting emotions, including fury and a deep and painful anguish. 'But if you think the ease with which I delivered myself up to you last night gives you the right to dictate my every move, then you are mistaken.'

Stuart threw her a black look. There was a scornful curl to his handsome lips and his words were as cutting as steel when he spoke. 'As your husband I have every right—and I ask this of you for your own protection. Do not forget who you are.'

'How can I do that when you will not let me?' she bit back.

Stuart ignored her remark. 'As long as you are on board this ship your life is in danger. Should the crew discover your true identity then I may not have the power to save you, such is their contempt for Nathaniel Wylde or any pirate who threatens their subsistence and their lives. Do you understand what I am saying?'

Smarting under his words, Cassandra nodded and swallowed down a hard lump that had risen in her throat, the futility of her situation bringing her very close to tears. 'Perfectly. I will play the part of a dutiful wife. I will give you no cause for reproach. But for how long are we to maintain this charade?'

'For the time it takes us to reach home. I am merely trying to spare you what will be a very painful and embarrassing ordeal. It is not going to be easy for either of us.

But that is how it must be. I will decide what is to be done then.'

Cassandra's ire at his condescending superiority was almost more than she could contain as she uttered angrily, 'Then it would appear that my fate is in your hands, Stuart.' She was unable to prevent the scalding tears from rising to her eyes and spilling over her lashes. Dashing them away with her fingers, furious with herself for allowing her weakness to show, she took a deep breath and threw back her head defiantly, her eyes dark and glaring at him like twin daggers.

'But why wait? Why not dispose of me now?' she cried, her voice breaking into a strangled sob, pointing to the knife he wore in his belt. 'You have a knife. Why don't you kill me yourself—or hand me over to your crew and let them do it for you and be done with the whole sorry affair? Anything would be better than your injustice.'

The bitter words rebounded through the cabin, ricocheting off the walls, reverberating in the silence. Weakened by the sight of her tears, Stuart looked at her and a flicker of emotion registered on his granite features, but then his face hardened once more and the implacable coldness was back in his eyes. 'I see no injustice, and were you not a woman and my wife I would already have done so. But I am a fool,' he growled. 'Despite all you are guilty of, I do not wish you harm.'

'When you married me I thought it was me you wanted. Does it really matter who my father was?' she asked forcefully.

'In this case, yes, it does. Before this, to me you were one person—now you are someone else. I cannot reconcile myself to that just now.'

'I realise how difficult it must be for you and I do not ask your forgiveness at this present time. But no matter who or what my father was, it does not make *me* less worthy. My feelings for you remain unchanged. Can you not feel the same? Can you not feel the same as you did last night and accept me with all my faults—all my disgraces? Must you despise me?'

The pleading sadness in her voice and her obvious distress made Stuart pale and he moved slightly, as if to go to her, but he checked himself quickly. 'Last night I was not aware of your disgraces when you so easily excited my desire. But having possessed you so ardently—and since learning who you are—I cannot help feeling that I have betrayed my brother's spirit. Now I can only reproach myself. At present I cannot say what my feelings are, but I do not despise you.'

'And despite coming from a family you have every reason to hate—you do still want me?' she dared to ask, with hope beating in her breast. Raising her hand, she unconsciously pushed back a gleaming lock of hair that brushed her cheek, brandishing the beautiful ring he had given her that caught the light, mocking them both and their situation.

Waiting for his answer to her question, Cassandra stared at him with her glorious blue eyes, darkened by apprehension and unhappiness. An inner passion flashed in Stuart's sombre eyes and the impulse to go to her and clasp her in his arms was written so clearly on his face.

He did go to her, but in sudden anger, not in love. Brutally he seized her by the shoulders, drawing her close. His face was suffused with rage and he looked with blazing eyes down into her own. She flinched and uttered a small cry of protest as she felt his fingers hurting her, and she struggled to free herself from his fierce hold, but he was too strong for her.

'What man, having possessed you as I did last night, would not?' he hissed through clenched teeth, his face, contorted almost out of all recognition, close to her own so that she could feel his warm breath on her cheeks.

'I admit you have bewitched me. I am obsessed by you, and I do want you. But I will do everything within my power to overcome my desire for you both now and in the future. When your father murdered my brother, he tore the heart out of my whole family. I will not allow you to poison my life as he has done. If I were to kiss you now I would not be able to tear myself away from you, and in so doing I would lose all self-respect and despise myself.'

Stuart let his hands fall from Cassandra's shoulders and she shrank back from the look on his face, defeated and deeply shaken by his words, thinking with bitterness that if this rancour was to continue then they would end up destroying each other like mortal enemies.

Drawing herself up, she raised her head proudly. 'You have made it perfectly clear what you want, Stuart. You needn't worry. I shall keep out of your way as much as it is possible to do in so confined an environment. And now I think you'd better leave before you do something you will have cause to regret.'

Without pausing, he left the cabin quickly and Cassandra stood absolutely still, listening to his footsteps dying. When she could hear them no more she slumped into a chair and let the tears run uncontrollably down her face, feeling so wretched and helpless she did not think she could bear it. She wanted to run after him, to tell him he could do what he liked with her, as long as she did not lose him.

But as the tears subsided she seemed to see before her, with terrifying clarity, the proud eyes and the arrogant smile of her father. She raised her head and wiped her eyes as a new determination began to take hold of her. The daughter of such a man could not demean herself and beg for a love that was denied her.

So, Stuart thought he could set her aside, did he? If he thought he could turn his back on her and coldly ignore her until he decided which course their marriage was to take, he was going to learn differently. He would soon realise she was neither meek nor sad. She would be as charming as her broken, empty heart would allow her to be, until he missed what they'd had together in each other's arms so badly he wouldn't be able to stand it.

The *Sea Hawk*'s crew settled down to the homeward journey. The air was balmy, the trade winds set fair as she was propelled along under full sail, following two cable lengths behind Captain Tillotson's *Spirit of Enterprise*, all hands getting the best out of her. Stuart and his officers saw that the ship was as well run as on naval lines, with able men who would accede to the discipline on board and were of as good a character as could be vouched for.

Sickness also had to be dealt with. The greatest threat to any seaman was disease due to bad sanitation and diet, and the death rate on any ship at this time was high. Dysentery and smallpox often took a heavy toll, as did yellow fever—or yellow jack, as it was commonly called—which was an acute infectious disease of tropical climates, caused by the bite of a certain mosquito.

In trying to prevent from spreading the diseases contracted in the Caribbean that he thought might be contagious, the ship's surgeon, Mr Patterson, took care to isolate the cases he thought posed a threat to the other seamen. So far two men had died of yellow fever, but the rest who remained sick were suffering from other illnesses—hopefully less contagious.

After no more than a week of leaving Barbados the winds failed and the cumbersome convoy of merchantmen drifted. Progress depended upon whatever breeze could be found. This involved the helmsmen bringing the ships in the convoy on to a different tack, and a good deal of patience from everyone as they waited to see if the ships caught the wind that would spur them on. In the warm calm surrounded by a vacuum of languid peace, the crew of the *Sea Hawk* had little to do but eat and drink, mend the sails and carry out minor repairs.

Determined to keep up the pretence of their marriage, Stuart was always polite and courteous towards Cassandra when in the company of others, and in this he succeeded, but the charade did not fool Rosa, who kept a quiet, dignified profile and her distance, determined not to exacerbate the tense situation that existed between the three of them.

Cassandra's feminine hope was that by retaining intimacy with Stuart for long enough on board ship, she would eventually manage to break down his coldness towards her. Stuart had taught her the true meaning of love. Her body had surrendered to his totally and utterly, not just with the physical, overflowing need that was a part of love, and the satisfying of it, leaving her craving for more, but the tender, emotional love, the caring, that two people in love feel for each other.

The physical separation between them became intolerable as the days slipped by, and she was often tempted to go to him, to get him to speak to her, even if it roused his anger. Anything was better than this.

Each evening she dressed with care, and the moment she appeared to take her place at the large table in the after cabin where they took their meals with some of the ship's company, she was immediately surrounded.

Her presence always enhanced the company and the officers drank deep of their liquor while Stuart sipped, drinking slowly, watching as his wife charmed and dazzled every man at the table with her polite conversation. She was an enchantress, full of light and laughter, and the evenings always grew merrier and noisier as they progressed, only becoming subdued when Cassandra excused herself and retired, taking Rosa with her.

Each time he was in her presence, watching her, in his

wretchedness Stuart would feel a pain stir in the region of his heart. He was tortured by memories of their lovemaking, which gave him neither rest nor respite. His feelings towards her were complex. He both loved and hated her and, no matter how he tried, he couldn't banish her from his thoughts. Without warning, a pair of fiery blue eyes would rise to his mind and mock him—devil take her.

She had the power to rouse his temper to violent rage, or to melt his heart with love. He couldn't get her out of his blood, and he didn't know how long he could stand it. She was like a witch who had entered his heart like a sword. It was agony to have her there, and an even greater agony to pull her out.

He would watch her with a hint of admiration in the depths of his dark eyes, and he could not deny that never had a woman with so much beauty graced his dinner table. She made a charming and decorative hostess. Seated at the opposite end to her, he would allow his gaze to linger on the perfection of her features and the tender, irresistible curve of her lips as she happily conversed with the gentlemen around her, ingratiating herself into the ship's company with perfect ease.

That she was completely at home surrounded by seamen and the sea was one cruel reminder of the time she had spent with Drum O'Leary aboard the *Dolphin* following Wylde's execution. Often she would sense him watching her and meet his gaze. Her eyes would narrow and she would arch her sleek brows in silent question.

Life was tedious on board ship, and when an attractive nineteen-year-old midshipman by the name of Daniel Stark began paying Cassandra more attention than was seemly towards the Captain's wife, she saw little harm in being charming in the face of such politeness. Unfortunately, Stuart was not of the same opinion.

From across the table one evening during dinner his eyes rested on his wife with angry reproach. Stuart found it impossible to take his eyes from her as she indulged in light repartee with the young midshipman. She leaned towards him, her lovely eyes alight with pleasure as she laughed delightedly at something he said close to her ear, seeming to exclude the company around them. Stuart's blood boiled at the liberty Stark was taking with his wife. Those gathered round the table would have been dumbfounded to know that, as he languidly toyed with the stem of his goblet, he was seething inside.

Cassandra's attentiveness went to Stark's head quicker than the wine he drank. Clearly he was quite besotted, and so naïve was she that his charm blinded her judgement and she trod the trembling ground with an innocent's boldness, without realising the trouble she might bring to the young midshipman. Out of the corner of her eye she observed Stuart's brooding look of deep displeasure, and, meeting his gaze head on, she ventured to put on an expression of considerable amusement.

Leaving the gentlemen to their brandy after the meal, Cassandra and Rosa went on deck where, as was usual at this time, the crew was relaxing. After they listened to the spellbinding quality of a man singing a ballad, the ship's fiddler began scraping away vigorously at a merry jig, at which there came a rousing cheer and everyone became infected with feverish gaiety as men began clapping and dancing with each other.

Cassandra was astonished when Daniel Stark came on deck and boldly caught her about the waist and whirled her into the dance. At first she laughingly protested and held back, for, being the Captain's wife, she never entered into any of the frivolities and was always happy to observe from a distance. But, seeing the merry light in her partner's eyes, and that Rosa was already enjoying the dance with a lively young seaman, the temptation to dance and lighten her heavy heart was too much to resist.

The whole ship rang with lusty cheers of appreciation from the crew as she proceeded to enter into the spirit of things, having no conception as she did so of the anger it provoked in Stuart when he came on deck and saw her partaking in the merriment, with the crew clapping and stamping their feet in accompaniment in the circle of light cast by the lanterns hanging in the rigging.

As he stood in the shadow, his eyes became riveted on his wife as she danced with gay abandon. The tempo was quick and, with skirts swaying, her nimble feet flashed over the deck. There was something vibrant and passionate about the way she moved—easy and agile, taunting, tantalising and lovely to watch. She threw back her head and laughed with innocent delight into the eyes of young Stark, causing the young midshipman to look at her in a way that made Stuart's temper difficult to control. A searing stab of jealousy pierced his heart. If she had not been his wife he would have been enthralled by her wild beauty, but as it was he became possessed of a blinding fury.

When the dance had finished, Cassandra laughingly declined to dance some more. As the merriment continued she sauntered away, letting her gaze wander into the shadows. Her breath caught in her throat when she saw Stuart's still figure watching her and, despite the distance between them, she could feel his anger coming to her in waves. Deciding that confidence was the best way of dealing with his moods, she walked towards him, Daniel Stark close at her heels.

Chapter Eight

'Why, Stuart. You find me enjoying myself,' Cassandra remarked breathlessly.

'So I see,' he replied coldly, taking in at a glance her hair tumbling about her shoulders in an aura of disarray, her flushed face and shining eyes. He wondered if it was her exertions that made her look so radiant or the lingering feel of Stark's arm about her waist.

His expression was impenetrable, bearing no hint of what he was feeling—only his eyes did that, and what Cassandra saw in their black depths was infinitely more terrifying than the marble severity of his face. Daniel shifted uneasily beside her, and Stuart favoured him with a withering glance.

'You may leave us, Stark. My wife has danced enough for one evening.'

Realising he might have overstepped the mark by taking too much liberty with the captain's wife, and not wishing to antagonise him further by staying to offer words in his defence, Daniel acquiesced with a slight inclination of his head and made a hasty retreat, knowing he would be severely reprimanded for it later.

Stuart moved away towards the rail, out of earshot, away from the light and the noise of the revellers and curious eyes. He sensed, rather that saw, Cassandra follow him, and that she stood behind him, staring at his taut back.

'Stuart! What is the matter?' she asked, sensing the tension vibrating inside him.

He turned and looked at her. Her eyes glimmered into his as she closed the distance between them. Her neck was bare and the lanterns' glow turned her skin down to her breasts to the sheen of gold. He wanted to reach out and touch her, to feel the warmth of her, the beauty of her, but if he did that he would be lost. They would both be lost. Focusing his gaze on the blackness beyond the ship, he moved away from her to recover himself. He needed to have some distance between them, since his male body, no matter what he might say, didn't give a damn.

'You cannot be angry with me for dancing. I could hardly resist Mr Stark in such high spirits and it was so good to dance.' It seemed like an eternity before Stuart turned, and she cringed before the naked anger glowing in his eyes.

'It would seem young Stark has acquired a boldness otherwise unknown to him. To act so free with the captain's wife is not acceptable. It is intolerable. I will share many things, but I will not share my wife.'

The brief drift of happiness Cassandra had experienced in the dance melted away. Regaining her composure, she struck a huge lode of stubbornness at least as rich as his. 'Come now, Stuart. You cannot be serious. It was harmless—a moment of jollity—nothing more. Mr Stark was merely being polite. I enjoy talking to him and he makes me laugh. And, anyway, why should you object when you are no longer interested in what I do?' she reminded him with a bitter smile.

Stuart glared at her. Most of what she said was true—though not the last part—and what was she guilty of other than enjoying herself? But he was angry and his anger made him cruel. Nothing had prepared him for the shock, the intense resentment he had felt on seeing another man pay her such close attention. 'The fact remains that you are still my wife,' he stated with lethal calmness, 'and I would kill any man who became your lover.'

Cassandra's temper erupted. 'I may be your wife, Stuart, but you have cast me aside. If I so wished, I would take whom I please to my bed and be damned to you.' The words were flung at him without thought, the sheer absurdity of them making a nonsense of them. For her to take anyone else other that Stuart to her bed was unthinkable.

Stuart's reaction was instant. His face had gone white beneath his tan, his eyes harder than ice. 'If you ever think of doing any such thing,' he said in a low, savage voice, 'you will yearn for the days before you met me.'

'I am beginning to do so already,' she was quick to retort in retaliation, instantly regretting the lie and wishing she hadn't said it. She sighed heavily. 'I'm sorry, Stuart. I didn't mean that. But there's precious little to do on board this ship—especially when my own husband treats me like some kind of pariah. But I have no wish to argue with you over this. It's too ridiculous for words.'

'Ridiculous? I think not.'

Tilting her head slightly to one side, an unconsciously provocative smile suddenly curved Cassandra's lips. 'Why, Stuart,' she taunted softly, moving within his arm's reach, the subtle smell of her perfume wafting over him in a cloud, 'from your behaviour and the way you speak, anyone would think you are jealous of Mr Stark.'

Her barb struck home, which only succeeded in increasing Stuart's wrath. His eyes glittered dangerously. 'Jealousy is not something I can be accused of—and I will never admit to so base an emotion with no other reason than to flatter your vanity. I am neither blind nor dim-witted that I cannot see what's going on. That young pup follows you

with eyes like a lovesick calf from stem to stern, and you—
you behave like a silly, giggling girl. The fact that you do
nothing to discourage him infuriates me. I find the time you
spend in his company offensive. How dare you think you
can make a fool of me in front of the entire ship's company?'

Cassandra stared at him incredulously, momentarily
stunned by what she considered to be an unwarranted accusation. Her cheeks became flushed with indignation. 'I
was not aware that I had,' she retorted, clenching her fists
under the folds of her dress to calm herself, the freezing
contempt in his eyes having brought a rush of anger.

'That you should behave so brazenly with every man of
your acquaintance I will not tolerate. But then,' he said,
speaking with quiet, icy precision, 'being in the company
of villains as often as you have—men lacking in both mor-
als and principles—there is no telling what you will and
will not do.'

They were both breathing hard as their eyes clashed, hers
blazing as hot as his. 'Your accusations are ill founded and
unjust—and I will not stay to be insulted by my own husband.' With a scornful toss of her head she turned and
walked away.

'Cassandra, wait.' Her head turned at the cool authority
of his tone, but to Stuart's astonishment she ignored it. He
marched after her, his hand moving as rapidly as a striking
snake as it closed cruelly around her arm and spun her
round. Her glorious hair fell across her neck and shoulders
and over his hands. Hot blood stained her cheeks red, and
her angry eyes were shining with tears. Her chin tilted ob-
stinately. Confident of her love, he had thought her pliable
to his demands, but she outfaced him, her tempestuous nature ready to do battle with his.

'Damn your treacherous heart,' he hissed between
clenched teeth, wishing she didn't look so unbearably beau-

tiful, so young and vulnerable, facing him in her outrageous mutiny. He was on the point of fury where all reason had left him. 'I warn you, Cassandra, I will not tolerate you making a spectacle of yourself again. Is that understood?'

'Why—what will you do? Throw me overboard? Feed me to the sharks? Lock me in my cabin?'

'If necessary. And if you so much as glance at young Stark, I shall have him keelhauled.'

Cassandra blanched at his threat. 'You wouldn't.'

'Try me.' His voice was hoarse, strained with anger. He towered over her, his eyes so full of blazing fury that Cassandra feared he would strike her.

When she looked at his satanic features, at his jaw taut with rage, she saw a stranger, a violent stranger, of whom she was suddenly very much afraid. She stared at him, her mind in turmoil. She could actually feel the savage, scorching fury that was emanating from him. It was as if, by her abandoned behaviour, she had unleashed some untamed force inside him that she had never dreamed existed in any human being.

'Disobey me, Cassandra, and you will soon learn what I can and cannot do.'

'Disobey you? How dare you remind *me* of my vows? It is I who should remind you of yours.'

'You are my wife and will behave as such. You will follow my instructions for your behaviour until this voyage is over. Is that clear? And until that time I suggest that your evenings are spent in conversation with your companion—with whom, considering your backgrounds, you have much in common—and, when the meal is over, refrain from coming on deck at this time.'

'You cannot mean that?'

'Why not?'

'You mean that you would have me cooped up down below every evening—in all that heat?'

'Exactly.'

The delivery of his words was cold and lethal, leaving no doubt in Cassandra's mind that he meant what he said. 'So—I am to be punished.'

'It is not the word I would use—but if that is the way you see it then I will not argue. I think you have created enough diversion for the members of my crew for one night. Go below.'

'And you can go to hell, Stuart Marston.' Cassandra turned on her heel and strode off across the deck.

Having been a sharp-eyed observer of the incident, and not unaware of young Stark's captivation for Stuart's beautiful wife, James Randell approached him, leaning against the rails, calmly puffing at his clay pipe and sending up small clouds of smoke, which went drifting away into the night sky.

'Forgive me, Stuart, and I know it's none of my business, but I am aware of the attention young Stark pays your wife. The poor lad's smitten. Would you like me to have a word with him?'

Stuart shook his head slowly, his anger of a moment earlier subsiding. 'No—there's no need, thank you all the same, James. I believe he is aware of my displeasure and will trouble my wife less in the future.'

'If you're sure.'

'Confined as we all are on board this ship, and my wife and her companion being the only females, it is only natural that members of the crew find it difficult keeping their eyes off either of them.' This was true, but Rosa was not as beautiful in the accepted sense as Cassandra was. Cassandra was exquisite, with the kind of beauty that made every man she came into contact with sigh with longing. She drew men to her like bees to honey, and always would. 'Good Lord, James, I don't expect them to go around in blinkers, but I suspect young Stark wants a good deal more from my wife than merely to converse. I have seen the look in his eyes.'

James chuckled, speaking casually. 'Aye! But what about the look in the lady's eyes? My observations tell me she is quite uninterested. She is too much in love with her husband to have eyes for anyone else.'

Stuart glanced at him sharply, but before he could say more James had sauntered off, still puffing at his pipe.

Cassandra had thrown Stuart off balance by boldly succumbing to Mr Stark's attentions, and his threat to confine her to the cabin was not an idle one. She had been playing with fire, she could see that now, and it must stop. She wouldn't risk angering Stuart to the point where he would carry out his threat and have her removed entirely from his presence. It was important that she remained close to him so that she could stoke the flames of his desire.

Determined to make matters no worse than they already were, she took great care after that to avoid the companionship of Daniel Stark.

When Rosa failed to appear in Cassandra's cabin one morning, as she usually did before they took a turn on deck, she went in search of her, surprised and concerned to find her young companion collapsed on the bed in her cabin, retching spasmodically and her usually cheerful face pale and drawn.

'Good gracious, Rosa,' she said, going to her in alarm. 'You are unwell. How long have you been like this? You seemed all right last night at dinner.'

Rosa sighed, closing her eyes and letting her head fall back on to her pillows. 'Yes, I was. It came on suddenly—shortly after I came to bed.' Her words were slurred and she spoke with effort.

'Do you suppose it's something you ate at dinner?'

'No. If it was, I dare say others would be ill, too. But don't worry, Cassandra. I'll be all right when I've rested a while.'

'You should have called me,' Cassandra reproached gently, pouring some water into a basin and bathing her friend's face, noticing how dry her skin was and how her forehead burned with fever. She tried to sit up, but Cassandra pushed her back on to the pillows. 'Don't even attempt to get up, Rosa. I'll fetch Mr Patterson. I'm sure he'll be able to give you something to bring your fever down and make you feel better. I won't be long.' She went out, her heart pounding hard, more concerned about Rosa's condition than she dared to admit just then.

Stuart was on deck when Cassandra appeared. Observing how distraught she looked, he strode towards her. 'Cassandra, wait,' he commanded.

At the sound of his voice she stopped and turned as he approached.

'What is it?' he asked sharply, looking down at her anxious features. She stared up at him with eyes wide and fearful, in a face out of which every hint of colour had fled. 'Is something wrong?'

'Yes—it's Rosa. She's ill—very ill. I'm so concerned about her.' If she had not been so worried about her friend, she would have seen that Stuart was regarding her seriously, with a look not devoid of concern. 'I must find Mr Patterson immediately. I am hoping he can give her something to make her feel better.'

'How long has she been like this?'

'She became ill during the night. At first I thought it might be something she ate at dinner, or even seasickness due the sudden squall that took hold of the ship when the wind rose during the night—but she's a good sailor and has never been troubled by it in the past.'

'Then go back to her. I'll have someone locate Mr Pat-

terson and send him to attend Rosa directly. Has she a
fever?'

'Yes. She's also vomiting.'

'Are you all right?'

Taken aback by the sudden softening of his tone, Cassandra looked at him. The rare moment of tenderness
touched a corner of her heart. He looked concerned and,
after enduring many weeks of cold indifference, she was
pleasantly surprised.

'Yes,' she replied softly. 'Yes. I am perfectly well.'

Fearing some contagious disease was about to burst out
on the ship, which could turn out to be a disaster on a
massive scale if not checked immediately, Stuart set about
locating Mr Patterson and sending him to attend Rosa. He
waited with increasing dread in the cabin next door whilst
the surgeon examined her. After several minutes Mr Patterson appeared, his features set in grave lines of concern.
He was followed by an extremely anxious-looking
Cassandra.

'What is it, Mr Patterson?' she asked anxiously. 'What
is wrong with her?'

Mr Patterson looked at her from beneath heavy brows
drawn together over his nose in a frown. 'She hasn't been
well since boarding the ship at Barbados, you say?'

'No. In fact, since going to Barbados she seems to have
been susceptible to weakness.'

'Mmm. The climate frequently has that effect on people.
If one doesn't possess a strong constitution to begin with,
they often have difficulty getting over even the slightest
ailment.'

'But living all her life on the Cape Verde Islands, Rosa
is accustomed to such a climate, so it can't be that. She
will get well, won't she?' Cassandra asked hopefully.

Giving a faint shrug, he shook his head slowly. 'It's impossible to say. She may—she may not.'

'Is it possible that she has cholera, Mr Patterson? Please tell me.'

'No. I don't think so. I have to say the suddenness with which it has developed might lead one to think it might be—but she doesn't have the symptoms of cholera such as the agonising cramps in her limbs and abdomen. Nor do I think it's typhus, because there is no rash, which usually accompanies the disease, to suggest this.'

'Thank God for that,' uttered Stuart with immense relief, for the last thing he wanted was an epidemic of typhus on board his ship, which would decimate his crew considerably. 'Then what do you think it is?'

'It can be any one of a group of mysterious infections characterised by high fever. It is possible that she may have eaten something contaminated—or become infected in any number of ways, which, because of the depressed state of her mind and body, has brought on the fever.'

'Is there anyone else ill on the ship with the same symptoms as Rosa—and, if so, are any of the fevers contagious?'

Mr Patterson shook his head. 'We had two cases of yellow jack at the start of the voyage—both men died, as you know, but that was some time ago. We were fortunate to contain it, because usually the disease spreads rapidly. Since then I've had nothing more serious to contend with other than the usual dysentery, shipboard injuries and the occasional mild fever. How are you feeling, my dear?' he asked with sudden concern, for her natural anxiety for her companion made her look pale and wan. 'Do you feel well?'

'Yes, thank you, Mr Patterson. I feel quite well.'

'Nevertheless, the fever may be malignant and highly infectious. If you insist on nursing your companion, there is every danger of you falling sick yourself.'

'Then I shall order Rosa to be moved to the sick quarters,' Stuart suggested sharply, 'where you can keep an eye on her.'

'No,' said Cassandra, turning on him fiercely, her eyes flashing with a savage brilliance, her features charged with emotion. 'It's a little too late for that, don't you think? I have already been exposed to whatever is wrong with Rosa. She will stay here where I can look after her myself.'

Angered by her bold resistance to his authority, Stuart's eyes narrowed. 'I insist on her being moved. For God's sake, Cassandra, be sensible,' he admonished harshly. 'You heard what Mr Patterson said. It is possible that the fever is highly virulent. If you do not expose yourself further, there is every chance you will not become infected. Rosa must be removed to the sick quarters at once.' His face was white and his eyes challenged her dangerously to defy him.

Feeling her blood pounding in her temples, Cassandra stood her ground and met his challenge defiantly, giving no thought to Mr Patterson's presence. 'Spare me your concern,' she scorned, her face twisted in anguished bitterness. 'Your sudden consideration for my well being is a travesty after all the agonising weeks of indifference I've been forced to endure.

'Rosa is my responsibility. If you are concerned that the disease will spread throughout the ship, then you can make sure no one else comes near her or me. If I am to succumb to the disease, then so be it. In fact, I shall meet it with a happiness you could not possibly imagine—for it will free me from you and this mockery of a marriage.'

Without looking back, Cassandra spun on her heel contemptuously and stormed from the cabin, leaving Mr Patterson staring after her in pure astonishment at her outburst, and Stuart with an expression as hard as iron. His hands were clenched into tight fists at his sides as he struggled to stop himself from going after her and physically dragging her away from Rosa's bedside.

* * *

The heat was unbearable inside the cabin as hour after hour Cassandra nursed Rosa. She lay on the narrow bed, twisting restlessly from side to side and rambling incoherently in her delirium, showing no sign of improvement. In fact, if anything, her condition grew much worse. Her eyes were dull and expressionless, her hair and body drenched with sweat. Cassandra worked ceaselessly, her mind torn with anguish as she poured the herbal posset Mr Patterson had given her into Rosa's mouth. She was constantly wringing out cloths in cool water and placing them on Rosa's face and body, which the fever had boiled dry.

The day dragged on, the afternoon drawing to evening, and Cassandra had no thought for anything as she watched Rosa suffer, fervently praying to God not to let her dear friend die. If anyone had to die, then it should be her—for was she not the reason why Rosa had gone to Barbados in the first place, the reason for her being on board this ship?

On the edge of her conscious mind she heard someone knock on the cabin door but ignored it, hoping that whoever it was would go away and leave her in peace to tend to Rosa, whose face was sunken against the pillows, her eyes hollow in deep purple sockets, her pulse rapid and her breathing so shallow that Cassandra had to place her hand on her chest to feel if she was still moving.

With the dark a fresh period of waiting began as Rosa began to slip away from her. By midnight she had fallen into a coma and by dawn she was dead. Cassandra was numb with shock. It had happened so quickly. As she stared down at the waxen face of her companion, her friend, the young woman who had become more like a sister to her over the past months and was now beyond her, her heart was torn apart. With a trembling hand she reached out and stroked her cheek.

'Rest, dear Rosa,' she whispered before turning away, choking on a sob as a tear splashed down her face.

She stumbled towards the door, desperate to leave the foetid atmosphere of the cabin and feel the cool morning air on her face. Dragging herself up the companion ladder and on to the quarter deck, she was vaguely aware of seamen moving about around her and aloft as they went about the ship's routine work.

Fearful of spreading infection, she moved away to an empty part of the deck and stood looking at the shimmering expanse of water all around her as far as the eye could see. Silver streaked the dawn sky and a fine mist floated on the surface of the sea, heralding the heat of the day. Her head ached as if it were about to split in two. She breathed deeply, filling her lungs with air. Bone weary, she felt so tired that she couldn't think. But she didn't want to think any more. All she wanted was for the rest of the world to go away and leave her entirely alone.

Stuart scarcely recognised the woman standing by the rail, swaying slightly, with lank strands of hair hanging down her face and her clothes dirty and stained with perspiration. From the moment she had locked herself in the cabin with Rosa, refusing to open the door to anyone, he had lived through one of the worst nightmares of his life. Patiently he had waited for her to emerge—and, as the crew of his ship had discovered to their cost when he had vented all his anger on them, patience was not one of his virtues.

The last rage-filled words Cassandra had flung at him before rebelliously locking herself in Rosa's cabin had reverberated again and again in his mind as the hours slipped by so that he thought he would go mad.

He was tormented by the devastating thought that by nursing her sick friend through the fever she too would become infected, and if so there was every possibility that she might die. He didn't know what obscure feeling prompted him to torture himself in this manner over the well-being of a woman whose father had murdered his brother, but seeing her so wretched and dejected filled him with compassion and his heart went out to her. Her distress was real and pitiful to see.

Cassandra was not aware of Stuart's presence until he stood beside her. Numbly she turned and looked at him, her eyes glazed.

'How is Rosa?' Stuart asked gently.

Cassandra met his dark eyes without flinching. 'Rosa is dead. She died just a short while ago.'

'I see. Then, for what it's worth, I'm sorry.'

His words seemed to come to Cassandra from afar, penetrating her mind slowly. She looked at him as if seeing him for the first time. Struggling to come to terms with Rosa's death, and feeling frustration at her own inability not to have done more to save her, she turned the rage that had been simmering in her breast ever since Rosa had fallen ill on her husband with full force.

'Sorry! You are sorry? I do not believe you. Ever since you became aware of who we are you have treated her with the same disdain and contempt as you did myself—as if we were lepers. You didn't know Rosa. You never tried to get to know her, and your insufferable, overbearing pride and arrogant manner did little to endear you to either of us. Rosa was so good. So caring. She deserved to live more than anyone I know. And now she is dead.'

Stuart looked at her with a grim seriousness. There was so much violence in her unpremeditated outburst of feeling, so much hurt. 'I know, and your grief is understandable. But you are upset—overwrought. Come—let me escort you to your cabin. When you have washed and eaten perhaps you will be able to look upon her death in a better light.'

'Better light? Never,' she whispered fiercely, returning her self-recriminating gaze to the sea. 'You don't understand. How could you? You see, I can never atone for what I have done to Rosa. It's because of me that she's dead. If I had not foolishly taken it into my head to go with Drum when Nat was executed, she would still be alive.

'Because of the hurt I have caused it should be me lying dead. But don't worry,' she said with a scornful twist to her lovely lips, spurred on by a sense of outrage. 'With any luck at all I shall have contracted Rosa's fever and will be dead within twenty-four hours.'

Her words pierced Stuart to the heart. His expression softened. 'You little fool. Don't say that. There is every chance you will not have become infected.'

'Maybe—we will soon know. However, perhaps you should not come too close to me, Stuart, otherwise there is every chance that you will become infected, too. But it would suit you, wouldn't it, if I contracted the same illness as Rosa—if it became fatal? At least then you would be rid of me, which would save you the embarrassment of explaining who I am to your family and friends. I know you have much to forgive—but I no longer care whether you do or not.

'Our marriage is ridiculous and a mockery and I should never have let myself be charmed by you. Let us say that the Caribbean cast a spell on us both, a spell that lost its enchantment the moment we left Barbados's shores. In the beginning I hoped things would be different between us and that you would come to accept me as your wife, despite who my father was. But I realise now that it can never be.'

Stuart listened to her outburst in grim silence, stiff and wary. He realised her grief over Rosa's death and his own treatment of her had wounded her deeply but, no matter how much he wanted the matter to be resolved between them, he was unable to put the past behind him just yet. It was too soon. But neither did he want to lose her.

'I told you I need time to come to terms with who you are.'

'Time! How much time? A lifetime? I am not prepared to wait that long, Stuart.' Her gaze became sad as she looked at the sea. A haziness blurred her vision, and the pain inside her head was growing stronger. 'You have no idea how much I have wished with all my heart for things to be different between us. I cannot help my past—and I deeply regret it. But your treatment of me has been cruel to the extreme and I cannot bear it. That is why I have decided to be mistress of my own destiny. I will not live with a man who finds me repellent.'

She did not tell him of the nights she had lain awake in her bed, knowing he was sleeping just behind the bulkhead in the adjacent cabin, just a few short steps away, or how she had hoped he would come to her, and how she had eventually fallen to sleep with her yearning unfulfilled.

'You know perfectly well that you do not repel me—quite the opposite, in fact—but it would seem you have given the matter much thought, Cassandra.'

'During the past twenty-four hours I've had plenty of time to consider my future—a future without you.'

'Then, please, tell me what you have decided?' he asked carefully.

'When the first land is sighted I want you to put me ashore. You will go on to England without me—and forget me, if you can. I don't want to go on without you—I don't know if I can. I don't know how I will bear it.' Her voice was low but steady, and in her eyes as she looked at him was the profound truth of her love for him.

Stuart was deeply moved by her words and the look in her eyes. There was a pain in his heart and his arms ached to hold her. He had to keep a tight rein on his emotions, on his feelings for her. He must not let her see what was in him, for he had made up his mind not to touch her, and she might weaken him. At length, he said, 'And if I refuse to do as you ask?'

'I shall jump overboard if I have to. You see, Stuart, I have no mind to let you take me to England where, should my identity become known—as there is every chance it will be—I shall be hanged. I cannot deny that the dread of discovery dwells heavy on my heart.' Her lips curled with irony. 'In that respect I am a coward, you see. So…will you agree to do as I ask—should I live that long, that is?'

Despite the barrier her relationship to Nathaniel Wylde had erected between them, the idea that they must part for ever was not to be borne. 'Ask anything else of me, but that I will never do,' Stuart answered, speaking in a controlled voice, forcing himself to remain calm. To show anger would achieve nothing at this time when she was grieving for Rosa. His eyes were like ice, but apart from that his expression betrayed no emotion. 'I shall have you shackled in irons if need be when we near land. You are my wife and will remain with me.'

'I would not insist on taking you to England if I knew you faced arrest. Apart from Samuel Tillotson, who has given me his word never to speak of it, I am pretty confident no one will discover your identity.'

'You are wrong, Stuart. If you recall, I told you that several of our neighbours in Chelsea know who my father was. He always went to great lengths to conceal his identity—always coming to the house quietly and seeing me in private, but servants are not stupid. They talk.'

'Then you must not go back to Everson House. As far as your neighbours are concerned you went to Barbados to visit your cousin and to all intents and purposes there you remain. And think about it, Cassandra. Why would anyone, knowing the reason why, believe that I was the man responsible for bringing one of England's most notorious pirates to the gallows, would make his daughter my wife? So let there be no more talk of you going ashore. However, this is neither the time nor the place to discuss such matters. Come. I will escort you below.'

Had he exploded with anger at her request, or responded with more force, Cassandra would have understood, but the deathly quiet of his voice unsettled her. A hard lump rose in her throat. She loved him to distraction and could not think of a world in which he did not exist. But she could not remain with him and not have his love. She would find some way of leaving the ship. She must. How she would survive the pain of leaving him she knew not, but her mind told her coldly that, if she was to retain her sanity and any dignity in her life, this was what she must do. Overcome with an intense feeling of weariness, she turned from him.

'Thank you—but I am perfectly capable of finding my own way down to the cabin.'

Stuart could see she was far from capable of going anywhere without assistance as she swayed against him. She had eaten nothing and had been without sleep for over twenty-four hours, and she was worn out with looking after Rosa. Taking one look at her flushed face and bright eyes, it was clear she had come to the end of her strength.

Suddenly everything seemed so far away to Cassandra. 'I'm so tired. I—I think I'll lie down for a while,' she murmured, placing a hand to her aching brow. Beneath her clothes sweat damped her body. Her stomach contracted and a wave of nausea robbed her of breath. She summoned the strength to move. Her movements were clumsy and each step was a concentrated effort of will. The deck seemed to sway around her and she staggered and would have fallen, but Stuart stooped to lift her up in his arms. His face, white and wiped clean of all but a hideous fear, was the last thing she saw before darkness claimed her.

Chapter Nine

Cassandra's collapse struck terror into Stuart's heart. His chest heaving with exertion and his heart hammering in a frantic rhythm, he carried his beloved burden across the deck, oblivious to the stricken, fearful faces of the crew. Reaching her cabin, he began to try to make Cassandra comfortable, driven by desperation, all the while fear that she might die clawing at him. Stripping her of her gown, he settled her back on the pillows. Her eyes were closed, her breathing laboured. Without another woman on board to nurse her—and refusing to even contemplate sending her to the sick quarters for Mr Patterson to tend, for a man other than himself to touch her—he knew it was up to him to look after her.

During his time on board ship he had learned a good deal about sickness and cures. He wasn't concerned about contracting the fever. He'd been struck down himself four years ago and survived, and he was a firm believer that some fevers didn't visit a body twice.

The rigors that often precede a fever soon set in and Cassandra began shivering violently. Gathering her up, he held her firmly in his arms, hoping to transmit some of his warmth to her flesh, which was clammy and cold. 'There,' he said, rocking her like a baby, stroking back the hair from her face and placing his cheek against her head. He spoke no more, but the softness and tenderness of his arms seemed to soothe her to a quiet sleep.

But it didn't last. Her flesh was soon burning hot and she was violently sick. Placing a cold compress on her forehead, Stuart was moved by compassion. When he'd done everything possible to make her comfortable he ordered the cabin boy waiting outside to fetch Mr Patterson, and to arrange for Rosa's body to be disposed of.

The surgeon confirmed his fear. Cassandra had contracted the fever from Rosa. Stuart informed Mr Patterson that he would look after his wife himself, so the surgeon left him to it, supplying him with the same potions he had given Cassandra to help bring Rosa's temperature down.

Alone with his wife—the cabin already taking on the oppressive odour of a sickroom—trusting to instinct, good sense and Mr Patterson's medicine, Stuart began the job of saving Cassandra's life. He pressed the cup to her lips to force the posset down her throat, drop by precious drop. 'Come now,' he breathed when she would have turned her head aside. 'Drink it, Cassandra. Fight it. You can. I won't let you die. You are going to get better.' Her eyes were wide and staring and she looked at him but did not see him.

The minutes became an hour, and then another, and finally a day and a night. Stuart waited, listened and watched, trying to rid himself of the despair that wrapped itself around his heart, suffocating him. Trying to infuse his own strength into her, he clutched her limp hand, determination driving him to talk to her ceaselessly.

His voice came to Cassandra from somewhere in the darkness. She tried to concentrate on what he was saying to her, but her mind was too tired. Death was all around her, but she was too weak to fight it. She remembered tell-

ng someone that she wanted to die, but she didn't die, and
he was frightened.

That same someone was speaking to her from afar, tell-
ng her that he wouldn't leave her, that he would stay right
eside her, and she wanted to hold on to that person, for
im to take her hand and fight off death until her strength
eturned for her to do it herself. In the swirling darkness
he called out for Stuart, but it was just a forlorn whisper
n her mind, for she recalled, as from a dream, that Stuart
idn't want her, but she wanted him so.

The fever took hold of her and consumed her. As Stuart
ursed her and night followed day, it was impossible for
im to detach himself from her suffering. His heart ached,
nd every fibre of his being willed her to live. Every half-
our he forced liquid and possets between her lips, all the
while shrugging off his increasing exhaustion. There were
imes when he closed his eyes, but he did not sleep—as if
e could, when Cassandra might need him. He sat or
neeled for hours, gazing at her, watching her, his elbows
n the bed, his own face a mask of suffering close to hers.
His meals and anything else he required were left outside
he cabin, and apart from that he had no contact with any-
ne.

He kept a constant vigil, his fear for his wife etched
leeply into his drawn features. He wiped her brow and
poke soft words of comfort as she rambled incoherently
n her delirium. Her body was on fire. Unlike many people
who believed that the only way to fight a fever was to sweat
ut the badness, Stuart did the opposite. He sponged her
aked body hour after hour with cold water in an attempt
o bring the fever down.

Miraculously she began to respond, and it was after midnight on the third night when the fever finally broke and
he lay quiet, no longer a part of that nightmare, delirium-

filled world in which she had struggled. Stuart's heart lightened, his hope renewed. He was convinced that now she would live.

Seated beside the bed, he gazed down at her serene face, unable to believe she had come through. The softness of her slightly parted lips, the curve of her cheek and the sweep of her dark lashes concealing her sparkling blue eyes, brought back a vivid memory of a laughing girl, full of love and teasing humour, and he remembered how magnificent she had looked as she had danced on deck with young Stark. Exhausted beyond measure, he placed his elbows on the bed and bowed his head, resting his face in his hands and closing his eyes.

As she floated in a comforting grey mist, Cassandra was aware of the sound of the ship's creaking timbers first. Then came the breath of a gentle breeze wafting in through the open window. The last thing she remembered was how much her head hurt, and that a terrible weariness was dragging her body down. Now it had been replaced by languor. She clung to this blissful state, because it allowed her to escape the fears and haunting memories lurking on the perimeter of her mind like nameless, threatening shadows.

The sheet covering her felt cool against her bare skin— she found it strange that she was naked, and couldn't work out how she came to be so just then. Her mind was fuzzy and her throat and lips dry. Lying perfectly still, she sensed someone was close to her. There was the light touch of fingers on her brow, so tender it barely disturbed her. Feeling strong enough, she opened her eyes and blinked, trying to focus, but her vision was blurry. She blinked again to clear it, and saw Stuart looking down at her, his ebony eyes hard and assessing as they regarded her with a serious expression.

Perched on the edge of the bed, Stuart's heart throbbed

vith renewed life and he thanked God that her eyes were
lear of delirium. He smiled, the light from the window
evealing the relief in his haggard, handsome face. 'Wel-
ome back.' His voice, quiet and tender, pulled Cassandra
ack to reality. 'You've been very ill.'

'H—how long has it been?' Her voice was hoarse, her
hroat parched.

'Three days.'

Memory flooded back. Spontaneous tears burned her
yes and a lone tear trailed its way slowly down her cheek.
Rosa,' she whispered faintly. 'Poor Rosa. She—she died.
remember.'

'You too succumbed to the fever. You'll get stronger.'

Cassandra closed her eyes to combat the struggle of her
rief. After a few moments she licked her dry lips and,
rawing a laboured breath, found the strength to ask,
Where is she?'

'You do understand that because of the risk of infection
preading throughout the ship, Rosa's body had to be dis-
osed of quickly, into the sea, don't you?'

'Yes.' She swallowed down her tears. 'Please can I have
ome water?'

Stuart helped her to lift her head and pressed the cup to
er lips. She drank a little, feeling the cool water soothe
er throat, making her feel stronger. Resting her head back
n the pillows, she closed her eyes. The effort had caused
er head to spin.

Compassion made Stuart's chest ache. Her hair was
pread over the pillows and her face was ghostly pale. 'You
hould rest now. You're very weak but you're over the
vorst.'

'Who looked after me?'

'I did.'

Her eyebrows rose delicately. 'All the time?'

He nodded, studying her with some intensity.

'Did—did you remove my clothes?'

'I am your husband. Your life was at risk. Preserving your modesty was the last thing on my mind. In such cir cumstances your hair would have been cut off to conserve your strength. I couldn't bring myself to do it.'

'Thank you. I—I must look a sight.'

He grinned, rubbing the dark abrasive stubble on his chin. 'So do I.'

Cassandra observed his exhaustion was real. She curbed the impulse to reach out and caress his tired face, to smooth away his weariness. Her love for him rose up like a painful throbbing ache. The shadow line of his beard accentuated the angular line of his jaw and the cleft in his chin. He looked worn out, and with his hair falling over his brow in damp waves, he looked younger and for once vulnerable.

'You must be feeling quite exhausted looking after me. Weren't you afraid you might get the fever, too? You still might.'

He smiled faintly, pushing his hand through his thick tumbled hair. 'Don't torture yourself. It wasn't your fault that you fell sick. Someone had to take care of you. I stayed because I wanted to.'

'But I can see that I have been a nuisance. I am sorry you have neglected your duties.'

'I have every faith in James Randell's ability to run the *Sea Hawk* equally as well as myself. Besides, we are be calmed once more, so there is little to do. How are you feeling?' he enquired gently.

'Tired. There was a time when I thought I was going to die. But then I heard someone talking to me, willing me to live and keeping the demons in my brain at bay, and realised I wouldn't die.'

Her words were so softly spoken and so utterly disarm ing, that Stuart reached out to lay the back of his hand against her forehead to test her temperature. He was gazing down at her with a lazy smile, then he said, 'You were obviously hallucinating.'

Cassandra tried to ignore the treacherous leap her heart gave at the sight of that enthralling, intimate smile. 'Was I?'

'Maybe not.'

This time there was no mistaking the husky timbre of his voice. Cassandra couldn't free her gaze from his. 'Thank you for saving my life.'

Something stirred in the fathomless depths of his eyes, something hot and inviting, and Cassandra's pulse quickened, even though he no longer touched her.

'You're welcome,' he murmured softly.

Her eyelids suddenly felt like lead weights and began to close against her will.

Seeing that she was about to drift into slumber, Stuart got up from the bed. 'You've talked enough for now. I insist you get some rest. When you wake you can eat.'

Struggling to look at him one more time before sleep claimed her, Cassandra gazed at the deeply etched lines of fatigue and strain at her husband's eyes and mouth and embarked on her own concern. 'You look like the very devil yourself, Stuart,' she pronounced bluntly. 'Might I suggest you do the same?'

Two days later Cassandra rose from her sick bed—weak, but she was young and strong and her strength was returning quickly, and with it her impatience to go up on deck. She grew restless and hated the enforced inactivity, but, afraid there might be a danger of them infecting the crew, both Cassandra and Stuart had to await Mr Patterson's permission before they could leave the cabin.

Cassandra missed Rosa terribly, and her distress over her death was real and anguished. The pain and the guilt that had seized her as the spirit of the woman who had been her comfort and strength for such a short time had slipped away to another world, where for mysterious reasons of his own God had not allowed her to follow, could have been sustained within the arms of the man who had nursed her through the fever. But it was not to be.

Now that she had recovered, she would like Stuart to be like he was when she had opened her eyes, when she had seen his fear for her etched deeply into his drawn features, when he had spoken to her in that soft and tender tone, when he had looked at her with love and concern in his eyes, but he had withdrawn from her, reverting to how it had been between them before she had fallen sick, remote and detached, but without the acrimony.

Most of the time he was at his desk in the main cabin, silent and absorbed as he poured over maps of latitude and longitude and wrote in the ship's log. From where she sat in the adjacent cabin, trying to immerse herself in a book or employ her fingers with needle and thread, she watched him through the open door. Sometimes she would venture into his abode, and without a word he would reach forward a chair for her to sit down, before carrying on with his work.

The day was fading and the *Sea Hawk* was rolling steadily before the trade winds when there was a change in the weather. A storm was brewing. Dark, angry clouds hung down so low they touched the sea, obliterating the other ships in the convoy. The sea began to swell, causing the bowsprit to dip and rise perilously. Enormous smooth waves lifted the ship high out of the water before she sank into a trough, only to rise again and take the full force of the increasing wind that filled her sails, the masts and yards groaning under the strain.

Spray rose and showered the waist of the heavily laden ship and soon the decks were awash. The experienced crew worked to make fast any movable objects and batten down the hatches, whilst Stuart, up on the quarterdeck, his expert eye on the sea and sky, knew they were in for a severe blow.

He ordered the bosun to strip the masts of canvas and the helmsman to hold course. Any footwork on the tossing deck was precarious enough, but aloft in the massive rigging, where seamen clung to ropes and had their arms stretched out along yardarms, one false step and they would be pitched into the sea.

Stuart's eyes were caught by Cassandra clinging to the port rail for support, the wind whipping her skirts and hair wildly about her. The crew was well conditioned to stand the violent motion. She was not, and she was still not fully recovered. Infuriated and cursing angrily, he went to her immediately, taking her arm and almost dragging her to the top of the companion ladder.

'What the devil do you think you're doing? Haven't you the sense you were born with? Go below at once,' he ordered, the wind whipping the words from his lips. 'The storm is likely to get much worse and you're not strong enough to withstand it. You'll find yourself washed overboard if you remain on deck.'

'But I don't want to go below,' she cried, having to shout to make herself heard. She had no fear of storms at sea and felt the inactivity of watching out of the stern window impossible to contend with.

'You selfish, stubborn jade,' Stuart thundered. 'We have enough to contend with without having to keep an eye on you. Don't make things more difficult. If you refuse to go below, I will have you taken there by force if necessary.'

Cassandra turned away from his ferocity and nodded dumbly, tears welling up in her eyes. 'I'm sorry. You are right. I'll go below. I won't place yet another burden on you or the crew with my stubbornness.'

Stuart watched her climb safely down the ladder before returning to the more urgent task of keeping the ship on the right course, but all the time his mind kept going back to Cassandra and how dejected she had looked, her trembling lips and tears as she had surrendered to his order and turned and gone below reminding him of her low spirits.

When darkness shrouded the ship and the storm showed no signs of relenting, everyone braced themselves against the pitch and roll, knowing it was going to be a long night. To make matters worse, a sheeting rain swept in from the sea. No matter how hard he tried, Stuart could not cast Cassandra from his mind, thinking of her alone down below in the cabin, and his concern deepened. For his own peace of mind, and not intending to be absent from his duties for more than a few minutes, he left the ship in James Randell's more than capable hands and went to her.

The main cabin was in darkness with no sign of Cassandra. Frowning, he looked around, seeing that the door to the cabin where she slept was closed. Sighing, he turned away, intending to go back on deck, thinking that perhaps she was asleep, but suddenly he paused, certain he had heard a noise coming from the other side of the bulkhead. Moving towards the door, he stopped and listened, straining his ears against the roar of the storm. It came again, a soft muffled sound of someone crying.

Stuart stared at the closed door, torn between his longing to go to his wife and his duties back on deck. The harder she cried, the more difficult it was for him to leave her. Pushing the door open, in the dim light he saw Cassandra lying face down on the bed, sobbing into her pillow as though her heart would break.

Never had he heard anyone cry with such profound distress. Swamped with pity, he felt a surge of deep compassion at her obvious pain, which drew him from his own desolation. Crossing over to her, he sat beside her and lifted her up, drawing her into his arms and cradling her against his chest as he would a child.

'Don't, Cassandra. Don't cry so, my love,' he murmured in a deep, velvety voice. He held her trembling body tenderly, his strong hands stroking her hair, unaware that his shirt was soaking wet from the spray and wetting her thin shift as he held her close.

The words of comfort slipped from his lips quite naturally and he did not try to check them, because here, in the intimate confines of the cabin and holding her in his arms, all the rancour between them seemed not to exist. He knew that along with the grief she suffered over Rosa's death he was partly to blame for her misery, which only added to his own wretchedness.

Conscious of his presence, of him holding her in an embrace she had despaired of ever feeling again, Cassandra's heart missed a beat. She couldn't believe he was there, radiating warmth inside her, which swelled and throbbed. Embarrassed that he should find her in such a distressed state, she averted her gaze.

'Don't look away,' he whispered, and she forced her gaze back to his. With her lips moist and half open, she raised her head a little and looked at him, astonishment and surprise registering in her tear-filled eyes on seeing concern and compassion written on his handsome features, darkly shadowed in the dim light. His eyes looking into hers were as black and soft as velvet.

'Stuart!' she breathed. 'Are you not still angry with me?' she asked with quiet gravity.

'No, but I was when I saw you on deck. You little fool,' he admonished gently. 'With your seafaring knowledge I thought you of all people would be aware of the dangers of being on a heaving deck during a storm. Had you remained, there was every danger of you being washed overboard.'

Something stirred in the fathomless depths of his eyes, something hot and inviting, and Cassandra's pulse quickened. Lowering her head, she placed it on his chest. 'I believe I told you once that I can swim,' she reminded him gently, amazed and deeply touched by his concern. She sighed, aware of a pleasurable drift of happiness seeping into her heart.

'So you did. But I doubt even the strongest swimmer could survive the sea the way it is tonight.'

'Why are you here? Aren't you needed on deck?'

'I was concerned about you.' Without knowing how it happened, Stuart found himself lying rather than sitting beside her on the bed as her weeping ceased.

Cassandra's eyes were closed but she could feel him breathing hard against her. His arms were around her and her head was close to his chest where she could feel his heart beating hard. She lay quite still, praying he wouldn't get up and leave her, as she felt all the demons that he'd aroused inside her when they had first made love hungrily demanding to be satisfied. Her breathing quickened and slowly she raised her face, feeling his lips and breath warm against her wet cheek.

Knowing what would happen if he stayed a moment longer, Stuart thrust her away and stood up, combing his fingers through his hair. 'This is madness. I must go.'

Quickly Cassandra rose from the bed and stood, blocking his way to the door. Stuart stared at her shimmering form. Fully intending to leave, he tried to slide past her, touching her. It was as though a bolt of lightning had struck them both, a shock that spread through their bodies like ripples on a pond. Stuart could do nothing to avoid their closeness. The fragrance from her body, her hair, drifted about him, settling on his senses, and he knew he was lost.

Cassandra's restraint broke before Stuart's did. With a quiet moan she slid her slender arms around his neck and kissed him with all the passion building inside her, pressing herself against him, glorying in the shudder that racked his body as her mouth opened over his, and their lives, already so irretrievably entwined, streamed together in a never-ending tide. Her hold was weak and could have been broken in a second, but Stuart's heart had been invisibly seduced, making her hold as strong as any of the iron links in the anchor chain.

The roar of the tempest outside went on and was deafening and the body of the ship shuddered and creaked as it was tossed about on the turbulent sea, but, having dragged his beautiful wife on to the bed, Stuart was deaf and insensible to it now, impervious to the consequences should he stay too long.

There was so much loveliness and appeal in the face so close to his that he knew he could not leave her yet. He was impelled by a desire stronger than himself, a desire that had sprung up inside him the moment he had opened the cabin door and seen Cassandra lying on her bed weeping.

Breathing hard, his heart beating wildly against her own as his mouth closed over hers, he was half demented with desire. Cassandra's slender arms clung to him. His lips were warm and firm on hers, and they became fused together as their bodies were drawn closer by a mutual need.

With all reason slipping away and his control beginning to deteriorate, Stuart was possessed of one thought only: to satisfy his aching need for his wife, a need that had almost driven him insane over the many weeks of separation—a separation of his own making. Quickly he tore away her shift before removing his own clothes and lying beside her, his strong arms holding her to him as his lips devoured her, kissing every inch of her beautiful body stretched beside him, his fingers caressing, stroking and burning her flesh.

Moaning with absolute pleasure at his tender assault on her body, Cassandra threw back her head, closing her eyes and yielding to all the aching pleasures vibrating inside her, pleasures that spread and swelled so much that she thought she would die of them. When his urgent and desperate need became too strong for him to control, when his weight pressed down on her and she found herself crushed beneath his powerful body, she clung to him, the heat of his naked flesh and unconcealed, unbridled passion, overwhelming her.

However briefly he was to be hers, she clasped him to her, loving him with her body, with all her heart and all her soul, yielding willingly, slowly, to the overwhelming crescendo of her love that went surging through her limbs, which were wrapped around him in a frenzy of passion. Their bodies became moulded together, straining, becoming one.

The noise of the storm was challenged by sighs and moans of ecstasy, violent and wonderful, lifting the lovers to heights of indescribable pleasure neither had dreamed of, until at last they felt a bright, shattering bliss and lay spent in each other's arms.

Cassandra felt Stuart's body tremble against hers and, opening her eyes, she could see he was looking at her as one awakening from a trance.

Propped on his elbow, he was staring at her stretched out in languid repose beside him, the lingering signs of their lovemaking evident on every inch of her glorious body. How achingly lovely she looked in the dim light, her breasts firm and thrusting and darkly tipped, her skin as soft and smooth as the finest silk. He allowed his eyes a moment to devour her as she lay, relaxed and glowing, with the wild tangle of her hair spilling over the pillows, and her eyes heavy lidded and soft in the gloom of the cabin. Quickly he tore his gaze from her, recollecting himself and the peril his ship was in.

Slipping from the bed, he dressed with haste and, without a word, left her.

Cassandra sighed heavily as she watched him go. With her arms above her head she stretched her naked body, which still throbbed from his touch. Utterly fulfilled, she closed her eyes and, with warmth spreading through her veins, fell to sleep, and not even the ferocity of the storm that continued to rage throughout the night could wake her from the happiness that temporarily freed her from her wretchedness.

When Stuart came up on deck it was as if all hell had broke loose. The night was pitch black and the wind screamed through the rigging. He'd experienced many storms in the Bay of Biscay and the Atlantic and the tropical storms in the Caribbean, but nothing like this.

The sea was an angry, heaving mass of white creamy froth, whipped up to a frenzy by hurricane-force winds, the crests and troughs enormous, the circling peaks of the crests crashing and breaking against the ship and falling on to its decks in an avalanche of water. The whole ship was awash and completely exposed to the full blast of the wind. Stuart's main worry was keeping the vessel afloat, his next the cargo. He prayed the water would not seep into the holds, although, if the storm continued for much longer, he would have to consider throwing overboard some of the heavier guns and provisions to lighten the ship.

Filled with apprehension, he yelled orders through a hatchway to the helmsman controlling the whipstaff on the deck below to hold course, and shouted orders to the crew, who were adjusting ropes with their usual diligence, manning the pumps and baling out the water with buckets.

Nobly the *Sea Hawk* fought to stay afloat. Each time the huge bulk of the ship went down into a trough, everyone on board thought the huge wall of water all around them would swallow them up. But still they came sweeping up to the top, the forecastle disappearing beneath the black water as she dipped and rose again, spouting water like a gigantic whale from her decks.

At one point there was a loud crack and everyone looked up in absolute dismay to see the top of the foremast come crashing down. Immediately the ship began to steer off course and every man was united in a silent prayer. They battled their way and gallantly fought to keep her afloat and stay before the wind—and to stay alive.

It was not until the faint glimmer of dawn broke on the horizon that the storm abated and the wind died down to a low buffeting. In the silence that ensued, in absolute dismay everyone assessed the colossal damage that had been done to the ship, and it soon became evident that, being forced to run before the wind, they had been driven to the south-west and over a hundred miles off course. In fact, the storm had so completely dispersed the convoy that none of the *Sea Hawk's* companions was in sight.

'How many men have we lost?' Stuart enquired of James Randell when he came to stand beside him as he surveyed the damage on the quarterdeck.

'Four. They must have gone overboard during the storm.'

'Poor devils.' Stuart sighed wearily, shoving his hair from his face. 'Even had they been able to swim they would not have survived in those waters. Order the bosun to hoist what sail is possible, James. With the foremast and the mizzen damaged we won't be going far until they've been repaired. But one thing's for certain,' he said, casting an uneasy eye over the large, empty expanse of water towards the distant horizon, 'we can't languish in these waters. Without the protection of the convoy it won't be long before we have every pirate ship in the mid-Atlantic bearing down on us.'

Chapter Ten

Unaware of the ferocity of the storm that had raged throughout the night, Cassandra washed and brushed her hair until it shone before going up on deck, totally unprepared for the devastation that met her eyes. She saw Stuart immediately, bare headed and unshaven. His white shirt and black breeches were somewhat wilted, having been wet and dried on his body several times during the past twenty-four hours. With his hands on his hips, he stood looking up at the damaged foremast with extreme annoyance and consternation.

Seeing Cassandra, he strode towards her. Her face was fresh from a night's sleep—a night's sleep that he hadn't had. He observed there was a strange serenity about her as she came to meet him in a swirl of bright green silk, moving with unconscious grace and a soft smile curving her lips—the time they had spent together at the height of the storm responsible for this transformation. Gazing up at him, she was an innocent temptress, a delight to see after the wretched experiences of the night, but when Stuart remembered how eager he had been to bow to her charms, to forget so easily all that stood between them, he was furious with himself.

Their eyes met and Cassandra flushed beneath his searching gaze, her smile fading as she beheld the hardness on her husband's taut jaw and the cold glitter in his eyes. This was not the welcome she had hoped for, and the light that had entered her eyes on seeing him went out, for it told her that nothing had changed, despite his moment of weakness earlier, which he clearly regretted.

'I see you suffer no after-effects of the storm.' Stuart fixed his stony gaze on the shimmering expanse of water to escape the bewitchment of her wonderful deep blue eyes.

'No. It must have been severe,' Cassandra replied, surveying the deck littered with all manner of debris, from buckets and ropes to overturned barrels of tar and torn sheets of canvas.

Stuart jerked his head around and looked at her in absolute amazement. 'You mean you slept through it?'

She nodded, fighting to hide a wayward smile. 'I think your visit to my cabin gave me a much-needed tonic, Stuart,' she said softly, summoning up all her courage to refer to the incident uppermost in both their minds, determined not to let him behave as though nothing had happened.

Stuart's eyes glared a warning at her gentle reminder, the muscles of his face clenched so tight a nerve in his cheek began to pulse. 'Forgive me. I quite lost my head, for which I have reproached myself severely. It was a mistake, and I would be grateful not to be reminded of it, Cassandra. You can rest assured that I will not allow my desire for you get the better of me again.'

Dismayed, Cassandra sighed, but she would rather die than admit to him how much their brief reunion had meant to her, and that she had foolishly allowed herself to hope he might have decided to put the past behind them. 'Very well. But you cannot blame me for thinking your attitude towards me might be softening.' She expected him to utter some sarcastic jibe, but instead he frowned and looked about him.

'Forgive me if I don't indulge in conversation just now. As you can see, there is much to be done. The storm has blown us a hundred miles off course so it's imperative that we get underway with whatever sail we can hoist. Pirates infest these waters. It's dangerous to languish too long without the protection of the convoy.'

'Then at least let me help tend the wounded,' Cassandra offered, seeing men who had been injured during the storm lying about the deck.

He nodded. 'Go ahead. I'm sure Mr Patterson will be glad of it.'

Cassandra had just finished tending a young seaman with a broken leg when her attention was drawn to another matter. As usual lookouts were posted fore and aft of the now crippled ship, but it was from the watch at the masthead that the cry of 'sail on the horizon' came.

A ship was sighted coming out of the sun on the port bow. All eyes became focused on it and tension was evident in every member of the crew. The distant ship, clear on the horizon, was too far away for them to make out whether it was friend or foe, but all on board the *Sea Hawk* prayed it was a vessel in the convoy coming to their assistance. Only as it came closer under a full spread of canvas did they see that it was accompanied by two more ships following close in her wake. None of them was a merchantman, and they held their breaths collectively as the evil fate in the shape of a pirate ship moved steadily closer to menace them.

Standing at the port rail watching the approaching vessels become clearer with each mile, Cassandra felt the blood run cold in her veins. The leading vessel she recognised immediately. It was one she had never thought to see again—the *Dolphin*, her father's ship, now Drum O'Leary's, and she had no doubt he would be at the helm.

Instead of feeling a rush of warmth at the impending meeting with her father's long-time friend, after all that had transpired since their parting at Trinidad, and the change she had undergone with regard to his indefensible profession, Cassandra now regarded him as an enemy.

Recognising the beautifully carved and gilded shape of the *Dolphin*'s low hull, and the spread and curve of her white canvas, she tried not to let the sentimental memories the ship evoked weaken her resolve to stand firm against its owner. The pirate ship had her colours flying brazenly, a blood-red ensign emblazoned with a death's head above two cutlasses at the topmast head. Blood red was the preferred colour for pirate flags, its purpose being to instil terror into the hearts of its victims. The white winged ship raced gracefully through the water in a cloud of white foam, running down the wind towards the stricken *Sea Hawk* as bold and easy as a thoroughbred.

Cassandra shivered, her eyes riveted on the ship. Turning her head, her eyes searched for Stuart. He was close, his body ramrod straight, his expression hard and set, but he wasn't looking at the ship, he was looking at her, watching her reaction closely, and she realised with a sinking heart that he too had recognised her father's ship. He approached her slowly, and she felt his presence as menacing as that of the *Dolphin*'s. His eyes, locked on hers, were mocking and cold.

'Well, well. Who would have thought it? What a coincidence. Out of the countless predators that roam the world's oceans it has to be Mr Drum O'Leary who comes upon us in our moment of weakness.' He smiled thinly. 'Why the stricken look, Cassandra? Can you not try to look more cheerful on seeing an old friend? Behold, your ship,' he jeered, with an elaborate flourish of his arm in the *Dolphin*'s direction, 'if I am not mistaken.'

'She is not my ship, Stuart. She belongs to Drum O'Leary, as well you know. I'm surprised—shocked, for I never imagined I would see the *Dolphin* again. I never wanted to. You must believe that.'

'I do. But now I think you are about to get a taste of what it's like to be on the receiving end of a pirate ship.'

Cassandra blanched. 'You mean there will be trouble?'

'I'm certain of it. To be captured by a pirate ship is a terrifying thing to experience. Prepare yourself to see ruthless savagery. After all, she's hardly likely to insist on escorting us back to the convoy now, is she?' he said with grim irony. 'But worry not, my dear. I'm sure that when the *Dolphin* overpowers us you will be treated with the utmost chivalry by its captain. As for the rest of us—from past experience we know we cannot expect such leniency.'

As Stuart spoke he could see by Cassandra's deathly pallor that she was afraid of what the outcome might be if there was a fight—and not least for the fact that she was the only woman on board. In all truth, this worried him also. If the ship was captured and boarded he would not be able to save her if the pirate captain turned out to be other than Drum O'Leary—and he had no illusions of what they would do to her. She would be given over to the pirate crew and raped and only death would release her from her pain.

When Stuart thought of his lovely young wife being handed from one filthy pirate to the next he was conscious of a hideous, impotent anger searing through him like hot iron. If he had any reason to suspect that O'Leary was not the captain of the *Dolphin*, then he would be tempted to finish her here and now to save her from such a terrible fate—but then again, he thought with bitter cynicism, perhaps when she told them who she was, Nathaniel Wylde's daughter would gain their respect in time to save her.

Cassandra knew nothing of Stuart's thoughts and would have been surprised and elated to learn his concern was as much for her safety as it was for his ship and crew.

'But the *Sea Hawk* is equipped to outgun the *Dolphin*, isn't she?' she asked.

'Yes, she is. But would you approve of seeing Wylde's ship blown to smithereens?'

'I told you, it's Drum's ship now—and, yes, I think that would be a fitting end for a ship that has been used as a tool for so much evil.'

'The *Dolphin* is nowhere near as powerful as the *Sea Hawk*, but combined with the force of her cohorts,' Stuart explained, referring to the two ships following in her wake, 'and with a full complement of men—for the pirates will total more than three times our number and will be armed to the teeth—it gives her an overwhelming, formidable superiority.

'Because of the *Sea Hawk*'s weakened state, the *Dolphin* is more than a match for us and strong enough to inflict serious damage. Crippled as we are we cannot sail with any great speed. We are not manoeuvrable and cannot hold our lead sufficiently to stave off the *Dolphin*. In fact, you could say we are a sitting target,' he said quietly, his expression grim. 'When the time comes we will either have to surrender or fight.'

'So our chances of escaping are slender. Do you think she will sink us?' whispered Cassandra.

Stuart cast her a sharp glance. 'Not if she knows who we have on board,' he replied drily. 'Drum O'Leary would not fire on Nathaniel Wylde's daughter. But fear not. I have no doubt her guns will be aimed high to bring down what is left of our masts and cause havoc in the rigging. It is not her intention to sink us—at least, not until we have been ransacked from stem to stern and relieved of our cargo.'

James Randell came to stand beside them, deeply worried about the whole situation. 'She's a pirate. She means trouble.'

'I know. Raise the flag of truce, James. We're in no position to fight. Have her come alongside for a parley.'

'And if she refuses? Is it your intention to surrender?'

'No,' Stuart replied firmly, watching the three ships bearing down on them. His mind was running clear and sharp, but after battling throughout the night against the storm, like every other bleary-eyed man on board he was overwhelmed by weariness. But to surrender at this point was out of the question. 'If she doesn't agree to parley, then there's nothing else for it. We will have to fight. Stand by to hoist the red flag just in case. Load the guns and have them run out—and instruct every man to be sure not to waste a shot.'

By now small figures could be seen scurrying about the *Dolphin*'s decks. The ships accompanying her sailed away from her in opposite directions, taking a wide arc, their intention clearly being to come at the crippled merchantman from all sides. The *Sea Hawk* hoisted the flag of truce, but the *Dolphin* had ideas of her own. When she was just within range, with a puff of white smoke she put a shot across the *Sea Hawk*'s bows, splintering the bowsprit, and leaving everyone on board in no doubt as to her intentions.

Orders rang out and, as everyone scrambled to, it was clear they were in for a desperate fight. Ports on the two gun decks were opened as shot and buckets of powder were brought for the guns. Eager to be of help, Cassandra assisted the young boys of the crew, carrying powder up from the magazine in the bowels of the ship, which was strenuous work for it involved clambering up and down innumerable ladders between the decks, but she was glad to have something useful to do.

'She means to have us, James,' Stuart said grimly, standing beside his first mate on the poop deck. 'And I fear she may do just that.'

James looked at him seriously. This was James's first voyage on the *Sea Hawk*, but he knew all about Stuart's previous run in with the threatening vessel, and his dealings with her one-time captain, Nathaniel Wylde.

'I agree with you. I don't think much of our prospects either. I understand this is not the first time you have encountered the *Dolphin*. You've had dealings with her in the past, I believe.'

Without taking his eyes off the fast-approaching ship, Stuart nodded slowly. 'We're old friends, the *Dolphin* and I. Although in those days she sailed under a different captain—Captain Nathaniel Wylde. You've heard of him?'

His expression grim, James nodded.

'No doubt Mr Drum O'Leary, its present captain, is just as ruthless. After our last encounter I prayed never to set eyes on that ship again.'

'Wylde acquired the reputation as being something of a gentleman, owing to the fact that he treated his victims with courtesy. I know you were the man responsible for his capture—and subsequent execution.'

'I was—but he was no gentleman, I can assure you, James. He was a vicious, murdering barbarian, as ruthless and cruel as any other sea rover who chooses to live by infamous means.'

'But how can you be sure this O'Leary you speak of is the captain of the *Dolphin*?'

'I can't.' Stuart's face set in grim lines as he turned away to inspect the loading of the guns. 'But I sure as hell hope that for my wife's sake he is.' He spoke these words to himself, not intending them to be heard, but James had sharp ears and heard them clearly, and although they puzzled him he did not query them.

The *Dolphin* had retreated just out of range of the *Sea Hawk*'s guns, leaving it up to the other two ships to fire on her, which they did, their first rounds falling wide of their mark and plunging into the sea. The *Sea Hawk* responded immediately, making the whole ship shudder violently as a huge broadside was delivered at the ship closest to her, finding her target with superb accuracy.

But as the ship began to roll there was no cheering from the crew of the *Sea Hawk* for by now the *Dolphin*, back in range, and the other ship opened up a withering fire upon the *Sea Hawk*, most of the rounds falling wide of their mark but coming closer with each fresh outburst of fire.

When fired the *Sea Hawk*'s guns recoiled violently, kicking backwards from the open ports. Cassandra had never seen guns used on a ship before and was unprepared for the acrid smoke that belched into the air, choking her and making her eyes stream with tears.

One shot from the *Dolphin* splintered what remained of the bowsprit and another hit the mainmast with accurate precision, causing it to crack and splinter. With a great crashing of timber it tumbled on to the deck, bringing with it her cordage and canvas and flinging men from her rigging into the sea.

Crushed beneath the massive weight, men screamed out in pain as others fought to drag them free, carrying them to the surgeon's quarters. Cassandra went to help Mr Patterson tend them as best she could. Blood was everywhere, the stench unbearable, but she worked diligently, trying to shut the noise of the thundering guns from her mind, until what seemed like hours later Stuart found her and pulled her outside.

The guns were still pounding and the crew's movements were impeded by cordage, which littered the decks. The two undamaged ships were almost upon them, the other still rolling slightly but managing to edge closer. Cassandra could see men with gaudy-coloured scarves knotted around their heads, barefoot and armed to the teeth with cutlasses and pistols, swarming about their decks.

The pirate ships had showered round after round at the *Sea Hawk* with shattering effect, piercing her hull in several places. But surprisingly she had responded, managing with great difficulty to slightly alter what tack was left in her desperate struggle to stave off the inevitable and fire back. But the nimble, easily manoeuvrable *Dolphin* remained virtually unscathed. Nathaniel Wylde would have been proud of her performance.

The sight of Cassandra appalled Stuart. Her clothes were torn and covered with the blood of the wounded, her face smudged with powder and grime from the guns. But he admired the way she had found something useful to do and had not gone to pieces at the first sound of cannon fire, as most women would have done. He had not seen her for several hours, and he had sought her out to reassure himself that she was unharmed—although his features revealed none of his concern and were set hard, refusing to let her soft appealing eyes weaken him even at this moment of crisis.

Cassandra looked up at her husband in consternation, knowing he had come to tell her the battle was almost over. With powder marks on his face and shirt, his dark eyes, looking out of his strained features, stared down into hers. Her fingers ached to reach up and push a rebellious lock of hair that dipped over his eyes back, but she checked herself, knowing he would not welcome the intimacy. The lack of warmth in his voice when he spoke confirmed this.

'All is lost,' he said gravely. 'It is only a matter of minutes before we are boarded. My intention is to surrender—they leave me with little choice. There are those who wish to fight to the bitter end, but I think enough lives have been lost. However, there may be fighting so I want you to go below, out of the way until it's over.'

'No,' Cassandra cried in sudden alarm. 'Please don't send me from you, Stuart—not now.'

'I must,' he said, his tone sounding harder than he intended, but his instinct was to protect her, and he could not do that if she remained in full glare of the pirate ships. 'If you stay on deck, you will only be in the way.'

'And what if you are killed?' she asked in desperation, having difficulty in suppressing her tears, for she knew that if she went from him now she might never see him alive again.

It was a question Stuart was unable to answer, for in all probability that was exactly what might happen.

'I won't leave you, Stuart. Whatever happens I want to stay here—to share your fate,' she protested passionately, thrusting herself forward and clinging to him, oblivious to the looming, menacing presence of the *Dolphin* edging her way closer, with men clinging to the rigging ready to jump on to the *Sea Hawk*'s decks at the first opportunity. The only thing that mattered to her at that moment was this man, her husband, whom she loved above anything and anyone. 'For pity's sake, must you reject me even now when we might both be killed?'

Stuart saw the anguish on her face, how her mouth softened as she pleaded with him, and how her eyes misted with tears, begging for forgiveness, like an animal punished through no fault of its own. With an iron force of will he took her arms and held her away from him, looking hard but with compassion into her eyes and willing her to be strong.

'I am not rejecting you, Cassandra,' he said fiercely. 'You must believe that, but you seem to be too ready to forget that I had a brother I adored, whom your father killed. Yes, I've reproached myself for making you my wife, as if it is a crime against his spirit. But, at this moment, above all else I want you to be safe.

'Can't you see they are stronger than we are? We none of us know what they have in store for us, but one thing is certain—if Drum O'Leary is not on board the *Dolphin*, then from past experience, where sea rovers are concerned, the unenviable treatment of females who fall into their hands fills me with alarm. As a precaution I want you out of the way when they come on board, and with any luck I might be able to reason with them.'

Hope began to beat a steady rhythm in Cassandra's heart, and a light entered her eyes. 'But if Drum is on board—perhaps when he sees me I will be able to speak to him. He can be reasoned with. I know he can.'

'Maybe. But I doubt his leniency will extend to me. To my crew, perhaps—especially those with specialist skills who can be of use to him. In exchange for their lives, others may decide to join the pirates—but do not forget that he has a score to settle with me. I was the one who sent Nathaniel Wylde to the gallows. Drum O'Leary will not deal with me lightly.'

'But if he has never seen you then there is little chance he will know who you are.'

'If you think that then you are a fool. I would wager the price of the cargo that he already knows who he's been up against for the past few hours. It was no secret that the name of the ship that hounded Nathaniel Wylde across the Atlantic was the *Sea Hawk*. The name will be emblazoned on his soul and will have been staring at him ever since he came within range of the ship.'

'But when he knows you are my husband he will—'

Stuart's face darkened. 'No, Cassandra,' he interrupted fiercely, his eyes blazing with fury. 'I don't need any woman using her favours to help me. I will not have you plead with that barbarian on my behalf.'

'I will if I have to,' she cried brokenly, holding out her hands to him in desperation, gripping his arms in an effort to get close to him, to communicate the fever that possessed her and to penetrate the armour he had built around himself against her. As tears she could no longer suppress began to flow uncontrollably over her lashes, it was clear to her by the tormented look that ravaged his face that this was the only thing that could save them all. But his stupid arrogance and pride continued to stand in the way as he refused to humble himself.

'Listen to me,' she implored, almost choking on her tears. 'Please, Stuart. In spite of everything I love you. I love you more than I have ever loved anyone—and even if I am to die my soul will go on loving you. I will go down on my knees to Drum if I have to so he will not harm you. Please let me help you. Just give me one single chance to speak to him. I beg of you.'

'No,' he said with blunt cruelty, trying hard to remain unmoved by her tears, by the pain he saw behind the defiance in her eyes, and by the sincerity of the words she spoke, which had the power to break him. 'Don't make it harder than it already is.'

'How can it possibly be harder?' Cassandra protested desolately. 'I love you. Don't push me away.' She wished he would say it back to her, even though he didn't mean it.

Stuart tried to distance himself from her, loosing the hands that gripped his arms and pushing her from him, when all the time he secretly asked for nothing more than to hold her, to crush her to him and bury his face in her beautiful mane of sweet-smelling hair and protect her from harm. He turned his head away wretchedly, angered by these feelings that threatened to weaken him at a time when he needed to be strong, when so many lives depended on his ability to remain calm and in complete control of his senses.

'For God's love, Cassandra,' he rasped, combing his hair back from his brow. 'Don't torture either of us like this.'

'Why not?' she demanded wretchedly. 'If we are to be parted, then help me to understand why you will not let me help you.'

'Stop it. I insist that you go below and give some thought to the seriousness of your own situation.'

In the agony of her grief over the critical nature of Stuart's plight, his words barely penetrated Cassandra's mind. She stared at him in bewilderment. 'Why—what are you saying?'

'Think, Cassandra,' he said fiercely. 'When it is revealed who you are, you will have more than Drum O'Leary to contend with. I cannot vouch for the conduct of my crew— because when the men realise they have been harbouring the infamous Captain Wylde's daughter on board, their treatment of you will be as severe as any you will receive from the pirates—should O'Leary not be there to save you.'

His words sounded hard and cruel, he knew, but, fearful for her safety, his instinct being to protect her the only way he knew how, Stuart was trying to inspire into her some of the indomitable spirit she had possessed when she had sailed on the *Dolphin*, and which had served her when she had colluded with O'Leary to steal it from under the very noses of the Admiralty and have her father's body cut down from the gallows, before travelling to the Caribbean and braving all the odds.

His words brought home to Cassandra the seriousness of her situation and a trickle of cold sweat ran down her spine. Her voice trembled with fear and from the depth of her hurt when she spoke. 'You are right. I have given little thought to my own situation—to the effect of who I am will have on others. Dear Lord,' she cried in an agony of sheer frustration, 'am I never to be free of it? Am I to be trapped forever more by a past inflicted on me by others?'

'A past you were willing to adopt,' he reminded her harshly, cruelly. 'A past you cannot blame others for regarding with abhorrence. A past which created in you an illusion that all pirates are misunderstood beings who never really mean any harm. I suppose you can be forgiven because of your youth and naïvety—but you really must try to understand that forgiveness for such crimes as your father committed is impossible to achieve for those who were unfortunate enough to have been his victims. Now, do as I say and go below.' His dismissal was as cold in this final moment they were together as the way he had conducted himself throughout the days of their marriage.

Cassandra felt as if he'd slapped her, but her pride brought her chin up. If he could speak to her like this, then all was lost between them. Despite his earlier insistence to the contrary, he did continue to reject her and could not wait to be rid of her—even at the moment of death. She drew herself up, showing him that she too could be hard and cold.

'Very well. I shall go below before I make an even bigger fool of myself. Go and do your duty, Stuart.' She left him then without another word, treading carefully over and around the many obstacles barring her path with as much dignity as she could muster, unable to shake off the burden of doom.

Stuart watched her go, deeply shaken by her passionate outburst of love, and he realised that his own feelings were not so very different. Only now, when it was too late, did he realise how deeply he had come to feel for her. She had succeeded in finding a way into his heart and mind as no woman had done before. He had never felt this way about anything or anybody, except his ship and the sea. Not even his mother, whom he revered greatly, or his dear departed father and brother had commanded the love he felt for his wife. But his inability to accept her because of who she was continued to divide them—although never would he be strong enough to reject her completely.

The thud of a grappling iron thrown from the *Dolphin* landed at his feet, splintering the boards of the deck and bringing a savage oath to his lips. He turned his attention to what was happening all around him. The *Dolphin* was alongside, and the fearsome-looking pirates that crowded her decks were armed to the teeth and poised to jump on board the *Sea Hawk*.

After a volley of musketry, the pirates swarmed over the bulwarks, armed with short swords and cutlasses. Panic-stricken, some of the crew jumped into the sea in the hope of escaping the vicious onslaught by this murderous, fiendish band of men. With a pistol in one hand and a sword in the other, suffused with an indomitable spirit and determination, Stuart entered the fray, thrusting and sinking his blade into the heart of one of the pirates who wielded a cutlass above his head with such lightning speed that the man was dead before he hit the deck.

Confusion reigned as fighting broke out, with men ferociously hacking and chopping with their cutlasses at anything that confronted them. Pistol shots, a profanation of yells and the clash of steel on steel resounded throughout the ship, and then Stuart was confronted by a hideous-looking specimen of a man. Recognition came to each man simultaneously. It was Drum O'Leary and Stuart knew he meant to kill him.

Not until she was alone in her cabin did Cassandra allow her stiff back to bend and her reserve to crumble. She felt totally abandoned by the man who had sworn to love and cherish her until the day he died. With a sob she fell on to the bed, burying her face in the pillows and weeping tears of bitterness and absolute despair. Her ears were completely deaf to the frenzied mayhem on deck, and it was only as the sounds began to penetrate her consciousness that reason seeped into her brain and she pulled herself together and considered what had to be done.

A deadly calm stole over her, as cold and fathomless as death. It was as though a voice spoke inside her head, unravelling her thoughts and placing them in perfect order so that she could study them and rationally throw off any challenge the arrival of the *Dolphin* had flung at her. Only when she had come to a decision did she strip off her filthy clothes and pour some water into a bowl to wash herself.

Along with her dress she threw caution to the wind in her determination to do what she could to save her husband, despite his insistence that she stay out of the way. Behind the smoothness of her face was the savagery of a lioness defending her young, but in Cassandra's case it was her husband she would defend, and woe betide anyone who stood in her way. She would kneel and kiss the ground Drum O'Leary walked on to save Stuart from death if need be. And afterwards—what then? She would let fate or Drum O'Leary take care of that.

Chapter Eleven

t didn't take long for the fighting to go against the crew
of the *Sea Hawk*, and when Cassandra arrived on deck it
was to a scene of utter devastation. A grey canopy of smoke
hung over the ship and slaughtered and wounded men lay
everywhere, with blood soaking into the wooden planks—
dark evidence of the ferocity of the battle that had been
waged on the *Sea Hawk*'s decks. The remaining bloodied
crew of the merchantman had been rounded up by the pirates, who kept a careful watch on them.

Cassandra quickly looked for her husband, praying with
every part of her being that he was still alive. And then she
saw him, surrounded by gleaming cutlasses, his arms held
behind his back by a bare-chested brute of a man. She was
alarmed to see a wound inflicted on his torso, but the ferocity of his curses and the way he struggled with his tor-
mentor told her it wasn't life threatening.

She sent up a silent prayer of thankfulness to God that
he had seen fit to spare him, but no emotion showed on
her face as she moved through the men thronging the deck,
an inanimate object which moved with a conditioned reflex,
with one single thought—to save her husband's life. Her

unexpected appearance shocked the men who were still fighting into immobility.

The pirates who had sailed with her on the *Dolphin* recognised her immediately. When they had recovered from their initial shock, the air resounded with their raucous cheers of welcome, causing the crew of the *Sea Hawk* to stare at each other in absolute bewilderment. Unafraid and contemptuous, Cassandra's gaze swept over the pirates, before coming to rest on Drum O'Leary.

As straight and slender as a young sapling she moved towards him. There was a look of fragility about her—but there was nothing fragile or frail in her manner as she looked at the pirate captain, remote and untouchable in her icy calm. The tenacious pride bred into her by her father forbade her to show fear, as boldly she drew back her shoulders and held her head high. No one seeing her could have doubted her courage and determination. All eyes were focused on her, for she cut a compelling figure indeed.

Stuart was as mesmerised by her presence as everyone else, and he could not believe that this was the same smoke-grimed, bloodstained woman he had sent to her cabin just a short while ago with tears in her eyes. Before him now stood a vibrant, haughty young woman, looking every inch a lady of distinction in a gown of gleaming gold satin. Her unbound sunburnt hair tumbled down her back—a plaything for the breeze that teased and tugged the silken strands. She met his gaze proudly as he soaked up the sight of her, completely unprepared for the surge of admiration that flooded his whole being.

Even now, after all this time, she still had the power to strike at him with a strength that both surprised and frightened him at times, and he was confounded by his own mixed emotions. But his admiration was soon replaced by fury over the way in which she had taken it into her head to openly defy him.

Ramrod straight, with a pistol shoved into his belt and a bloodstained cutlass clutched in his hand, Drum O'Leary watched her approach. Staring at her in absolute incredulity, he paled beneath his brown weathered skin, as if he were looking at a ghost.

Cassandra stopped in front of this devil in human shape, avoiding Stuart's eyes, and yet knowing they were fixed on her. The pirate captain had the look of one who was a predator among men, with all the marks of precocious vice. His mutilated face was hideous, his scar a vivid trail against deep brown skin, drawn tight over a living skull. He looked fearsome and his permanent smile was evil. His pale eyes glittered with a singular malice. They were cold and full of cruelty—like a snake's, she noticed, suppressing a shudder of revulsion. Why had she never seen it before? Why had it never disturbed her?

Her memories of him were of the kindness he had shown her in the past, but she found it difficult to tally that with his vicious attack on the *Sea Hawk*. She felt nothing in his presence now but a deep and utter loathing. The strong breeze blew from behind him, billowing his baggy scarlet shirt like the wings of a giant bird of prey, adding to the terrible apparition that was Drum O'Leary.

Drum's eyes were locked on Cassandra's in a burning, searching gaze, piercing the secretive veil of her covert thoughts. He assessed them correctly and was disappointed. 'Are you having trouble recognising me? I have no such difficulty in recognising you—despite your fine gown and the animosity I see in your eyes when you look at me. You are not happy to see me, Cassandra.' His mock reproof reawakened all Cassandra's anger against him. He laughed, a noise that was more like a wheeze than a sound of mirth.

'I recognise you. You have a brutal way of making your presence felt, Drum. And you are right. I cannot say that I welcome you.'

Drum's face remained singularly calm. 'So, you've turned sour on me. It grieves me to know that. I can see you've changed much since I left you at Trinidad—not so much the innocent. I've a soft spot for you—you have always known that. You've got pluck, for all the knocks you've had. But—where is my daughter? Where is my Rosa?' he asked, looking over her shoulder, hoping to see his daughter behind her. 'She is here with you, is that not so? You ensured me you would take care of her.'

'Rosa is dead,' Cassandra stated flatly, but she was not without a heart. Knowing how much Drum had loved Rosa, she felt compassion for the pain and sadness he must surely feel on receiving this grievous news.

Am unbelieving, stricken look entered Drum's eyes, but his expression remained blank. 'What scurvy trick is this?' he hissed. 'You're lying.'

'I would never lie to you, Drum,' Cassandra said quietly. To feel anger for his attack and the killing of the crew was one thing, but to slash at him with words about Rosa was another. Not given to moments of weakness, Drum turned and faced the sea. Cassandra moved to his side. 'Rosa became sick on board ship,' she explained. 'She—died of a fever. There was nothing any of us could do. Your bombardment wasn't to blame—in case you should think that.'

'Did she suffer?' His eyes were clouded, his voice strangled in his throat.

'I don't think so—at least not much. She was delirious for most of the time. I...know how much you loved her, Drum—we both did. For the short time we were together we became close—and I miss her terribly.'

Because of the life he led Drum had seen and been responsible for the deaths of countless men and women, but the death of his daughter hung heavy on his villainous heart. He turned and looked at Cassandra, who saw his eyes clear, and his face settle into an expression of lifeless formality. 'You say you loved her, and yet you look at her father with so much hatred in your heart. Why? Have I not always shown kindness towards you? Have I ever hurt you?'

'No. But then, being Nat's daughter, you wouldn't, would you? 'Tis a pity the same cannot be said of the men on board this ship—the ones you murdered.'

The accusation fell between them like a cannon ball. Drum's face closed up instantly and he moved away from her. After no longer than a moment, in charge of himself once more—he would mourn his Rosa later, in private— his hideous smile broke his expression as his eyes swept over those on deck. Suddenly he burst out in a spontaneous roar of laughter that rent the air—a cold, thin sound, which caused a prickling to break out on the flesh of all who heard it.

Cassandra was acutely aware of Stuart's presence close to her. He was standing without moving a muscle, his face hard and implacable as he watched and listened, omnipotent and contemptuous of his enemy, emanating a wrath so forceful that even the man holding his arms was wary. She stared at Drum, feeling neither fear nor intimidation. 'When we parted at Trinidad I hoped never to set eyes on you or the *Dolphin* again. Are you not surprised to see me on board the *Sea Hawk*, Drum? Have you not asked yourself what I am doing here?'

'Aye. I confess I did not expect to find you on board this particular ship.' Drum looked meaningfully at its captain. The fight between them had been fierce as each had fought for mastery over the other, but when the *Sea Hawk*'s captain had smashed through Drum's guard, Drum's men had intervened and overpowered him.

''Tis obvious that you're returning to England after visiting your cousin on Barbados, but you cannot have been aware, when you arranged passage on the *Sea Hawk*, that its captain was the man responsible for Nat's capture and death. Knowing this, perhaps you will enjoy witnessing the way in which I intend to avenge my friend—your father. So, what is it to be?' he said, pointing at Stuart with a long quivering finger, hoping to goad him to further anger.

'I expect you have it worked out already.' There was a quaking in the pit of Cassandra's stomach.

'I promise you he will be so much carrion flesh before the day is out. Shall he be flayed, hanged outright—which I do not consider painful enough—or keelhauled?' Drum rasped with a savage sneer, wiping away the sweat stinging his eyes with the back of his hand. 'But then, if we administer the latter, there is every danger that he might drown if the rope becomes snarled on the barnacles beneath the hull. His death would be too quick and I have clamoured for his blood too long. I am determined that he will provide my men with pleasure. Come, Cassandra, the choice is yours, unless you wish to combine all three—or, better still, you would like me to suggest some other torture more horrible.'

Appalled by the obscenities Drum's hideous mouth spewed forth, Cassandra paled, but her expression did not alter as she listened to the horrendous tortures he intended inflicting on Stuart. 'I am certain there are a thousand tortures you can think of that would turn even the strongest stomach. And I am equally as certain that practice has enabled you to perfect your barbaric entertainments.'

'You are right, there is nothing I would not do. I will have my vengeance as I have dreamed ever since that day at Execution Dock. Remember?' The word was spoken fiercely and caught Cassandra and slapped her. Drum's smile was evil when he saw her blanch, and a light of madness gleamed in his pale eyes. 'I see you do. Now, at last, the plaguing dream will be real in body and torment, culminating in triumph—vengeance realised.'

'And in so doing you will make me suffer. Is that what you want?' Cassandra's voice was low and hoarse with indignation.

Drum turned his attention on Stuart, and face to face the antagonists stood. Drum was tall, but his prisoner towered over him. Stuart's whole body was rigid, his face so expressionless it might have been carved from stone. Pressing the blade of his cutlass to Stuart's chest, Drum locked his gaze on his. 'To see him squirm, crawl and die will be a pleasure.'

Stuart's eyebrow tilted sardonically and his mouth curved thinly. 'Put away your cutlass, O'Leary,' he said, oblivious to the cold touch of death at his chest, 'and we'll see who squirms.'

'Have a care, Marston,' Drum snarled viciously, his body quivering slightly with anger and rage, his lips drawn tightly against his teeth. Lowering his cutlass, he took a step back. 'There is nothing I would not do to make you suffer.'

Somehow the bitter knowledge of his helplessness gave Stuart the strength to struggle free of his captor and thrust himself forward. He dismissed the malicious, leering face of Drum O'Leary with a look of loathing and contempt, refusing to allow his threats to intimidate him. That he meant to kill him by some grisly method he did not doubt, but he did not want his wife to have to witness it. His eyes snapped on to Cassandra, who recoiled in shock from the full force of the scorching fury directed at her in his eyes.

'What do you hope to achieve by this—this madness?' he hissed through clenched teeth, his blazing rage frightening to see. 'I ordered you to stay below. If you ever,' he warned savagely, 'dare to defy me again, I won't be responsible for the consequences.'

Cassandra longed to fling herself into his arms and tell him that she wanted to share his suffering, that she was trying to save his life, but she knew his survival depended on her keeping her emotions in check and remaining calm. 'Ordered!' she exclaimed. 'Stuart, I am not one of your crew or some—some trained chattel or underling to do as she is told. I am your wife, and my place is to be here— by your side.'

This revelation caused Drum to step back apace, clearly appalled by her disclosure, but then he threw back his head and laughed out loud at the absurdity of it, the sound an unnerving rumble in his chest. 'Wife!' he roared. 'Wife, you say?'

The face Cassandra turned on Drum was white, but her eyes blazed. 'Yes, wife—and I am hardly likely to enjoy watching the spectacle of my husband being keelhauled or hanged,' she flared.

Stuart was fully aware that his crew knew who Cassandra was by now. They were beginning to shift uneasily. Tension was evident among them and, briefly scanning their faces, he saw they were bright with hatred and a sense of betrayal. 'Cassandra, I command you to go below,' he ordered in a low, deadly voice, throwing her a warning glance, which caused Drum to laugh even louder, his entire body shaking with mirth. Indeed, he found the situation so amusing it had brought tears to his eyes.

'Anyone knowing her would know better than to command her to do anything. 'Tis not in the nature of Nathaniel Wylde's daughter to bow and scrape to any man.' He ceased laughing as his eyes slid to Cassandra, full of irony suddenly. 'How a marriage between the two of you came about baffles me and must be a strange tale, one that must have Nat laughing in his watery grave—one I shall find extremely interesting. But did you know Marston was Nat's implacable enemy when you married him—the man responsible for bringing him to the gallows?'

'And with good reason, Drum. When I married Stuart I

was not aware of the part he played in bringing Nat to justice, any more than he knew who I was. It was not until after we were married that we became aware of it.'

'Then knowing what you do about each other must make for strange bedfellows,' Drum chuckled.

Stung by Drum's amusement, Cassandra glared at him. 'Nat got what he deserved, though it grieves me to say so— as you will when the law catches up with you. Your luck will run out one day.'

Drum scowled at her. 'It disappoints me to hear you speak like this, Cassandra. I never thought you would dishonour your father's memory. Nat loved you. He would have been disappointed in you.'

The tone of his voice and the way he was looking at her made Cassandra feel like some faithless, flawed creature who had failed her father, that she was not the daughter he would have wanted. She blinked back the tears of remorse and self-denigration that suddenly sprang to her eyes and looked away, feeling terrible. For the first time since Stuart had discovered who she was and told her of the horrendous crime her father had inflicted upon those on the stricken vessel on which his brother had met his death, guilt that in her thoughts she had betrayed Nat filled her, made her feel physically sick.

'I loved him in my own way—he was my father, after all—but I do not feel duty bound to honour the memory of a man who lived by inflicting misery on others. He was cruel and unscrupulous—and he had no right to make me a part of it.'

'You knew the nature of his profession, but as a source of protection you clung to your ignorance because it suited you to do so at the time.'

'Maybe you're right,' she admitted. 'Now I know better. But, listen to me, Drum.' Moving closer, she softened her tone in an attempt to appeal to his better nature. 'I am asking you to spare my husband's life. If you care for me at all, do not place this horrendous memory between us.'

Faced by the soft appeal in her lovely eyes, Drum's face closed instantly and he felt anger, for, like her father before her, he knew she had the power to make him weaken. 'No. I can't do that, Cassandra. Not even for you. You'll find another husband—you'll forget.'

Contempt was written broadly in Cassandra's eyes. She raised her head defiantly. 'I am Stuart's wife. I will have no other man, for there is no other.'

'He deserves to die. Do not forget the man he hounded and saw hanged was my friend.'

'And my father,' she countered fiercely. 'If I can forget, then so can you and every man who sails with you. Nat was responsible for the death of Stuart's brother, Drum— on a vessel bound for the Caribbean that he attacked and plundered before watching it sink beneath the waves with nearly every man, woman and child on board. I have no doubt that you were a party to that. Can you in all honesty blame Stuart for wanting to see him brought to justice? Do you think killing him would be what Nat would have wanted—for you to avenge his death in this cruel manner by hanging his daughter's husband?'

Drum looked at Stuart and examined him more attentively. 'This ship your brother was on, what was it called?'

'The *Evening Star*—although you will have plundered and sunk so many ships since then you maybe don't recall the name.'

Drum's doubtful glance went from Stuart to Cassandra and back to Stuart. He sensed an injustice here somewhere—one that had blackened Nat's name more than it was already. 'Do you take me for a simpleton, or do you think I've lost my memory?' he growled, moving closer to Stuart and fixing him with a hard stare. 'I remember the vessel—became detached from a convoy. I was with Nat that day on the *Dolphin*. We were operating with another ship captained by a man named Jacob Yeats—an altogether different character from Nat, who cut such a figure that imagination cannot form an idea of a more frightful fury from Hell. It is clear your accusations are not borne out by the facts, Marston.'

A look of indescribable disgust twisted Stuart's face. 'If you are about to tell me that Wylde played no part in the attack, then save your breath. There were witnesses. Some of those on board managed to survive in the water until they were picked up by the convoy, which arrived too late to help the stricken ship.'

'Having stripped the *Evening Star* of some its cargo, Nat abandoned the vessel and left the scene—thinking Yeats would do the same. The mist was heavy, as I recall—the two ships became separated. As far as I can remember, the *Evening Star* was still seaworthy when we left her, and no harm was done to those on board—that was not Nat's way of doing things. He attacked, looted and then he vanished, only punishing those who resisted. He was not notoriously cruel. It was not until later that we learned Yeats had stayed and blown a hole in the ship's hull.'

'And I am supposed to believe this?'

Drum shrugged. 'Believe what you like. It is the truth.'

'And Yeats?'

'Dead—killed when he launched an attack on a Spanish merchant vessel a year back.'

Stuart remained unmoved by Drum's revelation. 'Try to absolve Wylde all you like, O'Leary, but it changes nothing. Nathaniel Wylde was a villain, callous to the feelings of humanity, who got what he deserved.'

'It changes nothing where you are concerned either, Marston.' Drum's eyes shifted to his crew. They were watching him with fearsome expectancy, brandishing their knives.

'Look at them. If they are to be denied your blood, there is no telling what they will do.'

Having listened to Drum, what he had told them about Nat had reinstated him just a little in Cassandra's estimation. However, it did not take away the bitterness from her heart, nor it didn't lessen the danger facing Stuart, and that was what was important at that moment. Her laugh was one of mockery edged with scorn as she swept her gaze nonchalantly over the villainous rabble. She was alarmed to see the crew of the *Sea Hawk* closing in around her, their faces dark and contorted with malevolence, but she did not flinch. She stood straight and erect, as if carved from stone, her gaze settling coldly on Drum once more.

'Why, what is this? Are you not master of your own ship?' she taunted, challenging boldly, her small fists plunked into the small of her waist. 'If you are to be dictated to by your crew, then you are not the Drum O'Leary I remember.'

Some members of the *Dolphin*'s crew edged closer, their nearness threatening. The hostility on board seemed to escalate to frighteningly tangible proportions, but in frozen, mute rebellion Cassandra ignored them and continued to fix her gaze on their captain, flinging back her head, her eyes gleaming defiance, until Drum capitulated. She looked so like Nat. He might be dead, but he lived on in his daughter. She had the same indomitable fighting spirit that had possessed him.

Triumph thwarted, Drum sighed deeply. 'What has happened, Cassandra? We confront each other like enemies.'

'It is of your making. If you kill my husband, I will never forgive you. Never. You have only to say the word. The decision is yours entirely.'

Her look remained challenging and hard and she had the satisfaction of seeing a softening enter Drum's eyes and his shoulders droop a little in subjugation. A feeling of relief and something like triumph stirred deep inside her. Perhaps when he realised what her intention was if he agreed to do as she asked—that she was condemning herself irrevocably and for all eternity to a life without the man she loved— he would be swayed completely.

'I have something to ask of you.'

Wary, Drum's eyes narrowed. 'What?'

'I want you to take me with you when you sail from here. But you must understand that I cannot do so with my husband's blood on your hands.' From the corner of her eye she saw Stuart start forward and heard him shout with rage, 'Cassandra, for the love of God, think what you're doing,' but the sound of her thundering heart drowned out anything else he said. Brutal hands forcibly restrained him. She felt his helplessness, his fury. It draped over her like a death shroud, and she couldn't bring herself to look at him.

Looking at her in astonishment, Drum could not begin to imagine the self-sacrifice that had gone into her request. His eyes shone and his hideous smile widened. 'As my enemy or my friend? I'd rather it be the latter, but—whatever.' He shrugged. 'I'll be glad to have Nat's daughter on board again. 'Twill be a little like the old days, eh?'

'Never that,' Cassandra replied coldly. 'If I go with you, it will be because I am left with no alternative. Will you grant my request? Stuart will not be harmed?'

Trying not to look at the ugly faces of his crew, for he knew the situation was extremely sensitive and explosive, Drum nodded.

'And the crew? Does your leniency extend to them also?'

'They will be kept under guard until we have left the ship.'

Aware that they were about to be cheated of their cruel entertainment, the pirates surged forward like a storm-tossed sea, the sun flashing on the steel blades of their raised weapons. The moment was ugly and one of extreme tension, but with a swift gesture of his hand and in sole command once more, Drum ordered them to stop.

'I have made my decision. We will take as much cargo as can be stashed on to our ships—along with her guns and anything else that takes your eye. Because of my past association with this woman and her father, Marston and his crew shall not be harmed. Is that understood?'

Reluctantly the men drew back, taking consolation in the spoils to be had in the holds of this heavily laden merchantman. Immediately they began swarming all over the ship like ants on an ant heap.

Having struggled free of his captor, Stuart moved closer to Drum, only to find his arms seized once more, and though he struggled violently, his face contorted with rage and sheer physical determination, he was locked in an embrace of hell. 'I'll kill you if you lay a hand on my wife, O'Leary. By God I swear it.'

Drum motioned Cassandra forward, smiling smugly into the rage-filled eyes of the man he had been cheated of killing. 'You have what you want—your ship and your crew. Now I will take what I want. Your wife.'

'You can go to hell,' Stuart retorted. 'She's going nowhere with you. You'll have to kill me first.'

Drum shrugged. 'Don't tempt me.' Pulling Cassandra away, out of earshot of her seething husband, he looked at her quizzically. 'Do you not submit to your husband with wifely obedience and consider your place to be by his side?'

Cassandra looked back at Stuart through a blur of tears. She could almost feel the anger seeping out of every pore of his body. 'I can think of nowhere I would rather be, but little did I know when I left London that I would turn my life into an irretrievable disaster. Unfortunately I was seen on the deck of the *Dolphin* when she sailed down the

Thames, and as a consequence I have a price on my head to equal yours. I have no illusions,' she said, a trace of sadness touching her lovely eyes. 'If I return with Stuart to London, like my father before me, there is every possibility that I will hang. So you see, I am left with little choice.'

'And what about the bond that attaches you to this man? If he is alive you will never be free of him. To finish him now would—'

'No,' she cut in fiercely, already feeling the wrench of her separation from Stuart like a knife piercing her heart. 'Apart or together, I remain his wife. Nothing will ever change that.'

Stuart was suffering all the torments of hell for, like the surviving members of his crew, he was helpless as he watched the vicious rabble from the *Dolphin* and her co-horts tearing his ship apart, penetrating every deck and cavity of the massive vessel, carrying off anything they could lay their thieving hands on.

Weariness lay upon him like a weight, pressing intolerably upon his heart and soul. As he watched O'Leary, he considered rushing at him and keeling him overboard, but the brute with his cutlass levelled at his chest, and the sheer number of the pirates, told him the dice were heavily weighted against him succeeding. But he was not so mindless that he did not realise that the sole hope of preservation of every life on board the *Sea Hawk* depended on his wife. No one could accuse her of lacking courage.

But she could not mean it when she said she would go with O'Leary. The mere thought of being without her, of not being able to look upon her lovely face, was like a physical, unendurable pain. Followed by O'Leary, she came back to him.

'What you intend is madness, Cassandra. You will not set one foot on that ship,' Stuart said, his voice low and trembling with fury. He stood towering over her, his whole body taut. 'You cannot go with this man. I absolutely forbid it.'

Cassandra raised her face imploringly to her husband's, and then she looked at Drum. 'Leave us together for a few moments.'

Reluctantly Drum moved away, and with a movement of his head indicated that the pirate holding the cutlass to Stuart's chest was to do the same.

'Don't be angry with me, Stuart,' Cassandra said when they were alone. 'I've made my decision. Please don't make it any harder for me. At least you will be safe now— you will live, you and your crew, which matters more to me that anything else.'

Blind with rage, Stuart reached out and seized her arms, gripping them hard and shaking her to try to instil some sense into her stubborn, foolish head. 'You little fool. I would rather have my life disposed of than for you to go with O'Leary and his murdering band. Death would be preferable to being connected with such a bunch of vile miscreants. For God's sake, Cassandra, think about what you're doing. If you leave now, you're condemning yourself to a life of hell.'

A spasm of pain contorted Cassandra's lovely face, but her voice was soft and steady and inflexible. 'I'm condemned already, Stuart. Every man on board this ship knows who I am. If I were to return to England with you, it is inevitable that one of them will inform the authorities to claim the reward.'

'Aye,' he growled, 'and I swear they shall not live to boast of it.'

'Nevertheless I could not bear it. I really have no alternative. I have wrestled hard with my decision, Stuart—it is a decision I have not made lightly, and I believe I have chosen wisely. My love for you I do not doubt—but because of who I am, and the shame your association with me will bring to you and your entire family, I must go for both our sakes.'

Her face was filled with such utter conviction that Stuart became afraid that he was about to lose her forever. His grip on her arms tightened. 'It doesn't have to be like this. By running away you will be making matters worse. If you return to London with me, you can be sure that I shall do everything possible to make the Admiralty see that the only crime you are guilty of—if it is a crime—is one of association. I am a man of position, and my good relations with some of those at the Admiralty will count. An opportunity may occur, and if it should you will be there to take advantage of it.'

'I'm not altogether sure of that,' Cassandra said with a sad little flicker of a smile. There came the temptation so powerful as to be almost irresistible to give in, to cast herself into Stuart's arms and stay there, without further thought. She needed him so much, his warmth, his strength, but she must not yield.

'My life is at stake—the things I am accused of too serious to be set aside. Moreover, I am wholly convinced that the Admiralty has acknowledged my involvement with the stealing of the *Dolphin* and the disappearance of Nat's body, and wants to teach me a lesson. The worst I have ever done in my life was to sail on a pirate ship. Apart from that, I know I have done nothing wrong but regardless of those who speak in my defence, in the eyes of the Admiralty I am guilty.'

Stuart realised with a terrible, sick despair that she could not be persuaded. The realisation of failure invaded his brain and body, almost robbing him of strength, so that his hands relaxed their grip and fell to his sides. She stood before him, slender and lovely, looking at him with sympathy and understanding, and a great sadness in her tear-washed eyes.

'I love you, Stuart, and I shall die loving you. I could not change that even if I wanted to. It has become an integral part of me and I cannot begin to explain or analyse it.' She searched his eyes with eager tenderness for some sign that would tell her he felt the same. Her throat swelled with pain. 'I would accept anything life had to throw at me, misery, suffering and even death, if just once you would tell me you felt something—that you do care for me just a little.'

Unable to resist the appeal in her voice, in her eyes, which were brimming with tears, Stuart seized her roughly by the shoulders and pulled her towards him, his face, only a few inches from her own, contorted with a mixture of rage and desire.

'I do care for you—more than I have ever cared for any other woman in my life. Night after night on board this ship I thought I would go crazy with wanting you, knowing you were close. If I didn't feel anything for you, I would not have these feelings. But I fought the urge to go to you, hoping that with time my desire would lessen—that I would become stronger—but it was just the opposite. Each day I would look upon your face. You were there. You never left me, not for a moment, your presence and your beauty tormenting me—haunting me.'

Confounded by his revelation, Cassandra felt a warmth begin to spread throughout her body and she shook her head in incredulity, her eyes wide open and soft. 'Why— Stuart! I—I never dreamt—'

'How could you?' he said fiercely. 'I cannot explain what it is that binds me to you. It goes deeper than our marriage vows. It is more than a combination of your smiles and glances and feminine gestures that fires my blood and torments me so I believe I shall go mad with wanting you.'

Her eyes bright with wonder, Cassandra stared up at him, hardly daring to believe his words. Surely if he could speak like this, with so much feeling and passion, then he must love her a little.

'But when I remember my brother,' Stuart went on, 'all the fiends from hell rise up to torment me, to mock me, for making the daughter of one of the perpetrators of his death and countless others my wife—for, whatever the truth of what happened that day, Wylde played a major part in bringing it about and cannot be exonerated.'

'I know, and for what it's worth I cannot blame you.'

'Don't you see that I haven't the right to love you?' Stuart said, his dark eyes blazing with anger and frustration at not being able to alter the hopeless state of affairs that existed between them. 'But nor do I want to be without you. The thought is intolerable to me—and yet I cannot bear to look upon your face without remembering who you are. The scars are still too raw. I do care about you, Cassandra, deeply, and if I were in a position to do so I would do everything within my power to stop you going with that villain.'

Cassandra was deeply moved by his confession, which made their parting harder for her to bear. 'You are right. The barriers that separate us are formidable and I cannot see how they can ever be overcome.' Lifting her hand, she looked at her wedding ring and removed it slowly, holding it between her finger and thumb. Raising it to her lips, she gently kissed the bright jewel and handed it to him. 'Keep this for me, will you? It's bound to catch the eye of one the pirates if I keep it with me.' She smiled sadly, bravely. 'They would steal the teeth out of your head if they could.'

'And these are the people you are to live with.' Reluctantly Stuart took the ring.

'For a time.'

'And then where will you go? Where will you live?'

'I have a mind to live on the Cape Verde Islands. There

are people there that I got to know when Drum went to see his family. That was where I first met Rosa.'

'Please don't do this,' Stuart said in one last desperate attempt to make her change her mind. 'Whatever happens when you return to England cannot be worse than living among this bunch of murdering savages. Come back with me and we will face it together.'

Cassandra smiled her gratitude, for he would never know how much his offer meant to her. 'Bless you, Stuart, but no. My mind is made up. But—there is one thing you can do before we part,' she said, looking at him in a passion of love and pain.

One of Stuart's dark brows rose in question. 'And what is that?'

'Will—will you kiss me goodbye?'

Stuart did not need to be asked twice. Immediately he gathered her into his arms. 'I will kiss you gladly—but not goodbye. Never that—and if you should need me I will come to you. Only death will prevent me from doing so.'

And then his lips found hers, soft and yielding beneath his own as she returned his kiss. He crushed her to him in the wild hope that physical contact might accomplish what words had failed to do and break her resistance. When her arms came up to encircle his neck, for a time he thought he had won. She clung to him in desperation as time and the world around them ceased to exist. They became one entity, encapsulated in a timeless circle of enchantment that swayed in the light breeze blowing off the sea.

It was Cassandra who broke the spell. Placing her hands between them, she gently pushed him away, looking into his face with deep concentration, as if for the last time, trying to imprint its image on her memory forever. Stuart did not try to draw her back. He realised he had no choice but to accept the inevitable, and he steeled himself to let her go.

'At least I was fortunate to win your love,' he murmured.

'I disagree, Captain Marston. I would say you lose in every direction,' laughed Drum, coming to stand beside them once more, having watched their two bodies merge into one.

As he drew himself up straight, there was a hard glitter in Stuart's dark eyes, but his gaze went past Drum O'Leary and he smiled, a slow, curiously triumphant, satisfied smile, his teeth flashing in the darkness of his handsome face.

'I don't think so,' he said softly. 'Victory is not entirely on your side, O'Leary. Look over there and tell me—what do you see?'

All sails filled with air, two ships came racing down the wind to the *Sea Hawk*'s aid, their ensigns fluttering proudly in the wind, the sunlight gleaming ominously on the muzzles of the guns protruding from their ports. So preoccupied had everyone been that they had failed to notice the ships bearing down on them. Cursing loudly, Drum immediately ordered the pirate crews off the *Sea Hawk*, knowing they stood little chance of surviving a confrontation with two heavily armed merchantmen.

There was a bright flash from one of the oncoming vessel's bow guns as she fired a shot, aiming wide so as not to damage the *Sea Hawk*, but threatening enough to send the pirates scuttling back to their own ships and preparing to sail, leaving most of the *Sea Hawk*'s cargo intact.

Drum took hold of Cassandra's arm to escort her on board the *Dolphin*. The contact inflamed Stuart. 'Take your filthy hands off her,' he raged, lunging towards him, only to find a knife materialise, pressed to his throat by the brute of a pirate who had restrained him earlier, whose look and savage grin made no secret of the fact that he would dearly like to slice it open.

Cassandra spun round in alarm. 'Don't worry about me, Stuart. I know I have to make a new life for myself, but I shall never lose hope that one day you will be able to look on me and see me as I am, for myself alone—and not as the daughter of Nathaniel Wylde. Goodbye, my love.'

Stuart reached out and tried to take hold of her, to prevent her from leaving him, but he felt the warm trickle of blood run down his neck as the point of the pirate's curved blade pierced his flesh.

'Go, if you must, Cassandra,' he called after her, his voice vibrant and resolute, 'but I will not give you up. I will search for you and there will be no place on God's earth where you can hide from me. My determination to find you will be as great as it was when I hunted down your father. I swear it.' He steeled himself to watch her go, which she did with a terrible effort of will and without looking back.

Stuart did not know how long he stood at the rail, because his heart, like his mind, was void of everything but his loss. It was only when James touched his arm that he turned.

Like everyone else on board the *Sea Hawk*, James was now aware of Cassandra's identity and his face was devoid of every emotion except sympathy and understanding. 'What can I say? I didn't know. None of us did. I am sorry—for both of you.'

Stuart nodded, his expression grim.

'It's better this way,' James went on, aware of how wretched Stuart must be feeling. 'Being the daughter of Nathaniel Wylde, had she remained on board the crew would have mutinied—you must know that. She did the wisest thing, Stuart. If she were to return to England, in all probability she would hang. Not even you could save her from that.'

Stuart nodded wearily. 'We will never know, but—you're right, James. She did the wisest thing, and in so doing saved all our lives. We have all need to be grateful to her for that.' He turned to see the two ships of the Company ready to draw alongside, Samuel Tillotson's *Spirit of Enterprise* ahead of the other.

Stuart remembered very little of what happened after that. Like most merchantmen, the *Sea Hawk* carried spare gear and a team of craftsmen, who worked round the clock to repair the damage done to the masts and spars by the storm and the pirates, enabling them to sail for England, but much time had been lost.

Chapter Twelve

Cassandra's parting from Stuart had left her a desperate and broken woman. She existed in a deadly calm and a coldness encapsulated her heart in the same way as it does a corpse. It was a situation she believed she would never recover from.

She hated the *Dolphin* and all the men on it, but she endured it as best she could, rejecting all attempts at friendship by Drum and other members of the pirate crew. The men who sailed on Drum O'Leary's ship were a brutal and dissipated band of men, who bore little or no respect for her as a woman. It was only the fact that she was Nathaniel Wylde's daughter and under Drum's protection that saved her from being molested.

The *Dolphin* sailed to the Canary Islands off the north-west coast of Africa, putting in at Tenerife so that she could be careened. Careening was a major operation that involved beaching the vessel and scraping the barnacles and weeds off the hull, giving Cassandra plenty of time to bask in the hot sun and try to bring some semblance of order back to her mind.

When the ship finally sailed south for the Cape Verde Islands, her face was set implacably against the future.

There were people on the islands she knew, people who knew her—searovers' families of all nationalities, people she had hoped never to set eyes on again, believing she would never have to. She would live there and let time run its course until she had decided what to do. But fate had a cruel way of turning things about.

Two heavily armed British naval vessels, cruising in the area to protect British shipping—mainly the huge East Indiamen leaving the trading posts on Africa's west coast—hove in sight. Drum tried to dodge and outrun them, but the *Dolphin* was no match for naval vessels of this strength, which could both outgun and outman it.

They set more canvas and endeavoured to escape, but the *Dolphin* was unable to throw them off. The two ships gained on her and, when they recognised her, knowing her to be a pirate ship, they began firing their guns. The *Dolphin* was hit badly; when the naval vessels drew alongside the fighting was fierce. Few of the pirate crew survived the fierce engagement. Many were killed, including Drum O'Leary, who was felled by a single blow and sank to the bottom of the ocean with his ship.

Few prisoners were taken—just four men and one woman—and in no time at all the naval captain of the ship Cassandra was taken on to realised he had captured a valuable prize indeed. Nathaniel Wylde's daughter had a price on her head large enough to make it worth his while taking her back to England.

The tale, which had become exaggerated with the telling—of how she had cocked a snook at the Admiralty and stolen her father's ship from under their noses, and cut down his corpse from the gallows at Execution Dock before one tide had washed over it, let alone three—had given her a larger-than-life image and inspired awe and admiration in many.

It had also inspired a certain amount of envy. Because it was a woman who had committed these crimes and had escaped from the laws and conventions that governed their own lives and sailed away to live on sun-drenched shores, it made some people inclined to forget that pirates were ruthless barbarians.

Being a woman—and a beautiful one, as rumour had it—she did not conform to the popular image people had regarding pirates. The drama had created avid interest among the public at large—and caused acute embarrassment to the Admiralty. The fascination and magical aura of Nathaniel Wylde, which had captivated the public during his time as a searover, had been transferred to his daughter—a woman the lords of the Admiralty were determined to capture and see hanged from the same gallows as her father before her.

On reaching London, Cassandra was taken to Newgate prison. It was a new prison, only recently completed; the old Newgate had burned down in the great fire of '66. Its outward appearance was splendid, but the sumptuousness of the outside did not signify that its interior was as grand. Here misery and pain went hand in hand.

Cassandra lived in a perpetual state of numbness, showing not the slightest emotion. She was put in a dark, underground cell, one that was usually reserved for murderers and other serious offenders. It was stinking and filthy and infested with vermin—rats, black rats, their eyes shining bright when they caught the light of the single tallow candle, which burned in her cell.

Heavily shackled, so fatigued was she that she collapsed on to a pile of filthy straw and slept the sleep of the dead, utterly confounding her jailers. But when she emerged from the mists of sleep hours later, memories returned to torment her with a cruel vengeance, and she was plunged into a world of hell.

* * *

Cassandra had been incarcerated in Newgate prison for two weeks when Stuart arrived back in London with the convoy, unaware of the fate that had befallen his wife. The *Sea Hawk* was carefully manoeuvred up against the quay before a noisy and colourful crowd of people that had come to welcome them home, a familiar enough sight when any convoy of ships returned from east or west.

After seeing to the unloading of the cargo, Stuart left the *Sea Hawk* for the last time—it now belonged to the Wheatley and Roe Mercantile Company—and went immediately to his house in Bloomsbury, eager to see his mother.

He had not been at home long when a footman admitted an extremely agitated James Randell into the hall. Curious as to what could be so important to bring James to his home when he had parted company from him just a short while ago, Stuart excused himself to his mother and took James into a small anteroom.

Refusing Stuart's offer of refreshment, James came straight to the point, aware that what he had to disclose was too important to keep from Stuart a moment longer. 'Forgive my intrusion, Stuart, but after speaking to an acquaintance of mine at the Admiralty, what I have to tell you is grave news indeed and cannot wait.'

Stuart frowned, a feeling of doom invading his whole being as he looked at James, whose normally placid face was drawn with tension.

'What is it, James?'

'It—it concerns your wife.'

Stuart became motionless, as if turned to stone. 'Go on.'

'It appears that the *Dolphin* was intercepted by two naval vessels off West Africa. The *Dolphin* tried to outrun them and so they fired on her. After what appears to have been a fierce struggle she sank—taking almost every man on board, including her captain, Drum O'Leary, with her.'

Stuart stared at him hard, and for an instant everything

seemed to go dark around him as James haltingly explained the circumstances leading up to the sinking of the pirate ship. All the blood drained out of his face as he steeled himself to ask the question that exploded and almost shattered his mind.

'And Cassandra—my wife? Are you telling me she is dead?'

'No. She survived and was brought back to London.'

Relief swamped Stuart, but it was short lived. When he thought of the fate that awaited her, then he could not help thinking that perhaps it would have been merciful if she had gone down with the ship.

'Where is she? What have they done with her?'

'She is in Newgate, awaiting trial. Owing to the fact that she is Nathaniel Wylde's daughter, a great deal of public interest has been aroused already—and because of it the Admiralty wants it over and done with as quickly as possible.'

Other than a tightening of Stuart's jaw, he gave no visible reaction to this staggering news. Striding to the window, he stared out, his eyes filled with a scolding rage, his stance like that of a man who was being stretched on the rack. He could see nothing but Cassandra as she'd looked on the *Sea Hawk*—courageous, proud and lovely when she'd confronted O'Leary, and the look in her eyes when she'd confessed her love. A spasm of pain tore through him at the thought of her having to endure the horrendous conditions of Newgate prison, with nothing at the end of it but the gallows.

'So,' he said at length, 'it would seem she has been condemned without a hearing. She has automatically been found guilty and her trial will be a foregone conclusion.'

'Unfortunately, it certainly looks that way. Already the lawyers and the lords of the Admiralty are preparing their case—although it would seem there are few, if any, witnesses for them to interview. This may stand in her favour. They can find no merchants who can testify that she took part in any of the raids Wylde or O'Leary carried out on their ships.'

'Is she allowed any legal representation?'

'No. I do not believe so.'

'I must go to her immediately. I must see her,' Stuart said with a note of urgency in his voice. 'Thank you, James, for bringing me this news. I know I can be assured of your secrecy on this matter. It is imperative that for the present any connection between myself and Cassandra is not made public.'

'You have my word on it, Stuart—although I cannot speak for the rest of the crew.'

'I realise that—but with any luck, after leaving the ship they will all have fallen into the nearest taverns and will be drunk out of their skulls for a week at least.'

When James had left the house Stuart stood for a long time, thinking of Cassandra, hoping to God she hadn't been hurt. What he saw in his mind was his last image of her— the wrenching look on her face. The memory of that haunted him. It tore at him, along with other worries about her. Over the weeks since their parting he'd tortured himself constantly, wondering how she was. He had tried to put her out of his mind before he went insane—even then she had invaded his every waking thought.

It suddenly occurred to him that she was going to need all the help he could give to get her through this, and to keep the Admiralty from badgering her and charging her with collusion just to terrify her into admitting things that weren't true. A sense of urgency banished the defeated despair that had clouded his thinking since their parting, and his mind began to work furiously.

Making his excuses to his mother, he left. An hour later,

after lining the turnkey's pocket with a generous purse, Stuart was admitted to Newgate Gaol.

Never had Cassandra thought London could possess an establishment as grim and hideous as Newgate Gaol—a habitation of violence and absolute wretchedness. Alone in her cell, the walls running with water and slime, she was acutely aware of the sounds of the prison above, below and on all sides of her—of screams and groans, the rattling of chains and even laughter, which sounded quite bizarre to her ears.

The stench of centuries of rot was appalling and made her feel sick, giving her no appetite for the stale prison food her gaoler brought her—although of late she had reason to believe her sickness was caused by something other than the unappetising prison food: she was certain that she was carrying Stuart's child. At any other time she would have reason to rejoice, but with death looming ever closer the only emotion it inspired within her heart was one of dread.

After a few days she was allowed to leave her solitary cell and mingle with the other inmates of the prison—a curious mixture of felons and debtors, whores and cutthroats and the like, and, because of her exploits, she had already acquired a certain popularity. But she remained as distant from everyone as it was possible to do in the overcrowded prison as she awaited her fate with a courage that deceived everyone but herself.

Her wrists and feet were still shackled and sore but, thankfully, they were not so uncomfortable that she was unable to move around the women's ward where she was housed. In the confused chaos she lived each day in an atmosphere of foetid corruption, where every kind of wickedness and vice flourished. She soon realised that everything had a price and that existence within this grim establishment could be eased somewhat if a person had money.

And so it was with reluctance that she sold a gold ring to the greedy gaoler for a meagre sixteen shillings.

It had been a gift from her cousin Meredith on her eighteenth birthday and was worth ten times that much, but she did not expect to live beyond her days spent in Newgate so she might as well see them out with what little comfort could be bought. Besides, there were people who would slit her throat while she slept for being in possession of less.

She took little comfort from her appearance. Not since the *Dolphin* had sunk had she had enough water with which to wash herself properly. Her clothes were filthy, her body and hair were filthy, and like everyone else in this miserable place she was infested with lice. In fact, she looked no different from all the other miscreants who inhabited Newgate.

Keeping herself aloof from the other prisoners, she was constantly worried about her child since gaol fever was always present. The death rate was high and babies born in Newgate rarely survived in the foetid atmosphere for long. There was an ample supply of alcohol within the prison and gambling and prostitution were routine. People came and went all the time for there was no restriction put on visitors or whole families of the prisoners' entering, providing they offered a generous purse to the turnkey.

One day the warder brought Cassandra a bundle that had been delivered to the prison by Meredith. It was accompanied by a letter begging her forgiveness, for Meredith had neither the desire nor the courage to enter Newgate Gaol. She expressed her shock and grief on learning of Cassandra's incarceration in such a dreadful place, and she would pray constantly that she would be shown mercy and exonerated from all charges brought against her.

Cassandra expressed a feeling of guilt and self-reproach at her utter disregard for Meredith's feelings in the past, and as she looked sadly back at her life—to the time when she had suffered such harsh treatment at the hands of her aunt and uncle—she realised that Meredith had always been there for her. Meredith had deserved better from her. She should never have gone off to Barbados the way she had, without a word, without a thought, even—just a brief note.

The bundle contained some much-needed clothes, and Cassandra could not suppress a smile for, true to Meredith's character, they were warm and practical. There was also a large woollen shawl, for which she was especially grateful—not only because the prison could be so very cold at night, but also because it would help conceal her steadily thickening waistline.

Cassandra expected no visitors and wanted none. She had no wish for anyone to see her in such wretched circumstances, so she was surprised to hear the warder call her name one day. Looking in his direction, she saw him being followed by a tall gentleman shrouded in a black cloak.

The gentleman spoke her name, and his familiar voice struck straight at her heart as she watched him come towards her adoringly, feeling her heart fill and almost burst with the joy of seeing him. He was just as she remembered, tall and broad shouldered, with lustrous, unruly black hair, and when she looked up at the lean, bronzed, formidable face, the instant she met his dark eyes she felt a shaking begin in her limbs.

Stuart's presence swept away the ugly prison walls and once again she could see the blue sky and smell the sea and almost feel the wind on her face and taste the salt on her lips. In an ecstasy of love she wanted to cast herself into his arms, yet her heart had already made its choice between distancing herself from him and the happiness that could be hers for a moment in his embrace.

There was something inside her that refused to weaken,

for the depth of her love was too great to allow him to ruin himself on her account. She had to be strong—cruel, even—to send him away from her, no matter how it would kill her to do so. Pulling her shawl around her to hide her condition—which was not yet so noticeable, but she had no wish to give him any reason to suspect she might be carrying his child at this time—she drew herself up straight and, with as much pride as she could muster, looked at him squarely.

'Forgive me if I do not welcome you, Stuart, but as you can see I am not dressed for company—and nor am I in the mood for it either. What are you doing here? I thought never to see you again—and, indeed, I had no wish for you to see me in such wretched circumstances. Have you come to say farewell? Is that it—to gloat at my wretchedness and to see how well I am coping with life in Newgate? Well, as you see,' she goaded with a trembling little smile, indicating her surroundings with am exaggerated flourish of her arm, 'I am surviving well enough.'

Stuart's face darkened with anger, but he was not deceived. Looking down into her eyes, he read what was behind this show of bravado.

'You little fool. You know perfectly well why I am here. What did you expect me to do when I heard what had befallen you?' he said fiercely, appalled by her miserable state. He was sickened by what he saw, but his pity overrode his reaction to her surroundings. In his anger he wanted to tear the shackles from her wrists and feet. Although, despite this and the rough and tumble of her life, she was cloaked with an innate air of dignity. 'You are my wife, for God's sake. I have every right to be here.'

'No,' she replied, with a fierceness that surprised him. 'I am your wife no longer. If you feel anything for me at all, then you will go from here and forget me. Forget I ever existed. I can bring you nothing but shame.'

'I will be the judge of that.'

He cast an angry look at the other prisoners who, in their ghoulish curiosity, were closing in on them, leering and laughing with amusement, hoping to discover who this fine gentleman could be. Muttering a curse beneath his breath, taking her arm, Stuart drew her to a corner where they could converse with more privacy. The stench inside the prison was indescribable, but he was unaware of it or his surroundings. Nothing mattered to him at that moment but seeing his wife.

Looking down at her, he saw that, apart from her wrists rubbed sore by the manacles, she showed no after effects of the terror that must have gripped her on her capture, but, looking more closely, he realised that was not quite correct. In her wonderful eyes he detected a terrible anguish and despair, and it was this that struck him the most.

He was unable to believe that the filthy creature with her mass of greasy hair falling about her pale and strained face was his lovely young wife, and yet, beneath the dirt and grime, her pure and perfect beauty shone through and her manner and bearing distinguished her from the rest. A knot formed in the base of his throat, for she was still lovelier than any man could bear to look at.

'You have no idea how I loathe the thought of you being here—alone and defenceless.'

'Not so defenceless. My exploits have made me something of a celebrity among these criminals, and because of it there are those who treat me with something akin to reverence. No doubt they will shift their allegiance when someone more notorious than myself arrives.'

'Nevertheless, on my departure I shall leave sufficient means to ensure that your time in here is made easier. I cannot tell you how shocked I was to learn of your capture on my return to London. But be assured that no matter what the outcome, Cassandra—or this foolish charade you are playing in an attempt to shut me out of your life—I will not let you face it alone.'

'But you must,' she cried, her voice trembling and sounding like that of a lost child as she struggled to retain her self-control. 'Don't you see, there is nothing you can do? I will not be vindicated—I would be a fool if I thought that. For your own sake you must not divulge that I am your wife. It would be folly to do so and you know it. You must protect your family from scandal and disgrace.'

Stuart looked at her hard, but he did not contradict her.

'Go away, Stuart. Leave me to my fate. I don't want you to stay—and God knows you have excellent reasons for staying away. I am trying to resign myself to dying—and your coming here will only exploit my weakness and seduce me to breaking point. Don't you see that I have to remain strong to withstand this? You must understand that my feelings must be suppressed—that I must forget everything, for it is the only way I can survive these remaining days left to me.'

As Stuart studied her, his eyes clouded and his expression was transformed to one of impotent rage that she had been brought to this. Unable to look at the tragedy in her eyes, he reached out and took her hands, holding them so tightly that he hurt her.

'Listen to me, Cassandra. You are right. You must remain strong, but do not expect me to leave you here and forget you. That I cannot do. I want you to be safe—to be free of this place and the threat of death hanging over you. Whether we are together or apart, I desire only your peace and happiness. You must never forget that.'

'Happiness? With you?' She gave a sad flicker of a smile, her determination to stand firm against him beginning to falter in her eyes in which tears were beginning to form. She found his presence and the warm pressure of his strong hands holding hers both welcome and reassuring.

'That's just a dream. Even if the men who will judge me show mercy, because of who I am we could never know happiness together. But I shall remember to the end that brief time God granted—when we met...the cave, and our wedding...and the night that followed. I shall never forget how you loved me then. No one can take that away from me.'

Hearing the anguish in her voice, Stuart felt a wave of pity and tenderness sweep over him. 'I am hardly likely to forget that time, either,' he uttered hoarsely, deeply moved by her words, for they made him remember how wonderful it had been between them, also. Placing a finger gently beneath her chin, he tilted her face to his. 'You were beautiful as a bride, Cassandra—in a shimmering gown of creamy white silk embroidered with tiny pearls. You still are. But tell me—how are you really? Are you afraid?'

Pain clouded her clear blue eyes. 'Yes,' she admitted quietly. 'I am afraid. I'm not afraid of death—but I am afraid of dying. Who is not? Will you tell me what will happen? I need to know the procedure so that I will be prepared.'

'Yes, of course. But understand that I do not intend sitting back and waiting for sentence to be passed on you without doing everything in my power to have you vindicated.'

'That would be most unwise.'

A slow, lazy smile swept across his face, lightening the moment. 'Nothing I have ever done has been wise, so why change the pattern of a lifetime? Tell me first about your capture. When the *Dolphin* was overpowered by the naval vessels, were you harmed at all?'

She shook her head. 'No, I was not harmed, but there is little to tell. We were sailing to the Cape Verde Islands when we were attacked. The naval vessel was powerful— we stood little chance of escaping. The *Dolphin*'s crew put up a fierce fight, but most were killed—Drum, also. He went down with the ship.'

Stuart's eyes searched her face for some sign of remorse over the loss of her father's friend. 'And how did that affect you, Cassandra? Were you saddened to witness the death of such an old friend.'

'He was not my friend, Stuart—not after what he did to the *Sea Hawk*, what he threatened to do to you. But, despite the cruel life he led, I felt no sense of relief when he was killed—merely remorse and, extraordinarily, sadness, for the man who had been my father's friend for many years, and had once shown me as much kindness and concern as if I had been his own daughter. I cannot forget that.'

Stuart nodded. Regrettably it could not be ignored that both the ship and the man had been a part of her life. Like Nathaniel Wylde, O'Leary had come to care for her—as much as it was possible for a man of his ilk to care for anybody. In her ignorance and childish innocence Cassandra had given her father her love and O'Leary her trust, but when she had become fully aware of the evils of their profession they had whipped the rug of childishness from beneath her feet, turning her trust and confidence to disillusionment and disgust.

'Have you been questioned by anyone from the Admiralty—or anyone else, come to that?'

'No.'

'And you have no idea when the trial has been set for?'

'No. What will happen?'

'As you will remember from your father's trial, the legal procedure for dealing with captured searovers will be heard by the Admiralty and three or four common law judges. Any crime committed on the sea or in any harbour or river is not subject to the rules of civil law. I believe you will be tried by a Court of Admiralty at the Old Bailey.'

Cassandra smiled wryly. 'You are well informed, Stuart.'

'As owner and captain of a merchantman, with years of experience behind me and dealings with searovers and the like, it was my business to know such things. I shall make enquiries at the Admiralty, but James tells me there is a shortage of evidence against you. The merchants who were attacked by Wylde and O'Leary cannot testify to your being on board on any of their raids.'

'That's because I never was. How could I be when I was at home in Chelsea? Both John and Meredith will testify to that.'

'So the only charge against you will be the stealing of the *Dolphin* from her moorings and removing your father's corpse from Execution Dock.'

'Yes—and I know the serious nature of those charges alone are enough to condemn me,' she whispered. 'How long will the trial last, do you think?'

'I believe you can be assured the proceedings will last no longer than a day. However, in accordance with the usual practice, you will not have any legal representation, so you will have to conduct your own defence. Fortunately, unlike the majority of seamen brought to trial who have little or no education and are ill equipped to defend their case, you are well schooled and capable of doing that. Is there anyone you can think of who can be called on to testify to your character?'

'No. Only my cousin John—Meredith would be too terrified. But as far as I am aware he is still on Barbados. Perhaps the trial can be deferred until he returns.'

'I doubt the Lords of the Admiralty will be prepared to hold up the proceedings. What happened caused them severe embarrassment and they are anxious to make an example of you and get the trial out of the way with as little publicity as they can.'

'Then there is not even the faintest flicker of hope that I will be reprieved.'

'While you are alive never lose hope, Cassandra,' Stuart said fiercely, still gripping her hands, trying to infuse some of his strength into her. 'Unfortunately there will be witnesses to testify that they saw you on board the *Dolphin* on the night she was taken. But unless statements can be obtained from the seamen captured with you, it is unlikely there will be any member of a pirate crew to speak against you. Can you remember who they were?'

She nodded. 'There were four men who were captured along with myself. Drum took them on board when he stopped to careen the ship at Tenerife.'

A flicker of hope shone in Stuart's eyes. 'Are you certain of that? Think, Cassandra,' he urged. 'It could be important. Were they on board before that?'

She shook her head. 'I don't believe so.'

'Then that will be in your favour. O'Leary was a vicious character. Who is to say that he did not engineer the whole affair? You cannot deny being on the *Dolphin* that night, but anyone with eyes in their head will see you could not possibly have committed the crimes you are accused of.' He uttered a low curse on seeing the gaoler who had admitted him beckoning to him, indicating that he'd had enough time with the prisoner. 'I have to go, Cassandra. I promise I shall come again very soon, but in the meantime keep your wits about you at all times, and say nothing to incriminate yourself. I shall pay a visit to the Admiralty office and glean what information I can about your case.'

'But—they will want to know why you are showing an interest. You must not let them know I am your wife, Stuart.'

He shrugged casually. 'They will know soon enough. Don't forget the entire crew of the *Sea Hawk* know you are my wife. It will not be long before the whole of London knows it.'

'And your mother? Will—will you tell her?' she asked hesitantly, observing how his expression became tense.

'Yes. I must. I intend telling her immediately—before she learns of it from someone else.' Hearing the gaoler rattling his keys impatiently, he sighed, tenderly touching her cheek with his hand in one final caress. 'Goodbye, Cassandra. It seems I must go. Be strong—be brave. Your survival will depend on that.'

With tears on her lashes Cassandra watched him go. Automatically her arms wrapped themselves around her abdomen, wondering what Stuart would say if she were to tell him about their unborn child. Dear, sweet, merciful Lord, she prayed fervently, don't let them hang me until after my child has been born.

Chapter Thirteen

Stuart rode his horse hard back to Bloomsbury. The stark horror of the conditions Cassandra was forced to endure inside Newgate Gaol tore at his heart, and the fact that she was being hounded by the Admiralty because she had made them look foolish caused a surge of sickness and disgust to engulf him like a tidal wave of emotion.

As he entered the house, the luxury and elegance of the stately residence struck a stark contrast to the filth and squalor of the establishment he had just left. After scrubbing the stench of the prison from his flesh and changing his clothes, he went in search of his mother. She was in her apartment, sitting at her desk writing some letters.

Subjecting Stuart to a close scrutiny when he entered, she rose, full of concern. Anxiously studying the deeply etched lines of strain and fatigue at his eyes and mouth, she moved towards him, looking deep into his troubled eyes.

'What is it, Stuart? You look terrible. I'm not one to pry into your affairs, you know that, but ever since you came home you've been on edge. Is there something you want to discuss with me?'

'I must speak to you on a matter of great importance,'

he replied grimly, walking over to a side table and pouring himself a liberal glass of brandy.

Lady Marston's dark eyes narrowed into a slight frown, a pensive expression which heightened the similarity of features between mother and son. Of medium height, she was a woman with strongly marked features. Her skin was flawless and she had lustrous dark hair and eyes. Seating herself on the nearest chair, she watched as Stuart took a long swallow of his drink and calmly waited for him to begin.

Lady Marston listened quietly and with imperturbable calm as he began to speak. Stuart was aware of her still figure and close scrutiny, sensing how hard she was trying to quell the anxiety building up inside her as she struggled to take in the extraordinary tale and the enormity of it. The telling of his marriage to Cassandra in Barbados, her identity and association with Drum O'Leary, and the circumstances of her arrest and imprisonment, was long and difficult, because Stuart knew it would revive and force his mother to relive that painful time when Stephen, his elder brother, had died at the hands of Nathaniel Wylde. It would be like re-opening a still raw wound.

Usually Lady Marston's reaction to most things was one of calm and dignity, but what Stuart told her now affected her deeply. When he told her he had married Nathaniel Wylde's daughter—the villain who they had been told had been responsible for the death of her beloved son—her fine nostrils flared and she gave an angry exclamation, but that was the only sound she uttered as she continued to listen tight lipped.

When he had finished speaking, the echo of Stuart's words still reverberated in the room, and without saying anything she rose and moved away from him towards the window, turning her back and looking out in quiet contemplation as she tried to recover from the shock of what he had just told her.

Stuart respected her silence. After a while she turned and looked at him. There was no reproach or blame in her eyes, only pain and a deep unhappiness. It was clear to her now that ever since he had discovered who Cassandra was, he had been tearing himself apart with remorse.

'There is no one who could wish you happiness in your marriage more than I, Stuart, but I do have my objections,' she told him quietly. 'Nathaniel Wylde killed my son and almost wrecked my life—and yet, still he has the power to reach out and inflict further pain on me from his watery grave. To have you married to the daughter of the man who was responsible for Stephen's death I shall find extremely difficult to come to terms with.'

'I understand. I know how you must feel, Mother, and believe me when I say that I would not have inflicted this on you at any price. I know it won't change the way you feel towards Wylde, but I can tell you that he was not the one responsible for the sinking of Stephen's ship. It was one of his cohorts—a vicious individual by the name of Jacob Yeats. He fired on the *Evening Star* after removing her cargo. Wylde had left the scene, believing Yeats would do likewise.'

'Who told you this?'

'Wylde's friend—Drum O'Leary.'

'The man who attacked you?'

Stuart nodded.

'And you believe this man?'

'Oddly enough, yes—yes, I do, but my opinion of Nathaniel Wylde remains unchanged. I blame myself entirely for my actions, but it is done now. I only hope you can find it in your heart to forgive me. It won't be long before my marriage to Cassandra becomes common knowledge. You don't know how wretched I feel. I would not have hurt you for the world, Mother—you know that.'

'Yes, I do. I cannot deny that I am shocked by what you

have told me, but clearly it was not of your making. Although how you could have married any woman on so short an acquaintance—and knowing virtually nothing about her background—baffles and astounds me. It is unbelievable that you of all people could have been driven to do such a thing. You are not usually so impulsive, Stuart. Quite the opposite, in fact.'

'With Cassandra it was different. Never have I taken such trouble to secure a woman. From the very beginning we were attracted to each other.' He paused and walked towards the fire, where he stood, gazing down into the flames. The tense silence that stretched between them was shattered when he said softly, almost to himself, 'I adored her. Marriage seemed a natural conclusion.'

'Yes, I suppose you are right.' Lady Marston crossed the room and stood beside him. 'You say she took no active part in what her father did?'

Stuart turned and looked at her. 'No. She was as much a victim of his profession as those unfortunate enough to cross his path. Because of her strict and oppressive upbringing within her uncle's household, thirteen years old when her father made his first appearance in her life, naturally, she was entranced by him. What could be more exciting to a young and impressionable girl than to listen to tales of strange and exotic empires, of people as exciting and colourful and completely uninhibited as those he knew?'

'And her cousin, Sir John Everson. You say he is a proprietor of the Wyndham Company?'

'Yes. Cassandra was visiting him in Barbados when we met.'

'Wasn't she afraid of travelling all that way?'

A warm glow entered Stuart's dark eyes and he smiled slightly when his young wife danced into his mind's eye. 'No. She saw it as just another exciting adventure. Cassandra is not like other women, Mother.'

Her lips curved slightly in a wry smile. 'I'm beginning to realise that. Tell me about her.'

'When I saw her for the first time, she was unlike anyone I had ever known. She is incredibly beautiful and quite remarkable. She was still so very innocent and vulnerable—exciting to be with, warm and lovely, witty and quite wonderful. The attraction was mutual. I couldn't believe it could be like that between two people.'

'And now? Do you regret marrying her?'

He shook his head and looked down at the flames once more. His raw, agonised voice was so low that Lady Marston had to move closer to hear it. 'I cannot answer that. For some strange reason I cannot find it in my heart to feel any different towards her. I have tried—God knows how hard I've tried, but I cannot.' He looked at his mother, his face twisted into a mask of anguish, eyes bleak and fierce. 'When she left me to go with O'Leary I was the most wretched of men. I tried not to think about her, for I realised that was the only way I could keep a grip on my sanity.'

Stupefied, Lady Marston gazed into his tortured eyes and nodded, understanding, thinking he must love her deeply if just speaking of her could instil so much passion into his voice and bring so much hunger and pain to his dark eyes. 'She must be someone very special to mean so much to you. It's perfectly obvious to me that you love her desperately.'

'Yes,' he admitted quietly, wretchedly. 'I think I must. She stole my heart the instant I set eyes on her. But my love and the fact that she is Nathaniel Wylde's daughter do not sit easily side by side. Whenever we are together there is this frightful thing between us that I cannot ignore. It lurks in my mind like some concealed enemy. But—dear God, I miss her. She haunts every hour of my life. Sometimes I wish I'd never met her—never set eyes on her—and then I contradict myself.'

'If you truly love her, Stuart, love her enough, then you will have to accept her for who she is. Only when you cease to struggle against it will you know true happiness together.'

'And how can either of us know that when she is under sentence of death? Without any legal representation, she will be found guilty and will hang. I cannot bear to think of her in that place and I shall endeavour to do all in my power to save her from death—whatever sacrifice I have to make. She is trying so hard to be strong, to be brave, to face her trial with fortitude. Her courage is remarkable, but deep inside she is terrified.'

Stuart shook his head dejectedly and looked at his mother. 'It is hardly an appropriate marriage, is it, Mother? Not the marriage you had in mind for me. I realise how disappointed you must be—that this is very difficult for you—but not for one moment did I mean to hurt you. You must understand that.'

She smiled slowly and her lips trembled. 'Give me time, Stuart. As well you know, I have always been less concerned by conventions than most. It is your happiness that is my chief concern. But one thing I do know—that I have learned from bitter experience—is that no one should be held responsible for the actions of their parents. However…' she sighed, her eyes clouding over '…I have to say that I would find it easier to accept Cassandra had her father been someone other than Nathaniel Wylde.'

Some women faced with a situation of the kind Stuart had just presented to Lady Marston would have reacted violently, refusing to meet a woman whose father might have been responsible for the death of a beloved son, but she was not like most women. Her upbringing had been harsh and she'd had to deal with many things during the years of Civil War—and one thing she had learned in the most cruel way was that children should not have to account for the sins of their parents.

It was over thirty years ago, when Civil War had torn England apart, that her own father had raised a troop of horse to fight against the King. He had been a hard and brutal man throughout his life, utterly despised within the community in which he lived, but, being a dutiful daughter, she had never questioned this.

She had adored him and would have done anything to gain his attention and his love, which had made her blind to the true nature of his character. But she had quickly come to learn of the brutal acts he committed under the cloak of war. Because of him, she had lost the man she loved and was to have married, the man whose family fought for King Charles and whom her father had had arrested and imprisoned—a family who had never forgiven him.

It had left a well of hurt and bitterness inside her—made worse by the hatred her father had incited within the community in which they lived, which had become directed against herself and other members of her family. It was not eased until Stuart's father, Lord Marston, had come along and she had fallen in love again.

Alone, she thought a great deal about Cassandra Everson. No matter what she felt about her, she demanded attention and could not be ignored. Whatever the case, she was now her daughter-in-law. It would be unjust to presume she was equally at fault as her father. Moreover, Lady Marston had absolute confidence and trust in her son. He was no fool and it was unlikely he would be drawn to any woman unless she was worthy of his attention. Uninfluenced by emotions or personal prejudices, perhaps she should see for herself what kind of woman this wife of his was.

Cassandra became accustomed to spending her days consorting with murderers, rogues and thieves of all kinds, at the mercy of brutal and greedy turnkeys and malefactors alike. The days were long and passed in agonising slowness. She was deeply apprehensive. Tension was mounting and the clouds of suspicion hanging over her became heavier and more desperate by the day. Her trial loomed ever closer and her concern for her unborn child weighed heavy on her mind.

She longed to unburden herself of the responsibility, wanting so very much to tell Stuart of her condition, to have him advise her of what to do, but she knew she must keep it to herself for the present. All her hopes were based on insufficient evidence being produced at her trial, so that whatever charges were against her would be dropped.

If the worst should happen and she was found guilty and sentenced to hang, only then would she disclose her condition, hoping that in doing so her sentence would be postponed until after the birth of her child—which was usually the case for condemned women—after which time her sentence might be transmuted to one of transportation to Virginia or Maryland.

Beyond the prison walls the sun disappeared behind a thick blanket of cloud in the west, the darkening patches of light penetrating the small, high windows, prompting more candles to be lit, when Cassandra's visitor arrived. At first she thought it must be either the prison chaplain, who often visited her to preach and persuade her to repent of her sins and see the error of her ways, or Meredith, who might have managed to overcome her aversion to Newgate, but when the person came into view she saw it was neither.

She saw a woman, quite tall and impressive, dressed from head to foot in black with a thin black veil covering her face. But Cassandra felt the piercing eyes behind that veil scrutinising her and she was sure they did not miss a detail.

Clutching her shawl tightly about her, Cassandra watched the woman come closer. She attracted scant attention from the other prisoners as visitors of every class and distinction were regularly to be seen visiting relatives and friends in Newgate. Cassandra was glad she had worn one of the two dresses Meredith had provided, which, despite its plainness, was reasonably clean, although she realised she must still look a sorry sight with her lank hair, which she had managed to secure in a knot at the back of her neck, and her unwashed face.

Stopping in front of her, the woman raised her veil to reveal her face. Cassandra's heart lurched violently on recognition, for nothing could have prepared her for this meeting. Introductions were hardly necessary. Her visitor was too much like Stuart to be anyone other than his mother. He must have told her of their marriage after all. The two women's eyes locked and Cassandra fought to keep the tension of this unexpected visit inside her.

There was a pain in Lady Marston's heart when she stood face to face with the daughter of the man who had played a part in Stephen's death—Stuart's wife. The beauty he had spoken of, revealed by the dim light, made the pain worse. For a brief instant she wanted to lash out at the lovely face, but she stiffened, reminding herself that she was not going to judge her because of who she was.

There was an air of authority and vigour about Lady Marston's face that inspired trust, but, suspecting what was passing through her mind, Cassandra held her head high, unyielding and proud, looking nothing like a supplicant whose brief rebellion when her father had been hanged had placed her in this unfortunate situation.

Lady Marston was secretly intrigued by Cassandra. She felt a stirring of admiration and a good deal of curiosity as she held her steady gaze, which surprised her, for initially this woman's relationship with her son had not suggested friendly feelings. A dawning light entered her eyes as she recognised something intractable and self-contained that secretly impressed her. After a long moment she spoke.

'I had to come—to see for myself if my son's wife is as he described. Despite your background, Stuart speaks highly of you. It would seem your father has brought you little but trouble and sadness.'

'As he has to you,' Cassandra answered stiffly.

'Yes. Sadly, that is the case.'

'Forgive me if I seem surprised, Lady Marston, but you are the last person I expected to visit me here. As you can see, it cannot be described as a hospitable establishment,' she said, indicating her surroundings with disdain, knowing Lady Marston must find the stench appalling and the din deafening—with most of the commotion coming from a corner where a violent dispute had erupted over a game of cards.

'I agree. But it is no different from what I expected,' Lady Marston replied after taking no more that a cursory glance around her, her eyes holding an alertness and imperturbability. In fact, she seemed oblivious to it, which made Cassandra suspect that Lady Marston might fare better than herself in this place, that she would be well able to defend herself against the bullying and robbery that prevailed.

'I realise you must be greatly shocked, Lady Marston, by what has happened—but I assure you it was not intentionally done. Please understand that when Stuart and I married we were ignorant of the tragedy that affected both our lives.'

'Yes, he told me. He also told me it was probably not your father who sank the vessel carrying my son, but one of his cohorts. Whether it is true or false is neither here nor there. After all, he did attack the ship, so he had a hand in what happened. I cannot exonerate him from blame.'

'No, I would not expect you to do that.'

'I know how my son feels about you, Cassandra—but what of you? What were your feelings when you discovered that he was the one responsible for bringing your father to justice and ultimate execution?' she asked, the steady gaze of her dark eyes compelling honesty.

'Naturally, I was horrified. Indeed, after that, I truly believe I began to hate my father. But he was not always a pirate,' she said quietly, even now finding it difficult not to offer some words in defence of the man she had adored for so long. 'He was raised in the church and fought hard for the King during the Civil War. It was only when he became a fugitive and was captured by pirates himself that he forgot God and fell into a state of sin. I never meant to cause Stuart unhappiness, Lady Marston, but now I feel that he looks on me as his most bitter enemy.'

Her words extracted a cynical smile from Lady Marston. 'Give him time. He will revise his opinion. His hatred of Nathaniel Wylde is not as great as his love for you.'

Her candid remark sent colour flooding to Cassandra's face. 'He—he said that? He told you that he loves me?'

'He didn't have to. It's perfectly obvious.'

Cassandra lowered her gaze. 'Then he will resent it bitterly. I have caused him so much pain that he must rue the day he ever set eyes on me. I have little hope of a reprieve, Lady Marston, and in order to protect the good name of your family I have asked Stuart to keep his association with me secret.'

'It's too late for that. Since the entire crew of his ship knows of the marriage between the two of you, it won't be long before those in high places are informed of it. Stuart knows that. He has many friends at the Admiralty. Ever since he learned of your arrest he has been seeking ways of getting you acquitted—and if the fact that you are his wife will help you, then he will not seek to conceal it.'

Tears sprang to Cassandra's eyes and her heart began to beat more quickly. 'He—he would do that for me?'

'Stuart loves you very much—more that you realise, perhaps.'

'And more than I deserve,' Cassandra said softly.

Lady Marston's dark, assessing eyes rested on the young woman a long time before she answered, nodding slightly, 'Maybe. I don't know you well enough to contradict you. But what I do know is that he would sell his soul to save you from having to suffer the same fate as your father. However, having been on the receiving end of his villainy, depriving me of my eldest son, he deserved his fate.'

Hearing the sadness and bitterness in the tone of Lady Marston's voice Cassandra lowered her eyes, unable to look on the hurt in her eyes. 'How you must despise me, Lady Marston—and—I cannot say that I blame you.'

'I am the Dowager Lady Marston, Cassandra. You are Lady Marston now. It may surprise you to know that I do not despise you. I have not the right to judge you—for if I were to do that I would be apportioning blame, and I—more than most—accept that you cannot be blamed for what your father did. He was the sinner and he has been rightly punished. You loved him, didn't you? Your father.'

'Yes. But it would seem that I loved a man who did not exist.'

Lady Marston nodded her head slowly, understanding more than Cassandra realised what lay behind that statement. 'By his own actions he destroyed himself, and when he decided to make himself known to you—for whatever selfish reason and regardless of the damage he was doing to you and to your future—oh, yes,' she said, when Cassandra looked at her sharply, 'Stuart has told me everything about you that he knows. Your father, and your father alone, is responsible for this sorry situation you find yourself in.'

Cassandra was touched by and also curious about her attitude, knowing instinctively that she was undeniably sincere in what she said. 'Forgive me, Lady Marston, but I am quite bewildered.'

'Oh?'

'Yes. You see…not only am I astounded that you should come to visit me in this dreadful place, but I would have expected anger from you—hostility, even—certainly not understanding.'

Lady Marston's eyes narrowed and her voice became low when she next spoke, as memories she had tried hard not to recall came back to plague her. 'Be assured that I was angry and bitterly disappointed in Stuart's choice of wife. What mother, having suffered as I have, would not be? But the truth is that only a woman who has undergone a similar experience as yourself could understand what you are going through now.'

'A-and you have?' Cassandra ventured to ask.

She nodded. 'Yes,' she answered stiffly.

Suspecting that she had touched on a raw nerve, forcing her to recall something she would prefer to forget, Cassandra was immediately contrite. 'Please forgive me. I—I did not mean to pry or to upset you.'

'You haven't,' Lady Marston replied firmly. 'Besides, it was so long ago now that it's passed into the annals of history—and there I prefer it to remain. And now I will leave you. I wanted to see you and, now I have done so, I can quite see why Stuart fell in love with you. Whether or not we meet again will be for the court to decide. But please believe me when I say I wish you well.'

'Does Stuart know you have come here today, Lady Marston?'

'No. He would have been against it and tried to prevent me. Goodbye, Cassandra. I shall pray that the judge shows leniency towards you and you are exonerated from whatever charges are laid against you.'

Cassandra already knew that the date of her trial had been set for the following week when Stuart came again to Newgate. He approached her with energetic strides and she watched him with desperate eyes, searching his darkly handsome features for some sign that would give her hope, but there was none.

Seeing him again caused a painful ache to wrench at her heart. She loved him, wholly and completely, inside out for every hour, every second of every day. He was her reason for living, the one thing in her life that helped her to get through each miserable day in Newgate. She noted with alarm the lines of worry on his forehead and his tense expression.

'How are you, Cassandra?' he asked, devouring her features with hungry eyes. A shaft of light cut through the grime of a small window high up in the prison wall, highlighting the perfect beauty of her face. Looking down, he searched her eyes, seeing there all the misery she was being forced to endure. The blue depths were still and sad, but her mouth trembled into a little smile that almost broke his heart. He felt anger and protectiveness begin to simmer inside him—emotions that had been leaping into a steady flame with each new day.

'As you can see, my condition could not be much worse. But it's surprising how one adjusts to life in Newgate when one has no choice. But, what is it, Stuart, that causes you to look so worried? Do not spare me, I beg of you. Is the news you bring me very bad?' The grim look he gave her was enough to send a chill through her heart.

'It is not good. That is why I've delayed in coming. My time has been taken up with going from one Admiralty department to another. Come, sit by me,' he said, taking hold of her hands and pulling her down on to a bench in a quiet corner. Seated side by side he looked at her, his eyes holding deep compassion.

'Before we discuss the trial, tell me first how you are. I left a generous purse with the turnkey on my previous visit to ensure your shackles were removed and that you get decent food. Does he abide by that?'

'It was an immense relief to get rid of the irons and I am fed well enough,' she replied, which was hardly true, for the food she got to eat was only slightly better than the unappetising prison food. 'I think it's the lack of water to wash in that I miss the most. But is there anything new I ought to know about the trial? You know it has been set for next week?'

'So I believe. As you are already aware, the charges against you are based on eyewitness accounts of those who saw you on board the *Dolphin* on the night she was taken from her moorings. That evidence alone could not condemn you, but it would seem it has been reinforced by one of the seamen captured with you—one Jeremiah Price. Price is willing to testify that not only were you on board that night, but that the crimes committed were on your orders.'

'Which, to my regret, I cannot deny,' she whispered. 'I confess that I inspired Drum to do it, but I did not physically take part in it.' Suddenly her face became a mirror of confusion. 'But—I don't understand. I told you that the only seamen captured with me were the four Drum took on at Tenerife. This man Price cannot possibly know anything about that night.'

'That's what I thought. He also claims that during the time you sailed on the *Dolphin* with O'Leary you assisted in the attack and raid of a British merchant vessel off the north coast of Trinidad.'

All the colour drained out of Cassandra's face and she swallowed hard, staring at his shadowy face in disbelief, unable to believe she was hearing correctly. 'But—he couldn't say that,' she protested. 'No vessels were attacked while I was on board. Drum would never put Rosa's life at risk, or mine. Jeremiah Price is lying. But why would he lie?'

'To save his own skin. By Price giving evidence against you, his sentence will be changed from that of hanging to one of transportation.'

'And he is believed?'

'Unfortunately, yes.'

'But—what do the seamen who were captured with him have to say? Have they not been questioned? It can be proved that he is lying.'

'No, Cassandra,' Stuart said quietly, his face set in grave lines. 'It is too late. His comrades have already been hanged.'

Cassandra's features froze. 'Then there is no hope,' she whispered wretchedly.

'It is the only positive evidence they have against you.'

'And the most damning. With this I imagine there will be a charge of piracy against me.' As the words tripped angrily off her tongue she had no idea how close she came to the truth. Only when Stuart did not reply did she stare at him as one struck dumb. 'Oh, dear God! I'm right, aren't I? I have already been charged with piracy?'

'I'm afraid so.'

'And have any witnesses come forward from this vessel I'm supposed to have raided—if it exists at all?' she retorted bitterly.

'It does, but as yet no one has come forward.' Seeing the hopeless look of despair in her eyes, Stuart gripped her hands. 'All is not yet lost. I shall demand an audience with the Lord High Admiral himself if need be. It must be made known that this man is prepared to perjure himself under oath in order to get his sentence reduced.'

'Stuart, do they know I am your wife?'

'Not yet—which surprises me. I really did think that by this time the crew of the *Sea Hawk* would have been quick to divulge such a fascinating piece of information about their captain, and that the gossip would have flown faster than rats leaving a sinking ship.'

That made her smile. 'Perhaps the men are more loyal to you than you realise. Because of the part you played in capturing my father, it is bound to cause some confusion at the Admiralty for you to show so much interest in me, his daughter, and will surely arouse suspicion—if it has not done so already.'

Stuart shrugged. 'I know—and I have to confess that my persistent enquiries have already given rise to a good deal of curiosity. But it's of little matter now. And who knows, the fact that you are my wife could vastly further your cause. I shall endeavour to have you freed at all costs,' he said in a tone of such utter determination that Cassandra's heart warmed and almost burst with love.

'Tell me more about the raid on this mysterious ship, Stuart. None of this makes sense. Where and when did it take place?'

'The vessel was the *Triumph* and she was attacked by the *Dolphin* three leagues from Trinidad on the first day of April last year. The assault was vicious, the captain and most of the crew killed. Unfortunately for the prosecution, no one can be found to testify who was on board the *Triumph* at the time. No doubt the few survivors have since become scattered and joined the crews of other ships. The sole evidence depends on the testimony of Jeremiah Price, and he is prepared to give a detailed account of everything that happened.'

Cassandra stared at him in disbelief, a dawning of hope beginning to flow through her. Suddenly all her nerve centres that had been numb by hopelessness and despair for so long were sharply reawakened.

'But—on the first day of April last year I was on the *Spirit of Enterprise* on my way to Barbados. I left the *Dolphin* when she put in at Trinidad in March. Drum's attack on the *Triumph* must have taken place after that—although how the *Dolphin* could have attacked any vessel in the state she was in confounds me. So don't you see?' she cried ardently. 'I couldn't possibly have taken part in the raid.'

Realising what this meant a hard, determined light of battle gleamed in Stuart's eyes. 'Cassandra—are you sure of this?'

'Oh, yes,' she said, her eyes large and luminous in the candlelight. 'Captain Tillotson will testify to it.'

The lines of gravity on Stuart's face began to relax as he was fired with renewed hope. 'Samuel! But of course.'

'Oh, Stuart, please don't tell me he's somewhere on the high seas and cannot be reached.'

'No. He is still in England at his home in the north. I'll leave directly and ask him to accompany me back to London. He will come, Cassandra—for you.'

There was so much tenderness in his last words that Cassandra felt a stab of elation.

Stuart folded her cold hands in his strong warm ones. 'Despite your background he always thought highly of you. With his testimony, I can see a strong possibility of you going free. As long as I have breath in my body, no power on earth will prevent me from saving you from the gallows.'

Cassandra's eyes were enormous with a sapphire blaze of tears, her soft lips trembling as she looked at him in wonder. 'Why, Stuart?' she asked softly. 'Why are you doing this? Why should my fate matter so much to you? Feeling as you do, would it not be better to be rid of me now?' She expected a harsh retort, but all he did was shake his head.

'You little fool,' he said, her two hands remaining locked in his. 'The last thing I want is to be rid of you. You are my wife. That is why I must save you. If you are found guilty, there will be no justice on earth or in heaven.'

'And afterwards?' she ventured to ask, hopefully, desperately, wishing he had said he was doing all this because he loved her and absurdly disappointed that he hadn't. 'Is there hope for anything between us? There is a bond—we both feel it—but will you be able to live with me as your wife when all this is over?'

There was a catch in her voice and a note of pleading, for the only thing that mattered to her now and always was this man, her husband, who she felt still rejected her. If he continued to cast her away from him when this was done, better that she be found guilty and hanged, for her life would be of no interest to her then.

Immediately a cloud descended over Stuart's dark eyes and his face became grim. He released her hands quickly, frowning as he rose and stepped back, hesitating as he gave her question some thought. His eyes held hers, but the look in them was inscrutable. At length he spoke, his voice sounding hard. 'At this moment the only thing I can focus on is obtaining your freedom—nothing else.'

'But what use is my freedom if I don't have you?' Cassandra cried wildly, anguish tearing through her voice, her lovely eyes, naked and defenceless, locked on his. She stood up, reaching out and gripping his arm in a futile attempt to stop him leaving her.

'For the love of God, Cassandra,' Stuart whispered savagely, his eyes beseeching her not to continue in this vein. 'Please stop it. Don't do this. Don't torture either of us in this manner. You know how I feel—how things stand between us. You are close to my heart—and, yes, rightly or wrongly I do care for you, deeply. I want you more than I ever thought it possible to want anything in my life. But don't ask anything more of me than this just now.'

'Then I will wait—and hope that one day—'

'No,' he interrupted fiercely. 'I cannot ask you to do that.'

'That is something you cannot decide for me.'

Gently he released himself from her clasp and turned away, intending to leave her, but, hearing a low, strangled sob tear from her lips, he again looked at her lovely, anguished face. 'Take courage, Cassandra, and try not to be alarmed,' he said, gripping her hands once more between his strong fingers.

'I—I cannot help it,' she whispered.

Even as she spoke, unable to stop himself—unable to look on her wretchedness—Stuart's hands cupped her face and drew it close to his, kissing her lips tenderly in an attempt to reassure her, to comfort her—a kiss so very gentle and without passion.

His expression was oddly touching and Cassandra felt her spirits lighten. With his arms wrapped around her she melted against him, closing her eyes, wanting to savour the moment, feeling that she had found a safe harbour. But his embrace was brought to a swift conclusion when the turnkey returned, forcing them to part.

Stuart released her and stepped back. 'Goodbye, Cassandra.'

'You—you will come back before the trial, won't you, Stuart?'

'Just as soon as I return to London.'

When he had left, cast down once more into the gloom of her surroundings, Cassandra was engulfed in a sudden, frightened loneliness. Alone in the corner where Stuart had left her, she turned to the wall and made no effort to hide her tears, which were no longer droplets and flowed in abundance. Was it just a dream to hope Stuart would want her to be with him if she was exonerated? And what would his reaction be when he found out about her condition? Would he reject their child also?

Chapter Fourteen

Stuart left Newgate knowing there was need for haste if he was to ride to Nottingham and return to London with Captain Tillotson in time for the trial. All his bodily senses were concentrated on getting Cassandra pardoned. He must not allow himself to weaken by letting his thoughts dwell on her wretchedness or her parting words and the throbbing plea in her voice when she had asked him if they would have a future together should she be reprieved.

It was a question he had asked himself many times, a question he could fight no longer. From the moment he had become aware of who she was, he had not allowed himself to think of a future for them together, but now, realising that he was on the brink of losing her forever had reawakened him from his mental stupor. It was like being resurrected—as if a light had been turned on in his soul.

He already knew what it was like to be without her and the misery it created. When she had left him to go with O'Leary, he had told her he would not rest until he found her again, that he would never give her up, and, looking back, he realised that that was the moment when the truth had dawned on him—that while ever they both lived he was powerless to leave her. She was his wife. They would not be parted—except by death itself.

'So,' Lady Marston said, when Stuart told her of his visit to Newgate and his intention to ride to Nottingham, 'you intend to claim Cassandra openly as your wife?'

'It is what I want and the right and proper thing to do.'

Lady Marston rose from the chair by the window where she sat do to her embroidery, and crossed to where her son stood by the fireplace, staring absently into the flames. His face had a bleak, forbidding cast to it. 'Once it is made public, your marriage will be certain to cause a great deal of speculation and scandal. People will talk.'

'Let them. It will not bother me overmuch. It's too late anyway. Cassandra is my wife and I have no intention of divorcing her—or living apart from her, for that matter—should she be reprieved.'

Lady Marston smiled affectionately. 'You always were obstinate, Stuart. So like your father. But—tell me, if she is reprieved, have you given any thought to where she will go? Where you will live?'

'I've thought no further than the trial. But I suppose I must.'

'Then I think she should come here—or perhaps to Charnwood—until the gossip that will be sure to surround the trial dies down, and she ceases to be looked on as something of a curiosity,' Lady Marston suggested, having reached a decision, knowing she must put her son's happiness before all else. 'I find it quite nauseating how people gather to witness a potentially scandalous spectacle and leave when the promise of bloodletting has disappeared.' When Stuart stared at her in incredulity and amazement, she smiled softly. 'Where else would you have your wife go? What would happen to her if she didn't come here?'

'I expect she would return to Chelsea to live with her

cousins. But would you mind her coming here, Mother? I am not insensitive to your feelings and will only allow her to do so if you permit it. Would it not be too much of a strain for you living under the same roof?'

'I was shocked when you told me you had married her— because of who she is. But neither of us can make her the instrument for our revenge because of the crimes committed by her father. The impulse to hate will eventually erode our minds if we are not careful.'

'But old hatreds die hard.'

'Only if we let them. It is time to lay Nathaniel Wylde's ghost to rest, for no matter what misery he has caused us it was not of Cassandra's making. I do not make harsh judgements, Stuart—especially when I know how deeply you feel for each other. I do try to understand and make allowances.'

Stuart turned his dark, introspective eyes on her, sensing there was something she was not telling him. 'You always have. On that you cannot be faulted. But how can you know how Cassandra feels when you have never met her?'

'Because I went to see her. Forgive me, Stuart,' she said quickly when she saw him start, 'but it was something I had to do for myself.'

He was astounded. 'You went to Newgate?'

Her expression was grim. 'Yes—why not? Life has taught me to make swift judgements and I liked what I saw in Cassandra—despite her ancestry. She is everything you said of her—lovely and quite charming, with courage I cannot help but admire. She is well mannered and seems to have been well brought up by her mother's family. Of course, there is bound to be surprise among our friends by your choice of wife—and my acceptance of it.'

'And have you accepted it, Mother? In your heart, I mean?'

She looked at him levelly, hiding her own secret grief

that Stephen's death had caused her to suffer and the cruel manner of it, for she knew that life must go on. 'As well as I am able to do just now. In time, I would like to think that Cassandra and I can become friends.'

Stuart stared at her. His mother never ceased to amaze him. The gratitude he felt towards her for her good sense and understanding was quite overwhelming, but he did wonder how he would have taken it had her wishes run contrary to his own. 'Thank you. I cannot ask you to be fairer than that.'

It came as a crushing blow not to find Samuel at his home in Nottingham. He and his wife had gone to visit their son and his family in Newcastle and were not expected back for another two weeks. Samuel was due back in London to take command of his ship in a month's time.

Stuart was devastated. Nothing had prepared him for this. There was absolutely nothing he could do. If he were to go after him, there was no way they could reach London before the trial. He must return and try to persuade the Admiralty to defer it until Samuel's return or until other seamen who had been on board the *Spirit of Enterprise* at the same time as Cassandra could be traced. But time was of the essence.

Cassandra was locked in a state of perpetual suspense as she waited for Stuart to visit her again before the trial, but he failed to do so, which gave rise to all manner of terrible thoughts in her already tortured mind. Why did he not come? Never had she felt so abandoned and alone. It would seem, she thought bitterly, that fate was taking a malicious pleasure in making her suffer to the very limits of her endurance.

On the day of the trial, Cassandra was shackled and taken the short distance from Newgate prison to the Old Bailey

Sessions Court. Although her legs trembled and there was a weakness inside her enough to bring down the stoutest tree, there came to her a strength that made her walk steadily into the courtroom.

The crowds had gathered. Trials and executions had a grotesque fascination for the public, and the spectators who had come to stare, filling the Old Bailey to capacity, expected to see lively action. There was an air of festivity to the whole proceedings. Because she was the daughter of the infamous pirate Nathaniel Wylde, whose own trial was well remembered and still talked of from the meanest tavern to St James's Palace, the case was to prove sensational. It was a day that would decide the entire course of Cassandra's life.

She was nervous as she scanned the faces of those present in the courtroom for the one she loved, the one she hoped to see most of all, but it would seem that he had truly banished her from his life in her hour of need. But why? her tortured mind asked over and over again. Why had he abandoned her so cruelly? But, sunk in her misery and degradation, she realised that perhaps it was too much to ask for him to burden himself with a wife who was a common criminal, someone who had inherited nothing but evil.

As Stuart had told her, she was to be tried by a Court of Admiralty presided over by an Admiralty judge—a man in middle years with a severe expression and cold eyes, and three grim-faced common law judges. After all present in the packed courtroom had been made aware of the evils of piracy and the wickedness of all who practised it, the trial began—a trial full of traps for someone as unwary and innocent as Cassandra.

'You are Cassandra Everson, are you not, daughter of Nathaniel Wylde, the pirate hanged for his crimes?' she was asked.

'Yes. I am Cassandra Everson,' she replied calmly, looking directly ahead of her, trying her best to ignore all the ugly faces around her.

Her identity confirmed, the Register of the Court proceeded to read out three charges against her. She was accused of stealing the *Dolphin* from where it had been impounded by the Admiralty in the Thames, and the removal of Nathaniel Wylde's body from the gallows at Execution Dock in November 1671. The third, the more serious charge, was that of piracy—which, like murder, carried the death penalty.

'How do you plead?'

Filled with physical terror, Cassandra trembled, the cold eyes of the judges doing nothing to allay her fears. Exhaustion was beginning to take its toll, but despite this and her shackles she stood straight and proud, no one but herself aware of her inner torment. 'Not guilty,' she replied.

Despite the grime of incarceration covering her, her deportment filled most of those present with admiration. She was without the jewels and pretty patches, or the powdered hair and sumptuous clothes of a lady of distinction and refinement, but even without these artefacts, like a magnet, she held the eyes and attention of everyone in the courtroom.

It was as if she had weaved a mysterious and mesmeric spell around them, like some kind of sorcery, for how was it possible for a woman to look so beautiful when she was clothed in the filth of Newgate? Her blue eyes were wide, seeming to lighten the room like the sun coming out after darkness, and her proud bearing revived for many the memory and excitement that had so gripped the trial of Nathaniel Wylde eighteen months earlier.

But the atmosphere inside the courtroom was beginning to weigh heavy on Cassandra as she listened to the witnesses for the prosecution, hearing nothing serious enough to condemn her to the gallows—until the dreaded moment arrived when the seaman who was to testify against her, Jeremiah Price, was brought forward.

Cassandra vaguely remembered him. He was a man of medium height, thickset and with a massive barrel chest and long arms, which gave him a grotesque appearance and compelled all eyes to stare at him in fear and fascination. His lank hair fell about his face, which was huge and deeply pitted with pockmarks, his eyes deep set and malevolent.

He gave a formidable and graphic description of the attack on the merchant vessel, the *Triumph*, three leagues off the north coast of the island of Trinidad on the first day of April in 1672, stressing that Cassandra Everson had been a willing member of Drum O'Leary's crew, and actively involved in the working of the *Dolphin* and the assault on the *Triumph*—at which time she was seen to be armed with a pistol.

Cassandra listened in stunned disbelief as the man calmly and deliberately perjured himself, condemning her with every word in the ever-watchful presence of the court. It was a tale he must have been told and remembered from members of the *Dolphin*'s crew—and he was incriminating her in the hope of obtaining a lesser sentence for himself.

Tension was mounting inside the courtroom with spectators commenting noisily on the proceedings. Every ounce of humiliation was wrung out of Cassandra as she was subjected to cross-examination, when questions—endless, probing, intimate questions—were fired at her mercilessly, about her relationship with her father, and the night when she had taken it upon herself to steal the *Dolphin* from the place in the Thames where it had been impounded by the Admiralty.

Expertly they tried to trap her into betraying something that would assure them of her guilt, and when she was asked if she had anything to say in her defence her eyes again swept over the mass of quiet, mesmerised onlookers in the courtroom. She was hoping to see Stuart, but there was still no sign of him. Bravely she raised her head, looking directly at the judge and speaking composedly.

'I am absolutely innocent of the crime of piracy with which I have been charged here. I adamantly deny any involvement in the raid on the *Triumph*.'

She argued her case cleverly and with a simple courage that drew increased admiration from all present, but it was not enough to convince the judges of her innocence, who listened with closed ears.

When she told them she had left the *Dolphin* at Trinidad in March to take passage on the merchantman captained by Captain Samuel Tillotson bound for Barbados, and that she could not possibly have been involved in the raid on the *Triumph*, and begged them to defer the trial until Captain Tillotson could come forward to testify to this, her interrogator thrust his face close, looking her straight in the eye.

'Do not forget,' he expostulated, his red lips parting viciously between a forked black beard, 'that you are under oath. Do not add wilful perjury to your other crimes. If, as you say, you took passage on board this other vessel before the assault on the *Triumph*, then why has Captain Tillotson not come forward himself to testify before now?'

Swamped with hopelessness, Cassandra lowered her head, remembering how Stuart had told her that the courts were unwilling to hold up proceedings to enable witnesses to come forward. The Admiralty welcomed the propaganda value of trials and executions of pirates as a reminder of the fate that awaited others who had a mind to make piracy their profession.

After five hours the jury retired to consider the evidence, and they had little difficulty in reaching a verdict quickly—

Jeremiah Price had seen to that. When they returned, Cassandra knew, with the instinct of an animal in an abattoir about to come under the butcher's knife, that all was lost.

She stared at the men whose eyes were cold and expressionless, all the blood draining out of her face and leaving it deathly white. Everything seemed to dance before her eyes and she was possessed of a desperate fear as she waited, hardly daring to breath, for the presiding judge to speak.

'It has been unanimously agreed that beyond all doubt, you, Cassandra Everson, are guilty of robbery and piracy in the first and third charges. Can you offer any reason why sentence of death should not be passed upon you?'

Her mind a total blank, Cassandra listened in a kind of haze as the damning words passed over her. It was all so unreal. It couldn't be her this was happening to. It must be someone else. A muffled roaring began in her ears and a violent thudding in her heart. Her exhaustion was complete, and before any words could pass her lips her sorely tried nerves gave out and she fainted away.

When she regained consciousness, it was to find herself sitting at the bar and leaning against the hard wooden bench. Through a haze she became aware of a commotion and she opened her eyes, thrust once more back into brutal reality. But she soon realised that the sudden weakness that had overcome her was not the only thing that had created a disturbance inside the courtroom.

Rising unsteadily to her feet, she clutched at the bar for support. Across the courtroom a man had entered—a man accustomed to instant attention, with implacable authority in his manner and bearing, and he was tall, taller than most present. He pushed his way through the crowd with an irresistible force, as easily as a ship cutting through the waves, anger and frustration burning so savagely inside him that he was heedless of the watching eyes as he strode towards the judges.

His clothes and boots were travel stained, as though he had been riding long and hard. His dark eyes glowed hot and fierce out of features bronzed by sun and wind, his lips drawn over brilliant white teeth and his thick black hair falling about his face in a tangle of waves. He looked wild and furious and incredibly handsome—giving everyone present the romantic impression that he was a gypsy or a pirate who had come to rescue his ladylove in her hour of need.

'Stuart,' Cassandra breathed, happiness giving her renewed strength. She gazed at him with joy and disbelief, filled with self-reproach for having doubted him. Clearly he had good reason for not coming to her before, and no doubt she was about to discover why, but in that instant of seeing him her terror was replaced by happiness, and everything but the wonderful glow of her love was swept away.

He was prevented from approaching her, but their eyes met and locked, and for a brief moment time stood still and nothing else existed. There was concern in the dark depths of his eyes, but they also burned with a love and passion Cassandra had despaired of ever seeing again, giving her back some of her courage.

No one watching him could be unaware of his anger and frustration at having come too late, or how silently enraged he was to see Cassandra so humiliated, shackled and surrounded by guards. When he had entered the courtroom, what he had seen in her face had drawn him up sharply. She was ashen, her hands clasped together trembling, and she had been looking at the judge with huge, unnaturally dark eyes in which he could clearly read her terror.

In an agony of despair he had seen her collapse, and now he was unable to tear his gaze away from her tragic form as she struggled to regain her composure. Fighting to contain his anger, brusquely he recollected himself and drew himself up sharply, looking towards the judge who had just pronounced her guilty of piracy and was about to pass sentence. The judge looked at him irritably, displeased by the interruption, although he was not unaware of Stuart's identity or the part he had played in the downfall of the prisoner's father.

'What is the meaning of this interruption?' he demanded, trying to make himself heard above the loud ripple of applause from the spectators packed inside the courtroom, who sensed the drama was far from over and were enjoying it to the full. Their mouths agape, they stared at the newcomer, whose powerful presence commanded their attention and admiration.

'I would like to be allowed to speak on the prisoner's behalf,' Stuart said, in an awful voice and piercing deep. 'As I was made aware on my entrance to the Old Bailey, precious few have come forward to speak for her.'

'Perhaps that is because there is no one,' the judge replied coldly. 'Let me remind you that the accused is no pathetic innocent, as she would have us believe, but the daughter of Nathaniel Wylde—a vicious pirate justly tried, sentenced and hanged for his crimes, from whom she no doubt learned her trade. And, I will also point out, that when we have rid ourselves of such corrupting influences as this woman, the world will be a far safer place for the rest of us in which to live. I am aware of who you are, but for the benefit of the court will you give your name, if you please, sir.'

Stuart seemed to be able to hold himself aloof from the world and yet, with his mere presence, dominate the scene around him. 'I am Sir Stuart Marston—until recently owner and captain of the ship, the *Sea Hawk*, which is now the property of the Wheatley and Roe Company.'

'And what is your connection with the accused?'

'She is my wife,' Stuart announced quietly and firmly, to the absolute surprise of all present, rendering them silent, but then a gasp seemed to erupt from every throat as Stuart's eyes met those of Cassandra's and she smiled softly. Never had she loved him as much as she did at that moment.

The presiding judge's eyes narrowed after registering some astonishment, this latest information having taken him completely by surprise, for he was not aware that the accused had a husband—especially not a man who was held in high esteem by both the Admiralty and the Wheatley and Roe Mercantile Company. Nevertheless, he could not let this interfere with the course of action.

'Your wife? Correct me if I am wrong, sir, but were you not the man responsible for bringing about the capture of Nathaniel Wylde, the accused's father?'

'I was. But this trial is not about Nathaniel Wylde,' Stuart pointed out forcefully. 'As you said yourself, sir, he was tried and justly sentenced for his crimes.'

'As Cassandra Everson has been—or will be, shortly,' the judge replied imperturbably, his thin lips twisting in an expression of disdain.

'Her name is Cassandra Marston,' Stuart corrected him coldly. '*Lady* Cassandra Marston.'

'Of course it is, and I realise it is only natural for a husband to defend his wife—what man would not? However, I sense you are influenced by personal emotions and nothing more. So—if you wouldn't mind, sir, I would appreciate it if you would stand aside and allow myself and these other gentlemen present to proceed with sentencing the prisoner.'

'And I ask to be allowed to speak for her,' Stuart persisted, speaking authoritatively but with all due respect.

'You should have done so earlier.'

'Because of my efforts to trace a vital witness who would be able to vouch for both her character and the fact that she was not on board the *Dolphin* when she attacked the *Triumph*, I was unable to be here—and Cassandra Marston had absolutely nothing to do with it. I defend her because she is innocent of any crime and must be acquitted. I tell you, sir, and all present, that she stands unjustly accused. She is only guilty of being Wylde's daughter—and if that is a crime in itself, then over half the population of England would hang for the sins of their fathers.'

The spectators loved it and roared out their approval, drowning out the orders for silence. The courtroom was loud with applause and cheering, becoming all confusion, noise and madness, and the presiding Admiralty judge was far from pleased. As he half rose out of his seat, his voice thundered out to still the uproar. He gave Stuart an angry look.

'The trial is over. The accused has been tried and found guilty of piracy.'

'And I say that she has been found guilty on the evidence given by a villain who has perjured himself under oath to suit his own ends,' shouted Stuart, determined to fight for Cassandra to the bitter end. 'Jeremiah Price did not join the *Dolphin*'s crew until just days before she was attacked and sunk. If you condemn my wife to death, then I ask you, sir, are you prepared to burden your conscience with murder—for it will be nothing less?'

'Enough,' the judge expostulated, rising fully to his feet, his features becoming scarlet with sudden fury.

In fierce desperation Stuart was driven on, refusing to be deterred by the judge's anger.

'She spoke the truth when she told you she boarded the *Spirit of Enterprise* captained by Captain Samuel Tillotson at the island of Trinidad in March of last year. I have been trying to trace him for several days now to come here and testify, but he has left his home in Nottinghamshire for the north to spend time with relatives before he has to return to London and his ship. He is expected back in London a month from now and so I beg the court to adjourn the trial until then—or until others who were on board the *Spirit of Enterprise* at that time can be traced.'

The Admiralty judge was implacable. Captain Marston's violent interruption to the proceedings had caught him on the raw, angering him greatly, and he was determined not to swayed by it. 'It is only natural that you should speak up for your wife, but the trial is over,' he said with icy precision. 'I order you to be silent, otherwise I will have no choice but to have you bound over for contempt of court.'

He fixed his cold eyes once more on Cassandra, who felt her heart quake. She drew herself up instinctively, knowing there would be no deferment. She stood calm and erect, as if carved from stone, as she listened to him pronounce judgement, saying the doom laden, time-honoured words.

'You, Cassandra Marston, are to go from here to the place from where you came, and from there to the place of execution, where you shall be hanged by the neck till you are dead. And may God in his infinite mercy have mercy on your soul.'

A deathly hush descended on the courtroom, but why everyone should appear amazed by the judgement of the court surprised Cassandra, for it was no secret that the trial was a foregone conclusion before it started.

'No,' Stuart protested vehemently, his face becoming convulsed by a spasm of violent anger and exasperation as he faced the presiding judge, causing all eyes to turn in his direction and two guards to move towards him, and others to close in around Cassandra. 'The sentence of this court is unjust. She is nothing more than a victim of circumstance and guilty of no wrongdoing.'

'Silence,' ordered the judge, looking once again at Cassandra. 'Have you anything to say before you are taken back to Newgate, where the prison chaplain will come to prepare you for death?' he asked coldly, impatient for the trial to be over and the courtroom emptied of what he could only describe as a vociferous rabble.

Cassandra tore her eyes away from her husband and fixed them on the judge, knowing the moment had come when she must divulge her innermost secret in order to save her life and that of her unborn child. Drawing a deep breath, she did not look at Stuart. She dare not, but she was vividly conscious of his eyes on her.

'Yes—there is something I have to say. I—hope the court will show mercy when I tell them that I am with child.'

This stirring pronouncement brought a collective gasp from the mouths of all present. It sounded like a low hiss, followed by a stunned, heavy silence that descended on the courtroom like a blanket. Unconsciously Cassandra's eyes sought Stuart. His face was like a marble mask, betraying no emotion. It was as if he could not credit what he had heard. Suddenly the courtroom was in uproar, with people shouting in jubilation and laughing all at once.

At last Stuart's composure finally snapped and a flash of anger shone in his black eyes as, in the chaos that ensued, the guards turned their attention on the surging, heaving crowd in an attempt to restore order, and he found he was able to move closer to her.

'Am I to believe this? Is it true?' he hissed, so harshly that Cassandra trembled, quaking at the sight of his clenched teeth and flaming eyes. She drew her shawl tighter, wrapping her arms around her waist as if to protect her unborn child from this monster who was looking at her so accusingly, as if he hated her.

Steeling herself, she held her ground before his stare.

'Yes. It is true.' Brutally roused from the joy she had experienced on seeing him earlier, she raised her face imploringly to his. His jaw tensed, his eyes probed deep into her own, as if seeking something to weigh and to judge.

'You should have told me,' he rasped savagely, a vein beginning to throb beneath the skin in his right temple. 'You should not have kept this from me, Cassandra.'

Faced with his wrath, Cassandra lowered her eyes. This was not the way she had wanted him to find out about their child. She was swamped with dismay and severely disappointed by his angry reaction, perceiving in his words and manner so much anger and bitterness that she experienced a feeling of apprehensive foreboding.

Suddenly she wanted to burst into tears, understanding his anger, for was it not hard enough having to come to terms with and having to accept the daughter of Nathaniel Wylde as his wife without the added burden of a child, in whose veins his blood would mingle freely with that of his most hated enemy?

'Forgive me,' she whispered.

'How could you do this?' he admonished coldly. 'I just cannot believe it. Truly, Cassandra, I thought you were more intelligent than to keep such an important matter from me? '

'I—intelligent! How?' she asked, her eyes clouding with bewilderment.

'Had I known, I would not have gone chasing off to Nottingham. Can you not see that there would have been no need? Your condition would have been sufficient to have the trial deferred to a later date—to the time when Samuel has to return to London and his ship.'

'Oh—Stuart—I am so sorry. I did not realise,' she said wretchedly, her blood beginning to pound in her temples when she saw what a silly, utterly stupid, thoughtless fool she had been, and that she should have told him about the child after all. Without blinking, he continued to look at her with hard eyes, without expression, so that she was unable to read what he was thinking. The vein in his temple began to beat harder.

'It's too late for reproach. We can only hope it gets you out of this mess,' he rasped coldly and brutally before looking away.

Fearing that a riot was about to break out, immediately the Admiralty judge ordered the courtroom to be cleared, and not until then did he speak.

'Why did you not reveal your condition to the court at the beginning?'

'Because I was hoping I would be found not guilty and reprieved,' she answered, again seeking her husband for reassurance, for understanding, but seeing in his dark eyes only a blazing fury and a questioning doubt, which did not go unnoticed by the judge.

'Then you were wrong,' he said, his eyes moving to her waist, its thickening carefully concealed by the large shawl she had draped about her person. 'And, unless my eyes deceive me, your condition appears to be a surprise to your husband, also. However, you are not the first prisoner to be accosted and become impregnated inside Newgate in order to plead her belly to escape the gallows—and nor will you be the last.'

Cassandra's cheeks flamed with scarlet indignation at the intended insult, which went a long way to restoring some of her pride and courage. When she replied, it was to Stuart that she looked, wanting to reassure him that the child was his, and to reassure herself that the look he had given her a moment before hadn't been because he doubted. 'It is my husband's child I carry. No one else's.'

The judge nodded with indifference, having little interest in who the father was. He was only annoyed that the proceedings were to be prolonged by this unwelcome turn of events. 'As you say. And when do you expect the child to be born?'

'I—shall be full term in four months.'

'Very well. I have no alternative but to send you back to the prison where you will be subjected to an examination.'

As Cassandra was being returned to Newgate, she could not see, over the sea of heads, the coach that halted outside the Old Bailey and two people get out, a man and a woman, who struggled to get through the surging crowd and enter the courtroom.

Chapter Fifteen

Her pregnancy confirmed, Cassandra was returned to the courtroom, which was strangely quiet now, with just the presiding judge and Stuart and two more people besides, who she recognised at once and could not believe her eyes. It was Meredith and John, her dear cousins, who must be suffering all the tortures of the damned on her account. Immediately her eyes filled with tears and she felt strangely comforted and strengthened by their presence.

Meredith's face was white and strained, for the weeks of Cassandra's confinement had been like torture to her tender, caring heart. A smile curved her lips and her dark eyes were sweet and loving and full of pity when they rested on her young cousin. She would have liked to go to her, but the judge had ordered them to remain quiet until after the proceedings, which would not be long, for, after conversing with John and Sir Stuart Marston during Cassandra's absence, it had been made clear to him that there had been a miscarriage of justice.

John had arrived back in England the previous day, and Meredith had lost no time in informing her brother of Cassandra's sorry plight and the charges against her. Much as John would have dearly liked to visit Cassandra in Newgate to reassure her he would do everything within his power to help her, there was no time. Immediately he had set about trying to find Stuart but, failing to do so, he had enquired as to the whereabouts of Captain Tillotson, remembering the name of the captain on whose ship Cassandra had travelled to Barbados from Trinidad. She had spoken highly of him and he was convinced he would be willing to testify in her defence.

Having no joy in this either, in desperation he had successfully sought out some of the seamen who had sailed on the *Spirit of Enterprise* on her last voyage—which was what Stuart had intended doing, given more time—seamen who testified under oath that Captain Tillotson had indeed taken Cassandra and her companion on board in March of the previous year when they had put in at Trinidad.

Presented with such positive evidence, the judges were at last convinced that she could not possibly have been on the *Dolphin* when she had attacked the *Triumph* off the coast of Trinidad in March. They were also convinced that Jeremiah Price had perjured himself, which would add to his other crimes.

Having become an object of compassion, Cassandra listened in stunned silence as the Admiralty judge told her that because of insufficient evidence presented at her trial, and in the light of her pregnancy, justice was to be tempered with mercy and she had been reprieved.

Cassandra could not believe that her nightmare was over, that her ordeal was at an end. The nervous tension that had been ever present during the last few days finally snapped, leaving a crushing fatigue. Stuart ushered her quickly outside where the crowd was beginning to subside, but people continued to gape in curiosity.

'For God's sake, let's get away from here,' he said with obvious impatience.

Cassandra hesitated, looking back towards the courtroom

where her cousins had paused to have a word with the Admiralty judge. 'Please wait for John and Meredith.'

Noticing that Stuart's fingers holding hers were icy cold, Cassandra looked up at him. His face was closed and set and a hard line had settled between his black brows. From the moment he had found out about the child a change had come over him, making her realise that what she had hoped would bring them closer together might only have succeeded in driving them further apart.

Silently her whole being cried out to him not to turn away from their unborn child, to accept it as happily as she had, and when she spoke she tried to compose herself and ask with patience, 'What is it, Stuart? Have I upset you?' She saw how strained he looked, as if he, too, had gone through a great ordeal these past weeks.

'Upset me? How could you do that?' His tone was incredulous.

'When you found out about the child—your—your reaction was not the one I'd hoped for.'

'And what reaction did you expect?' he asked, sounding harsher than he intended, the joy and relief of her freedom overshadowed by this startling, shattering news about a child.

'Certainly not one of anger. I can see you aren't pleased. You don't want it, do you, Stuart? You don't welcome a child—or—perhaps it would be more correct if I said my child,' Cassandra said quietly, her eyes losing some of their lustre.

Her expression was so sad and wistful that Stuart was prompted to place his hands on her arms and look deep into her eyes. But how could he tell her how he felt when he didn't know himself? His feelings were mixed. 'Why didn't you tell me you were pregnant? In all truth, I don't know how I feel. My mind has been occupied for so long with the trial and concentrating on getting you acquitted, that anything else for the moment is hard to take in.'

'I can see that.' Shrugging his hands from her arms, she stepped back. The thin veil of joy and happiness she had secretly nursed since becoming aware of her condition evaporated before the harsh reality that Stuart did not feel the same—that he might reject their child. Rebellion and the fierce urge to protect it brought her out of her reserve, and as she looked at him her expression hardened and her cold eyes cut back at him.

'It is evident to me that the hot blood of feeling that so possessed you at the time of the child's conception has gone cold, for your look is devoid of memories or emotion. Perhaps it meant nothing to you after all. Perhaps it meant nothing more to you than an appetite satisfied—a return to carnal pleasure after an imposed abstinence imposed on both of us by you.'

'That is not true,' Stuart objected fiercely.

'Isn't it?' Cassandra flared, giving way to a sudden, almost uncontrollable burst of wrath. 'And you are sure about that, are you? I have just endured the most horrendous few hours of my life—when I truly believed everything was lost and my life was about to end, that I was going to have to suffer the tortures of being hanged like my father. When I was told I could go free it was like being reborn—but now I see that I am to be made to suffer yet again. No sooner do you arrive than you set yourself up as judge and jury when you discover I am with child. How dare you?' she said in a choked voice, fighting tears and struggling to keep her voice under control.

Stuart stared at her, white faced. After all she had been through, why did he have to hurt her—and in so doing hurt himself? 'It is not my intention to make you suffer any more than you already have. I would not do that to you.'

'Then could it be that your anger and air of tragedy is

because you believe—like the judge—that the child I carry is not yours? Are you trying to pretend that on the night of the storm, when you came to my cabin and made love to me, that it never happened? Because, if so, let me remind you that you were a willing partner—however much you have come to regret it since.'

'I don't need reminding. How could I forget? How could I forget something that was so perfect?'

'You must have known when you made love to me that a child could result from our union. That, Stuart, is how babies are conceived,' she said with cold sarcasm, enunciating each word.

'I do know that,' he rasped between clenched teeth, his voice filled with frustrated passion, 'but I was so carried away by my desire for you that I could think of nothing else. Yes, I admit it, I have hungered for you—but I just wish you had told me, Cassandra, that I didn't have to find out about our child this way, in a courtroom full of people.'

'So do I.' She raised her stormy eyes to his. 'But you see, Stuart, I dared to hope that when I told you the moment would be one of joy and exultation—a moment that would obliterate the tragedies of the past. I can see now that I was wrong. It's a blessing that John has returned from Barbados, that he and Meredith are here today—otherwise the situation would be one of immense awkwardness for you. I realise that.'

Stuart heard the bitterness in her tone and tried to get rid of the anger within himself. The people milling around only added to his frustration. He realised that Cassandra was suffering from shock and exhaustion, that it had been a long and gruelling day for her, and that she was unable to put the sentence that had been passed on her before her reprieve from her mind. But he could not dispel the shock of her announcement, which he was trying hard to come to terms with.

'Awkward in the sense that, without John's intervention, I would have had one devil of a job convincing the judge of your innocence. I cannot express my gratitude to him enough—which, might I remind you, you must do yourself. After all,' he said curtly, 'it was your own foolishness in the beginning that brought about this whole sorry business and must have caused him a great deal of worry and embarrassment.'

Wounded by his words, Cassandra felt all the pain of his harsh reproach, first with shock and then with fury—mistakenly believing that it was the knowledge of their unborn child that had driven him to accuse her so cruelly. She hardly dare look at him, yet, looking once, she was unable to look away. She drew herself up proudly, her ire ill suppressed, her eyes blazing a painful deep blue in her pale face.

'Yes—you are right. I was stupid. I more than anyone see that now—but I do not need you to remind me of it, Stuart. Especially not now,' she retorted with quiet anger, refusing to bow before his cruel accusation. 'To save my life I acted out of necessity. I had no choice but to disclose my condition to the judges—which I am now beginning to regret. Perhaps it would have been best for all concerned if I had kept it to myself and let them hang me and our unborn child. That way you would be rid of us both.'

The atmosphere between them was laced with bitter condemnation as they faced one another, each acutely aware that all the old bitterness was still there sparking between them, threatening to destroy any hope either of them had of a future together. But Cassandra knew that if Stuart rejected their child then she must formulate a future without him.

Her heart twisted agonisingly at this thought and she asked herself how she would survive the pain of parting from him forever—but her mind told her coldly that she would have to. She stood before him frozen to a slender sliver of ice. Everything about her had the appearance of cold transparency, her lips and her skin bloodless, her eyes narrowed and like frosted glass.

'Why your aversion to a child, Stuart? I know how difficult it is for you having to come to terms with marrying Nathaniel Wylde's daughter without the total change a child of his blood will bring to your life. But this is our child. It is nothing to do with my father. It was conceived out of our love and is a gift from God. Do you expect me to give birth to a monster?'

Stuart's hard eyes never wavered from hers as he stepped closer. 'What a dreadful creature you must think me.' His tone was cutting and contemptuous. 'What kind of man would be so unnatural as not to want his own child? To be deprived of its father because of the wrongdoing of its grandfather would be a dreadful penalty to exact on any child.'

'I am relieved to hear you say that because if, in your pride, you cannot overlook that, then I shall have no alternative but to accept it and make my own way…' She trailed off at the sight of the murderous look on Stuart's face.

'You really think that I would leave you? Don't be ridiculous.' Suddenly, uttering a quiet oath of exasperation, he reached out and grasped her hand. 'Come along. People are watching us. This is not the place to discuss such matters. It can wait until we are alone. After a brief word with your cousins, we will leave immediately.'

'Leave?' Cassandra asked stiffly. 'And just where do you want to take me?'

'You're coming with me to my home in Bloomsbury,' he told her with firm authority, almost dragging her towards a waiting carriage.

For some strange reason Cassandra found the prospect of going with him to his home most unwelcome. More than anything else she wanted to go somewhere that was familiar to her, somewhere quiet where she could lick her wounds until she was completely healed. A coldness stole over her heart. Lost in the complexities of the trial, she had temporarily put out of her mind what loomed ahead of her if she was given a reprieve.

'And—your mother? Are you telling me that she will allow me to live under her roof?'

'My mother is a woman of good sense and immense understanding—as you will discover for yourself when you become better acquainted.' When they stood beside the carriage he turned and fixed her with a hard stare. 'Why did you not tell me she had visited you in Newgate?'

'Because I thought she would prefer to do that herself. However, I—I am surprised she told you.'

'Why? What my mother does is her own affair. Far be it from me to tell her what she can and cannot do. But with you it is different. You are my wife and it is my wish that you come with me to my home. There I promise you will be given every possible care and consideration.'

Cassandra felt the anger that possessed him, and in the depths of her weakness and misery she might have let him persuade her, but then she saw Meredith coming towards her. With Meredith she would find the same warm, loving haven and affection that had protected her from Aunt Miriam and comforted her throughout her childhood and would help heal the wounds of these past months. With that, like the time when she had left Stuart on board the *Sea Hawk* and gone with Drum, the same strength that had helped her then came to the fore.

She twisted her arm from his grasp. 'Let go of me, Stuart. I am not going with you.' A hard gleam entered her husband's eyes and his features tightened remorselessly. In his arrogance he had been certain she would obey him.

'No? Then where will you go?'

'Home. To Chelsea.'

His lips twisted with irony. 'I was under the impression that when two people married their home was together.'

'The circumstances that exist between ordinary married couples hardly apply to us.'

'Maybe not, but enough of this. Don't forget, Cassandra, that I am not your cousin John.'

'You are right,' she mocked, infuriated by his imperious tone. 'Anyone listening to you now would believe you are my owner.'

Stuart drew back sharply, his dark eyes hard between narrowed lids and he spoke with chill precision. 'Does the thought of living with me in my house cause you such misery?'

His face was set implacably, and when she met his gaze Cassandra's heart was anguished. Unable to summon the fortitude to argue with him further, she lowered her head. 'No, of course it doesn't. But please allow me this.'

'Very well,' Stuart conceded on a gentler note. 'I have enough compassion for your wishes to agree to that. I will give you no cause to reproach me for playing the heavy-handed husband.'

Suddenly everything seemed too much for Cassandra. The excruciating terror of the trial seemed to have eaten into the deepest parts of her being and she stood beside him, almost too weak to speak. She wanted to cry, but the tears would not come.

'I am grateful, Stuart,' she whispered, 'to you and to your mother. But you must give me time to recover from this. I must have breathing space, somewhere to repose. The fact is that at this moment I can think of nothing but the simple matter of having a bath to wash away the stench and the filth of the past weeks. The memory of them may not be so easy,' she said quietly, unable to stem the involuntary shudder that swept over her. 'Anything else will have to wait. My mind is going round and round in worn-out circles so that I can no longer think or feel. I would be grateful if you would allow me to leave with my cousins quickly and without any bitterness.'

Stuart saw that her eyes were filled with a great weariness, the translucent skin beneath them smudged with shadows. He was deeply shaken and reproached himself severely for his anger at a time when she needed his support so desperately. He was ashamed. Hadn't she been tortured enough without him making it worse by wallowing in his own misery and inability to respond as a prospective father should when told that his wife is to bear his child?

A wave of tenderness and deep compassion overwhelmed him, and he was unable to resist doing the thing that came most natural to him. Reaching out, he gathered her into his arms, holding her tightly and stroking her head, trying to communicate to her his strength and his love, feeling her trembling against him like a crippled bird.

'Forgive me, my love,' he murmured against her wet cheek. 'I'm so sorry. I was angry—with myself mostly—with my inability to deal with a situation thrust upon me at a time when the only thing I could think of was obtaining your freedom. Throughout this terrible ordeal you have shown a strength and courage no one seeing you could help but admire. Not for one moment did I intend to cause you pain after all you have been through. But I have been driven almost out of my mind with worry.'

'I know,' she said, standing back in his arms and smiling up at him through the tears she could no longer withhold. 'I understand. These past weeks have not been easy for either of us.'

Despite the warmth of the day she began to shiver and, seeing this, Stuart removed his cloak and draped it around her. Taking her hand, he assisted her into the carriage where Meredith joined her, John climbing in and sitting opposite. Stuart looked at his wife steadily, with eyes heavy with fatigue, and when he spoke his voice was quiet and perfectly level.

'It may be for the best that you go with your cousins. They will take care of you. Perhaps when the events of the past weeks have been eased from your heart we can think about the future—to merrier times and the birth of the child.' Gently, he caressed her cheek with the tips of his fingers, his expression very tender as he gazed into her eyes. 'I'm truly sorry for what I said. It's just that I can't bear the thought of losing you again. I am delighted about the baby—' his lips quirked in a smile '—and so you don't doubt my loyalty or my love, we're going to have the most handsome child, with the biggest, brightest blue eyes you've ever seen.'

Blinking at the moisture that blurred her vision, Cassandra turned her face and brushed the palm of his hand with her lips. Her voice was hoarse with emotion when she spoke. 'I have a fancy for a boy who has his father's eyes and nose—but, providing it is sound in wind and limb, I shall be content.'

'Will you not come with us, Captain Marston, and see Cassandra settled in?' John asked.

Stuart stepped back from the carriage. 'No. No. Another time, perhaps. If I am needed, you know where I am.'

Deeply conscious of Cassandra's wretchedness, as the coach drew away Meredith took her hand and squeezed it affectionately. Cassandra's behaviour and casual disregard for Meredith's feelings following Nathaniel's execution had hurt Meredith, but that had not stopped her worrying about Cassandra and praying for her with all her loving heart.

'Everything is going to be all right now,' she said softly. 'You will get over this. I was most surprised when John told me of your marriage to Captain Marston—and I have to say that I like him. It is clear he cares for you a great deal.'

'Poor Stuart. Little did he know when he married me that he would come to grief. Oh, Meredith! Why does so much pain have to come from loving?' Cassandra murmured miserably.

'You must try and put all that has happened behind you now. You have the child to think of.'

Cassandra's lips trembled into a weak smile. 'Yes—yes, you are right, of course. I'm sorry, Meredith. I must look dreadful. Shockingly so.'

'Nothing a tub of hot water and some soap won't put right,' she laughed, as practical as ever.

Back in the large Elizabethan manor house in Chelsea, Cassandra's strength gradually returned. The awful spectres of terror and the stench of Newgate Gaol began to leave her, but no matter how an anxious Meredith fussed over her constantly, giving her accounts of their neighbours and everyday life in Chelsea in an effort to revive her interests and spirits, she failed to smooth the lines of worry wholly from her face.

Cassandra lived for the day when Stuart would come, and she clung to his parting words like a starving child clings to a crust of bread—that he would come to her and they would discuss the future, a future that was theirs to shape as they would—but deep inside her innermost self she was not convinced that he had meant what he said, that they were only words uttered to placate her in her distress. She was more than a little afraid that he would reject both her and the child completely.

Knowing very little of the unfortunate spate of events that had befallen her since her wedding in Barbados, or the part Stuart had played in bringing her father to justice, John and Meredith listened as she told them everything that had happened to her since they had parted. Naturally John was astonished, unable to believe the coincidences that had brought two people together who, unbeknown to either of them, were linked by tragedy, and he deeply regretted that he had unwittingly told Stuart that Nathaniel Wylde had perished at the Battle of Worcester, and in so doing heralding consequences he could not have foreseen.

The day was sultry and warm as Cassandra and Meredith walked along a narrow lane. The sleepy meadows on either side were strewn with daisies, the land shimmering in a haze of heat and evaporating on the horizon.

As a result of Meredith's generous compassion and care, and the peace and tranquillity she had found at Chelsea, the marks of Cassandra's imprisonment had been erased. Gradually she had begun to return to the land of the living, to look around her and appreciate everything there was to see with the kind of thankfulness and gratitude that can only be felt by someone who has been on the brink of losing everything.

They were heading in the direction of the house when they saw John strolling towards them accompanied by a gentleman. Cassandra's eyes opened wide, disbelieving, everything around her vanishing in a haze when she recognised Stuart. His long muscular frame was well turned out in a slim-fitting scarlet coat and breeches, the coat curving away from his chest to reveal a matching waistcoat. Scorning the wearing of a wig, Stuart had his black hair tied neatly back with a black ribbon. White lace frothed at his throat and wrists and white silk stockings encased his muscular calves. Never had she seen him dressed like this, or look more handsome, and the transformation from a ship's captain to a gentleman was immense—and yet the change was more substance than attire, for he still had the look of a sea captain and appeared most worldly.

Her senses were heightened sharply by her growing awareness of him, and there was a quickening in her veins, which brought a sparkle to her eyes. She stopped and waited for him to come closer, conscious of only him, of the slight smile curving his handsome lips. His bronzed features still held that haughty arrogance she knew so well.

The child chose that moment to divert her attention when it stirred inside her, invading her consciousness and making her wonder if Stuart had come to Chelsea out of duty rather than willingness. Drawing herself up proudly, she created an impression of cool reserve, her eyes as calm as the sea on a quiet day, telling herself resolutely that she would not succumb to the small voice at the back of her mind that urged her to throw herself at his head—not until she knew his intent.

'She is looking a good deal better, is she not, Captain Marston?' Meredith, the first to speak, smiled.

'She is indeed. She looks glorious,' Stuart replied, his voice rich and deep. He devoured Cassandra with his brooding eyes, dark and formidable. 'Chelsea clearly suits her.'

There was a moment of awkward silence, but quick-thinking Meredith took her brother's arm.

'Come, John. Walk with me back to the house. I'm sure these two have much to talk about. I must also inform Cook there will be a guest for dinner. You will dine with us, I hope, Sir Stuart?'

'Yes—thank you.'

Smiling timidly from one to the other, Meredith tactfully fell into step beside John, the two of them walking on ahead and leaving them alone.

Chapter Sixteen

His brow raised as he took in Cassandra's detail, Stuart saw she was in the full bloom of her pregnancy, that its radiance reached right to the centre of her being. Her hair shone with a dazzling brilliance, pale and silver in the sunlight, and he was sure that her eyes, wide and clear, were bluer than he remembered. A deep contentment swam in their velvety depths. She had lost the tragic air that had been present when he'd parted from her, and the gaunt look and unhealthy pallor had been dispelled from her face. Her cheeks were rounded and a warm shade of pink, and there was a vulnerability that had been absent before. And yet the calm detachment in her eyes as she regarded him made him wary of her—wary of approaching too close too quickly.

With the sun shining on her proud head, her face upturned to his, she looked radiant and sensuous in her pregnancy. He looked at her appreciatively, thinking what a gorgeous, exotic woman she was as he let his eyes dwell languidly on the full creamy mounds of her breasts, showing delectably above the heart-shaped neckline of her lavender-coloured dress, the extra folds of material about the waist comfortably accommodating the child growing steadily inside her.

The silence that stretched between them seemed to last for an eternity. Cassandra was utterly composed, her eyes steadily looking into his with what he thought was total impartiality, and Stuart felt the first stirrings of alarm, for he couldn't tell what she was thinking or feeling. Three weeks ago he would have known, but now he didn't and he was both puzzled and perturbed by it. She had always been open and approachable, but now she was looking at him as if he were just a mere acquaintance.

'How are you really, Cassandra?'

Her delicate eyebrows rose. 'I am well, as you see, thank you, Stuart,' she replied lightly, somewhat bewildered by his own reserved manner, and his seeming reluctance to venture too close. His eyes lingered on hers, a yearning quality in their depths, but, regrettably, there was also a tension in his manner that suggested the struggle was unrelieved by the brief time they had spent apart.

As she had watched him approach she had almost become two people. One was governed by the hurt and pain that spanned the time since Stuart had discovered Nathaniel Wylde was her father, and the other consumed by love and her need to have him hold her. Unaware that his aloofness had been brought about by the change he saw in her, it was the former that greeted him, which was coupled with doubt as to the sincerity of his visit, causing her to receive him with calm detachment, terrified of inviting new conflicts between them.

'And what of you, Stuart?' she enquired softly. 'Would I be correct in assuming that by your grand attire you have not ridden from Bloomsbury?'

'Quite correct. It's such a lovely day I decided to come by river.'

'Forever the sailor,' she murmured. 'And are you finding life on dry land agreeable?'

'I must confess to finding it somewhat tedious. It always takes time to settle down after being at sea for so long—but no doubt I'll soon adjust—as you have, I'm happy to see,' he said softly, his gaze holding hers, 'to being exonerated of any crime, and to being free of Newgate.'

'Nevertheless, the time I spent in Newgate and my trial are still raw in my mind. It is not easy to erase something like that. I do not believe I could live through such torment again. My cousins have been good to me, and so very patient and understanding.'

Stuart nodded slowly, a chill beginning to settle on his heart. She certainly wasn't making it easy for him. Something was lost and he didn't know how to deal with it or this new Cassandra. How was it possible that she could have changed so much in just three short weeks? He thought he knew her, her emotions and how her mind worked, but this new Cassandra, a Cassandra who seemed perfectly at home in serene, rural domesticity, evoked his surprise and puzzlement, prompting his mind to cry out for the adventuress in her to return.

His mind flew back to the lovely young woman he had met and fallen in love with in Barbados, when she had been far removed from the restrictions that govern the lives of young English ladies. He remembered the time as if it were yesterday, of how she had dazzled him with her vivid beauty, how they had both been instantly and violently attracted to each other, and how he had acted as any warm-blooded male would have done and pursued her unashamedly.

He remembered the thrill of excitement he had experienced when they had made love in the cave, and afterwards when he had made her his wife. Even when he had been made aware of her identity, which had driven a wedge between them, not once had he failed to admire the vibrancy and liveliness of her spirit.

They walked a little way, Stuart being the first to break the uncomfortable silence that had settled between them.

'I wouldn't blame you if you are angry with me, Cassandra. I feel quite wretched about the way I behaved towards you on the day of the trial. My conduct and absolute disregard for your feelings after all you had been through were inexcusable.'

Cassandra half turned towards him and smiled slightly. 'Yes, they were. But what did you say that I did not deserve? I should have told you about the child, I know that now. But I wanted to wait until after the trial, should I be acquitted, not to use my condition as a means to an end— which is how it must have seemed to you.'

Stuart looked at her, determined not to fail her this time. Staring down into her wide eyes that met his steadily, he saw that they did not soften under his long gaze but continued to hold a detachment, a calm watchfulness, which he was beginning to find infuriating.

'I've thought of you constantly, Cassandra.'

'Have you?'

He nodded. 'I wanted to come before, but, knowing how much you needed to rest after all you had been through, I thought you might prefer it if I didn't.'

'And here was I in Chelsea thinking you might have given up on me. You have been very patient—and I am grateful—but I wish you had come to visit me sooner.' When she saw pleasure and relief light his eyes she ventured a little smile. 'What brings you here now?'

'Tomorrow I leave for Charnwood and I would like you to come with me. It is your home now—and it is only right that our child should be born there.'

His words caught all Cassandra's attention. She stared at him, experiencing a flicker of alarm, unable to credit what he was saying, unsure whether or not she could cope with another upheaval in her life quite so soon. 'Charnwood? Forgive me, Stuart—but I—I thought—'

Anger flared inside Stuart when he fully comprehended what it was she did think, and that it might go a long way to answering why there was this change of attitude towards him, and why she regarded him so reservedly. His jaw tightened and his eyes became as hard as stones, a dangerous light flickering in their depths, as he glared at her.

'Just what did you think, Cassandra?' he said fiercely, reaching out and grasping her arms with a grip so powerful that she felt the pain of it. He forced her to look at him as she tried to avert her eyes, becoming increasingly annoyed by her coolness.

'Did you honestly think I would desert you now?' he said with angry frustration, wanting to shake her out of her lethargy. 'I admit there have been times when I have been driven to the limits as I have struggled to come to terms with who you are—but my loyalty towards the child has never been in question. Even if I wished to do so, I would not reject it now—and I assure you it will not be made to suffer because of its ancestry.'

'And how can I be sure of that?' Cassandra cried earnestly, fired by the anger in his eyes, having lived with the fear of his possible rejection of both herself and the child for so long that it was difficult for her to grasp what he was saying—and yet wanting so very much to believe him. 'How can I be sure that you have swallowed your pride and misgivings and will allow yourself to raise a child of Nathaniel Wylde's blood?'

'Because I have said so, and because you must.'

'Why must I? Cast your mind back to the time when we first met, and how firmly you decided against me when you discovered who I am. Because of that I have every reason to doubt what you say. How can I be certain your acknowledgement of the child is one of willingness rather than duty? Forgive me, Stuart, but I have to know.'

Stuart's complexion became pale with anger and his black brows snapped together. He listened with an air that was void of any remorse when she so cruelly chose to remind him of his treatment of her when he had become fully aware of her parentage. 'Why? What difference will it make?'

'A great deal of difference to me. I may be your wife, but no chain binds me to you.'

Drawing himself up to his full height, Stuart's eyes blazed down into hers. He drew a long, harsh breath and said curtly, 'What are you saying?'

'That I am a woman with an independent will, which, although it would pain me greatly to do, I can exert and live apart from you if you feel that you cannot accept our child out of love.'

Stuart let his hands drop to his sides and he took a step away from her, looking at her incredulously. 'I would not keep you against your will, but I expressly forbid you to even consider such a notion—and certainly not whilst you are carrying my child. I can understand why you must feel that way, but I did not believe you would doubt my sincerity.

'I have many faults—which I readily admit to—and the feelings aroused by the discovery of your parentage and your deceit in keeping it from me were natural at the time. You could hardly expect me to rejoice in such a connection. But do you think that because of this I have no heart or soul—that I would reject my own child because it will bear the stain of your father? What a poor, despicable creature I must appear in your eyes.'

He spoke with deep contempt, the delivery of his words cold and lethal, which caused Cassandra to feel somewhat ashamed for having doubted him. In no mood for further argument Stuart sighed deeply, fully understanding the reason behind her fears. Cassandra's eyes were downcast, the thick lashes making half-moons on her cheeks. A faint breeze blew some strands of hair across her face to create a fine web, and gently his fingers drew them back, causing her to raise her eyes and look at him openly and with love, aware as she did so of scalding tears burning the backs of her eyes.

'Having had time for contemplation,' he went on, his tone less cutting, 'I now realise that anger and hatred seem futile—and to continue nurturing such emotions can only lead to a lifetime of bitterness. Your father was justly executed for his wrongdoings and it is time to lay his ghost to rest.

'For the sake of our child we cannot allow this to stand between us forever. It is over—in the past. It's the future that matters. Despite everything, I believe we can have a life together—you, me and our child. We must build our own happiness—at Charnwood. Do you still doubt me, Cassandra? Have you no faith in me?'

He fell silent, watching her soft profile intently, his gaze long and searching as he waited for her to reply.

For Cassandra the moment was unforgettable, his words unexpected and more than she had dared to hope for, but she had doubted for so long that they could have a future together that all the obstacles to their love and life together were not easy to overthrow. Thoughtfully she began to walk on slowly, the light that had come into her eyes on seeing him becoming brighter.

Falling into step beside her, Stuart drew his dark brows together when she did not reply immediately and made a gesture of impatience. 'It is what you want, is it not,' he demanded harshly, 'unless you thought to remain here at Chelsea?'

'Of—of course it is what I want,' she murmured hesitantly. 'Forgive me—only—well, it is all so unexpected. I confess that I had thought of staying here with Meredith and John—at least until the child is born.'

'There is no question of that,' Stuart said firmly. 'It is my wish that our child will be born at Charnwood, where he or she will be raised in love, honour and decency.'

'But—have you thought seriously about what it will mean?'

Sensing her compliance, Stuart began to relax and smiled down into her eyes upturned to his. 'I have thought of little else.'

'When your aristocratic friends and neighbours discover who I am you will be ostracised.'

Stuart paused beneath some trees and looked down at her, his face grave and calm. Taking her hands, he drew her towards him. 'Do you believe that would matter to me, Cassandra? You are already my wife—and besides,' he murmured, treating her to one of his old wicked smiles which she had always loved, 'with my mother behind us no one will dare to slight us.'

'Your mother approves?'

'Yes. None of this has been easy for her, but she does understand. She is wiser and fairer than either of us give her credit for. She may not be able to bring herself to visit us at Charnwood for quite some time—which is only natural considering the past, but she will come, in her own good time. You have no objections to this, I take it?'

'No. I am not asking you to forgive me for all you have suffered on my account, but if I come with you I must be your wife wholly and completely. However,' she said, averting her eyes, a soft flush mounting her cheeks as she continued, 'you must not expect too much of me straight away. We must take things slowly—one day at a time. Do—do you understand what I am trying to say?'

Stuart's eyes were dark and compelling when he looked

at her, fully comprehending her meaning, and Cassandra was overwhelmed to see a passionate desire leap in their depths. She found him scrutinising her with a thoroughness that made her feel undressed. His gaze moved unashamedly over her high, full breasts, then meandered leisurely over the length of her before returning to capture her gaze.

Unable to prevent himself, or to resist the soft light glowing in her eyes and the magnetism of her softly parted lips, placing his hands lightly about her waist, Stuart bent his head and brushed her lips ever so lightly with his own, which caused Cassandra's pulses to soar. 'I understand perfectly,' he murmured, his lips hovering just above her own, his warm breath caressing her mouth, 'but you cannot blame me for having erotic thoughts and wanting to pull you down into the grass here and now and make love to you.'

Filled with a tremulous joy and yet pretending to be shocked, Cassandra gasped and allowed her lovely mouth to curve in a soft, haunting, sweet smile, unable to stem her delight as the atmosphere between them became light-hearted. 'Stuart Marston! You are incorrigible!' she exclaimed, placing her hands on her swollen abdomen. 'And here was I, thinking my size would put you off.'

Stuart kissed the warm hollow of her throat where a pulse throbbed rapidly, his lips like soft velvet. 'On the contrary. You have blossomed way beyond my expectations. You, my darling, beautiful, pregnant wife, are adorable, and I am considering the frenzy you will create when I present you as my wife to my friends and neighbours at Charnwood.'

Cassandra leaned back in his arms, a mischievous light dancing in her eyes. 'Because I am a stranger to them?' she queried. 'Or because I am the daughter of a notorious pirate?'

Stuart's chuckle was low and gently chiding, his warm

gaze caressing her face. 'Both. Do you know just how beautiful you are?'

Cassandra was taken aback by his enquiry. 'Beautiful— as big as I am?'

'Aye, Cassandra, and still virginal for all that.'

A hot flush of colour burned her cheeks. 'You of all people should know better, and the proof of it is for all the world to see.' When she felt his arms tighten around her she laughed softly and pushed him playfully away, all the while thinking that perhaps they wouldn't have to wait too long to experience such pleasurable delights of the flesh after all. 'You must behave yourself. Someone might see.'

'And what is wrong with that, pray? What is wrong with a man wanting to kiss his wife?' He smiled seductively and, with a sigh of regret, reluctantly let her go. 'Oh—very well. But do not make it too difficult for us. Do not take too long. Patience never was one of my virtues.'

Observing the softness of her face, something inside Stuart began to melt, his anger of a moment before having vanished under the tender assault she had on his senses and his impulse to protect. The barrier he had sensed earlier had crumbled with his kiss and suddenly Cassandra looked so young, so innocent. They stood and gazed deeply into each other's eyes and each knew what the other was thinking. Something passed between them, something they both fully understood, and, no matter how much hatred and bitterness lay between them, there was a physical bond holding them together which neither of them could deny.

When Cassandra saw the change in Stuart and the softening in his eyes, a solitary tear ran slowly down her cheek, which he wiped away gently with his finger.

'You are right,' he said softly. 'Perhaps when you have settled down at Charnwood—when the child is born and we have introduced some gaiety and laughter into our marriage—there will be better understanding between us. Until then everything in its own time. I promise you that I will be the soul of courtesy. You must not be afraid of anything—especially not of me. I know how hurt you have been—and I would have you know that I would not hurt you intentionally. There was a time when I never thought we would be together—I couldn't see how we could be, but now we are I shall make damned sure I don't lose you. I love you, Cassandra—so very deeply. I cannot live without you.'

Cassandra trembled slightly beneath the intense, glowing look that had entered his dark eyes and averted her gaze. Stuart reached out and touched the hair tumbling about her shoulders, then very gently he drew his finger down the soft curve of her flushed cheek and placed it beneath her chin, tilting it up so she had to look into his eyes.

'And I love you, Stuart,' she whispered. 'I love you so very much.'

He contemplated her for several moments, his dark, brooding eyes riveted on her face.

'Just don't keep me away for too long. That's all I ask,' he said, with unconcealed passion, drawn by the tenderness in the depths of her eyes and her moist, slightly parted lips. His voice was as rich and thick as honey, which made Cassandra think of the last time he had made love to her, of his body and the way it had attuned itself perfectly to her own.

'What the future holds we have no way of knowing,' she whispered. 'The past is gone and whatever regrets either of us have, we have the consolation of knowing it will never come again.'

Reaching inside his tunic, he brought out a small box; opening it to reveal the ring Cassandra had given back to him when she had gone with Drum O'Leary following the raid on the *Sea Hawk*, the beautiful sapphire and diamond ring that had been a token of his love on their wedding day—the ring she had despaired of ever seeing again.

'This, I think, belongs to you,' he said softly, taking her hand and slipping it easily on to her finger, kissing the precious gems lightly with his lips.

The token made Cassandra gasp with delight. Looking down at her hand, she saw how brightly the diamonds shimmered and how the sapphire flashed in the sun's rays. 'Thank you,' she whispered. 'I do believe it looks more beautiful than it did on our wedding day.'

Stuart smiled, pleased with her reaction. Cassandra raised her eyes to his and, placing her hands on his shoulders, reached up and brushed his lips with her own. With a teasing scowl he stepped back, taking her hand and tucking it into the crook of his arm.

'I think we'd best be getting back to the house. I am reluctant to start something we cannot finish.' Cassandra laughed with a tantalising seductiveness that delighted him, for it was reminiscent of the Cassandra he had met in Barbados.

'Oh, I don't know. The meadow grass smells so sweet— and I am sure it is as soft as a feather bed—that I might just take you up on your offer after all.'

Any anxieties Cassandra might have harboured about going to Charnwood soon vanished when she saw the house. Nothing could have prepared her for the beauty of it. It was a large, Tudor manor house near Tonbridge, close to the banks of the River Medway. It was built of local stone—a rich golden yellow streaked with reddish brown and rising in stately splendour over a large lake. The surrounding landscape was gentle and peaceful, with large, undulating stretches of parkland.

Because none of the family had been in residence for some considerable time, the house retained a skeleton staff and the estate had been left in the capable hands of a bailiff. During the early days Stuart had little choice but to leave Cassandra very much to herself while he familiarised himself with estate affairs. He was kept so busy that he had little time to think about or miss his life at sea but, even if he did have any regrets, they were of little consequence now he had Cassandra by his side.

Cassandra found herself drawn more and more to the stables, which Stuart was slowly beginning to replenish with fine bloodstock, and he would laugh when he saw the yearning look in her eyes, knowing how eager she was to climb up into the saddle and ride hell for leather through the park.

'Will this child of ours never be born?' she once complained with severe frustration after one of her visits to the stables when he was walking her back to the house. 'You have no idea how I so long to ride again.'

Stuart looked down at her, a smile curling his lips, his lids drooping seductively over his smouldering black eyes. 'I think I have. But I would not dream of letting you climb into a saddle so near your time. I want you strong and healthy, my love, for later. We have a lot of catching up to do after your confinement.'

Fully comprehending his meaning she flushed prettily. 'Then for the time being I will have to content myself with the carriage,' she quipped light-heartedly, 'but it's not nearly as much fun.'

'I once remember you telling me that you rode like a gypsy—and I can well imagine you with your hair flying out behind you like the pennant attached to the mast on the *Sea Hawk*, and the wind on your face, dropping your cares like fancies along the wayside as you ride by. There will be time enough for me to show you the parts of the estate the carriage cannot reach after the child is born.'

If Cassandra had thought her marriage to Stuart would

ostracise him from friends and neighbours, she was wrong—in fact, it had quite the opposite effect and caused intense excitement. Everyone was intrigued by their strange marriage and more than a little curious to see if Nathaniel Wylde's daughter was as beautiful, and as wild, as rumour had it.

Those who saw her riding by in the carriage were not disappointed. With wry humour, Stuart pointed out on more than one occasion, which brought a smile of amusement to Cassandra's lips, that most of their bewigged and dandified neighbours, who considered themselves to be a cut above the rest, had more than one skeleton propped up in their ever-so-expensive cupboards.

Their son slipped into the world with relative ease, a big lusty boy with a cap of black hair and, as he suckled greedily at his mother's breast, he was blissfully unaware of all the pain and sadness that had almost driven his parents apart.

The moment Stuart picked him up and held him close in the curve of his arm, the infant entered his heart, holding it so tightly that he knew he would never let go. He was a beautiful child, as dark as a gypsy, with hair the same colour as his own. Briefly the image of Nathaniel Wylde entered his mind and he was thankful his son bore him no resemblance.

Cassandra's eyes were soft with love as they dwelt on father and son and tears of unbelievable happiness shone in her eyes, for it was a sight she had once, not so very long ago, despaired of seeing.

'He's a fine boy, don't you agree, Stuart?'

'Yes, a fine, beautiful boy, indeed.'

'And—and you will not blame him…' The question she had been about to ask trailed away when Stuart cast her a fierce glance, drawn towards where she lay by the dazzling brilliance in her eyes.

'Never. He is our son, Cassandra—yours and mine—no one else's.'

Cassandra cherished those early days after their son was born—basking in the closeness and intimacy and the long silent looks from Stuart as he went about his work. They spoke little, having no need for words with this new understanding between them, and their son drawing them closer with each new day. But when they were alone, Stuart made no attempt to touch her or draw her into his arms, for this new relationship, without shyness or restraint, was so wonderful that neither wanted to shatter it. They wanted it to go on and on, the days belonging only to them, where nothing else mattered but each other.

But it was the nights that were a problem, when each would go to their separate beds. It was a state of affairs that could not continue.

When their son was two months old, Cassandra decided it was time to take the initiative.

At Christmas they were to give a ball, the first major event at Charnwood since Stephen had died. Invitations were sent out to the local gentry and affluent guests invited from London. Even though the roads would be virtually impassable in parts owing to the dismal winter weather, few declined the invitation. Curiosity to see the couple who had married in adversity was too great to resist.

Stuart's mother had arrived at Charnwood after the birth of the child, determined to take a leaf out of her son's book and make the best of the situation. She had the wisdom and good sense to see that Cassandra would make him a loving and caring wife. Stuart was extremely fortunate. Despite the identity of the child's maternal grandfather, the Dowager Lady Marston adored her grandson to distraction.

When trunks were delivered to Charnwood—Stuart's property and Cassandra's own from the *Sea Hawk*, she had no difficulty in deciding what she would wear for the ball, insisting on keeping her dress a secret, no matter how hard Stuart tried teasing it out of her.

The evening promised to be a splendid affair. The house was filled with the sound of music and exotic flowers were sent down from London, with only the finest food and wines for the guests. As Cassandra dressed for the occasion she was nervous and oddly excited. Many of the people due to arrive had never seen her, and she knew they were in for a surprise—as was her husband.

Assisted by her maid, it was for Stuart that she bathed and anointed her body with lightly scented jasmine, before dressing in the shimmering gown of creamy white silk gauze embroidered all over with tiny pearls—the gown she had worn as a bride on her wedding day. She luxuriated in the delicious feel of it as it caressed her body. Her shimmering wealth of hair, brushed to a silky sheen, was unadorned, and hung down the length of her back.

When Stuart entered to escort his wife down to their guests, resplendent in black coat and knee breeches, white silk stockings and delicate white lace at his throat, he stared at her, at a complete loss for words. He had known her gown was to be something special, but he had not expected this.

She stood tall and proud, watching him calmly, as his eyes travelled from the top of her shining head to the slippers on her slender feet, with incredulity and disbelief, before meeting her eyes. They looked at each other for a long moment that stretched into eternity—each remembering the last time she had worn the gown, and the occasion, and

wishing, with love and longing, for the evening to end so
they could be alone at last.

'What can I say?' he murmured at length, moving to
stand in front of her. 'You look quite incredible and as
exquisite now as you did on our wedding day.'

Cassandra trembled, looking up into his dark, brooding
eyes, her face full of passion and her moist lips parted and
quivering, longing for the kiss she expected but did not
come. Instead he brushed her lips with the tips of his fingers, sensing her mood.

'If I kiss you now, my love,' he said hoarsely, his eyes
dark and filled with passion, 'I shall not be answerable for
my actions. But later, when our guests have gone, nothing
will keep me from you. I will make love to you until you
beg for mercy.' His lips curled into a smile at the warm
glow that shone in her wonderful blue eyes, which told him
he would be welcome. 'Now, come—let us greet our
guests. Everyone is curious to meet you—and I am convinced they will be impressed. Not only will you charm
each and every one of them—but you'll give them something to talk about for a long time to come.'

The ball was a huge success and it was almost daybreak
when the magic moment that would elevate Stuart and Cassandra out of time arrived, but they had been apart too long
for Stuart to hurry. Lithe of limb and graceful, Cassandra
raised her arms and began to remove her gown but he
stopped her, preferring to do it himself, to feel its silky
softness, and, lowering her arms, she happily gave herself
over to him.

He proceeded to do what his fingers had ached to do all
evening. Slowly and methodically he undressed her and
spread her hair like a soft, shimmering cloud over her
gleaming shoulders before gathering her up into his arms
and carrying her to the bed.

As he leaned over her, his warm, moist lips began to kiss every inch of her naked body and, overwhelmed by the intensity of his passion, Cassandra yielded herself to his soft, caressing touch willingly, clutching and clinging, and they came together as easily as night follows day.

They loved and slept and towards morning there was more love, and by the time the sun rose Stuart knew that the wonderful adventuress he had met and fallen in love with in Barbados had returned to him. She had not vanished, after all. She was there, just waiting to be resurrected.

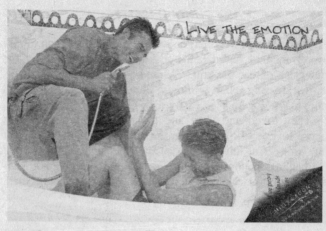

Modern Romance™
...seduction and
passion guaranteed

Tender Romance™
...love affairs that
last a lifetime

Medical Romance™
...medical drama
on the pulse

Historical Romance™
...rich, vivid and
passionate

Sensual Romance™
...sassy, sexy and
seductive

Blaze Romance™
...the temperature's
rising

27 new titles every month.

Live the emotion

MILLS & BOON®

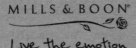

MILLS & BOON®

Live the emotion

Historical Romance™

ONE NIGHT WITH A RAKE
by Louise Allen

Beautiful widow Amanda Clare woke in a strange bed, next to
a tall, dark and very handsome stranger. Knocked out in a
stagecoach accident, they'd been rescued and it had been
assumed they were married! Amanda had no idea who the
man was – and, intriguingly, neither did he.
The gentleman had lost his memory...

Regency

COLONEL ANCROFT'S LOVE
by Sylvia Andrew

When Colonel John Ancroft is persuaded to escort an elderly
widow to Yorkshire, he has no idea that the lady in question is
heiress Caroline Duval. Her disguise is revealed when he happens
upon her swimming naked in a pool, and his self-control is severely
tested as he confronts this bewitching flame-haired beauty...

Regency

THE ELUSIVE BRIDE by Deborah Hale

12th century England

To protect her home and people, Cecily Tyrell would marry the
devil himself – and if rumour held any truth, she might just have
to! Lord Rowan DeCourtenay was a knight of some renown –
but a widower of some repute. Still, he was the warrior she
needed – but was he the man she wanted?

On sale 3rd October 2003

*Available at most branches of WHSmith, Tesco, Martins, Borders,
Eason, Sainsbury's and all good paperback bookshops.*

0903/04

FREE
2 BOOKS
AND A SURPRISE GIFT!

We would like to take this opportunity to thank you for reading this Mills & Boon® book by offering you the chance to take TWO more specially selected titles from the Historical Romance™ series absolutely FREE! We're also making this offer to introduce you to the benefits of the Reader Service™ —

- ★ FREE home delivery
- ★ FREE monthly Newsletter
- ★ FREE gifts and competitions
- ★ Exclusive Reader Service discount
- ★ Books available before they're in the shops

Accepting these FREE books and gift places you under no obligation to buy; you may cancel at any time, even after receiving your free shipment. Simply complete your details below and return the entire page to the address below. *You don't even need a stamp!*

YES! Please send me 2 free Historical Romance books and a surprise gift. I understand that unless you hear from me, I will receive 4 superb new titles every month for just £3.49 each, postage and packing free. I am under no obligation to purchase any books and may cancel my subscription at any time. The free books and gift will be mine to keep in any case.

H3ZEC

Ms/Mrs/Miss/Mr ....Initials ....
BLOCK CAPITALS PLEASE

Surname ....

Address ....

....

....Postcode ....

Send this whole page to:
UK: FREEPOST CN81, Croydon, CR9 3WZ
EIRE: PO Box 4546, Kilcock, County Kildare (stamp required)

Offer valid in UK and Eire only and not available to current Reader Service subscribers to this series. We reserve the right to refuse an application and applicants must be aged 18 years or over. Only one application per household. Terms and prices subject to change without notice. Offer expires 31st December 2003. As a result of this application, you may receive offers from Harlequin Mills & Boon and other carefully selected companies. If you would prefer not to share in this opportunity please write to The Data Manager at the address above.

Mills & Boon® is a registered trademark owned by Harlequin Mills & Boon Limited.
Historical Romance™ is being used as a trademark.